The Big Both Ways

The Big Both Ways

JOHN STRALEY

Alaska Northwest Books®
Anchorage · Portland

Library of Congress Cataloging-in-Publication Data

Straley, John, 1953 –
   The big both ways / John Straley.
     p. cm.
   ISBN 978-0-88240-739-5 (hardbound) — ISBN 978-0-88240-732-6 (softbound)
1. Labor movement—Alaska—Fiction. 2. Inside Passage—Fiction. 3. Alaska—
Fiction. 4. British Columbia—Fiction. 5. Washington (State) —Fiction. I. Title.
PS3569.T687B54 2008
813'.54—dc22   2007051440

Second printing 2008

The Caribou Logo is a registered trademark of Alaska Northwest Books®.

Alaska Northwest Books®
An imprint of Graphic Arts Center Publishing Co.
P.O. Box 10306
Portland, OR 97296-0306
(503) 226-2402 * www.gacpc.com

President: Charles M. Hopkins
General Manager: Douglas A. Pfeiffer
Associate Publisher, Alaska Northwest Books: Sara Juday
Editorial Staff: Timothy W. Frew, Kathy Howard, Jean Andrews,
  Jean Bond-Slaughter
Editor: Ellen Wheat
Cover design: Karen Lybrand
Cover illustration: Ray Troll
Interior design: Jamison Spittler
Production coordinator: Susan Dupèrè

Printed in the United States of America

For Robert DeArmond,
who has opened windows to the past
that will stay open forever

AUTHOR'S NOTE

The Big Both Ways is a tall tale, meant to be told around the fire. There are some historical figures and events included here, but mostly this book is a product of my sometimes feverish imagination. All mistakes or possible screwy interpretations in the text rest with me and not the many people who inspired and assisted in the writing of it.

My heartfelt thanks to:

Robert DeArmond, who rowed a dory from Sitka to Tacoma in order to get to college in 1931. He made the trip alone and some sixty years later wrote the tale in his fine book *Voyage in a Dory* (Arrowhead Press, Sitka, Alaska). One of Alaska's preeminent historians, Robert's advice was indispensable to me.

Olga Klietzing, Bill Hills, Fred Matson, Emmett Watson, Curtis Morrison, John McClelland, Ken Dola, Rosemary Ahern, Sara Juday, and Ellen Wheat, for their help, advice, and wisdom.

Curtis Edwards and Hugh Straley for giving me the writing tools.

Ray Troll and Karen Lybrand for the extraordinary cover art.

Gary Gouker of Gouker Custom Machine Shop for giving me a job during the lean years of writing this book. No writer ever had a better patron.

Finally, to Jan Morrison Straley and Finn McHattie Straley, who listened to all my doubts and gave me back more confidence than I could ever muster by myself. Thanks are not enough. I can only take comfort in my belief that their love is a big river and it flows both ways.

ONE

~~~

Even though she had never traded sex for money, she was nothing now but a whore with a bloody nose. It was a hard fact to accept . . . but there it was.

She looked at the man curled in the trunk of the car, blood oiling over his white shirt. She had his broken watch in her hand, its intricate guts at a standstill, the second hand trembling between two painted tick marks on the face. It was only then that she started to cry. Her sobs leaked between her bloody fingers as she tried to stifle the sound. A mile to the west a car hissed over the pavement, and somewhere in the woods a screen door slammed.

She stepped toward him then. Tears flecked off her chin as she lifted the cold arm to place the watch back around his wrist. She was thinking that he might as well keep it, for however stupid it seemed, even in a world gone mad a broken watch could still be right twice a day.

It was May 1935. In April, Amelia Earhart had set a speed record on a solo flight from Los Angeles to Mexico City, and when she took off again she set another from Mexico City to New York. In the American southwest, a blizzard of dust scoured the tired farmland and the Roosevelt administration began relocating dust bowlers to communal farms in the Territory of Alaska. In August, Will Rogers and Wiley Post were to set off in their Lockheed Orion for Point Barrow, and on June 24, the miners of the Alaska-Juneau gold mine would riot when scabs started marching up the street to the hiring hall. All of these things would take on a new meaning to Slippery Wilson in the months to come, but just then he was looking halfway up a big-butted Douglas fir tree listening to his bull buck tell him something through a wad of chew.

His given name was Jack, but his parents had called him Slippery. Like many people during the Depression he wanted to be hopeful. Others had told him that life was hard but he had not seen it that way. He had always been stubborn in his optimism. But now he was beginning to wonder.

"Well, I guess you better scamper up there and cut him down," the bull buck said as he spit out a stream of tobacco juice onto the duff. They were standing in the northern woods of the Skagit River drainage, in Washington State. The wind was sour with the smell of pitch. Seventy feet up in a broken tree, Jud White was slumped dead from his climbing rope, where a partially rotten limb from the fir he was topping had hit him square in the chest. High up in the tree, Jud's torso was at a sickening angle to his waist, his axe swinging from its lanyard attached to his belt.

"You better get up there and cut him down," the bull buck repeated.

It was just after sunrise and the tired men around him had stopped rattling through the brush. Gray jays flitted in the slash of tangled branches. The hook tenders, who had already oiled up their bones with the first hard half hour of clambering down the cut, stood watching him, their faces toward the sun, like flowers in their round hard hats. "No, I'm sorry," he said to the bull buck, who was standing flat-footed amongst a tangle of rigging cable. "I'm going to draw my pay." And he started walking out of the woods.

It had been three years since Slip had left the failing ranch in eastern Washington. Roosevelt had promised reclamation and electrification. The high desert country east of the Cascades would be a new Eden. Slip had watched the men hitchhiking with cardboard suitcases to the dam sites. He had picked apples, put up hay, and milked his family's cows for his entire life, but when his father died and the bank took it all, he decided to follow those men up the river. As if to show him the rightness of his choice, the old cow kicked him one last time while he loaded her into the buyer's truck, and even then he thought only of the thick, sweet milk she had given.

He sold his logging boots for five bucks to a cowhand with a cleft palate who had been killing himself working on the rigging crew in his slick leather boots. Slip rolled his two changes of work clothes and a black suit he had used for funerals into a burlap bag that he tied off with a hank of rope. He pulled on his red mackinaw, grabbed his cap, and slung his bindle of clothes around his back. The last thing he did before walking out to the highway was to pull up the loose floorboard near his bunk. Tucked between the joists, Slip had hidden his tool kit. It was a long, open box with a few of the tools he had gotten from the farm before the men from the bank had come for their inventory. There was a fine Swedish handsaw, a brace, an assortment of bits, and a set of chisels that had never been abused. He had a square and a plumb line, a long-handled framing hammer, and a smaller claw hammer for finer work. He had a trim saw and a folding rule. There was an assortment of punches and nail sets and a carpenter's level. He had a handmade knife with his initials stamped into the leather sheath. The box had a strong leather sling and a canvas cover so he could travel easily without fear of spilling his tools on the ground.

He dug into his toolbox for a tobacco tin. He opened the tin and put two twenty dollar bills inside. This forty dollars represented his pay for the last two weeks, minus the money the company took out for their trouble. With that forty dollars he had well over two thousand dollars saved, and two thousand dollars could buy a future, with any extra going toward happiness.

Jud White had loved logging and was eager for Slip to love it too. Jud believed in it, he loved the bunkhouse and the tools. He loved the sweat and the smell of it. The rest of the boys worked for their wages and to build something somewhere else. Jud had been right square in the middle of his life. He woke up each morning exactly where he was supposed to be. He had been fully alive cutting trees, right up until the second that one killed him.

Slip shouldered his way past the men crowding toward the foreman's shed. Already word had gotten round about two jobs that might open up. The skinny men drifted out of the brush like scarecrows come to life. They had been tenting off in the woods or in dry sections of culvert waiting for just this: someone to die or someone to quit. They didn't care. They needed the work.

He grabbed some letters for friends in the bunkhouse, promising to post them when he got to a mailbox. He shook hands with the Filipino cooks and bent down to shake the hands of the truck mechanics in the grease pit. He wished them all good luck, then he walked south and stuck out his thumb. The saws on the landing were rattling in the cut as a crew lowered Jud White's body down from the tree.

Dew was still on the grass alongside the road. The morning wrens and sparrows were calling to each other in the shade. Just under the whine of the saws, he could hear the white noise of the Skagit River roiling down the valley.

He got a ride with a kid from Sedro Woolley, who talked about his girlfriend and asked him for gas money. He got another ride from a salesman whose car was burning oil at an alarming rate, so

Slip asked to be dropped off by the river, preferring to walk a while rather than be stuck with the salesman when the car broke down. As the salesman drove away, a cloud of exhaust hung like a storm squall moving in.

He walked along the river, thinking of the dough in his tool-box and about a piece of ground he might be able to buy. Every time the thought of Jud White's body welled up from the sickness in his stomach, he choked it back down and would think instead of the place he would build, maybe along a river with a few fruit trees and a loyal cow of his own.

Slip had been an active baby, always trying to wriggle out of his grandma's arms. He arched his back, twisting and kicking at the cradling bath towel or the pair of strong arms reaching out for him. "This boy's slippery," the old woman had said, and the name stuck. Teachers heard his name and assumed he would try to get out of his studies. Girls chased him at church picnics instead of the greased pig. When he started working on the big dam project up the Columbia River at Grand Coulee, other workers assumed he was going to drop his rivet gun off the scaffolding. But he never did. In some ways his name was the anvil his personality had been forged against. If anything was true about Slippery Wilson, it was that he wanted to stick.

Near a bend in the river road, a new Lincoln was pulled over with its left front tire hooked down into the ditch. The Lincoln had wire wheels and fine chrome headlamps mounted outboard of the grill. The rear wheels had scuffed two ditches in the soft dirt of the road's shoulder. A blonde woman in a housedress and a cardigan walked around the back of the car, looking under the bumper and running her hands along the edge of the chrome. The wind riffled her short hair, and as she knelt down Slip could see the thick muscles of her thighs pressing against the fabric. When she stood up and turned, he saw the blush of rising bruises under her eyes and some redness under her nose as if maybe she were getting over a cold.

"You wreck your car?" he called out to her.

She turned quickly and almost jumped away from the trunk. "What?" she said, shielding her eyes to look at him.

"Oh, I'm sorry," Slip said. "I didn't mean to scare you."

"No . . . no . . ." the girl said.

It was then he noticed that her hands were shaking and her skin seemed sickly pale. "Are you all right? Would you like some help?" He waved at the front of the car and took off his wool cap with a short brim, aware now of how shabby he must look to this girl.

"Yes," she said, and he set down his tools.

It would take weeks for him to understand what he was feeling as he walked toward the blonde woman. There would be storms and killings to come, there would be beatings and long hours of recrimination, but still he would try to hold on to his original impulse: the sound of the river with a beautiful woman standing under a tree. All he wanted to do was help her in a way that he hadn't been able to help Jud, or his parents for that matter—or even himself. He wanted to make something right, on this fine morning when he was headed out for his fresh start. But, of course, by the time he recognized his mistake it would be too late. The future, like a breaking wave, would have washed over him.

"Somebody run you off the road?" he asked.

She looked up from where she was still running her hand along the edge of the rear bumper. She looked at her fingers and then up at Slip. "I hit a dog back a ways and I was just looking to see if there was any damage."

"Must have scared you," Slip said.

"What?" she asked, not taking her eyes off his.

"Hitting the dog. It must have scared you."

"Oh that, yes, it was frightening."

Slip walked to the front of the big Lincoln and bent down to look at the front bumper.

"Don't bother with that," she said, putting her fingers lightly on his shoulders. "Let's just get the car out of the ditch."

In ten minutes the Lincoln was back out in the road, engine idling and a thin haze of exhaust slithering along the road.

Slip was panting and gathering up his things when she walked over to him with a paper cup of river water for him. "Thank you," he said, "that's nice of you." Then he folded his kerchief and gestured down the road. "Can you give me a lift?"

"Oh . . . sure. Where are you heading?" She nervously wiped her hands on her dress and walked around to the passenger's side, and then seeing she was in the wrong place, walked back around the car with Slip following her.

"I'm headed to Seattle for a bit. I've got a friend who runs a barbershop," Slip said.

"You need a shave?" she said, still wiping her hands.

"I suppose I do," Slip said, and he doubled back toward the trunk to open it.

"I didn't mean it," she said, looking down at her feet. "You look fine."

Slip smiled at her, and he too looked down at her feet as if the answer to what was to happen next was down there somewhere.

"Here," she said, suddenly waking up. "Just put your things in the back here. I . . . I don't have the key for the trunk."

"All right." He smiled and opened the passenger door.

Slip settled into the front seat and she got behind the wheel. In reality the car smelled of cigarettes and whiskey, but Slip could only smell the cedar trees along the river. The woman's hair was dyed blonde and was showing dark roots. Her eyes were the cobalt blue of a medicine bottle. The steering wheel was about as wide as her shoulders and she gripped it as if it were the wheel of a ship. She looked around for the starter button down on the floor and before she remembered that it was already running, she pressed the starter, and it shrieked in distress. She jammed the gears, then with a grinding lurch wheeled out onto the road.

〜〜〜

Out in the woods the loggers liked to talk about sex. For some of them the very nature of their work, the felling and the skidding of timber, was erotic. Slip had sat on the butts of massive fallen trees and listened to the exploits of men who hadn't actually been with a woman for years. There had been many stories about sex and most of them were lies and exaggerations; he had even told some of them himself. But he was not a natural when it came to rough talk, while others made a kind of ragged poetry out of their lies.

He looked over at the woman driving the Lincoln. It had been weeks since he had been this close to a woman. He wondered why there had never been any stories about the curve of a woman's arm, about how it might look like a slender limb of a fruit tree. There were no stories about the softness of her skin or the smell of her scalp. There were no stories about the sound of her voice or the way she sat in a chair. There was never anything about what a woman said, or felt, or thought. As he thought about it driving down the road he wasn't surprised, for to mention something tender about a woman would cast a pall of loneliness on these men, who had long ago chosen their bunkhouse lives and the day-to-day heartache of ruining the woods.

The Lincoln lurched from one side of the road to the other. She jerked at the wheel and bounced up and down on the accelerator. Slip braced his right hand against the top of the open window frame and wedged his foot against the door for support.

They drove for an hour, the car tacking back and forth across the road. She drove so erratically that the cows along the near fences stopped in mid chew and watched her pass. Slip sat upright and watched the road. The miles ticked off and the young woman said nothing but stared through the windshield as if trying to bore a hole in the glass. To Slip, her bad driving was a testament to her innocence. He imagined that she was a farm girl who had snuck away with her brother's car. She was learning to drive to surprise her family back home, or her boyfriend.

"You drive really well," Slip said, his eyes darting back and forth from the road to the steering wheel, his left hand arching out a bit ready to grab for it.

"Look's like you've got something there," he said, and pointed to the front of her shirt.

"What?" She looked down.

The top three buttons of her sweater were undone, and she looked down to where there was a small smear of blood across the top of her chest.

"Oh . . . oh . . ." she said, and started wiping at the blood. The left tires crunched on the road apron. Slip reached over and took the steering wheel.

"Slow down and let's pull over," he said, straining to keep the car on the road.

She let up on the gas and her hands fumbled at the stain. The big Lincoln slowed to a stop on the side of the road, and Slip reached across her lap to pull on the brake. "You must have gotten some of that dog's blood on you after all."

"I've got a clean handkerchief in the glove box," she said, her fingertips twisting at the fabric of her dress. Suddenly she looked down the road to where there was a small gas station beside the river with a few cabins behind it.

"I need to rest," she said, and wheeled back out onto the road.

It was awkward watching the woman making arrangements with the homely boy wearing overalls. It was only the middle of the afternoon and she was renting a room. When she came back, she threw the key on his lap and lurched the car up to the first little cabin along the edge of the woods. She opened the door and her hands were still shaking.

"I'm sorry," she said, "I was only able to get one room with a small bunk." She didn't look him in the eyes. "You could stay on the floor, or you could wait for a ride out on the road. The boy here said there is a bit more traffic later in the afternoon." She pulled a leather bag out of the backseat and dug around in it. She pulled out a surprisingly big roll of bills and peeled off a ten dollar bill then waved it nervously in his direction, still without looking at him.

"For your trouble," she said.

"No," Slip said, "I think I'll stay."

She held out her hand. "My name is Ellie Hobbes," she said.

He took her hand, and though the skin was soft her grip was much stronger than he expected.

There was a tin stove in the corner of the cabin, one bed, and one chair next to a table that stood beneath the only window. Slip brought in his bindle of clothes and his toolbox and set them both under the table. Outside, the river slid past in a constant rush. The water was a light emerald green, and the spring current turned the rocks in the riverbed so that there was a consistent chunking and chortling above the sizzle of water. Slip started a fire in the stove with some cedar chips and a couple of pages from a magazine. Then he added splits of dry fir. They crackled inside the stove sending whiffs of smoke puffing out the seams until the flue started to draw.

Ellie sat on the narrow bunk. The metal webbing creaked underneath her and she seemed even smaller than she was. Her hands cupped around her elbows as if she were trying to hold herself in. Slip sat on the floor in the corner of the room. He propped his bindle behind him and leaned against it.

"Tell me about yourself," she said. She shivered even though the room was warming up and the dampness was retreating through the cracks in the walls.

He told her that his friend had died in the woods earlier in the day. He had been topping a tree. He told her because he believed that women were sympathetic, but all she said was, "bastards," very softly under her shivering breath.

"Tell me about what you want to do," Ellie said, breaking the awkwardness between them. So he told her about working on Grand Coulee Dam. He told her his plans to go back east of the mountains and get land to start a ranch. He told her about electrification and power to pump water, about irrigation and how the Great Basin country would soon be a productive paradise. He talked about how beautiful and green the fields would be and how there would be nothing like it anywhere in the world. He was happy talking about this fantasy he told himself was his future, for he really didn't know how to talk about Jud's death.

He talked about his friend Andy who had worked alongside him on the Grand Coulee Dam, and about how they had talked about going in together on a place, about how Andy was a good worker and had been saving up some money by working in his uncle's barbershop down in Seattle. He explained that he was intending to go to Seattle and round up Andy, and as soon as they could get a truck and a few materials together they'd head straight over Stevens Pass and start looking for a place.

Ellie laid down on top of the covers. She lay on her side with her hands for a pillow. Slip knew that she was only partially listening but he didn't mind. He stopped talking, thinking she was asleep. But as soon as he did she opened her eyes, staring intently toward the stove.

"I don't mean to talk so much," he said.

She closed her eyes softly once and then opened them again. In the darkening room he noticed she had faint scars under both eyes, fishhook size, right in the spots where the bruises were rising.

"What do you do?" he asked softly, not sure he really wanted to know. A bird walked on the tin roof, its small claws ticking into the room.

Ellie looked straight at him. "Let's not talk about what we do."

"All right," Slip said, and he pretended to be looking over his fingernails as if he had some intention of cleaning them.

"I want to fly an airplane," she said. Even though her voice was soft and sleepy, there was resolve running underneath.

"I was up in one once. On the takeoff I thought the whole thing would fall apart right there rolling along the ground. But then . . ." and she raised her hand slowly out over the edge of the cot, "we rose into the air." She was smiling out into the atmosphere of the room.

"Did you fly it yourself?"

"Oh my no. It takes lessons, lots of lessons to learn to fly. I was with a barnstormer, a guy just passing through. I married him."

"Did he teach you to fly?" Slip asked.

"No. He . . . well . . . he took off with another young girl." And then she smiled ruefully, the curled scars under her eyes strangely bittersweet.

"You got a family?" Slip kicked his feet out toward the cot a bit more.

"I had a sister but now she's dead."

She took a deep breath and shifted so the springs shrieked. She looked at Slip, curled on the floor. His eyes were open, staring at her as if he knew her, but of course he didn't.

"I'm sorry," he said once again, the words turning sour in his mouth.

"No," she said. "That's all right. She was married. She and her husband died in a house fire."

"That's hard," was all he could think of to say. But his mind wandered to his parents' graves alone in a dusty field now wholly owned by the bank.

"I'm tired of talking. I need some rest," Ellie said. "Just a little bit. Then we'll get going."

And she closed her eyes.

It was dark when he woke up and the tin stove was barely warm. She was lying against him on the floor, her arms curled around him. She gripped him tightly with the same surprising strength he had felt in her handshake.

"What time is it?" she asked, her breath warm in his ear.

"I don't know. It's dark."

"We better get going," she said, and she sat up, pulling her coat around her shoulders. "I need to take care of the car."

They stood up and awkwardly straightened their clothes. Slip fussed with the stove, doing anything he could to get past the anxiety of waking on the floor with this woman he did not know.

Outside, the river kept at its work and the rocks tumbled one after another down the riverbed. The lights from the gas station spattered up through the trees and Slip could see the red taillights of cars gliding down the road.

He grabbed up his bindle and toolbox, then walked out the door behind Ellie. She walked directly to the driver's side door and Slip walked around the back end of the car. A sliver of light cut through the trees from the gas station and ran across the car, which was parked on an incline, its nose facing uphill toward the cabin. As Slip walked past the trunk, he stopped short. There was a sour smell in the air, like the musk from a big animal, a black bear or a dead bull in a ditch. The breeze stirred and the smell of the cool river slid around him. Then he looked down at the rear end of the car where the light sparkled on the bumper.

The Lincoln had a carriage-style trunk, and down near the latch a dark line of liquid traced along the bumper and a fat blob of liquid hung from the edge of the chrome. He knelt down and touched it with the tip of his finger. It was blood.

They didn't speak while driving. A light rain began to fall as the sunrise poured over the fields and forests. Farmhouses showed dim lights through rippled windows. In one of the fields, Slip could make out the form of a lanky kid walking behind the loose-limbed cows ambling toward the barn.

Still they didn't speak. Slip kept rubbing his fingers together. He simultaneously thought of the soft flesh of her body and the blood on the bumper. He wanted out of the car and at the same time he wanted to drive with her straight through the night and on over the pass to the Columbia River country. He rubbed his finger against his thumb where the stickiness of the blood was still rough. Maybe it was just blood from that dog she hit back up the road, but the instant he thought it, he knew it couldn't be true.

After a few hours they traded places and Slip drove. Every once in a while Ellie would nod her head and tell him to take a particular turn. He didn't know where they were going, but it didn't matter because each mile gave him more time to think.

Eventually there were street signs and small houses on little lots laid out in straight lines.

"Pull in here," she said, and he aimed the Lincoln into the driveway of a clapboard cottage with a willow tree dripping over the front porch. The ground beneath was a mâché of narrow yellow leaves no one had raked up the autumn before. An ugly terrier with an infected cut across his snout pulled against his chain in the corner of the yard. When they drove in, the dog stopped pulling and sniffed the air blindly. When Slip opened his door the dog began to growl.

A screen door slammed against its hinges and a tall man in a wool coat came out on the porch.

"What the fuck took you so long?" the man asked. He stared at Ellie from under the brim of his hat.

Slip kept his eyes on the man. He was out of place on this sad little dairy farm. His hands were big and fleshy, with a Masonic ring girdling one of his fingers as if it were meant to cut it off. His shirt was clean but his tie was pulled aside. He gave the nervous appearance of someone who had been waiting a long time in a place he didn't like. Slip didn't know him and didn't even know his type, but he was dangerous, of that he was certain.

"And what the hell happened to your face?" the tall man barked.

"I ran into a wall," Ellie said, as Slip set the car's brake.

"I see you also got some help," the tall man grumbled. "That wasn't in the deal we talked about."

"I got the car stuck and needed the help. He doesn't know a thing about our business," and she opened the car door. "We could use some breakfast," she said and started walking up to the porch.

A short, fireplug of a man in only his shorts and undershirt walked out behind the tall man. The little man was unshaven and carried himself like a heavyweight boxer who had been shrunk down in the wash.

"You get me what I want. Then we'll talk about breakfast."

"Just some coffee, and a biscuit if you have one. That's all we need." She looked over at Slip, whose eyes were darting back and forth between the two men. Her expression was pleading, her eyes begging him to say nothing.

A young woman with stringy black hair stepped out onto the porch. She held a baby cocked on her hip in a way that made Slip think she had lots of babies in the house. The short man rolled his shoulders toward her and hissed, "Get that child back inside, Ida." The tired woman turned and went back inside. When the screen door banged against the unpainted door frame, the baby in her arms started to cry.

"We won't be long, I promise," Ellie said to Slip, and then walked behind the car and opened the trunk with a key. She rummaged in the back. Another dog came slinking around the corner of one of the sheds and growled at the rear end of the car.

"Hush now," Ellie said to the dog. Then she slammed the trunk down hard and walked back toward the porch holding what looked to be a leather attaché case. "This is all of it."

The tall man produced a toothpick from his coat pocket and put it in his mouth. He didn't reach for the case but let her put it on the porch at his feet. He appeared to be about to say something, but he looked at Slip and just nudged the corner of the case with the toe of his leather shoe.

"Everything else still in there?" he said, nodding to the car with the damp end of the toothpick.

"Yes it is, and like I said, we'll take care of it right after breakfast, unless you'd like me to leave it here and we can take the train to town."

Slip stepped away from the car. He wanted to get his clothes and his tools out. The two men on the porch were like bare wires and the air was charged between them. He half expected lightning to strike.

The tired woman came out on the porch holding a rusty tray of food. She timidly walked down the steps and handed Slip and Ellie cups of coffee, then handed them each a fried egg sandwich. Slip took the food tentatively like a dog stealing meat, thanked her, and sat on the steps. Drops of egg yolk spattered his jacket as he bit into the sandwich.

The tall man bent down and picked up the case Ellie had brought from the trunk. Slip could see there was blood smeared on the smooth leather. The man opened the case and pawed through the papers. He stopped and looked at his right hand, which seemed to have a smear of red on the palm. He stared down at the two of them eating their breakfast. Slip noticed that the man's eyes were gray, his face was pale, and there was the chill of winter about him.

"You sure this is everything?" the tall man blurted out, not really speaking to anyone but giving voice to his growing frustration.

Ellie did not look up at him as she ate her fried egg sandwich. "Everything," she said.

The tall man walked off the porch and around the back where he had parked his own car. In a few seconds he was gone, leaving nothing but the oily smell of exhaust.

The tough little man went back inside and didn't come out again. Slip finished the last of his coffee, poured the grounds out onto the mud, and put the cup on the porch. Inside, the babies were crying, and Slip could see the tired woman staring at them through the water-stained curtains. He waved as she backed into the dark and the curtains fell together.

The sun was breaking over the hill behind the house when they pulled back onto the main road. The low-slung rays of light lit up the grass making a sparkly haze and wisps of ground fog rose straight into the air. The earth seemed to be holding on to the silence of the night. Off to the east the mountaintops glowed silver, and the first light poured across the coast to the ocean where salty air was beginning to rise.

As Slip drove, Ellie sat closer, and now when she told him to turn the car she touched his shoulder lightly with the tips of her fingers. They drove about an hour and came to a fenced area on a slough. There was a barge landing with a ramp built out over the water. The loading area was deserted, and the window of the guard shack was as dark as a missing tooth. She pointed up the ramp and Slip drove the Lincoln to the edge and got out. She reached under the front seat and took something out from under it. It was a green file folder with a few pages of yellow paper wedged inside. She clutched the folder to her chest a moment then reached over the backseat and took out a black wool coat and her leather bag.

"Don't forget your things," she said, and opened the back door from the inside. She stepped out, circled the car to the driver's side, let off the parking brake, and pulled the gear shift into neutral. Slip grabbed his tools and bindle.

"Do me a favor and grab the registration from around the post under the steering wheel," she said to Slip.

He had set his gear down. The car was starting to roll. The car door was open. A small light was lit under the dash beside the glove box. On the steering wheel column was the car's registration. He ripped it free as the car began to gain speed. Stepping back, he looked at the paper in the leather case in his hand. All he read was "Floodwater Security" before she took it from him, and they stood there watching the big Lincoln as if they were launching a ship.

The great car eased slowly toward the slough. As the front tires went over the lip the undercarriage smacked down on the ramp. There was a loud scraping of metal on metal for two seconds and then the car stopped.

"Come on. She just needs a little help," Ellie said. She threw the file folder onto the grass beside the shack, then she walked over, grabbed the rear bumper, and put her shoulder against the trunk. There was just a rind of dried, brownish blood along the bumper. Slip could see a vein of it widening and branching out toward the seam of the trunk. He put his hands on the bumper and set his feet firmly beneath him.

They were face to face as they pushed. Slip could smell the coffee on her breath. She hadn't changed clothes back at the house but had washed her face in the water from the garden hose. Damp hair rimmed her face and it struck him that her eyes were changeable—perhaps they drew the blue out of the day—because now they seemed to be a colder blue, like the water in a high lake, inviting but cold enough to numb.

They lifted and pushed against the bulk of iron. When it gave way the Lincoln pitched into the water, then bobbed to the surface and stayed upright for several heartbeats until it eased into the current accompanied by gurgling and garlands of bubbles.

"There!" Ellie slapped her hands together and pushed back her hair. "That's done." She walked back to the grass, picked up the file folder, and put it into her black leather bag.

Slip watched the car. He wanted to say something. He wanted to apologize to whomever or whatever was in the trunk. He would have liked to somehow correct the situation. To do something decisive and right. But where to start, without a new day or a way to travel back in time?

When they got to the shack she tapped the file folder against her thigh, then gripped him by the neck and kissed him on the lips. It was a soft kiss: coffee, fried egg sandwich, the warmth of her body came into his mouth. She tilted her head back so as not to bump her nose.

She leaned away from him and looked straight into his eyes. "It will be all right," she said. "You had nothing to do with this."

"I better get going," Slip said, pushing away from her.

"Okay," she said. "You are going to walk to the road and about a mile south you can catch the interurban train." She reached down into the file folder and took out an envelope that was fat with cash. She pulled out five ten dollar bills and stuffed them in his shirt pocket.

"For your trouble," she said, this time looking him in the eye. Then she reached inside her jacket pocket and took out a revolver. She held it for a moment with the stubby barrel pointed straight at his heart.

Slip felt nothing so much as sad. It was the sadness of reality descending on him. This woman was not the girl by the river. She was going to kill him. She was going to take the whole thing away: the cabin, the river, and the future too. He reached for the gun.

"This is the last favor I'm going to ask," she said. She handed him the gun while she reached into her bag and took out two pieces of paper. One was a flyer advertising some kind of meeting, the other was ledger sheet with names and figures.

"Put these papers in your toolbox. Bring them to me in Seattle. The address is printed on the flyer. Bring the gun or throw it away if you want. Just don't get arrested with it. Do you understand?"

Slip took the papers and nodded stupidly, as if this strange life were just too hard to comprehend.

"I'll give you five hundred dollars if you deliver these papers to me day after tomorrow."

"Why don't you just take them?"

"It's complicated," she said.

Of course it is, he thought to himself.

All she did by way of saying good-bye was pat him twice on the shoulders. Then she turned and walked into the shack and pulled down the window shade.

Slip walked out past the empty watchman's hut. He stuck the revolver in his pants and covered it up with his coat. The morning birds had stopped singing and the early ground fog had cleared away. Just over the hump of the wooded ridge he heard the mechanical hum of the city. He slung his bindle over his shoulder, picked up his tools, and walked toward the clatter of the city, happy to be walking in any direction away from the still gurgling car.

T W O

~~~

George Hanson lived on a crooked road overlooking Lake Washington. His wife had wanted to live in the country but he still needed to work in town, so this house above the truck farms of the Rainier Valley was their compromise. Above the lake, white clouds floated on the winds like battle cruisers, while in the blackberry bushes song sparrows flitted through the vines on their pipe-cleaner legs.

George drank his coffee and idly turned the page of his newspaper. The free-flowing river of the revolution in Russia had been dammed and diverted by the Politburo, and the fascists were gaining power in Europe. The world seemed on the verge of some monumental change, and this change, whatever it was, hung over everyone around the globe like a new season no one had ever experienced, wedged somehow between winter and spring.

George Hanson's father had been a broad-shouldered Finn who worked the Seattle docks during the wildest years of radical unrest. He had been a brawler and a speech giver who would often come home as cut up as a country tomcat. During the general strike of 1918, the Big Finn would stumble home with scars across his knuckles and blood scabbed across the bridge of his nose. Lying in bed, George would hear his mother's protests as the big man's boots thumped the soggy wooden steps. He would keep his eyes pinched shut as his father boomed up the narrow stairway to the tiny dormer room cut out of the roofline. The stout man smelled of newsprint, blood, and whiskey as he leaned over the boy's bed. He never said a word. He never touched the boy or straightened his blankets, but the battered man would back into the corner of the room and watch the boy pretending to sleep. The floor did not creak beneath his father's boots, and the door hung silently on its hinges. All George could hear was the Big Finn breathing through his broken nose. Then, after a few moments, his father would turn and rumble down the stairs into the steamy kitchen of his mother's boiling pots.

In 1919 the Big Finn had stood shoulder to shoulder with the Wobblies in Centralia and had faced the brickbats of the Legionnaires as they came to wreck the hall. He had run with Wesley Everest up the back alley toward the river and had swum downstream before Wesley shot Dale Hubbard with the broken pistol no one thought would work. Later that night the Big Finn had sat hunkered under the railroad bridge as the mob churned across Trower Avenue and Wesley's body was flung over the side with one end of a rope tied to a trestle and the other knotted around his neck. The Finn pushed himself back up into the darkness beneath the bridge as the crowd above him trained their rifles on the dead Wobbly, his corpse slowly turning on the rope like a counterweight of a clock.

From that day until the day he died of a bad heart on the floor of a meeting hall in Ballard, the Big Finn burned with a hatred for the Republicans and the Legionnaires. He'd hitchhike across the mountains to shout speeches to field workers in Yakima, and he'd make goulash in skid road rooms for men carrying explosives to San Francisco. As for why he was seldom at home, he used to say that every breath he took was for the revolution.

To George, his anarchist father made all other human beings seem small, even from a distance. The Big Finn loomed over all of George's elementary school teachers even though he had never set foot in the school. He dwarfed his high school football coach although he had never been to a game or practice. The Finn's flamboyance had caused his wife to send their second child, a fragile and softhearted girl, to live with an aunt. The Big Finn had missed most of George's childhood, and even though death separated them now, George had never really missed his father. But lately he had been haunted by the sensation of the old man crowding into the room where he slept, breathing through his crooked nose. The memory evoked the certainty that no matter what he would do with his life, whatever success he would have, or great accomplishments others would acknowledge, George would never be as vivid in this world as the Big Finn. The memory of his father made George feel as unsubstantial as a wisp of steam, even though he had become a champion boxer in his late teens and by his late thirties he was the best homicide detective ever seen along Seattle's waterfront.

When the telephone rang, he did not rise to get it. The birds along the fence startled up and away. Emily walked to their telephone in the entryway and answered. George watched as clouds scudded over the lake from north to south, and he listened for the voice of a boy playing in the street though he could not make it out.

"All right. I'll tell him," she said. "No . . . he'll be there. All right. Yes, good-bye." She hung up the phone and walked toward the kitchen wiping her hands on her apron.

"Who was it?" he called out finally.

"The office," she said absently as she flipped his eggs without breaking the yolk.

He waited, expecting more. "What did they say?"

"They said to come right away. I'll make you a sandwich."

"Thank you." He drank the last of his coffee and got up to put on his suit jacket, being careful to hold his tie back against his shirt as he rose.

"Did they say what it was about?" he asked her.

"Just that they found a body dumped near the slough."

"They say any more about it?" He was putting on his jacket.

"They just said it looked like somebody you knew." She handed him a sandwich and stood there, her expression blank as if she were already alone.

"That the body was someone I knew, or that the killer was someone I knew?" He wanted to move forward and give her a kiss but felt unsure of himself.

"I'm don't know," she said, turning away. "I think probably both."

Slip stepped down from the train. He had bought the ticket with some of the money she had given him, but he was going to need a bit more. He wanted to rent a room for the night, maybe a couple of nights, and he wanted a bath. He wanted to wash the memories of the day's events off his skin. He would use some money to stay someplace with a private bath. He would eat a beefsteak and maybe a bowl of ice cream before crawling between clean sheets for the first time in months. He had no intention of seeing that bottle blonde or her money again.

He found a mailbox near the station and posted the letters the boys from the camp had given him, then he ducked into an alley where no one could see his business. He dug his tobacco tin out from his kit. When he opened it up he felt hollowed out—sick to his stomach and icy cold. The tin was empty, all but for a single piece of paper. His two thousand dollars were gone. The woman must have taken his money while he slept at the cabin. The single sheet of paper was another flyer, the same as the one she had handed him along with the ledger page. The top of the flyer read, "Workers of the World Unite!" He stopped reading, and crumpled it up but did not throw it away.

He went looking for the meeting hall, but all he found was an empty house and he was sure the flyer must be wrong. He spent the rest of the day talking to bartenders and waitresses. He asked about Ellie Hobbes, if anyone knew where to find her. He talked to a few trainmen and a couple of busboys. They all said they didn't know her but in a way that made Slip think that they did. As soon as they heard her name they looked around, as if someone else was watching, then they would shake their heads and deny any knowledge of the bottle blonde who wanted to fly.

He was hungry and he didn't know how long he would need to make the money in his pocket last. He saw a handmade sign for a soup kitchen and followed the arrow. He turned the first corner and there was a line of men two blocks long waiting to get something to eat. A cop with a billy club walked up and down the line. Every so often he'd rap one of the bums on the shins with his stick and the little hobo would give a crow hop back onto the curb. When the doors to the soup kitchen opened, the line started shuffling forward with small steps as if they all wore manacles on their legs. Slip poked into the line to talk to some of the mugs, but they froze him out, thinking he was trying to cut in line. Eventually the cop came back, flipping his club by the leather strap, and told Slip to be moving along.

Black clouds were riding the back of the darkness easing in from the west. Slip walked down the hill toward the shipyards and the flat south of the docks. He would rough it for a few nights until he figured out what he was going to do. He would find a place to get out of the rain in Hooverville, but a bath and a beefsteak would be harder to find. As he headed down the hill he could see the sprawl of the slums coming into view.

The settlement was a vast collection of shacks and coops built on what had once been a pasture. Families who had followed the harvests and timber tramps back from the woods washed up here, and built shelters out of crates and pallets. There was no scheme to the pathways and lanes; people simply put up sheds wherever there was space. Once you walked into Hooverville it was easy to lose your way.

He carried his tools and bindle swung over his right shoulder. He kept a good grip on his tools. If someone were to lay into him, he was ready to let his clothes go but he was damn sure not going to let go of his kit.

Children scampered around the sheds, in and out of the pools of sputtering light from gas lanterns. A group of three tough boys chased a pig out of a woman's shack. She screeched at the ruffians and the group laughed and pounded on the animal's back with sticks. A drunk laid out against a dying tree shook his fist and yelled something unintelligible in a scolding tone. Slip hadn't planned on coming into this ragged part of town, but it was cheap and he could be anonymous.

He walked a hundred yards through the muddy labyrinth. The last of the sunlight shone thinly through the layer of clouds. The air held the promise of rain all mixed in with smells of human waste and wood smoke. He was looking for an empty shack, but there didn't seem to be any. Families lay sprawled on mattresses. Women sat on crates in the doorways as if to block any more people from coming in. He looked up at the clouds and hoped for any shelter at all.

He turned the corner of the muddy lane. He saw a stunted maple tree at a crossroads and a skinny man sitting on a coffin. The old man was rolling a smoke and looking up at the sky.

"You looking for someone?" the old man asked.

"I'm just looking for somewhere to duck in for the night," Slip told him.

"She's pretty filled up," the old man said, and he licked down the edge of his smoke. "I been hearing that the health boys and the bulls are going to start rousting folks out of here this afternoon. Chase 'em back up into the hills, I guess. When the good folks start complaining about the smell, the next thing you know they got to move us out. You got any fire?" He looked at Slip, and the logger unbuttoned the top of his tool kit to take out a box of matches he kept there. He struck a match and lit the old man's cigarette.

"I'll rent you this spot if you want." He smiled and rapped on top of the coffin.

"You sleep in this thing?" Slip asked.

"Hell, son, I figure it's good practice." The old man winked.

Slip shrugged his shoulders as if getting cold, and handed the man fifty cents.

A few raindrops spattered the ground, and the maple tree whispered as a fresh wind blew through the encampment.

He looked around, and opened the lid of the coffin. He sat on the lip, unlaced his boots, and climbed in, arranging his bindle under his head and his toolbox alongside his feet.

"Give me a hand there and pull the tarp over, would you?"

And the old man spread a canvas tarp over the opened lid so that it draped down like a lean-to.

The coffin was lined with a lurid red fabric that was surprisingly soft. The strangeness was in climbing in. But once in he felt tired and at ease . . . at least as long as the lid stayed open. The sounds of the hobo encampment crept under the tarp. The voices of parents calling their children in blended with the thudding of feet padding on the mud. Chickens clucked and occasionally a dog would bark. Somewhere men were playing cards and cursing their luck, and somewhere a teapot was shrieking its contents into the air.

Slip was tired. The world was strange to him now as he settled into the coffin for the night. He wondered if meeting Ellie Hobbes had somehow slipped his life off the tracks and into this waking hallucination that his life had become.

In the morning he was damp with the rainwater sluiced into his coffin around one corner of the tarp. He unfolded himself from the box, stretched, tucked in his shirt, and went to get a shave. Walking up the hill to the barbershop on Cherry Street, he felt that was as good as any place to start.

≈≈≈

"Good Lord, Almighty!" Andy stopped sweeping and stared.

"Hey, Andy," Slip said.

"You look like hell," Andy said, and he set the broom in the corner then gestured to the only barber's chair in the place.

"Well, I got robbed of my stake money and spent the night in a coffin." Slip flopped down in the chair and pushed himself back with a groan. "So, I figure, I've looked better."

"Not since I've known you, you ain't looked better." Andy set down his broom and smiled.

Slip and Andy had been running buddies. They had blown into the Seattle train yards together. They had both quit the dam job at the same time and had ridden all night shivering on the outside of a tanker car through the Cascades where the snow spit down on them like nails. They had been wet and shivering by the time they stumbled up to the little jungle camp along the river by White Center. Andy decided to ask his uncle for a job, and Slip thumbed it north to the Skagit. Slip and Andy had been a couple of the lucky ones. They had found work. Although Slip wasn't feeling particularly lucky anymore.

"Where's your uncle?" Slip asked.

"Up and died. Can you believe it? I'm working for Aunt Ruth now. She says I'm a part owner, but I don't see how I'm owning anything. It's more like I'm working for her."

Andy gently soaped up Slip's face. "Lord love a duck, how'd you get so beat up?"

"I ain't been beat up. I've just been logging." Slip kept his eyes closed as he spoke.

"Same difference," Andy said. He scraped up Slip's throat.

"You ever hear of a gal named Ellie Hobbes?" Slip asked, his lips making bubbles in the lather.

"Hobbes . . . I don't know her, but I've seen her. She's a Red, pal."

"The hell you say."

"I'm telling you the truth, son. You ain't mixed up with her are you? That's a good way to get your skull cracked."

"She's not a skull cracker is she?"

"Naw. Not her, she's a honey trap. But those who come around her end up with their skulls cracked."

"Who does the cracking?" Slip asked.

"Floodwater. They get paid to clean the Reds out of town. They don't give a goddamn if you're a Red or not. They see you hanging around a meeting hall or catch you with some pamphlets, they'll split your head open for sure."

"They got a tall one with a fancy hat?" Slip asked, thinking of the antsy man at the rundown house with the crying babies.

"Hell, son, they're all big. Ben Avery's the one you got to watch out for. He's killed his share of hoboes he thought was Reds. Killed 'em and let them die in the weeds."

"You're making this up now." Slip closed his eyes and breathed in the mint-scented soap. He relaxed under the touch of the razor, easing into what could only be a preposterous barber's lie.

"The hell I am," Andy said, as he wiped the soap on the towel draped over his shoulder. "You get mixed up with Avery?"

"I don't know. Got mixed up with Ellie Hobbes, though. That's for certain."

"Ah, criminy," Andy said. "I'd just blow town right now. You can't handle Ben Avery's kind of trouble."

"I tell you, Andy, I just got the wrong ride."

"I can believe that."

"I'd love to blow town but she's got all my money for the farm. She's got everything I've ever saved."

Andy nodded, wiping the razor with a towel. "You didn't give it to her, did you? 'Cause I'm just saying that was one stupid . . ."

"No, she took it."

"Strong-armed you, did she?" Andy was smiling as he lifted the tip of Slip's nose and moved the razor to his lip.

"I got an address and a time for a meeting. I've got some paper she wants. I got a gun. You want to come with me to the meeting and get the money? We can grab it and be up over the mountains before sunup."

"I ain't going to no Red meeting. I don't care about the oppressed masses. I'm hoping to be a proud member of the ruling class if my aunt ever signs this shop over to me."

"So you're not throwing in with me?" Slip asked, not really surprised but disappointed nonetheless.

"Look at me, partner. I'm a business owner. I got soft hands now and a taste for the good life. I am not going to milk some pig on the east side." He chuckled and gestured around his shop—the one broken barber's chair, the sink, a coal stove, a few soft chairs for waiting customers, and a small cracked mirror—as if it were a newly discovered paradise.

Slip tried halfheartedly to change his friend's mind, but didn't have the energy to see it through. He promised he would see him again before he left town, and Andy shook his hand. Slip tried to pay for the shave but Andy waved him off, and Slippery stepped out into the new Seattle morning. There was a breeze coming from the north with streaky clouds in a gray sky and across the Sound he could see whitecaps dotting the water.

He walked the waterfront for most of the day, trying to decide what to do. He had to go and get his money. But he knew that he was stepping into a hornet's nest if he did. There was no good luck coming from this. He held the revolver in his pocket and thought of throwing it off a wharf but he didn't. It might come in useful if someone tried to crack his skull, though he had never fired a pistol and wasn't sure he could, even in anger.

Around sunset he bought a glass of beer and helped himself to two free sandwiches on the back sideboard of a crowded bar. They were gray roast beef and mustard on stiff white bread. He started back for a third but the Irish bartender with a mustache like John L. Sullivan's gave him the thumb and told him to beat it.

Slip walked around looking for the meetinghouse for at least an hour. He ended up at the same sagging house he had visited the day before. But now there were six guys hanging out on the corner. The evening was cooling down with a damp breeze blowing through. The men were shuffling from one foot to the other while sharing a bag of tobacco. A couple of them had newspapers stuffed inside their suit coats for insulation. The house looked like it had once been a storefront. The big front window had been filled in with smaller window frames but none of the windows matched up. The whole place sagged a little like a rotten jack-o'-lantern.

"I'm here for the meeting," Slip said, nodding to them. One of the men offered him a smoke but he declined. The men said nothing. They didn't exchange names but kept stamping their feet, trying to avoid each other's stare.

Finally a nervous young man came walking up the sidewalk. He was tiny with a wiry build. He walked quickly, lifting his knees as if the pavement were red hot.

"Sorry to be late," he said in a hoarse whisper. "I'll let us in. I'll put some coffee on, then maybe I'll find some sinkers to go with it." He lunged up the front steps, unlocked the door, and went inside.

There were maybe ten chairs set up in the living room all facing the same direction. There was a piano and a birdcage, and sitting on the couch next to the window was Ellie. The red blotches on her face had darkened into purple bruises.

Slip walked directly over to her.

"Hello," she said, "it's good to see you." And she smiled in a way that momentarily made him forget that he was angry with her.

Slip was about to start talking to her when the young man came in with a plate of doughnuts and the men all pushed toward them. The tiny man stepped back as the bums rushed in around him, and he disappeared behind their shoulders.

"Got more of these," he said in his same raspy tenor. "I'll bring them out when the coffee is ready." The men shoved the doughnuts into their mouths. Some of them had faces sunken in by hunger. None of them had shaved that morning and none of them looked at any of the flyers laid on the chairs.

Ellie was turned in her chair and looking out the window to the street.

"Listen," Slip said to her, "I want my money back."

"All right," she said softly, "but the meeting is about to start."

"I'm not staying for no meeting," Slip said, looking around.

Ellie pulled him down into a chair. "Just sit here for a bit. I'm sorry I took your money. I will give it back to you, I promise. I needed you to come here. You've got the other paper I gave you?"

He nodded his head, and she patted him on the leg, stood up, and walked up to the front of the room.

The men ate as if someone were going to steal the doughnuts from their mouths.

"We'll have some coffee in a little bit," she said softly, flexing her fingers back and forth into a fist. The men looked down at their hands in their laps. One or two looked at Ellie.

She smiled silently until all the men looked up at her beautiful wrecked face. One old man let out a low whistle. No one else made a sound. Her dull blue eyes began to awaken, as if she had just taken a breath of mountain air.

"Gentlemen," she started nervously, "I'm not here to sell you anything. You don't have to believe a word I have to say and I'm not going to ask you for any donations. If all you get out of this evening are some doughnuts and coffee, then that's fine with me."

Ellie walked back and forth in front of the hungry men. As she walked, she played with her hair nervously. She smoothed the fabric of her clean blue dress down her legs, not looking at any of them.

"Now, you don't know me," she said and then stopped, staring each of them in the eyes. "But I figure that I'd like to get to know you," and she smiled sweetly.

"Fine with me," a man to the left of Slip called out.

Ellie smiled with as much coy charm as her bottle-blonde hair and bruised face would allow and she didn't speak for another long moment. The hinges of the folding chairs squeaked and someone cleared his throat.

Then she looked up at them. "You boys want beefsteaks?" Everyone smiled, and one man with broken-down leather shoes rubbed his hands together and licked his cracked lips. "Well, I can't afford beefsteak for you boys. I can't afford these doughnuts. I stole 'em in the first place."

"Somebody call the cops!" someone yelled, and everyone laughed.

"That's right," she said, "call the cops. But before they get here, let me ask you something. You boys like this life we got here for ourselves?"

Then she stopped and looked at the men shifting in their chairs, her blue eyes burning so hard inside that purple mask that no one wanted to look up at her. "Now come on. It's easy. Are you happy with what you have now? Do any of you have a house to go home to? Do your kids have plenty to eat?"

"Yeah, sure," a guy next to her grumbled, "and an ocean liner to keep it all on."

"Well, what's the matter?" she said, pushing up her sleeves and pacing in front of the room. "I was just looking around and there's lots of people who have plenty of everything. I've been peeking in the windows of those big brick buildings up on Queen Anne and Capitol Hill. I've been up in the neighborhoods looking out on the lake, and everybody out there's got tables just heaped with food. What's wrong with you men? Are you lazy?"

"Lazy . . ." somebody grumbled.

"'Cause that's what they say. They say you don't want to work."

"Course we want to work," the grumbler said out loud, and he looked up directly at the woman for the first time.

"Then you must be picky about what kind of jobs you'd be willing to take."

"Phooey," the grumbler said, and began to stand up.

"But I think there's probably a better explanation. Because I've also been snooping around the docks today, and I've seen the foremen getting bribes to put their friends to work. I've seen men working all day long for no more money than one decent meal for himself alone." The grumbler sat back down. "Yes I've been snooping. How else do you think I got this," and she gestured vaguely toward her face, "this nice eye makeup. How'd you think I come by this? I'm a woman. I'm naturally curious."

A laugh went around the room. "I have seen men getting hurt or killed every day and not one thing done for their family except maybe a smoked ham from the front office . . . and a card from the boss that his secretary signed."

She stopped and looked straight at them, "I know you don't believe this. But I believe in you, men. I believe in you."

The room was quiet then. The chairs creaked and men shuffled their feet. A sadness crept into the room.

"I know that you aren't lazy. I know you want to work. I know you want a decent life in this country that promises you a decent life every time it fights a war and you have to go off and risk your neck."

An old man coughed, filling the awkward silence.

She paused again until they were all looking directly at her. She seemed bigger now as if their attention made her grow in stature. "You could whip any nation on earth, because you'd be working together. You could march halfway across the world and beat the Germans or the French or just about anybody. And your wives and sisters would be proud and welcome you home with flowers and kisses." A couple of the men rubbed sore hands on their legs and gulped their coffee without taking their eyes off her.

"Then how is it we're here today, broke and alone, eating stolen doughnuts and drinking weak coffee? How'd it come to this?" She looked around, knowing that each man was casting for an answer.

"I'll tell you how it came to this. Those people up in those fine houses don't want you asking for what's yours. They don't want you to come together and demand a piece of that good life that they all got." She paused and looked around and some of them looked down at their feet and nodded to themselves.

"You deserve a good life. You know that, don't you?"

A couple of them muttered.

"You deserve a good life," she almost whispered.

"Just bring out the coffee," someone said, and the others laughed.

"It looks like you got what you deserved, lady," a feeble old tramp called out.

She looked at him and drew in a deep breath, but instead of launching back into her oratory she spoke with a soft, husky voice as if she were alone with the tramp.

"There's a lot we all deserve, isn't there?" And she looked at him with her blue eyes that seemed to make shadows wherever she looked. "Yes, we all deserve things. Good things . . . and then bad things," and again she gestured toward her face. "We're all probably due payment from both accounts. But aren't you getting tired of only getting paid for the bad? I know I am."

The men shifted in their chairs. The floor creaked under the threadbare carpet, and two of the men took off their hats and stared at the speaker, who looked at them each one by one, and she ended up staring directly into Slip's eyes and holding him there as if he were floating up out of his chair.

"Ain't it about time you got some of those good things you deserve?" She looked at them until they could bear it no more. Then she walked around the room shaking their hands.

Most of the men stood up and looked around for the food.

The little man brought out a coffeepot and some mugs and they gathered around as if standing at a campfire. A couple of them stuffed extra doughnuts into their pockets to be kept in reserve for the revolution.

Slip looked over and saw two men by the door motioning Ellie over to where they stood. Ellie refused to acknowledge them. Slip moved between the hungry tramps and tried to get her attention but she purposely ignored him now as well. Finally she handed the coffeepot back to the little nervous man, and walked toward the men by the door.

They were both several heads taller than she was, with wide shoulders, and one had a long, crooked nose that he aimed as if sighting down a barrel. Then he pointed his finger in her face. He appeared to be speaking slowly and urgently. Slip could not hear the words until one of them stepped back suddenly and said, "Fine, then!" And both the big men walked out the door.

Ellie walked slowly back toward Slip. Her hands were nervous once again, tugging at her clothes, and she seemed to have shrunken back to size.

"That wasn't so good," she said.

"Who were they? What did they have to say?" Slip asked.

"They're nobody. I meant that the speech didn't go so well."

"I've got to talk to you," Slip said to Ellie.

"I don't doubt it," she said softly, putting her hand once again on his lap.

"I got a friend who says you're going to get me killed."

"Your friend sounds like the nervous type," Ellie said. "Besides we got bigger troubles," and she nodded toward the door.

"You stole my goddamn money, sister." Slip blew up. "There ain't no *we* to this."

"I will give you back your two thousand one hundred and twenty three dollars. Trust me. You don't have anything to worry about," she said.

"Why should I trust you?" he asked.

Ellie was standing by the window holding the curtain back slightly so she could keep one eye out on the street. "That is a good question, and I don't really know the answer. I just know that you do. I know it because you had plenty of chances to walk away and you didn't. You do, Jack Wilson. You trust me."

"I do not trust you," he said with as much conviction as he could muster.

She squeezed his hand again. "We'll see," she said.

Slip felt like shaking the girl in hopes of waking her up, for it struck him that she was acting with an odd formality that he hadn't seen in her before. It was as if she were aware of someone else's presence and was consciously putting her best foot forward. Then for the first time, he noticed the birdcage on the piano. Inside the cage was a yellow bird with a crest that stuck up from his head and big red spots on his cheeks. To Slip it was an odd and beautiful sight as if the bird had just finished putting too much rouge on its cheeks. There was a little girl standing on the piano stool and poking her finger into the cage. The girl had long braids and glasses tilted forward on her nose.

"Hey, Buddy. Hey, Buddy. You want something to eat?" she cooed to him.

"Annabelle, honey, why don't you play in your room for a bit longer," Ellie said.

"Can I take Buddy with me?"

"Sure you can, doll," Ellie said, still keeping her eyes out on the street.

The girl hopped down and took the little round-topped cage with her and disappeared through the door.

"Oh, my dear." Ellie whispered, "Excuse me, Mr. Wilson, you still have the gun I gave you?"

"Yes, I do, and I'm not giving it back."

"That's fine," she said, and turned away from the window just as someone began pounding at the front door. "I just recommend that you keep it close."

Slip didn't say a word. The pounding continued and the glass window in the door sounded as if it were going to shatter.

"Is that Avery?" Ellie asked as she walked toward the back of the house.

Slip looked out the window and saw a man in a gray coat standing on the corner under the streetlight. The two men who had been talking to Ellie by the door were headed back toward the house.

"How the hell would I know?" Slip called out.

Ellie was buttoning up her coat and feeling her pockets for something in a hurry. "It's probably Pierce and Conner. They're going to want back in. But don't you let them."

"What the hell are you talking about?" Slip said, sounding more tired than frightened.

"Back door," Ellie said and walked out of the room.

"What about the little girl?" Slip called out.

"No time." Ellie was in the little kitchen peeking through the shade pulled over the window above the sink. A loud pounding from the front door shook the room. "They don't want her. She'll be fine. It will slow them down, if anything. We'll come back in a bit and get her."

"What do you mean a bit?" Slip stood flat-footed in the living room with his arms folded across his chest.

"One hour tops." Ellie had her hand on the back doorknob.

The pounding on the door stopped. There was a long pause and then there was the creaking sound of two men taking a step backward.

Then there was a shattering of glass.

"I'm getting out of here," Ellie said, as the doorframe began to splinter.

The frame gave way and Slip was running right behind the blonde. They were out the back door and into a small muddy yard. They ran to the low board fence and pushed through the gate. As they turned up the alley Slip noticed that the streetlight was not on. He turned and thought of going back to the house, but saw shadows of big men wobbling past the shades. When they went into the neighbor's yard, a dog started barking. They ran out into the next street over.

There was no one there waiting for them. The streetlight was on and it poured out a pool of serenity in the night. Slip took three steps backward when a man in a gray suit stepped out of a gate and took his arm. He was joined by others. None of them was the tall man from the dairy, but they were cut from the same cloth: bone breakers in worn-out suits and clean shirts. Nightmares in crepe-soled shoes.

"Easy now, bud," one of them said.

A slow-moving sedan turned the corner and came to a stop.

"Put 'em in the car. I'm going to take the both of them for a drive," he said with a growl the other mutts appeared to defer to.

"Want us to come along, Ben?" the man getting out of the car asked.

"Naw, I'm fine. These two don't have balls enough between 'em. We've got some talking to do. I'll see you back at the office tomorrow."

"If you say so," the gray suit said, and pushed Slip into the front seat of the sedan.

"You, logger. You drive," Avery said, and he pushed Ellie into the backseat, slamming the door behind her.

As they turned the corner on the darkened street where the meetinghouse stood, Slip looked up and saw Annabelle in the top window. She had the yellow bird resting on her index finger. The light from the window slid down the side of the building and spattered out onto the street like paint. As they turned the final corner, the yellow bird ruffled its feathers and looked as if it were going to fly.

THREE

~~~

Annabelle loved staring at the yellow bird. She could spend hours looking into his black doll's eyes, thinking about what it must be like to fly through the eucalyptus forests of Australia. Buddy was from Australia, or at least his parents were from there. The lady from the pet store said that Buddy had been born in the store and had never known any other life. He was a cockatiel and he would live a very long time.

Annabelle had won Buddy in a contest. All she had had to do was write her name very carefully on the back of a lid from a box of birdseed and put it in a jar. Ellie had given her the money to buy the birdseed in the first place. Ellie was good for those kinds of things. Surprises. Unexpected parties. Like buying a box of birdseed just out of the blue without much explanation.

Ellie was Annabelle's aunt, and though she was a good speech maker she wasn't much like a mother. Ellie was fun, but ever since her mother had died Annabelle had learned to do things for herself.

Annabelle loved Buddy even though when she first got him he would bite her hard enough to break the skin. Annabelle even suspected that the pet store lady had given him away in a contest because he was such a bad-mannered bird. Then the girl decided that it must have been a result of somebody being horribly mean to him. So Annabelle chose to be exceedingly nice to the cranky yellow bird. She fed him exactly what the books said to give him: nuts and sometimes some pieces of fruit. She gave him his food by lying for hours on the bed with the seeds cupped in her hand and her hand extended into the cage. For the first day Buddy would only shriek and hop from perch to perch, but the little girl would lie still, murmuring his name and saying, "It's okay, it's okay." By the third day he was eating out of her hand, and by the end of the week she could put him on her shoulder while she read a book.

Annabelle rarely spoke to anyone. It wasn't out of unfriendliness or fear. It was just that she felt that her words were like money and she wanted to spend them wisely. She loved reading books. In books there was a surfeit of words and to her a library was a kind of Fort Knox. She particularly loved books about animals. More than books and words she loved the animals themselves. There was a drawing of a leopard above the window where she stood and watched the man put Ellie and that other man with the sad face in the car.

They had been living in Seattle for a couple of years. Ellie had been in Aberdeen when Annabelle first came to live with her. They lived in her grandpa's bar, which worked out fine for a while but Ellie wanted to give speeches in Seattle. Leaving Aberdeen seemed to have been a mistake. There were fewer and fewer men turning out for her aunt's speeches, and more and more men coming around late in the evenings with whiskey on their breath. It had often occurred to her that one day Ellie might not be there in the morning, and this thought didn't particularly frighten her. It didn't frighten her like thinking about Buddy flying away, or thinking about Buddy flying into a windowpane, swooping down from some perch looking at that other yellow bird coming at him in the exact same motion. Annabelle knew about being alone. She just didn't want Buddy to die or become lost.

So when she heard the men breaking down the door, she took Buddy and hid underneath the bed, and when she stood at the window and watched them drive away she only thought about whether there was enough birdseed in the house.

The night passed as it usually did for Annabelle. Ellie was out. The sounds of the street secreted their way into her dreams, so that she sometimes saw birds driving milk trucks and when newsboys threw their papers they would become fluttering moths before hitting the porch. So it didn't seem odd to Annabelle that Ellie was home around daylight and was in a hurry to leave that next morning, just as the bruise across her aunt's face hadn't frightened her. Annabelle packed up her gear: a small bag of books, underwear, socks, two shirts, two pairs of pants, her heavy coat, and her umbrella. Ellie packed more of her clothes, furiously stuffing them into suitcases, and Annabelle walked slowly down to the kitchen and took down the big package of birdseed from the pantry shelf.

The car they were riding in was the same one in which they had driven away the day before. When Ellie opened the car's trunk, Annabelle saw a hand that looked kind of waxy white with blood on it. The rest of the person was covered with a blanket. All Ellie said was, "Don't look at that now," and she slammed the trunk shut. When Annabelle got in, she saw the sad man holding a cloth to his nose with blood dripping down on the seat. He said "hello" to her in a polite voice. It was then that Annabelle knew they were going on a very long trip and she was sorry she hadn't brought more books.

They drove on various small roads, trying to stay away from other cars or houses. Just before the sun came up, they came to a small yard near a muddy, fetid section of river. There were smokestacks behind them and rusty pieces of iron scattered in the mud. Ellie made a big point of talking to Annabelle while the man got out of the car and opened the trunk. Annabelle looked at her bird, the black dots of his eyes jittering around his cage, while just faintly along the edge of her perception she listened to the sound of someone dragging something across the mud.

Ellie started to cry and she couldn't stop. Her nose got all snotty and her chest heaved up and down with those big *boo-hooing* sounds that little kids make when they fall off the swings and get the wind knocked out of them or when they step on a bad rusty nail and know that they might die of lockjaw. Ellie cried like that, hard and sad, but when she was done crying, she acted as if nothing at all had happened. Annabelle kept one hand on top of Buddy's cage and she put the other hand on Ellie's shoulder. "It's okay, it's okay," she said, looking only at the bird.

The rest of the morning they drove around not going on any big street or in any one direction for very long. They stopped at a little house. Annabelle didn't even get out of the car because people were yelling and Buddy sat with his feathers ruffled as if the sound of the angry voices were a spray of cold water. The girl looked up over the bottom of the car window toward the house where the man with the broken nose was yelling at someone, while Ellie sat off by herself on the porch smoking a cigarette. An ugly man who looked like a strongman from the circus, only about four feet tall, came out and threw a case down on the ground. The case was empty and it sat on the wet lawn like a broken clamshell. The little strong man was saying that they would be lucky if they got caught by the cops. Buddy pecked at his bell and looked at his curved reflection in his little mirror and Annabelle cooed to him to reassure the bird that everything was going to be all right.

Then the ugly man told them all to get off his property, which they did.

They drove until they came to a spot where a bunch of cars were stopped and there was a police car. The sad-looking man said a bunch of bad words and turned the car around. Then he wanted to get out of the car once they got around the corner but Ellie wouldn't let him. So they drove back down toward the city where there were lots of cars, and the man with the broken nose said that he had had enough and he got out of the car even when it wasn't all the way stopped.

Ellie said that they couldn't go back to the house and they had to get rid of the car. She stopped at a gas station and made some telephone calls and then drove out to a market where a gray cat was sitting on top of the candy counter and a brown terrier was tied up to the water pump. Ellie stood outside the store and drank something from a bottle wrapped in a paper bag. The dog didn't even lift its head. Annabelle thought the dog didn't look very happy and she was thinking about going over and seeing if she could get it something to eat or maybe just scratch his ears for a minute when Ellie came back to the car and told her that they were going to have to walk for a little ways down to a barbershop. Which they did.

They walked down the street, away from the market, away from the gray cat on the counter and away from the sad-looking dog that lifted its head just an inch off of its paws to watch them go. They would come back for the car a little bit later but the dog would be gone, its chain lying tangled in the mud and its big footprints filling up with rain.

FOUR

~~~

Slip woke up sleeping on the ropes. He rolled over and felt a jab of pain from the cut on his hip. He looked down the row where some dozen other tramps were slung up on the thick lines strung above the warehouse floor. He wasn't the only one who had blood dripping from his clothes.

This was a warehouse where a shipping line stored the great mooring hawsers used for securing the big ships. The boys would stretch them across the width of the warehouse and make a kind of gigantic hammock out of two or three courses of the ropes. It wasn't comfortable, but it beat sleeping in the mud under the blackberries and was certainly better than sleeping on the wooden floor of the warehouse where the rats would chew on your shoe leather.

Slip woke up slowly. For a moment he lay relaxed, warm with the feeling that everything that had happened the night before had been a dream. He could hear the sound of the water slapping against the pilings under the floor. The images from the car swept back and forth in his mind: the sharp voices, the blows, and the knife blade, then the smell of gunpowder in the close quarters of the sedan. Some tramp fell off the ropes and hit the floor with a thud, and a coldness grabbed Slip. He knew it wasn't a dream. Ben Avery was dead. He put one foot on the plank floor and wadded his shirt up against the weeping cut on his side.

He had no idea what time it was. It was morning when he had gotten there but that didn't mean much. Guys came in and out of the warehouse at all hours looking for a place to hide from the cops. The bulls had swept through Hooverville just a day later than the old man with the coffin had said, so now it was easy to get picked up downtown on a vagrancy charge.

Downtown cops didn't care much for loafers or tramps hanging around where people were making money. In other parts of town it was a little easier to hide out in the brush or in a vacant lot. But the boys just in off the freights or looking for work on the docks had to lie low if they wanted to stay out of jail.

A couple of tramps came in from the train yards and said the place was crawling with bulls. "Christ almighty!" one of them yelped. "They got city cops, railroad bulls, and Floodwater ops going through every car. They got so much juice down on the flats there can't be any cops up here!"

One little hobo with a broken hand said he heard someone had killed a Floodwater op. Slip kept his collar up and his head down while he feigned sleep.

"Hell, I wouldn't kill me no private dick. Shit, they never had it in for nobody but the Reds. I'd kill me a railroad bull."

"I'd kill me a dock boss," someone else said.

Then came a clattering on the warehouse door, and cops with sticks lumbered in and started knocking shins. Large men in blue slickers walked down the line hitting the boys with sticks as if they were hoeing a bean field. Boys yelled and swore but none of the would-be murderers put up a fight.

Slip turned and swung under the ropes, crawling on his belly toward the corner. He got a better look and saw that these weren't cops but private security men, probably American Legion or local volunteers. They were yelling and standing guys up to get a look at their faces. One scuffle broke out when the little hobo with the broken hand smashed a bottle over someone's head. Slip stood up and dove for a hole in the floor, while blows rained down on the little hobo like wet snow sliding off a roof.

Slip caught his shoulder on a ragged nail on the way down, but he made it cleanly into the water beneath the warehouse wharf. He felt the weightlessness of falling and then the slap of the water. For a brief numbing moment he thought he was unconscious: no sound, no sensation of being either held up or held down. Then the coldness of the water began splitting his skin and he struggled to the surface. He gasped, choking and spitting as he came to the surface, then he started swimming back toward the shadows under the wharf.

Rats crawled over the rocks and over his clothes as he lay there bleeding and shivering. He listened to the footfall of the dicks dragging the tramps across the floor above him. There were some more shouts and scuffles but eventually the clamor subsided and the voices took on their usual tone of muttering complaints directed at no one within hearing.

Slip clambered up the rocks, then up onto the boardwalk that served as the sidewalk next to the warehouse. He slicked back his hair and tried to shake himself off as best he could. He reached in his inside pocket and took out the tobacco tin, opened it and checked his cash, which was still pretty dry. Slip straightened out his sore shoulder, put the tin back in his pocket, then tucked in his shirt to hide the bloodstain.

The avenue was clattering awake as he lumbered over to the steam baths. He paid a kid a nickel to run up to the barbershop and get a message to Andy to meet him at the Alaska Steamship Company dock as quick as he could.

Long hours passed as Slip waited for Andy. He went back to the ropes and took some dry clothes off a drunk, using the undershirt to bind up his hip and shoulder. He walked back out on the street. He kept his old mackinaw but was wearing a felt hat that was too big with a hole worn in the front brim. He wanted to go back up to the meetinghouse to get his tools but he didn't dare. Avery had found him there, so other Floodwater operatives were bound to be watching the place.

The rain kept falling between the buildings and the clogged gutters sprayed out like broken showerheads. He had no idea what time it was, but it felt like early evening by the time Andy came up the sidewalk to the spot where Slip was sitting back under the eaves of the steamship building.

"This looks like some kind of mess," Andy said as he ducked under the eaves.

"Yeah?"

"They are all over you. Couple of flatfoots came by my shop. Wanted to know where you are."

"What did you tell 'em?" Slip turned his head but didn't look Andy in the eyes.

"I told them I had seen you yesterday. Don't want to get caught in a lie right off. They probably been following you all along."

"I suppose."

"Well . . . did you kill him? Avery, I mean."

"It's a long story, Andy. All that matters is I'm in a hell of a fix."

"Yeah. You and that girl you were talking about. Just after the cops were by my shop she came in. Guess she's in the same fix, huh?"

"Ellie?"

"Hell, yes, though I got to say it looks like you got the worst of it."

"What did she say?"

"She wanted to know where you were."

"Was there a kid with her?"

"I didn't see anybody else. She just wanted to see you real bad. But I don't know. Everybody has their tit in a ringer about Avery. They found his car parked back up the hill and there was blood all over the trunk. They're pretty riled up, son. I've never seen anything quite like it. They're rousting out people who aren't used to being rousted. They're stopping cars on the streets and they say they got the docks and the trains shut down tight. This one flatfoot said that if you stick your broken nose out from under any rock in the city they will be on you like stink on shit. Hasn't hit the papers yet but it will tonight, tomorrow morning for sure."

"Got any ideas?" Slip looked Andy in the eyes now. He was bone tired and every part of his body seemed to hurt. Slip didn't know what he would do next if Andy didn't have something to offer.

"I got an idea. But I can't say you're going to like it much."

"I'm not picky."

"All right. You know where that little steam laundry is up at the far end of the beach? It's run by that Chinaman? Meet me there tomorrow morning early. First light. I'll get some stuff together."

"Andy?" Slip asked.

"Yeah?"

"If she asks about me again, tell her where I am, okay? Don't tell nobody else. Just her. You understand me?"

Andy shook his head from side to side. "Lord, Lord, Lord," was all he said.

Slip stole a loaf of bread and an apple from a vendor in the market and slept under the wharf near the Chinese laundry. He lay shivering as the rain dribbled down between the planking. He heard men talking in strange languages and their footsteps pounding along the walk. Each time he heard someone he held his breath, waiting for them to stop and start yelling for the police, but no one did.

That night passed as one interminable moment. Each splash of a wave seemed as loud as a siren, and each time he moved, the clatter of even the smallest rock rang like an alarm bell under the wharf. Finally he threw a crust of bread as far away as he could to draw the rats off and he listened to them scramble and fight for it. He could not close his eyes; he stared into the echoing darkness and begged for the sun to come up.

When it did, he was half asleep. The rain was a soft drizzle, and under the wharf he found himself in a dripping cavern of shadow set back from the world. With the daylight, the lapping of the waves against the tarry pilings seemed less threatening than it had in the dark. Even this little bit of greasy light gave Slip some cause for hope.

His hope was beginning to dim by the time Andy stood above him on the sidewalk and whispered his name.

"Hey, son, where the hell are you?" he hissed.

Slip rolled out and pulled himself up on top of the wharf.

"Come on," Andy said, and grabbed him by the elbow, rushing him around the corner and down the street half a block to a set of stairs that went down the far side of the laundry building to the beach.

"I won this from an old Norsky fisherman in a poker game about a month ago. He claimed it was plenty good and had caught him lots of fish." Andy was pointing down at the water. Slip stared after him but couldn't imagine what he was talking about. There were things down on the beach but nothing came into focus as an answer to his current problems.

"I put food and stuff in it. The old Norsky had all the gear. There's a lantern, a little stove. There's an axe and everything. He said he had some rum squirreled away in the kitchen kit. I even got your clothes and the toolbox out of the meeting hall."

"How in the hell did you do that?" Slip was looking all around him.

"I paid a kid to get it. It wasn't hard. The door was broken in. The bums had taken all the food but your stuff was fine. Just a few clothes, your suit, and a hank of rope. I had to buy the tools back from the kid. The little scamp wanted to keep them, but I figure you might need 'em for your voyage." Andy had a chuckle in his voice.

"What the hell are you talking about, a voyage?" Slip looked into the eyes of his old running partner, not angry but genuinely confused.

Andy pointed down to the water. "The dory, boy. They ain't going to be looking for you by water. They got the roads and the train stations all buttoned down."

"Maybe they're still looking for Avery. He could have just run off?" Slip said weakly, shivering in his wet clothes.

"He ain't run off. You and I both know that, Slip. They found his body last night dumped out in the weeds by White Center. Now I hear they got another body in a trunk of a car out past Edmonds somewhere, and everybody's just *real* excited." Andy did not look at Slip as he spoke. Slip wiped his nose with his hand and looked straight up into the sky for a moment.

"Who was in the trunk of the car they found sunk in the water?" Slip asked softly, and Andy just looked at him without speaking.

"Tell me!" Slip barked.

"Aw," Andy said, "it's just . . ."

"For Christ's sake, Andy, who was in the trunk of the car?"

"Some union boss. He was the guy that ran the docks up in Everett. It's just . . ."

"Well, what?"

"I never said nothing about the car being sunk in the water."

Slip threw up his hands "Ah, goddamnit, Andy. I got enough on my mind without you being suspicious minded."

Andy seemed more nervous now, gesturing vaguely up the hill with his right hand. "Anyway, they got every flatfoot and

Floodwater op on the West Coast in Seattle by now. I figure you just sneak north in this little boat and maybe get back onto the road system up above Everett somewhere and then slide on up into Canada for a spell."

"A boat?" Slip asked. This plan was taking a long time coming into focus. "Andy, I don't know a damn thing about boats."

"Well, it's about time to learn, son, 'cause I didn't win no zeppelin from that Norsky fisherman."

Slip looked at the dory, and walked over to it. It was built of narrow planks and looked about twenty feet long. There was his old roll of clothes. There were three long oars and a mast with a bundle of canvas lashed to the outer deck. There were three other canvas bags and one big metal box sitting in the bow.

"It's got an engine?" Slip asked, his voice trailing off into the rain.

"Better than an engine, it's got your two strong arms. Now let's get going so's I can go back to the shop just nice and normal so the guys watching it won't get suspicious."

The dory was hauled out on the cobbles below the laundry. Upstairs there were people coming and going from work. There were doors opening and closing. Lights were coming on, sweeping through the rain above their heads. Uptown he heard a trolley clanging its bell, and in the distance a truck chewed through its gears trying to pull a hill.

"Well, I thank you, Andy. I surely do. I'll make it up to you, I swear."

"Just get the hell out of here. We'll talk about what you owe me later."

"I'll pay you back, Andy, I swear."

Andy put his hand lightly on Slip's shoulder and they bent over the boat to inspect the provisions. There was the metal box with the food and the little gas burner stove. There was a bundle with a creased canvas tent along with a small metal jug for stove fuel and a wooden keg for fresh water. There was even some fishing gear: a rod with a rusty-looking reel and some lures that Slip could make no sense of whatsoever. There was a tube with charts in it. Andy pulled one out and then another until he found the right one. He had ducked in under the cover of the wharf and was trying to show Slip how to read a chart by pointing out where they were and which direction north was when they heard someone quickly walking down the steps.

There were Ellie, and the little girl with the yellow bird in a cage.

What Slip noticed first was that Ellie's hair was still as shiny as a pearl even when it was soaked through and plastered to her head. The second thing he noticed was that the little girl was dry because she was holding a very large black umbrella that seemed to encase both her and the bird.

The first thing he heard was Andy saying, "I'm sorry, Slip. I did what you asked of me. I told her where you were."

Ellie walked toward the boat, wobbling on the sharp rocks in her slick leather shoes. "You want some company, don't you?" she said. And she waved to Annabelle to start bringing down their luggage.

FIVE

≈≈≈

Annabelle held on to the handle of her umbrella. Buddy squawked and sat humped on his perch. The wet wind blew and the silver bell in the cage tinkled. Ellie looked up at them and smiled. She was nervous and had been drinking out of the bottle in the paper bag. Her words had that odd tone as if she were saying something funny but nobody laughed.

Annabelle liked her aunt, but doubted that she was what people thought of as a proper parent. She knew that Ellie was acting out her role as a parent. It was as if Ellie was memorizing lines from a play that starred a very good parent, but she wasn't going to get the part.

She wasn't always like that, though. When she wasn't speech-making about the revolution, Ellie would often sit on the floor of Annabelle's room reading books aloud. Mostly she chose books about animals: beavers building their dams, or arctic terns flying the length of the globe. Sometimes she irritated the girl by turning the life histories of the animals into parables about the struggles of human beings, but not that often. Usually Ellie simply sat with her, reading and napping on the floor, tired, the girl thought, of being an adult.

Sometimes Annabelle thought that Ellie didn't care that much about the revolution. Ellie just liked the company of working men and she liked to read books about airplanes.

Ellie wanted to be a pilot like Amelia Earhart. Annabelle once asked how wanting to be a pilot contributed to the workers' struggle, and Ellie said, "The way this revolution is progressing we're all going to have to learn to fly." Annabelle didn't know if that meant Ellie was pessimistic or optimistic about the coming revolt.

To Annabelle, wanting to fly was the one truly admirable trait Ellie possessed. She seemed to have the temperament for it. Like a bird, she was quick and fussy. She didn't like to settle in one place for too long. When she wasn't exhorting the workers to seize control of the means of production, Ellie liked having fun, all kinds of fun, like walking to the library on rainy days and taking money from the Party fund to go to the movies when she felt like it. Most important, Ellie liked talking about her future and Annabelle was always part of the fantasy.

"I think we should fly to New York City. You can be the navigator and I'll be the head pilot. We'll circle the Stork Club a few times and then set down right in Central Park."

"What can Buddy do?" Annabelle would mutter.

"Buddy can fly second seat. He'll watch the gauges while I fly the plane."

Annabelle and Ellie hadn't had a lot of money since they had moved to Seattle from Aberdeen. The revolution wasn't very profitable apparently. Sometimes Ellie worked late at night at jobs she didn't tell the girl about. Sometimes she disappeared, and came back with a small bundle of cash. There was talk of making changes and moving on to other jobs and other towns. But there had always been that kind of talk, and the girl became as accustomed to it as if it were the moisture in the air.

≈≈≈

The bell in Buddy's cage continued to ring as Ellie piled her suitcases into the middle of the little boat and Annabelle found a seat in the very front. The little boat was loaded down so it squatted on the rocky beach like a duck. The two men pushed it across the tide flat until the stern was resting in the water. The sad-looking man got in and fumbled with the oars while Ellie pushed them farther into the water. Ellie took one last long drink from the paper bag then threw it under the pier, where the girl heard glass breaking. Ellie pushed the boat away from shore and climbed in.

It felt as if the whole thing was going to flip over. No one could keep their seat until the sad man with the beat-up face started to row. He sat with his back to the front and pulled on the oars, staring straight at Ellie.

The rain was falling harder now as the sun broke over the Cascades. The raindrops made little plopping sounds as they tried to jump back into the air. All the drops made little circles and the circles all cut into one another, and sometimes a fish jumped right up through it all and back into the green. A little white diving duck, which Annabelle did not recognize, poked its neck down and disappeared. She leaned back under her umbrella and closed her eyes.

The little dory sat low in the water. Ellie was pulling clothes out of her bags and throwing the suitcases into the water. She was laughing but no one else was. Annabelle had her feet up on her own suitcase and the man who was rowing had a bundle of clothes resting on his outstretched legs. When Annabelle tilted her umbrella she could see only the shoulders and back of the man ducking his head and pulling against the oars.

Annabelle looked to the south where dark clouds rolled over the water. There was a bluff of black clouds churning up the water in its path. It almost looked as if bits of broken glass were being sucked up out of the sea. Annabelle hunched deeper in her spot.

Ellie called over the man to Annabelle, "Did I ever tell you about the little sailboat I used to have out on the lake near the Idaho border?" The battered blonde was waving gaily as if she were in a parade. "My sister and I could sail that boat anywhere." The little girl hunkered down in her nest. "No," she said softly, and added, "I think we're going to get wet." Then she closed her eyes tight and the wind stooped down on them like a falcon. She pulled her umbrella down and curled against the birdcage. As the wind tried to pull the umbrella out of her hands, the yellow bird began to sing.

S I X

George Hanson quit drinking about the same time Prohibition had been lifted. He didn't see the point of it anymore. He had been a cop for ten years and most of that time he had been chasing after the small-time crooks and grifters who had come down to the waterfront following the illegal liquor trade. There had been hidden warehouses and late-night schooners pulling up to unlighted piers. There were speakeasies where everyone knew the password and no one ever expected to be raided. There was never much pressure to solve cases. But now everyone was drinking anywhere they wanted, and Hanson was back to more disagreeable crimes: men killing their wives and sometimes wives getting a first good lick in. Hanson had tried drinking after they lifted Prohibition but he found it too damn depressing.

Hanson had grown up knowing the world of the docks. There had been stevedores and wharf rats coming to their back door for meals ever since he could remember. He had helped his father stitch up men who were unrecognizable from their beatings. His first few years on the force he tried to stay away from the waterfront, but gradually he ended up near the beach, drawn by the smell and the call of the gulls, drawn by the bodies that had a way of washing up there. George had seen the corruption moving into the labor rackets, kickbacks and bribes that flowed up the chain of authority in a way that would have sickened the Finn. The docks were becoming another grift, and he didn't mind putting the bite on some of these new union boys, but he still couldn't stand to be around Floodwater operatives.

Floodwater Security was an old company from the Midwest. The first office opened up in Winona, Minnesota, when the town was broken open by spring floods and the local authorities couldn't stop the looting. The first Floodwater ops were just a couple of thugs beating anyone they caught carrying goods down the street. After the First World War they started their own security firm and moved out to the West Coast. In San Francisco they worked the docks for the big shipping companies and hired more big boys who carried themselves like cops but never learned any other skills than sapping down looters in the mud.

Or so it seemed to George. He was thinking about this because his good leather shoes were sinking into a muddy bank somewhere the hell and gone out in White Center and a clodhopper of a shamus was preventing him from looking at a body some good citizen had bothered to find. Ben Avery had been the best of the Floodwater rat terriers on the docks and as such he was the worst of the thugs, but still, George thought, he deserved a few questions asked about his murder. He had hated Avery, but he harbored a special sliver of disgust for Avery's boss.

"Boss said I'm 'sposed to keep people away from here," the operative said from under the brim of his hat.

"I'm not people," George said, and he held up his badge and shouldered past the dick. He stumbled down the slippery bank over root wads and rusted rigging cables toward the sodden pile that someone had decorously covered with a raincoat. There were men in civilian clothes walking up and down the river, each of them carrying a kerosene lamp. The effect made George think of a bunch of farm boys looking for goats in the dark.

George was looking around for the body in all of the confusion. In the murky light he saw some Floodwater boys carrying a stretcher up the slope. He started to yell to them when he heard heavy footsteps coming up behind him.

"I wouldn't want to be the man who shot Ben Avery," a voice said, and George turned to see Tom Delaney standing in his raincoat with the brim of his hat dripping water.

"You know it was a man?" George asked, still looking at the body. "Wasn't Ben known to have a fairly complicated love life?"

"No dame is going to shoot Ben Avery with his own gun," Delaney said. "It was one of those goddamn Reds. They killed the trade unionist up north and they did this to Ben." Delaney walked around to the head of the corpse and squinted down into the dead eyes. "There's a shit storm about to come down on those Bolshevik bastards," he said.

There were two bodies in two days. One was this shit heel Ben Avery who was found in the grass out here in bumfuck White Center southwest of downtown. The other was the trade unionist they found in the trunk of a Lincoln in a slough up north. George had already heard the story of the trade unionist. Yesterday afternoon a kid fishing from a bridge twenty miles north of Lake City saw the fat tires of a new Lincoln poking up out of the muddy water and he ran home to tell his mother. When the locals came and pulled the car out, the trunk broke open from the weight of the water and the bloated body of Dave Kept flopped out like a dead walrus.

Dave Kept was a trade union organizer who had been making quite a stir along the Washington waterways getting the dock workers to both stand up for themselves and keep their jobs. Kept was considered the lesser of two evils by management. Now he wasn't worth considering at all.

Dave Kept's murder was being handled out of Everett, which was the next town of any size north of Seattle. It had been made famous in George's father's day when the Everett cops shot up a couple of boatloads of Wobblies trying to land at the dock for a rally. Kept had given a speech in Everett the day before his body was found. The Everett cops believed he had been killed in their jurisdiction and was then driven south. George had heard about the case from the investigating officer, who had called down to George's office wanting some background on Kept and the rest of the labor scene.

Delaney was probably right. The two murders were connected. But there was no way of knowing how. George believed that if Ben were still alive he would have told the Everett cops that his car had been stolen. Unless, of course, he was going to confess to murdering the union man, which seemed unlikely. No, there were only two dots right now. It wasn't worth even trying to draw a line between them.

George took out a small notebook and a nub of a pencil. "I'm going to need a list of everybody who's here on the scene and I'd like to get a look at their shoes just so I can make some sense of the tracks around here." George looked over at the Floodwater op and waited, his pencil poised.

Delaney turned slowly and stood up. He was looking down on George even though he was standing downhill. His jaw was set hard and he said nothing.

George dropped his hands to his side but he didn't put the pad and pencil away. "Tom, we'll find the guy."

"With all due respect, George, you aren't the man for this case. We'll take care of this and the situation up in Everett."

"You're saying I'm not the man for this case because of what?"

"Again, with all due respect to you and your father, George, we've got this covered. We've got authorization. We've got the governor and the senator on this. Hell, they can get right to the president if we want. You don't have to have it on your books and you don't have to waste any of your officers' time." Then Tom Delaney reached over and flipped George's notebook shut.

"They've brought this on themselves. You know it's true, George," Tom said almost tenderly.

The one thing George had inherited from his father was his hatred of private security goons. He hated their phony badges and he hated their air of superiority, particularly when the bastards knew nothing about being peace officers. Hell, they couldn't resolve a dispute between two chained-up mutts.

"Brought this on themselves," George muttered to himself, while he stumbled back up to his car. The Big Finn would have thumped that bastard Tom Delaney and dumped his body in a wood chipper. But George was a city employee. He would think of other ways.

He opened his notebook again and made a few notes. It was a body dump and Delaney had told him the killers had used Ben's own gun. Usually George would work this from the ground up. He'd have men all over the city looking for the car and shaking down Ben's contacts on the waterfront. But this was going to be different. George wasn't even going to call the captain. He knew it was true. It was not much of an exaggeration to say that Floodwater could get Governor Martin to clear a revenge killing. George was not going to fight that war. It would cause him to have to make promises to his bosses that he had no intention of keeping. As he got to his car George knew he was going to have to work from the top down.

"I'm going to bed," he said, then pushed the starter with his left foot. When the engine caught, George Hanson wheeled up onto the river road and drove home to his wife, his new electric icebox, and his nice dry bed.

The next morning brought a break in the rain and cold. Sunlight sprawled through his kitchen as he drank his coffee. Kids were playing up and down the street, and his wife stood at the window staring out at the soggy patch of grass that served as a yard.

"You going to be able to pick up a cake at the bakery tonight?" she asked.

"They got it in our name?" he asked without turning his head toward her.

She nodded, and he stood up to put on his jacket.

"You sleep all right?" she asked, as he was heading for the door. "It's like you didn't sleep at all."

George turned and looked at her, trying to recognize something in her tone, something that worried him.

"Yeah, I'm fine. I just have something on my mind." He walked to the door, and she turned back to the window where the sun dappled down mingling with the voices from the street.

"Okay then, just remember the cake. You want me to write you a note?"

"Naw." He moved over to her, paused, and quickly kissed her neck, then turned to go before she had a chance to face him.

In an hour George was knocking on an unpainted door up on Queen Anne Hill. A massive round-faced man with sleep in his eyes came to the door.

"Fatty! Good to see you, boy!" George said as he shouldered past him.

"Christ, George, I just got to bed."

"I'm sorry, Fatty, but you know us government workers. Regular hours and all that." George stood next to Fatty's chair, where his gun and Floodwater badge hung, glinting in the light. George absently fingered the heavy metal badge.

"You got any coffee?" George asked.

"I was asleep, I told you." Fatty rubbed his eyes and shut the door.

"Don't bother making any for me then." George sat in the straight-backed chair and dropped his hat over the toe of his shoe. "Listen, Fatty, I'm going to call in my marker."

Fatty Miller was not just overweight. He had a fat man's sad aura. He walked like a fat man, he breathed like a fat man, and he had the mournful slit-eyed countenance of a man whose personality was hiding deep down in his flesh. He padded across the bare wood floor into the bathroom, where he put on his pants and swung his suspenders over his undershirt.

"I know I owe you, George. But don't ask me what I think you're . . ."

"Tell me who you are going to finger for Ben's killing."

"Christ, George, you know I can't do that." Fatty was holding his socks from last night in one hand and scratching between his toes with the other. He had to strain to reach his feet with his arms fully outstretched.

"I know you can. I know you will. I still have the file, you know. Photographs I took down at the baths, witness statements, everything. It wouldn't bother me at all to turn it over to the District Attorney. In fact it would help me out. You know, I get a call from that boy's mother about every two months or so. She says he still walks funny. She says he can't breathe right through his nose."

Fatty didn't bother putting on his socks. "Jury's not going to believe that little fairy," he muttered.

"It doesn't really matter what a jury believes, Fatty. The people who know you . . ." George twisted a bit in his chair and made a show of polishing the shamus's badge with his sleeve. "The people you work with are going to believe him."

Fatty leaned back in the overstuffed chair, put his hands on his thighs, let out a long soggy breath, and didn't say a thing.

"Tonight," George said. "I'll meet you outside the baths. Six o'clock. It will be a good reminder of our friendship."

Fatty offered up some weak resistance as George walked out the door into the banana-yellow sunlight of a Seattle morning.

Three feet down the sidewalk, George winced. He had almost forgotten about picking up the cake for his wife, and the bakery was just down the hill. Not that he wanted the cake for himself, but she'd want to eat around six. She'd want to light the candles. She'd be sad of course but she'd still treat it like a birthday. She'd set the boy's picture in his place. It was almost too much to think about. If he was going to meet Fatty at six, George would have to be late for dinner, the cake and the candles. Maybe that was all right. Maybe he'd go to the bakery before the meeting. He'd pick up something for the fat man. Christ, he thought, he didn't want to go home.

Back at his desk, the first thing George saw was a letter from the captain saying that they had entered a memo of agreement with Floodwater Security regarding the murder of their operative Ben Avery. The death of Dave Kept would be handled by the Everett P.D., and George was directed to offer his "full and unqualified support in the joint effort to bring both cases to a quick and successful conclusion."

He set the paper down on his desk. There was going to be no "successful conclusion" to Floodwater's handling of this case. Until he got some news from Fatty, the best way to keep track of their investigation would be to watch the hospitals.

"There's water coming in back here," Ellie said without showing much concern.

Slip stopped rowing and grabbed a bucket from under one of the seats. The sockets for the oarlocks were sloppy and pulling loose from the rails of the dory. One oar caught the water and levered back into Slip's chest, almost knocking him into the water.

"Here," Ellie said. She stepped over Slip, grabbed the bucket, and started to bail. "Row, row, row," she hissed.

Slip grabbed both oars again and awkwardly started to scissor the water, splashing the surface a few times until he gained purchase, and pointed the bow downwind so that the small boat wouldn't make such a big target for the waves.

"Pull more to the left," Ellie said softly, while she bucketed the water out of the boat and the girl pulled even deeper into her umbrella.

"You should call it port," Annabelle said flatly from under her black umbrella.

"What?" Slip asked without turning around.

"When facing the bow, the boat's left is called port and the right is starboard. It doesn't matter whose left or right or what way they're facing. It's just the boat's port and starboard."

"Really?" Slip asked. "How do you know that?"

"I dunno. I read it somewhere, I guess." Annabelle's disembodied voice was floating out over the water. "P-o-r-t has the same number of letters as l-e-f-t and that's how you remember that port is the boat's left side."

"All right. If you say so," he mumbled.

Slip rowed through the rain for an hour and a half. They were around the first point, the clouds began to lift, and the rain tailed off to a light mist. By noon they could see distant mountains to the west and east. Puget Sound felt as if it were a broad river valley flowing north. He rowed in silence. Ellie sat in the stern wrapped in a tarp. Annabelle spun her umbrella and the yellow bird ruffled his feathers and squawked as if to register his disgust at the progress they were making.

George walked down the marble steps toward the morgue. His footsteps made a lonely echoing sound. The air smelled like iodine. Outside he could hear the rattle of a trolley rolling down the hill toward the water.

"When did he come in?" George asked. The attendant flipped through the sheets on his clipboard.

"I dunno, I guess a couple of hours ago," he said.

"Who brought him?"

"Ambulance from Edmonds."

"Edmonds? Why'd they bring him all the way down here?"

The attendant was a kid, maybe twenty, with his hair slicked back and a single spit curl in the center of his forehead. This kid was some kind of sheikh who only wanted to be done with work so he could get into his good clothes and dance down at Parker's Dance Hall. He had listened to only a few, but already he was growing tired of George's questions.

"You wanna just look through the paperwork yourself?" he said peevishly.

"Yeah, thanks," George said, and grabbed the kid's clipboard.

"Is this some kind of joke?" he asked the sheikh, who now had his attention on the inside story of a *Police Gazette*.

"What? I dunno," he offered.

"They've got this guy Dave Kept listed as an accident victim?"

"I dunno, why?" the kid said without looking up.

"They found his body in the trunk of a car sunk in a slough."

"Sounds like a *bad* accident," the kid said.

Looking at the last page, George saw the signature line where Tom Delaney had signed off on the transport for the stiff.

Without asking, George walked back into the cooler where two bodies were laid out on metal tables with a two-inch lip around the edges. One was uncovered. The dead man's mouth was wide open as if he were trying to gulp the harsh white light spraying down on him from above. The toe tag said it was David Kept, accident victim, the man from the trunk of the Lincoln found about a mile from the northern end of the interurban.

Dave Kept had been beaten with something heavy and fairly soft. There were the beginnings of large bruises across the side of his face and jaw. There were bruises on the hands and forearms. It looked like his wrists were broken and the thumb on his right hand was dislocated. Dave Kept had put up a good fight up until the last few moments when someone stepped up close to him and put a bullet through his brain. The entry wound was discreet and not big enough to collapse the skull or move a lot of meat around. The bullet was a fairly small caliber, probably a .38. The halo of powder stippling around the dark hole told George that the shooter had been standing close. The shooter had gotten everything he or she needed out of Kept before he was put down like a dog.

George made some notes and pulled back the sheet from the second body. Ben Avery's eyes were shut and his mouth was closed. Someone had cleaned the mud off of him from the dump site. Ben had a small hole in his right hand and another just below his rib cage. George took his pencil and worked the point into the entry wound below the ribs. The flesh was cold and stiff as clay so it took a bit of doing to get the pencil in, but it told him the small-caliber bullet had traveled upward through the body and that Ben had probably had his hand over the barrel when the shot came.

He flapped down the sheet so that it settled slowly over the features of the corpse, the accumulated air gradually escaping, the harsh light making the floating shroud almost transparent. The compressors for the coolers buzzed and rattled, and George threw his pencil away.

"Hey!" the kid at the desk yelled from behind him. "You got to get out of here. I'm locking up. Don't you guys have nowhere to go at night?"

"No," George said. He bent down to grab his pencil after changing his mind about needing it. "Goodnight," he said, and walked through the dirty swinging door.

The sun was going down behind the western mountains. The gray water of Puget Sound pulsed for a few moments with streaks of silver before a cool shadow eased toward the east. A brisk wind pushed the waves and the dory along. Everyone but Slip was asleep, curled on the floor of the boat and covered up with whatever they could find. Ellie was wrapped in the canvas tarp. Annabelle had pulled her umbrella down over the triangular seat in the bow and wrapped herself around the bird's cage.

Slip pulled on the oars. His hands were bleeding now and his neck ached from craning around to look where he was going. After several hours, he stopped looking forward and only scanned the water to the stern. He kept the dory's stern at right angles to the direction of the waves. If the wind shifted, so too would his course, but it didn't matter to him. They were making headway, putting distance between themselves and the muddy riverbank in White Center.

Slip took off his damp wool mackinaw and laid it over his knees, hoping to let it dry out a bit. While he did this, he set the oars inside and the dory drifted in the waves. He pulled his tool kit closer so that he could wedge his feet against it and the boat as he pulled against the oars.

"You don't like to get too far from your tool kit," Ellie said with a sleepy voice. She sat up in the stern, pulling the green canvas tarp around her as if it were a mink stole.

"Nope," Slip said.

Ellie's hair was tousled and her eyes seemed to take on the gray of the sky. She took a long breath and formulated a question. Then she stopped and leaned back against the stern of the boat.

"I'm sorry for getting you mixed up in this," she said. "But you know, you asked for a ride."

"Let's just get up the coast a bit and then we can go our separate ways," Slip said.

"All right," she said, and she wiped rainwater from her face.

"So who is this girl?" Slip nodded over his shoulder to the umbrella in the bow. "I can't figure you for a mother."

"I thought I told you. I had sister. She was sickly all her life. Then she got healthy and married an upstanding man, a minister in a country church. Then as goddamn luck would have it she and her husband died in a fire and Annabelle came to me."

"Quite a family," he muttered.

"Thank you," she said, still smiling.

Ellie and her sister Beth had grown up on the northern Idaho border. Their mother had thrown her first husband out after he could not give up drink. Their stepfather was a sober man who raised horses and mules for the government firefighters and the army. As soon as she could sit astride a horse, Ellie had begun breaking stock. She went with the men to move the winter herd in from the lowland range and helped cull them out in the spring. Beth had spent summers hanging on fence rails and handing her father his shoeing tools when he was bent under a workhorse with feet the size of dinner plates. The sisters had waded in the shallows of the nearby stream catching frogs in their hands and had built a swing that was long enough to carry them out over the deepest pool. The girls had not gone to elementary school, but their mother had managed their education by teaching them math while doing carpentry and memorizing poems from one of the leather-bound books she kept near the fireplace. Before she was ten, Ellie had been able to recite most of the first book of the *Odyssey* as well as the poems "Crossing the Bar" and "Hiawatha." Their mother taught them some Latin and Greek even while they learned their letters in English.

Newspapers made it out to the farmstead in weekly packets and the parents read them by the light of guttering candles at the table. The world was changing so fast around them that they couldn't imagine being able to keep their girls isolated on the shrinking island of their farm. They gradually came to the realization that the girls would have to go to school in town. They could be schoolteachers or nurses until they found husbands.

The two sisters reacted differently to the world beyond the farm. While Beth re-created the pastoral universe of her childhood by canning peaches for her timid husband's flock, Ellie scandalized her family by openly smoking cigarettes and using slang. Ellie had heard Helen Flynn give a speech in Spokane and had stood with her mother as the dour suffragettes marched in rank down the middle of the main street, their sashes proclaiming a woman's right to vote. She listened to the speeches and wasn't moved by the ideas, for the ideas seemed plain and self-evident, but she was moved by the tone and the posture of the women who spoke.

By the time Ellie was seventeen she had run away with the barnstormer to an airfield in Spokane, and when the barnstormer moved on, Ellie's mother had turned her wild girl out. Beth married the upstanding preacher and moved to Montana. Ellie rode a clattering freight train to the coast, looking for her biological father she had never met.

They were about two miles offshore. Waves humped up from the fifteen-knot wind and sizzled white as they crested near the boat. The air around the skiff was a rumble of wind and hissing waves. Slip was too tired to be afraid. He leaned against the oars, letting the weather fill the hollow of his skull. Three gulls with yellow legs flew upwind to meet the dory, landed in its wake, then dove for something unseen beneath the surface. Occasionally, small fish would slap the surface, drawing the gulls' attention. After a few dives the gulls pulled up into the air and rode downwind into the distance. Slip kept rowing. He shipped his oars just once to double-check his tobacco tin in his shirt pocket. Ellie had given him back his money and he wasn't going to lose track of it now. The night came on suddenly. The day was a gray twilight one moment, then the lights of Seattle were glittering like constellations in the dark. The whitecaps glowed in the darkness and their hissing seemed more pronounced. With the darkness coming on, the wind began to build, and soon the waves were breaking over the side of the dory. The seawater stung their skin with a burning kind of cold.

"We got to go to the beach," Ellie said from the floor of the boat. She was shivering now. "Pull us to the right."

"Starboard," Annabelle piped up from under her umbrella. The bird squawked as if in agreement.

"Starboard." Ellie stood corrected.

"I see a light on that black section of the beach. It looks like a fire." Ellie was up now, looking over the bow.

Slip didn't speak. His hands and back ached. He pulled on his portside oar and the wind cut across the stern quarter. Every third wave dumped water into the boat. Ellie bailed with the bucket, while Annabelle cupped her hands and heaved icy pearls of water over the side.

The dory ground onto the rounded stones of an exposed beach. Waves sizzled up the rocks and dumped into the dory. All of them were shivering now.

"What do you say if I look for a path to the fire? We can go up there together," Slip said, and without waiting he began stumbling toward the trees. He walked in a wide arc around the bow of the boat until he found what looked like a deer trail up into the beach fringe. "Let's go," he said.

Ellie tucked the girl into a wool blanket and a tarp in the bow of the boat, then walked through the beach fringe over slippery gray rocks clattering underfoot. Fir trees swayed in the darkness, their trunks creaking like a ship's mast in a blow. Up an embankment was a railroad bed with a single set of tracks running down the middle.

Soon voices boomed out through the dark, and they both saw the shimmer of a campfire painting golden lines on the underside of the trees. The roadbed ended at a small trestle bridge across a ravine, and beneath the bridge was an encampment of about ten men around a campfire. The flames lit up the unshaven faces of the men, who were squatting on their haunches and passing a bottle slowly around the circle. A shabby man with a game leg was breaking up a freight pallet with a hammer, feeding the wood into the fire. Sparks twisted up into the air and the fire made a popping sound.

They all turned their heads as Ellie and Slip walked toward the light. Two men stepped back into the shadows. One took off running. The others stared up at the couple in their wet clothes without speaking or offering any help.

"You got anybody chasing you?" the woodchopper asked in a monotone.

"We were in a boat. We saw your fire and pulled into the beach," Slip said.

"Got wet, did you?" the same man asked.

"Yes sir, we did. Mind if we share your fire for a bit?" Ellie said, stepping forward into the bubble of firelight.

The woodchopper paused and looked her over for a moment. "As long as you ain't bringing the bulls down on us, I suppose it would be all right. Got any smokes?"

Ellie reached into her coat pocket for her soggy tailor-mades. She didn't smoke cigarettes that often any more but she always carried them as a way to strike up a conversation with men on picket lines or in the alley behind a sweatshop.

"Got some but they're soaked through."

"We'll take care of that." A skinny man with a scarecrow hat reached across and took the pack, plopped it into a frying pan, and picked at it with a stick. "Papers might be ruined but we can come up with something," he said, looking hungrily down into the pan as he held it over the flames.

"You headed fishing?" the big man grunted.

"No, not really," Ellie said, running her fingers through her hair to dry it by the fire.

"I'm sorry we don't have much in the way of accommodations for you, ma'am," the little man said.

"This fire is more than enough right now." She caught his eyes and smiled.

"We've got some gear and one more person in our party. We've got some food in the boat we'd be happy to throw into some mulligan if you figure on cooking some up." Slip pointed with his thumb back toward the beach.

"Sounds fine with me," Jake said. "He got a big appetite, this other fella traveling with you?"

"Naw, she's just a little bitty girl. But I'm plenty hungry. I just took my first lesson in rowing a boat." Slip rolled his shoulders to try to make himself seem bigger. The big man smiled.

"Got a little girl with you. Heck, we should be able to come up with a good place for her to sleep. No sense a child should have to put up with this nonsense."

"We got some more wood up under the bridge we could build her a little crib," the skinny man said, holding out a shriveled cigarette to Ellie.

"Well, aren't you sweet." She smiled, taking the cigarette, then fishing a stick out of the fire to light it.

From the south came a rumble along the tracks and the big man fished in his pants pocket for a watch. "What the hell? There ain't a northbound train due until morning."

Some of the men shrank away from the fire. The moon was higher in the sky and its thin light showed the hoboes skittering away over the rocks and logs.

The rumble came faster and thinner than a heavy freight. "What the hell?" Jake said, looking up toward the tracks.

A little switcher engine pulling two small crew cars came to a stop. This was the kind of rig that usually pulled crews out to where the tracks needed repair. The engine stopped well short of the bridge. Its lights went out and the engine idled down.

"I don't like this," Jake said. As he stood up by the fire, the first cries came from the men in the darkness.

The moonlight caught the figures of men running in every direction. One man fell and others fell upon him with sticks flailing, arching toward the ground, the fallen man's legs kicking against the stones.

Slip grabbed Ellie's arm and turned to the south, back toward the beach where the dory and the girl were. The men swinging clubs against bone sounded like wood cutters. They mostly wore leather windbreakers and knit caps. There were at least three who appeared to be giving orders and they wore trench coats and fedoras. Some of them had badges but Slip could not see any uniforms. The thugs started to drag hoboes toward the fire. One of the men in a long coat had an electric torch, which he shined in their faces as they lay writhing on the ground.

Slip and Ellie ducked into the woods. They could hear sobs as men cried out in pain and they heard curses as the bulls barked orders. Ellie turned back and saw Jake lumbering after them. He made four strides before he was set on by two bulls who cracked him down and set to work on breaking his legs. She stopped running and started back.

"Ellie, what the hell?" Slip said.

"They're going to kill him," she said as she picked up a beach stone the size of a small coconut. Slip took two steps to follow her before his legs were cut out from under him by a stout little man using a pick handle for a club.

"Where you think you're going, fella?" the rat-faced man in a leather windbreaker said as he started in on Slip. He got three good licks in, the first searing against Slip's nose and splitting his upper lip. The second cracked a handful of ribs on his left side, and the third one he didn't remember, other than he heard the sound of another voice nearby crying out in pain.

S E V E N

≋≋≋

Annabelle wrapped the wool blanket around her shoulders. The smell of wet wool made her feel as if she were wrapped in the skins of dead animals. Buddy tapped his bell and the girl dozed off to a restless torpor, not sleeping but not awake.

She sat up suddenly to the sounds of the riot through the trees. Someone was walking down the beach. She could hear footsteps tumbling the stones. Some of the stones were big. Men were crying out in pain: once, twice, and the voice would go silent. The clattering beach rocks came closer. She stuck her foot out from underneath the umbrella.

"Ellie?" she whispered.

The voices blended with the waves swooshing up on the beach.

"Hey," she said weakly as Buddy started to sing and rattled his little bell.

"Somebody's here," she whispered and tried to sink down deeper into the bow of the tiny boat. Buried in the very bow of the boat was Slip's coat. In the coat was a .38-caliber revolver. She held it in both her shaking hands and pulled the hammer back with her tiny thumbs.

George Hanson remembered the cake. Now he sat at the table by himself. The kids on the street had gone in for their dinner and the silence that had followed sat like an unwanted guest at the table. The cake stayed on the counter wrapped in the blue box, the string still tied neatly.

He had known the cake would go uneaten. It had only been a year. This would have been the boy's tenth birthday. He didn't know why she had wanted to buy the cake in the first place. Why not just stay away from such things?

Benny had died of influenza and George knew it was pointless to start asking questions. But it bothered him that all of his investigative skills were useless in the death of his own son. Every second of every day was filled with risk, particularly for a boy born frail as Benny had been. The threats were everywhere and the opportunity for illness crowded around him like mosquitoes on a warm night.

George sat at the table trying not to ask any questions. Questions only drove him deeper into the dark. George had cried and had eaten the meals their neighbors had brought after Benny died. He had gone out by Green Lake to the cemetery and tended the plot during the summer. But that was as far as he was going to go. The rest of the grief he refused.

The clock ticked on the sideboard. Emily stayed upstairs. She said she had a headache and that may have been true, but George knew she was lying face down on Benny's bed both wanting and not wanting to vomit up the cold stone that her grief had become.

George left the dining room table, went upstairs, and stood by the bedroom door for a moment. He remembered the nights he had stood by his son's door and listened to his labored breathing. He felt the dread that had crept over him then. He felt it still as he listened to his wife's sobbing.

He turned from the door, went downstairs, and spread his case files out on the kitchen table. When Emily got up he would warm some supper for her.

Fatty had stood him up at the steam baths. Apparently the fat man was more afraid of Tom Delaney than he was of a felony assault rap. That was all right. Fatty was a man caught in the middle. He didn't really have the temperament for a Floodwater goon, and he certainly didn't have the aptitude for law enforcement. The facts of the steam bath assault were ugly enough that once Fatty was sure George would use them, the fear of the public scandal might make him lose some of his prodigious appetite. George would give him more time to get in good with the Ben Avery investigation and then would put the bite on the fat man again.

The cops in Everett had traced the car David Kept had been dumped in to a motor court up north of Sedro Woolley. A blonde woman had rented a cabin for herself and a man. She had paid cash, and she had forgotten to sign the register. The kid who had handed her the key said that the man with her didn't look right. He said he looked like a hitchhiker; he had a bindle of clothes and a box slung over his shoulder. She was driving a Lincoln and didn't look like a hobo. It just wasn't right.

The Everett cops had interviewed union members along the docks in Everett but no one was particularly helpful. There was a shop steward named William Pierce who had worked closely with Dave Kept, but Pierce (the report from the Everett P.D. noted) had "kept his mouth shut tighter than a bug's ass."

The only break in the case had come when one of the union boys had gotten so nervous about the questions he bolted and left town. When they went to his house to talk to the wife, they found a leather case that had belonged to Dave Kept. The case had blood stains on it and the wife claimed to know nothing about where it came from. Only that "a beat-up blonde and some palooka wearing a red logger coat" had dropped it off. They didn't take her into custody but had men parked out in front of the house to watch who came and went. George had taken notes from his conversation with the Everett police. On the bottom of the last page he had written the address.

George liked working at home, all the more so since Benny had died. Work felt like something useful. Work kept the sickness of grief at bay. He liked asking questions that had answers.

One of George's street sources had told him that just before Ben Avery had been killed he had been on the trail of Ellie Hobbes. Avery had been hunting her down, asking questions, frantic questions the sources seemed to think.

He looked at the thick pile of notes on this case he was not supposed to be working on, and just before he turned to the next page, he got up, opened the box, and cut himself a large piece of birthday cake.

With white frosting on his fingers he turned the page. A patrolman had taken the street lead and tracked the logger down to an old man down in Hooverville who had rented him a coffin to sleep in that night. "Oh, Lord," George said out loud, and licked his fingers. "What kind of mess did you get yourself in?" Then he took another bite of cake and sat up straight as he heard his wife coming down the stairs.

Ellie was twenty-eight years old and she liked men, in a vague and unenthusiastic sort of way. She liked men in the same way some people liked racehorses: it was fun to rate them and some of them were even beautiful, but you couldn't imagine yourself owning one. So now, standing above Slip with his head cracked open, Ellie felt a sinking kind of fear. Not so much for the man before her or the fact that he might die, but a leaden kind of despair that, like it or not, she had come into possession of this battered logger and couldn't simply leave him.

She had killed the man who had been beating him. She had picked up a stone and brought it down on top of his head. When he fell on top of Slip, she knelt over him and struck down three more times until she was certain he had stopped moving. There were men lying all over the field who were unconscious or worse. The Floodwater goon was dead and she knew she would have to carry the memory of killing him with her for the rest of her life. If she had any regrets about killing him it was only that: the blood and the sparkling red stone, the feel of his blood on her fingers would be with her forever now, like an unwanted lodger who had decided to stay.

They were far enough into the beach fringe that neither the firelight nor the moonlight would give away their position. She rolled the corpse off Slip and leaned over him in the dark.

"Slip, come on, get up," she said, as she slapped his cheek. "Come on now, they'll start looking for this guy soon. Let's get back to the boat." But there was no answer. Slip was warm and the blood from his nose kept flowing down his chin, so he must still be alive.

She tried to drag him by his arms but it was hard, particularly over the rough ground under the trees, and when she tried to drag him by his feet she could see that his head kept hitting hard against the stones and she figured that wasn't going to work. She had thought of him as thin but the tightly bunched muscles hidden under his layers of shirts made him much heavier than he looked. So she took off the dead man's belt and tied Slip's wrists together. Kneeling down, she draped one arm around her shoulder and let the other ride around front like a sling and then she stood up. She pulled down on his wrists to keep the weight up high on her shoulders, and by leaning forward she was able to drag him down through the beach fringe toward the boat.

Men were calling out and moaning for help as she fought her way through the tangle of woods below the railroad tracks. But there was no new outcry that she imagined would happen once they found the dead man with the leather coat next to the trees.

She fell once and came down hard on a small spruce tree, which knocked the wind out of her. Slip's weight lay so heavy on her back that she thought she might suffocate right there. But she rolled over and regained her strength. The wind was still hissing through the trees and the slushy sound of the waves on the cobbles was louder now than the voices of the men by the fire. She wanted to call out to Annabelle for help but she didn't dare, and she didn't want to leave Slip in case she couldn't find her way back before the goons found their dead comrade.

She lay listening to the soothing sound of the waves and the wind and she tried to let her mind lift up out of her body. She thought she had cracked one of her ribs, but she knew she had to pull Slip up and get him back to the boat.

Annabelle poked her head out from under her umbrella as the clattering of rocks came closer. She saw Ellie's legs truding slowly, with the bloody shoes and cuffs of a man dragging behind her.

Annabelle gently uncocked the revolver and set it back into the pocket of Slip's coat. The yellow bird rattled the bars on his cage. Ellie slung Slip onto the edge of the dory.

"Sweetheart, we've got to go. Right now," she said, and Annabelle didn't argue. Ellie flopped Slip down in the bottom of the dory like a dead fish. The little girl jumped out onto the shore and helped Ellie push the dory down to the water.

George Hanson sat uncomfortably on a broken chair listening to the tired-looking woman weep loud and hard. A baby slept in the overstuffed chair, a toddler sat as still as a stone next to her mother on the couch, and another baby climbed up her arm.

"I ain't telling you nothing," Ida said. She settled the climbing child into her lap. "I got these kids to think of. What's to say they don't come back?"

"Who?" George asked, brushing right past her reluctance to talk.

"Floodwater . . . or the Reds, for that matter. I don't know. I told him to stay clear of this union business. I told him to stay clear of them Reds."

"How long has your husband been gone, Mrs. Cobb?" George asked. He leaned forward gently so as not to lose his balance on the straight-backed chair.

"He left that day the tall man in the car came out here and got the papers. Ray left right after that."

"Who was the tall man? Had you seen him before?" George had to raise his voice to be heard over the sound of one of the babies crying on the couch.

"Raymond don't tell me nothing about his goings-on. He don't tell me nothing."

"Did he call him by name?"

"Nope. He just called him 'Boss,' that's all I remember."

"Boss. You sure?"

"Raymond ain't no Red, officer. I swear to God he ain't. He just joined the union a couple of months ago."

George looked down at his notebook. He wrote "Not a Red" in letters big enough for her to see. The baby on her lap stirred for a moment and then closed its eyes.

"Now, what did you say happened to the papers?" George asked.

"The tall man in the nice coat took 'em."

"Did any money change hands?" George asked.

She did not answer. Her silence told him there had been some money. Maybe not a lot. Certainly not enough. But there had been some money, and George hoped that she had it in a safe place. The Everett cops had asked her the usual questions about the cars and the license plates that had come and gone. They had harassed her for a better description of the tall man and the others in the car, but Mrs. Cobb had given them nothing. George considered taking her through it all again, but instead he thanked her and left. A dirty terrier growled at him as he got back in his car.

~~~

Off the beach, the wind remained steady, and the choppy waves came fast in the shallow water, pushing against the stern and slapping up into the boat. Puget Sound was dark, filled only with the howl of the wind and the crunch of white water breaking on the rocks. The wind would blow the dory past the hobo jungle where the thugs were cleaning up their mess. Men were carrying gas lanterns in their free hands, lowering them to their knees to get a look at the faces of the hoboes laid out on the ground.

Ellie settled in the middle seat and pulled hard on the oars, trying to cut across the waves, but the wind angled them down the beach right in front of the scene.

"Get down," she hissed. She and the girl scrambled for the bottom of the boat. Ellie peeked over the side of the dory and looked toward shore, hoping they wouldn't bump up against the rocks breaking white just off the hobo encampment.

The fire had been stoked now by the men with the clubs. Sparks zigzagged into the darkness and a man with a long coat and some papers in his hands brushed a spark away from his face. There were several men down on the ground, but Ellie could see only one person being carried on a stretcher from over by the trees where they had just been.

"Are we all right?" the girl asked in a steady voice.

"We will be. Soon."

And soon the little dory drifted past the fires and then into the dark mouth of open water. To the west lights twinkled up on the bluffs. Ellie's arms were cramping and her hands could barely grip the oars, but she gradually pulled the boat away from the beach. The dory moved up and down the swells as if it had found an easy gait. Ellie tried rowing downwind but kept missing the period of the waves and ended up turning the dory broadside letting the waves dump in.

Annabelle had an electric torch that she shined around the dory.

"Better turn that off, honey," Ellie said softly.

The girl's leg bumped against the canvas roll and the mast lashed to the narrow outer deck. Ellie reached to untie the line and began tracing the rigging as the dory wallowed in the seas. Her fingers scrambled over the sail, sorting and tracing the lines tied to the small step mast. Then she stood up and shoved one end of the mast into the hole in the seat just behind Annabelle and Buddy's perch.

The dory came alive with flapping canvas and thin ropes flailing in front of the boat. Annabelle cowered with the bird in the bow. Ellie tied off reef points in the canvas and then hopped to the bow to reach for the lines that were snapping the surface of the seas ahead of them.

"You know what you're doing?"

"I'm not sure. This is different from our little boat on the lake," Ellie said. "But my hands are cramped up and I can't row this thing fast enough with the wind like this."

Ellie gathered up the lines and brought them toward the stern. The dory tipped and dodged in the seas, but the weight Slippery Wilson contributed, lying on the bottom, helped its stability. The canvas kept flapping until she stepped over the prone man and wrapped a line around a cleat on the starboard side. Then the commotion stopped. The little sail ballooned downwind and the dory surged ahead. Ellie felt the rush of motion and it made her lightheaded for a moment. She pushed the oars away with her feet and felt the lift of the little boat flying. Then it turned abruptly to port and the whole enterprise seemed to be lurching into the sea.

"Put the oar in the stern!" the girl yelled.

Ellie had released the rope holding the sail and once again the air was alive with the popping of canvas and rattling ropes. She brought both oars in, and then set one in the water at the stern. There was a short piece of tarred twine to hook across the two posts that would keep the oar in place.

"Okay," she said, trying to sound sure of herself, "let's try that again."

She tightened the rope around the cleat again and the sail ballooned out. Ellie dug the oar down into the waves and the little dory surged forward like a plow horse in the morning. But the weight was wrong and waves lapped up into the bow and Annabelle came scrambling back toward the stern.

Ellie settled her in the stern. Annabelle had tied her blanket around Buddy's cage so he wouldn't get soaked. There was scarcely enough room for the three of them in the stern. The little bell in the cage tinkled through the fabric and the bird squawked like a crow. With the weight shifted to the stern, the bow rode out of the water and the dory slipped more easily through the waves. Ellie placed the oar under her right arm and grabbed the end with her right hand. She put her left hand gingerly on the girl's shoulder and left it there for a moment.

"You think he is going to be okay?" Annabelle asked, furrowing her brow and staring down at Slip in the middle of the dory.

"I don't know. He got clonked pretty hard. But if it was real bad he'd be dead already."

"Looks like his head is bleeding," the girl said, biting her lower lip and moving in closer to Slip to get out of the wind.

"It's a long way from his heart, honey."

The girl looked out into the darkness. The sea was humping up and hissing like an animal whose name she didn't know. She was cold now and frightened. They were both shivering and the girl's teeth were clacking together. But when she looked at her aunt clutching the makeshift rudder, she wanted to believe that this was just another kind of craziness they had both lived through before. So the girl wrapped herself in a tarp and leaned back into Ellie's chest for warmth and tried listening to her aunt's steady heartbeat.

Ellie Hobbes had moved in with her biological father when she was nineteen, and by the time she was twenty Beth had died and Annabelle came to her. Beth had specifically written this provision into her will, sensing perhaps the strength the child would need to be an orphan in this world. The old man ran the wildest saloon in Aberdeen, Washington, both before and after Prohibition. The Haywood Saloon was a marvel of curiosities. Early in the century when men around Aberdeen were cutting more timber than almost anywhere else in the world, there was an army of lumberjacks encamped in the area. Hundreds of these men preferred to get their mail, do their banking, and seek advice for most medical conditions inside the walls of the Haywood Saloon. News of the region was reliably reported there: which outfit was paying the best wages, who had been killed in the woods and how. Men would sometimes come in on a Friday and have to be carried out and loaded into the back of a company truck on Sunday morning. The church women of Aberdeen were scandalized that Ellie worked in the saloon, but she didn't care. No man, no matter how drunk, ever pestered her for sex in her father's place. They may have been rough, but to Big Joe's daughter they were courtly drunks who could be counted on for their manners.

Joe was six foot five inches and had been a faller of some renown until he lost his left hand when he caught it between a wire cable and a stump. He compensated with a stationary hook that fascinated children.

The Haywood Saloon had a stuffed alligator across the top of the bar. There was a lumpy stuffed polar bear with dust-scoured glass eyes in the back by the pool table, Indian headdresses hung from the ceiling, and a strange piece of curved ivory, which was said to be a fossilized walrus penis, served as a handle for one of the beer spigots. It was rumored that Big Joe kept the genitals of Wesley Everest, the Wobbly who had been lynched in Centralia, in a jar of alcohol under the bar. Even though Ellie never saw such things, she was not quite ready to disbelieve any stories about the Haywood where, after all, there was a mummified body resting in the basement on a shelf above the hard liquor.

Annabelle slept and fussed in a crib behind the bar while Ellie ran back and forth from the restaurant bringing food for the men who wanted to eat with their beer. She cleaned spittoons and sometimes acted as a banker by holding on to some of the regulars' wages so they couldn't drink them away in the bar.

They lived above the bar in a small apartment that smelled of cedar shavings and cigar smoke. There was never a night that Ellie and Annabelle didn't fall asleep to the clatter of billiard balls and glasses breaking.

She loved eavesdropping on the men's gossip and tall stories. They all had dangerous jobs and lived without the benefit of women. They talked so frequently and explicitly about sexual matters that the mystery of human anatomy was lost to her by the time she was twenty.

Men talked about sex. They talked about home. And they liked to complain about the rain and the steepness of the hills. They liked to complain about the dispositions of the camp cooks and the temperature of the coffee. But what working men liked to talk about the most was the stupidity of the educated classes. Thanks to the booze and the consistency of this complaint, the Haywood Saloon became a tight-knit community: for it was clear that everyone else, everyone outside those walls, was a stupid bastard.

The men in the front office, and the ones in the boardrooms in Portland and Seattle, may have gone to college, but they didn't know a goddamn thing worth knowing. Even when the topic shifted, this theme ran through all their stories: the assholes from everywhere else were robbing them blind and slowing down the progress of civilization. There were countless stories of perpetual motion machines that had been stolen from unwitting farmers, of men who wore two-hundred dollar suits and didn't know how to start their own cars, of engineers who hopelessly screwed up an entire construction job by ignoring the advice of the mechanic on the ground. The people who ran things didn't know what the hell they were doing. This story was told over and over again in the Haywood Saloon. This was the story that bubbled up between the floorboards of the little apartment where Ellie and the toddler slept. By the time Ellie was twenty-four she had accepted the story as gospel truth.

When Big Joe died, the bar ended up going to the bank and they shut it down for good. Ellie tried to borrow money to take over the bar, but the bankers locked her out. The night before she and the girl left Aberdeen for good, she let herself in through the windows. She curled Annabelle in her bed and slept on her narrow shelf, back near the icehouse where she used to listen to the men at their card games. It was silent then with nothing but the flutter of the gas lantern. She went to sleep with a head full of anger toward the dumb bastards who had taken her bar away.

Slippery Wilson opened his eyes and could see only Ellie's profile in the dark. Above her the heavy canvas sail fluttered slightly on its downwind run. There were stars above the dory that appeared to jog back and forth as the little boat lunged through the waves.

"You should have left me there," Slip said in a cracked voice.

"Jesus, you scared me," Ellie said, jumping back.

"You should have left me there," Slip said again.

"I know, I should have."

"But you didn't."

"Not yet anyway," she said, as she ran her fingers across his head feeling the greasy smear of blood in his hair. "We got to get you patched up." She pulled on the steering oar to swerve the dory toward a sand spit jutting out into the darkness.

They pulled the dory up the sand and into a tangle of alder trees and berry bushes. Back in the tunnel of brush was a hollow where it looked as if a black bear had bedded down. The air smelled stale with sour urine, and bits of fur were tufted on a few of the thorns. Annabelle threw the tarp over the dory and curled up to sleep.

Slip pulled a blanket out of the boat and settled in the bear's bower. Ellie hauled some fresh water from a nearby creek and tore up a skirt from her wet bindle of clothes. She sat beside Slip and started cleaning his wounds. Slip winced as she scrubbed his cuts. Her hands were cold twigs against his face, and the warmth of the blood was almost a comfort. When she finished cleaning his wounds she hugged him around his waist for warmth and they lay curled into each other.

The wind blew through the brush so that the sides of their bower pumped like a human heart. Slip listened for bears or men running toward them on the beach. Ellie pulled her shivering body close in under the cover of the wool blanket and a canvas tarp and they lay there silently for a half an hour, enjoying the flickering warmth of their tired bodies. Finally they stopped shivering, and they slept the sleep of the dead.

EIGHT

~~~

George Hanson was sleeping downstairs on the divan. He had had a hard time getting to sleep and was groggy when the phone rang sometime before five in the morning. A young man's voice he didn't recognize told him that Floodwater had a problem at a railroad bridge north of Ballard. They were going to clean it up this morning. George sat up. He was wearing the same shirt from the day before and his tie was still loosely knotted around his neck.

"Where?" he said. "How am I supposed to find it?" He cradled the phone against his shoulder and started to adjust his tie. He felt as if he had been caught napping in his office.

"Ask the railroad boys. They'll tell you," the voice said, and the line went dead.

Even if the train driver hadn't told him about a riot at the hobo jungle and transporting a body back to town, George could have followed the parade of Floodwater ops down to the beach. Their black cars were parked willy-nilly at the end of a sandy lane as if they were a bunch of clam diggers headed to the beach. George brought two cars of his own, one with three detectives and a station wagon from the morgue. From the tone of the caller's voice, George was certain there would be more than one body involved.

He walked down the muddy gut where the blackberry bushes had grown head-high and formed a tunnel. As his slick-soled shoes skidded on the clay he felt as if he were falling into a hole.

A fire pit smoldered in a clearing. George could smell tarry smoke mixing with the smell of salt water. It was a fine clear day with just a few clouds streaking across the sky. Finches sang in the berry bushes and the rocks were beginning to hold some of the day's heat. It felt like spring but George knew it wouldn't last through to summer. This was just a short respite from winter.

Men in raincoats stood near the fire looking at their clipboards. Tom Delaney had his back to the fire. He turned and looked at George as the policeman came walking across the clearing.

"What are you doing here?" Delaney asked, trying to stifle his irritation.

George didn't answer him but turned and waited for two detectives to catch up. One of them was dusting off his rear end where he had landed sliding down the trail.

"All right, I want you to start getting statements from these men. We've got a report of someone transporting a body out of here late last night. I'm going to look around by the woods." He pointed to the group of Floodwater operatives by the fire, then turned away from Delaney and started toward the woods.

Delaney caught up with him. "Didn't you get the message, George? We're handling this."

"I've got a railroad engineer who said he brought a group of vigilantes out here last night. He said he brought back one body. Kind of scared the trainman. Thought he might get in trouble if he didn't talk to the authorities. Can you imagine that?" George didn't look directly up at Delaney but kept his eyes ahead of him.

"Listen." Delaney was puffing to keep up with George. "There are no deaths. Everyone was transported to the hospital. They've been there and been released. Everything's fine."

George scanned the ground around him, following the contour of each rock and piece of driftwood. He moved his head back and forth methodically as if he were working a grid pattern on the ground. He reached into his coat pocket for his notebook with a stubby pencil stuck through the wire binding.

"Everyone's fine . . . except David Kept, Ben Avery, and now a squatty little man with a wife and three kids has gone missing."

"You don't know what you're talking about." Delaney's voice flattened out as if he were suddenly bored with talking about murder.

George stopped his scanning and looked directly at Tom Delaney. "The body they found in the sunken car, David Kept. He was an up-and-comer on the docks."

"That's what I heard." Delaney sniffed.

"Radicals hated him. He was making real progress getting the boys on the docks better pay. He was beating them at their own game and still making management happy."

"So?" Delaney acted as if he were also looking for clues.

"So, why was he killed with Ben Avery's gun?"

Tom Delaney stamped softly on the ground, then looked down at George Hanson and motioned him closer with his right hand. George noticed Delaney's Masonic ring, too tight for his fleshy finger.

"Listen, there haven't been any tests done. No one can say anything for sure."

"You can't do any tests because you don't have Ben's gun. But it sure looks like both Avery and Kept were killed with the same caliber." George stopped scanning and stared at something ahead of him and off to the left.

"How in the hell do you know that?" Delaney hissed.

"Christ, Tom, I'm a policeman. I've got to do something with my time." Then he took three quick steps forward. "You said everybody from last night's party has been treated and released from the hospital?"

"That's what I've been told." Delaney's voice was growing softer, backing away from his indignation.

"What's the name of the hospital?" George asked as he knelt down next to some dark blood spatter on some jagged rocks.

"Walk out of here, George." Delaney stepped behind him so that his shadow fell over the blood.

"I want you to go back to the fire and give your statement to one of the detectives. I want the names of everyone who was part of this last night and I want to talk with them."

Tom Delaney stood silently. Both of his hands were balled into fists. Then he took a toothpick out of his coat pocket and put it in his mouth. He was standing there weighing his next move, when George made it easy.

"Go!" he said, and Delaney did, though not to the fire but up the trail and back to the cars. He whistled as he walked and his men ran after him like sheep dogs headed to their kennels.

The cops who had come with George started to put up a fuss and one of them got out his cuffs but George waved him off. "As long as you got their names and contacts let them go. Send the boys from the morgue down here in case there is another body tucked away somewhere."

The Floodwater ops trailed off up through the blackberry tunnel. One of George's detectives pulled on a pair of leather gloves and started looking through the ashes around the edge of the fire.

"What do you think we might find here, George?" he called out over his shoulder.

"I'm not sure. Look for blood first. Look for big splashes of blood and see if they lead to anything," he called to his detective.

"Anything like what?" the man poking at the fire pit asked.

"Anything like a dead person," George hollered back.

George followed the blood spatter under the trees. He followed the rocks with blood and fresh dirt kicked up around them. He saw some rocks with their damp sides facing up. He saw broken sticks and drag marks punctuated by blood spatter. He walked through the woods away from the fire. Sunlight shimmered down through the trees and the smell of warm mud rose from the ground. George saw more drag marks and blood spatter leading toward the south. There was a piece of a cloth snagged on a fallen spruce lying across the path. The material was a cotton print fabric, possibly from a dress. There was a small splotch of blood on its edge. He found a partial footprint where a rock had turned in the soggy ground. It was a small pointed shoe, pressing down with way too much force: a small print deep down into the mud. Drag marks were next to the print, with blood spatter spaced every three feet or so. A woman was carrying a bleeding adult on her back.

George followed the tracks out onto the beach. The tide was up and the waves pushed lazily against the cobblestones along the shore. Two skinny spruce logs floated in the drift with a skirting of seaweed like a rubbery mat along the edge of the water.

George watched the tracks of a small, strong woman carrying a man on her back. He watched her drop him back in the woods, tripping on a slick log. He watched her struggle down the cobble beach, overturning some large rocks, blood dripping down from his dangling sleeve or his nose.

Then he watched her carry the bleeding man into the sea and disappear without a trace.

The dory sat in the bower for four nights. Slip lay in the brush and Ellie took care of him. They didn't build a fire and they didn't turn on a torch. They ate mildewed crackers and two of the cans of stew. The spit ran a quarter mile from the railroad tracks running along the Sound. They were somewhere north of Seattle and south of Edmonds. From the brush Slip could see the railroad bulls walking up and down the tracks. At night they took their switcher engines and traveled slowly back and forth shining their lights off to either side. A few boats passed by close to the beach and they could have been looking for them, but no one sent up a cry or came ashore. Ellie had gone down the beach early the first morning and brushed away their tracks in the sand using her hands and a spray of beach grass. That night Slip hobbled west with a bucket to get fresh water from the creek running through a culvert under the tracks. When he got back Ellie was curled on the tarp in the darkness of the bower.

"I thought you were going to sneak off," she said, and she rolled on her side propping her head with her elbow.

"I didn't think I could make it back." Slip winced as he sat down.

"You took a beating," was all she said.

"I've been thinking about taking out on my own." Slip sat beside her. "I can make it to the other side of the tracks through the culvert and then get up the bluff and into the woods. I'm sure to hit a highway if I head east."

She rolled against him and pulled his shoulder down. The damp canvas smelled musty, like animal sweat. Their clothes and blankets had begun to dry out in the spring sun. But still they were cold as she folded the tarp over the two of them.

"Stay," she said, and her hands reached up between the buttons of his shirt. His wounds were still exquisitely tender. Her fingertips brushed the gash in his side and he sucked in his breath.

"Ellie. I killed that detective back in Seattle. They're looking for the three of us. It would be better if we weren't traveling together."

"Stay," she said again, and she slipped off his shoes, undid his belt buckle, and pulled his pants down. Slip arched his back while she pulled them all of the way off.

"I don't know what kind of trouble you're in. I don't know who was in that car we dumped in the water and I don't know who

Pierce and Conner are and why they wanted to talk to you that night when all hell broke loose at the meeting hall. The truth is I don't want to know . . . because I know that there's nothing I can do to fix it."

Slip looked up through the tangle of the beach roses and his eyes glazed with tears. Moisture clung to the thorns so they caught the starlight like tiny knife blades. A nuthatch hopped through the thicket and Slip held Ellie's hands as she tried to kiss his tears away. He could smell the damp fur of the animals who had bedded down here. He tasted his own blood in his mouth. He wanted nothing more than to be somewhere else.

When daylight came Slip worked on the dory, cutting new sockets for the oarlocks from timbers he found on the beach. He fit them in place and by working some old screws out of the seats he was able to strengthen them so the sloppy pivot didn't rob the energy going to the oars. He spent an entire day working with his tools, using the chisels and the hand brace. Just hefting them, taking them out of their leather sheaths, made him feel better. Seeing the bright curl of wood lifting from the blades, feeling the grain of the wood, gave him some needed strength.

As the evening came on Slip grabbed his bindle and toolbox and he walked toward the bluff. He went through the culvert under the tracks and he crossed up into the steep woods. Ellie had given him his money back. She had taken her ledger sheet to keep. His tobacco tin was secured in his toolbox and held fast with a leather bootlace. That part of his future was secure at least.

The bluffs were made of gray clay, and it took him two hours to go the first two hundred yards up to a bench where he could look down on the bower. He wanted to make his way up the bluff and back to the roads running north. He thought that if he got the right rides he could be in Canada in a day.

He looked down at the bower. His head throbbed under the bandages that Ellie had tied. His ribs seared with each breath. He could only take three steps before having to stop to let the pain subside. The woods ahead were a dense tangle of blackberries and alder scrub. His hands and arms were freshly scratched and the cuts on his chest were open and bleeding again. He looked back toward the dory. *Maybe just a few more days,* he thought to himself, and he turned back down the hill.

As the sun was going down on the fifth day, Slip started loading the dory. The wind was calm. Ellie had done a good job keeping Slip's injuries clean but he bled every time she peeled the bandages off. Slip sat on the sand as Ellie and the girl pulled the dory out of the brush and eased its stern into the water. Ellie helped Slip climb in. Annabelle, who hadn't said a word to either of the adults for almost two days, brought Buddy out of the brush and got into the bow of the boat. Ellie pushed off and settled in the stern, facing the logger as he started to row.

The new night was warmer than the others. Slip's hands were stiff and his shoulders still hurt. His old cut from the nail in the warehouse had scabbed over but opened up when he started to pull on the oars. His head was full of bees. He rowed north as the sky above Puget Sound turned from silver to black with a flare of red over the Olympic Mountains. He rowed until his hands started bleeding again and he kept rowing as the girl and Ellie fell asleep. He pulled and the water mumbled something he couldn't quite make out. He pulled and the wind whispered something just out of reach and soon he too was asleep.

George Hanson had little left to go on. He had asked his men to keep shaking down the Floodwater ops who patrolled the train lines. He drove to every small port north of the hobo jungle to see if anyone had seen an injured man and a woman in a small boat. He even asked a pal of his with a fishing boat to cruise up and down the shore and let him know if he saw anything. George called the navy and the customs patrol boats, but he had gotten nowhere. He put the squeeze on Fatty but the fat man played cute. He had a pile of evidence, but his case was going cold.

He reviewed the Everett case files and wanted to reinterview the union boys from Everett to see where the nervous Raymond Cobb might have gone. The Everett cops shook them all down except two, Pierce and Conner, who had quit the country apparently, because no one would say where they were. George had opened a file on each of these new missing men. Each file had a name and a photograph and very little else.

He spent as little time at home as he could manage. Emily stayed to herself in her room. When he tried to get her to come down and speak with him she always promised that she would, but hours passed and the door never opened. He cooked her a pot roast on the weekend but it remained uneaten. One night he sat on the porch as the darkness came on. Kids were running down the sidewalk in the soft spring air. All he wanted was for her to come down from her room. The moths bumped against the screen door. A chill rode on the air from down the street. George turned off the lights and slept on the couch.

The horn blast shattered Slip's sleep. He sat up abruptly and held his hand to his forehead to shield his eyes. The sail hung limply at the front of the dory and the sun was just beginning to warm their clothes. A large black boat was bearing down on the dory. The sizzle of its bow wake was close enough to sound like a mountain stream.

Slip lifted the little girl and set her down gently on the stern seat. He stood up and waved his arms overhead. A man in a navy pea coat and watch cap stood on the flying bridge on top of the boat. He cranked the wheel hard over and the boat swung parallel about thirty feet from the dory. A gentle wake rolled under the two boats.

"I thought I had me an abandoned dory," the skipper of the boat called across the distance. "You need some help?"

Ellie was just waking up on the floor of the boat. She looked up at Slip, who was struggling to stand.

"We're doing okay. We were just taking a nap," Slip said.

"You got some fishing gear set out?" the driver asked, and he idled the big boat's engine down.

"No," Slip said, knowing that it wasn't enough. The boats rolled on the easy waves. A handful of gulls hovered above the stern of the black boat.

"You sure you're okay? It's kind of crazy you being out here like this."

"Naw, we're fine. Just . . . traveling north. Had the wind last night and thought we'd make up some time."

"Where you headed?" the driver asked, and he climbed down the ladder to the main deck.

Slip looked around Puget Sound. The mountains to the west seemed closer than before. The mountains to the east were hanging back in the distance. It was a mild day and only a few clouds were running south to north above them.

Slip couldn't think of anything to say. The man in the pea coat stared at him, passing a coil of line from one hand to another.

Ellie stood up suddenly in the dory and yelled across to the black boat. "We're headed to Alaska. Juneau, Alaska," she said in a firm voice. "We got work in the mine up there."

Slip glared at her as if she had suddenly burst into flame. "What?" he mouthed.

"Long ways north," the skipper said, looking at Slip's bleeding hands. He walked to the stern of the black boat and picked up a stern line. "I'm going north. I can tow you a ways if you want."

Slip started to shake his head when Annabelle stood up beside him. "Can I bring my bird on board?" she yelled.

"Well . . ." said the skipper, making a show of looking around his old wooden boat, "Seeing as how I left the cat at home, I don't see why not." He threw a line across the distance to Slip and began pulling the small boat closer.

She was an old wooden fishing boat with a great squared-off stern and a boxy house built on three-quarters of the deck space.

Her hull was made of massive oak ribs with cedar planking. All the lines on deck were coiled neatly and she looked to be freshly painted. She was called the *Pacific Pride* and her skipper was Johnny Desmond.

Johnny was headed north to a cannery up a fjord in British Columbia to deliver some lumber for making shipping crates. He had gotten this job through a cousin who knew the cannery manager. Johnny's house in Tacoma had become overrun with his wife's relatives, who had gone bust in Texas. Johnny had told her he was doing this one job and would be back in two months but the truth was he was scouting out a new place to live.

He had heard of a new town being built on the Alaska coast to the west of Juneau. A new town built for the fishing industry. It was called Cold Storage. He had heard about it from a Swedish fisherman in a Chinese restaurant near the Tacoma docks. A brand-new town, without in-laws in a place where freeloading Texans would not follow. Johnny wanted to go and see it for himself.

The *Pacific Pride* had left Tacoma two days before and Johnny had been hoping to pick up a crew in Seattle. His regular crew had taken off for jobs on a bigger, more profitable boat, and Johnny had not liked the looks of any of the men who were wandering the docks in Seattle. He had been planning to hire a deckhand somewhere up the coast, and when he saw Slip in the dory he figured he was a hand-line fisherman who might want to work his way north.

But when he looked down into the dory and saw the battered man, a blonde woman, and a little girl with a caged bird, Johnny sucked in his breath and considered cutting them loose. But he didn't like the idea of leaving that girl out there in the middle of the Sound.

"You need a doctor for that man?" Johnny called down to Ellie.

"I don't think so. I think he just needs to heal up."

"Can he walk?" Johnny asked, thinking more about asking whether he was going to live through the day.

Annabelle was the first to clamber up over the side. She smiled, said "hello" and shook Johnny's hand, then leaned over and asked Ellie to hand the birdcage up to her.

Ellie helped Slip on his feet. He whispered, "Juneau, Alaska? Why didn't you tell him we were going to the North Pole?"

Ellie narrowed her eyes at him. "Shush. It's fine."

Slip closed his eyes and tried to pull himself up the side of the *Pacific Pride*. With the first motion the pain from his ribs jolted down through to his legs and he buckled, so Johnny grabbed his arms and pulled him up over the side and laid him on the deck. Ellie climbed up and tried to get Slip back on his feet.

"He gonna die?" Johnny asked Ellie.

"Certainly not," she said, and waved dismissively. "We got jumped by some guys on a beach a ways back. He took a bit of a beating, but he'll be all right."

"Jumped you? Who?" Johnny asked.

"Just some boys camped out by the railroad tracks. They wanted our boat and whatever . . . you know. They were drinking." She said the word "drinking" as if it were turning sour in her mouth.

"We could put in up here a bit and you could talk to the police. Wanna do that?"

"No. Please, we don't want to cause a delay." The blonde waved her hand again. "It's over now. They didn't get anything. We pulled out fast enough. Police won't make anybody heal up any faster."

"Okay . . ." Johnny looked over at Slip and let his voice trail away. Then he looked over at the little dory floating next to them.

"How long you had the dory?"

"Just got her," Slip grunted from the deck, wanting to save some face. "Friend of mine won her in a card game and he let me have her cheap. I heard there was work up north and the first thing I knew, I had company for the trip."

"I know how that happens," Johnny chuckled.

"Thank you for stopping," Slip said, holding his hand out for an awkward moment until the skipper reached out his own and pulled him to his feet. The men shook hands quickly and a silence slipped between them.

"She'll be right then," Johnny said abruptly, as he took the dory's bow line from Annabelle's hand and tied a much longer line to the end. "She was made to trail behind a boat like this. Just give her what she wants when we get under way and make sure to shorten up whenever we slow down. Sound good?" Johnny smiled, and showed the girl where to attach the line to the big boat's stern. She smiled in full agreement even though she had no idea what the man meant.

"All right. North it is." And he went into the wheelhouse, put power to the engine, and cranked the wheel back around. Annabelle handed the line to Slip and ran into the warm wheelhouse.

Slip and Ellie walked unsteadily to the stern rail. Ellie leaned into him and asked, "Can you run a boat like this by yourself if you need to?"

Slip didn't answer. He didn't even respond with a look. He just let out the line until the dory trailed some sixty feet behind the *Pacific Pride*, then tied it off to a heavy cleat. He turned around to answer her but she was already inside standing by the oil stove.

It was late by the time George got back to his desk. It was long after dinnertime and he was afraid that he was going to have to stand for an ass chewing from the captain. He read through his messages. To his relief the captain had gone home earlier in the day.

He started logging his evidence into his locked file drawer, and was about to pick up the phone to call home when dispatch rang a call through to the anvil-shaped black phone on his desk.

"Did you go to the party up by the railroad tracks?" It was the voice of the same young man who had called him with the tip early in the morning.

"Yeah, I got there. Thanks for the help. You want me to get

your name and address if there is any reward offered?" It was a feeble attempt to get the boy's name but feebler things had worked in the past.

"Goodness is its own reward," the voice said. George could hear music in the background. Scratchy jazz on a Victrola, maybe.

"I suppose that's true," George said, and tried to make out any other background sounds before the person hung up on him. "Listen, it's been a few days since I heard from you. Can you tell me what happened to those people in the small boat that pushed off from the hobo jungle?"

"I don't know nothin' about that. They went up in smoke I guess."

George listened to the voice. There was something about it that pestered his memory.

"I do know something though." He paused. "The papers they got from the woman . . . the papers she got out of the car before she dumped it . . ." The voice paused again, maybe for dramatic effect, or maybe to make sure that George was still listening. "They weren't all there."

The voice was funny. Nasal or something, and it was like he wasn't sure what to say next. He might have been reading from a script but he couldn't read very well.

"How do you know they weren't all there?" George asked.

"The papers were notes of informant interviews. Ben Avery's informants. But the most important page was missing."

The young man's voice kept bothering George. He pushed too much air through his nose like he had a cold or something.

"Don't you want to ask me what was missing?" the kid asked petulantly.

"Yes, tell me. What was the missing piece of paper?"

"It was the informant key. You know what that is?"

The record in the background hit a scratch and started to skip: a clarinet trilled up from a backbeat, over and over again.

"Yes, I think so," George said. "When your agents gather information from informants on the street, they give the informants numbers or code names to protect them. The informant key has the name and profile of the informants themselves."

"Paid informants." The voice had a childish kind of emphasis. "Paid," he said again.

"That's right," George said, as if talking to a toddler. "Paid informants." George listened while someone in the background bumped the record player needle and the song continued. "So you're saying that David Kept had some Floodwater informant notes?" he asked into the phone, which suddenly seemed much heavier.

"Paid for their services. Just imagine that," the kid brayed and hung up quickly.

As he was driving up Madison, George was thinking about the day, images just rising up: the blood on the granite rock, the look of Tom Delaney as he turned and walked away, the tracks and drag marks walking into the water, and the good feeling he had when standing in the cool sunlight on the edge of those trees.

Just as he was relaxing into that memory of the beach, it struck him who the anonymous caller had been: it was Fatty's boy. The one whose mother said he couldn't walk so well or breathe right through his nose. Fatty's bathhouse boy. He was making the calls for Fatty so the fat man could stay out of the way of his boss. It also helped explain why the boy took so much pleasure at the notion of an operative paying for someone's services, for certainly he was not working for free. George was beginning to find a whole new respect for the fat Floodwater operative and the kid with the broken nose.

George parked on his street and sat in his car for a few minutes. It was quiet with just a few pools of light spilling out of the windows fanning across the grass. By craning his neck he could look up and see the stars blinking among the new maple leaves as the wind caused them to make a light rattling sound. He didn't want to go inside. His wife's grief seemed to suck the oxygen out of the house. He felt heavier there, weighed down, and his recognition of this made it all that much worse. He wanted to tell her something that would make it easier for her to bear up under the fact that Benny was gone. But he couldn't. He wished their lives could at least be like sitting on this dark and empty street. It was sad, sure, but there were lights on in the other houses, the dogs were sleeping by the stove, and soon enough it would be morning again. George just wanted to keep loving his son. He didn't want to feel punished anymore. He wanted to move from daylight, to darkness, to daylight again, and with each pulse of daylight the grief would become more rounded, less sharp.

But he couldn't tell her that. It sounded too much like forgetting. Like pretending it hadn't happened and she couldn't bear that.

A boy ran past rolling a tire down the street. His sister cantered behind laughing and shouting, "Wait . . . wait . . ." as he barreled ahead through one pool of light to the next until all that was left was the distant slap of their leather shoes on the bricks. He decided to tell Emily that he loved her. He would tell her they should go on a trip this summer, maybe over the Cascades where they could go square-dancing with her sisters in the Methow Valley and he could fish the cold streams. They could eat and dance and be back with her boisterous brothers and sisters there in the ranch house in that steep-sided valley she had grown up in. She'd like that even if she didn't admit it to herself. She would be hard pressed to say it wouldn't be nice. First he would tell her that he loved her, then he would apologize for being late.

He unlocked the front door and put his briefcase down on the table by the entrance. He called her name and walked up the stairs. Her apron was laid out on the bed along with the pants and cotton blouse that she wore while working around the house. She had changed for dinner. He put on a sweater and emptied the change out of his pocket and put his wallet and watch on the dresser. Her jewelry box was open and he closed it gently. She must have really gotten dolled up tonight.

He took off his leather shoes and slipped on a pair of elk-hide moccasins that his brother-in-law had given him three Christmases ago. Then he padded down the stairs.

He said her name again and he pushed against the swinging door that led into the kitchen. His shoulder stopped hard against the swinging door, and when he pressed with his leg he saw that there was something jammed behind the door. He pushed again, and then he looked up and saw there was something wedged between the top of the door and the doorjamb. He took one step back and kicked at the flimsy panel in the center of the door. With the first kick he smelled the gas pushing out of the room. With the second he could see Emily lying in her best dress on the floor in front of the open oven door.

NINE

≈≈≈

The *Pacific Pride* was warm inside, and Annabelle quickly found a place for Buddy and herself on a shelf near the stovepipe. To be so suddenly warm and safe, to be *inside,* seemed so strange to her that she didn't want to look around too carefully for fear that it might all disappear. So she watched Buddy ruffle his feathers and peck at the small bell hanging in his cage. She was glad to be on this big boat.

Her happiness felt like a big cup of hot chocolate.

To get from the back deck, a person had to walk through the galley and then up a couple of steps to the wheelhouse. Ellie and Slip sat on a bench by the chart table, just inside the wheelhouse. They slumped on the seat and tried to arrange themselves comfortably to enjoy the heat. While the warmth felt good to Slip, every slight roll of the boat sent pain shooting through his ribs and up into his head. When the boat rolled across the wake of a larger ship, he groaned and Johnny could see that the battered man was not going to ride well there. He motioned Annabelle to come to the wheel. She stood up on the milk crate Johnny had scooted in front of the wheel and peered out the rippled glass windows at the ocean that was sliding underneath her feet.

He showed her how to look for logs and how to slow the engines down. He showed her how to hold on to the wheel and how to pull the throttle lever, which was the lever with the red cap closest to the starboard side of the boat. "Just head straight down the middle here," he said. "If another ship comes toward you, let them pass on our left side."

"Port side," Annabelle said, more to herself than to Johnny.

"That's right, port side. Let them pass port to port. If you see a log or anything floating in the water, steer around it. When in doubt, slow the engine down and I'll come running."

At first the girl was nearly panic-stricken with the responsibility. She turned and looked at Buddy. She wanted back into the small world she was used to inhabiting.

"What's your bird's name, honey?" Johnny asked.

"Buddy," the girl whispered.

"Well, Buddy's right here and he's going to be watching too. I need your help steering for a bit. Just keep your eyes out there ahead."

Annabelle could hear the bell in Buddy's cage and she knew he was watching out over the water.

"Do I steer around every single thing in the water, or can we go over the small things?" Annabelle asked after giving it some thought.

Johnny thought about it for a moment and said, "Steer around anything you can't throw for a dog." Then he added, "I'm going to show your folks where to put their stuff. I'll be right back."

Then he took Ellie and Slip down some steep steps into the forward bunk area that Annabelle seemed to remember was called the forecastle, or fo'c'sle. She remembered the word because of all the apostrophes.

Annabelle slid her glasses up her nose and turned the wheel to port and the vessel gently shouldered to the left, then she brought it back around to the original course. She wondered if this was something like the sensation of flying. The big boat had a loud engine that growled under her feet, and the waves seemed like distant events beneath her. The dory had bucked through the waves, but the *Pride* seemed to stride along humming to itself. She scanned the water ahead and saw diving ducks pop up from nowhere and then begin to beat their wings on top of the water to fly away as the boat approached. She looked carefully to see their markings but quickly swung her eyes back to scan for logs.

Annabelle scrunched up her nose with a worried expression that always made her glasses slip. She looked north and the sky seemed to be hard and gray. Were they really going to go to Alaska? Wasn't Alaska too cold for cockatiels? Images of her imagined Alaska swarmed around her head like flies. There were polar bears she knew, very far north anyway, and people lived in houses made of ice. Could you build a fire in them?

All the while she was a conscientious helmsman, not taking her eyes off the course ahead even when Slip poked his head up from below and asked, "What are you doing?"

"He left me in charge," she said.

"You know what you're doing?"

"I steer around any sticks I can't throw for a dog, and if I have any doubt I just slow down and he comes running."

"Oh." Slip stretched and closed his eyes. The heat from the galley stove eased into his aching bones and made him drowsy.

"Aren't you sleepy?" he asked the girl.

"Not now," she said, and she took off her glasses to clean them with the tail of her shirt. With her glasses off she stared so intently over the bow that it looked as if she could will herself to see.

"I'm beat," Slip said. He closed his eyes and looked as if he were going to sleep right there with his feet half in and half out of the wheelhouse. "But I should probably check on the dory."

"Slip?" she asked.

"Yeah?"

"Are we really going to Alaska?" She turned the boat slightly starboard to avoid a raft of kelp up ahead.

"I dunno," he said, his breath becoming deep and regular.

"Are there jobs up there?"

"Probably."

"It's a long way to go in that little boat, isn't it?" the girl asked, while a black duck popped to the surface. It looked like a scoter but she couldn't be sure.

"It can't be that far."

The girl crinkled up her eyes. "I don't wanna be smart-alecky, but I think it's that far. I mean really, really far." She saw the horizontal edge of a log bobbing in a straight line above the jumble of the waves and she steered well around it.

"I suppose," Slip said.

Annabelle was about to tell him about a friend of hers whose grandmother had taken a steamship to Juneau and about how long it had taken her running day and night at a lot greater speed than he could row that dory. Then she was going to tell him about how far it was to Alaska, but before she could she saw that he was asleep.

Annabelle kept steering. She wasn't opposed to going to Alaska. She just wanted to know how far it was.

Johnny shook the sleeping logger awake and showed him to a bunk, then came up into the wheelhouse. He looked down at the tired little girl.

"I made up some bunks. There's one for you all the way in the very front." He stepped in front of her and took the wheel. He scanned their position, then reached forward and increased the throttle.

"Buddy likes your boat," she said as she pointed to the birdcage.

"He's a smart bird," Johnny said.

Annabelle smiled and sat up on a short bunk just under Buddy's shelf.

"Go ahead. Kick your shoes off and lie down. You must be as tired as the rest of them," Johnny said.

"What if you need me to steer?" Annabelle asked.

"I'll wake you up. But I've got it for a while."

"Okay." She lay down and for the first time she felt the fatigue pull on her arms and legs. Soon the same weight was working on her eyelids.

"Captain Johnny?" she said through the warm syrup that was forming in her head.

"Yeah?" he replied.

"They're not my folks."

"That's okay, hon."

"Johnny, my folks died in a fire."

"I'm sorry, hon. Try to get some sleep now."

"You'll let me steer the boat again?"

"Sure. I'll let you steer."

"Okay," she said. And when she tried to say something more she found that it just wasn't important.

Johnny steered the boat north. The winds and the tides were fair and he figured they could be in a good anchorage near the Canadian border by nightfall. He would sort out what to do then. He had wanted a crew to help him take the boat up the Inside Passage and now it appeared he was a hospital ship for a rough-looking bunch. He didn't really believe the story about the hoboes and the train tracks, but he couldn't see what business it was of his if they were lying. He had two guns on the boat: a .45-70 rifle he used for shooting deer on the beach and a .22 pistol that he kept in with his fishing gear in case he ever hooked a fish too big to land by himself. He thought about some of the stories he'd heard of skippers who had tangled with the wrong crew: captains who were shot while standing watch, their bodies weighted down and

thrown overboard, never to be found. Johnny didn't put a lot
of stock in these stories and this group of castaways didn't seem
to have the strength of kittens, but still, he'd do well to keep the
weapons secure and available only to him. He'd stow the rifle in
the engine room and the .22 would fit nicely beneath the instru-
ment panel in the wheelhouse.

He looked at the ship's clock, checked his tide table, then
scanned his position in the Sound. He wanted to go through San
Juan Channel at close to slack water so he adjusted the throttle and
sat back in the pilot's seat, scanning the way ahead. Behind him
the little girl was asleep with her mouth wide open, while above
her on the shelf the yellow bird began to trill. He was two days out
of port and already the trip was bringing surprises. He reached up
and adjusted the throttle upward a second time, but then thinking
about the fuel he was burning, he pulled it back again. It would do
no good to hurry.

George Hanson had the funeral two days later. The minister who
had performed Benny's funeral came by and offered to help George
with the memorial service. Emily's family from the Methow Valley
came late the day of the service, and one of her brothers got so drunk
he tried to pick a fight with George and the rest of the family had to
pull him off. The three brothers and two sisters came to the service
at the Lutheran Church, but they were so hung over and sorrowful
that they didn't linger around for refreshments afterward.

A few policemen attended the funeral. His captain had come
and had shaken George's hand with both of his. He told George
how sorry he was and that George should take whatever time he
needed before coming back. There was a neighbor lady and her
teenage son who came, but George didn't even know their names.
She cried softly, sitting in the back pew, and the son sat stone-faced
and uncomfortable in his wool suit. George wished the mother had
not made the boy come with her. He'd rather think of the boy

playing baseball in the empty lot on the corner than see him sitting inside being subjected to the wilted send-off for a woman who had taken her own life.

George walked back to his house from the church. It had rained the night before but the morning had cleared off into a bright emerald of a day. There were a few cherry trees in bloom along the street and their blossoms were like a frothy pink candy. Cars had been parked overnight under the trees and the rain had pasted them with a layering of cherry blossoms. In the morning, when the cars were driven away, they left bare black patches in the brushstrokes of wet petals. George stopped a moment and looked at the black patches.

George wandered up around several blocks, not wanting to go home by himself. He walked past the empty lot where no kids were playing ball but a couple of cats were chasing around the edges hunting birds that darted in the berry bushes. His boss had told him to "take the time he needed." How much time *was* that?

Andy was sweeping up the trimmings of his last customer when George walked in. It was a one-chair shop with only three soft chairs against the wall for men to lounge in while they waited. There was a cast-iron stove in the corner with a bin of coal next to it. A pot of water sat on top of the stove. An old man with a bowler hat fished in his coin purse to pay Andy his twenty-five cents as Andy swept up. Andy took the quarter and helped the old man into his overcoat and then the man wobbled out the door.

It was just a hunch that brought George to the shop. He knew the logger had been with Ellie Hobbes and he knew that he had been looking rough. A rough-looking logger running with a blonde would want a shave.

"You're just in time," Andy said to George, as he popped a towel across the cracked leather barber's chair. "Looking for a shave or a trim? I got time for both if you want," he smiled.

"I'm looking for a logger who was running with a blonde gal. A Red probably, but he might not have that part figured out. Might have been through here in the last week," George said, taking off his overcoat. "But you know, a shave might be just the thing." And he sat down in the barber's chair.

"Listen, I told you guys everything I know. I don't know no more." Andy attached the cape around George's neck.

"You didn't tell me anything, mister."

"I told that other detective at least three times. I'm serious, I don't know nothing more." Andy was stropping his straight-edge on the leather strap hanging from the arm of the chair.

"Floodwater?" George asked, as he reached into his pocket.

"They didn't really say but I didn't figure them for real cops." Andy dippered hot water from the stove into a wash pan and put a towel into the steaming water. He had two pairs of tongs to lift the hot towel and to wring it out. Then he gently wrapped the towel around George's face. George let out a sigh, for even though he didn't really need a shave, the warm bay-scented towel eased some of the strain that had been building up behind his eyes.

George lay motionless for a moment, letting the heat sink in past his eye sockets and cheek bones. Then he held up his brass badge in his right hand. "I'm a police detective, not a private eye," he said through the layers of hot fabric.

"Yeah, so that means you'll put me in jail if I don't talk to you," Andy said as he stirred his shaving brush inside the cup, "and they'll just kill me."

"I'm not going to put you in jail. I just need to know about this guy."

"What happens if I don't tell you?"

"Then I figure you know something pretty useful. You may know where he is right now. Or you might have helped him get out of town in a small boat."

Andy stopped soaping the shaving brush. He didn't move for several seconds. George could hear the tin pot on top of the stove rattling just slightly in the rising heat. He heard Andy shifting his weight back and forth on his feet.

"And . . . if I do talk to you?" Andy said finally.

George sat up a bit and took the towel off his face. "I guess that depends on what you have to say," George said, staring at Andy. He was thinking too long about what to do and now his hands were starting to shake, which was a bad sign for a man who made his trade with a straight razor.

"You haven't told anybody else about the boat, have you?" George ventured.

"Listen, mister, I don't know a damn thing about a boat." Andy was back to soaping the brush, but nervously now, faster than necessary.

"You better hope I find your buddy before the Floodwater boys do."

Andy said nothing.

George leaned back. "I can still use a shave."

Andy began lathering his face and then he gingerly pushed the tip of the police detective's nose away from his lip and began gently scraping downward.

"His name's Jack Wilson," Andy said, "but he goes by Slip."

"Where's he gone?" George kept his voice soft, to match Andy's.

"They'll kill him sure?" Andy asked.

"Uh-hmm," George offered.

Andy leaned back, stirring his brush once more in the soapy mug. "They almost killed him last night up north of Ballard. They may have, for all I know. I just know they made off in a boat that was small enough to put up on the beach."

Andy started in on the cheek. "Damn fool should have stayed well away from that broad."

"Just tell me where he's headed. I'll give him a fair shake. I promise."

"He's headed north. That's all I know." Andy daubed soap on the detective's face, then took up the razor.

"Does he have any kin? Is he going to go to someone for help?" George leaned forward and stayed Andy's hand with the razor in it.

"Naw. He's got nobody as far as I know. Folks are dead. Poor dumb bastard. He's in quite a fix, ain't he?"

George didn't answer. He just stared up into the shop light while Andy kept shaving and telling him everything he knew: How Slip showed up looking for the girl. How he was in some kind of jam with Avery. How Andy gave him the boat the old Norwegian fisherman had lost to him in a card game. He told him about the woman and the kid showing up with a yellow bird and getting into the dory just as Slip was about to push off.

George sat back and relaxed into the shave. The barber wanted to talk. His voice was rhythmic and steady. The words came out of his mouth as if they were blown forward by a dark pressure in his chest. Whatever trouble this logger had gotten into had scared the barber just by being close to it.

"Did Slip tell you if he killed the shamus?"

"No, he didn't tell me. I swear, he never said." Andy had finished the last section under George's ear and he prepared another warm towel.

"But what do you think?" George asked.

"I dunno," Andy said. "I think he's in deep. Even if he didn't kill him, he couldn't just walk away clean. I think he was tangled up somehow with that woman and her little girl."

"That would slow a fellow down all right," George said. He got up from the chair and gave Andy a dollar, then put on his coat and walked out the door.

Johnny Desmond was headed north to get away from his wife's relatives. Her brother and his wife had moved in that winter after they were put out of their house, and Johnny couldn't bear to have them underfoot. He had made just enough money for gas by rebuilding an engine for a friend's boat last winter. He had a line up on this box wood to sell to this Canadian cannery. So on the day he came home from the last day of putting the engine in and he found his brother-in-law eating the last of the roast while sitting in Johnny's chair by the fireplace, Johnny went down to the *Pacific Pride* and started getting ready to go to Alaska.

Puget Sound was a broad thoroughfare stretched out ahead of them. A cormorant stood on a drift log with its wings held out away from its body to dry. A merganser paddled along on top of the water, and far ahead a tugboat was pulling a barge full of stone.

"Are we going out in the ocean, Captain Johnny?" Annabelle asked, without taking her eyes off the course ahead.

"We'll just poke our nose out a bit. But mostly we stay to the Inside Passage. Its islands and inlets protect a boat all the way north. If you go far enough, you have to cross some big water to get to the Queen Charlottes and then there's Dixon Entrance. But it's mostly sheltered waters."

"So there's nothing . . ." and the girl bit her lip for a moment, "there's nothing bad that can happen to this boat."

"Well . . ." Johnny thought for just a moment, letting his imagination count all the potential hazards, then said, "You mean like a typhoon or a hurricane or something?"

"I guess."

"We'll always be able to get into a good safe place to ride out a storm."

"That's nice," Annabelle said, and smiled out at the water ahead.

"There are the tides. Big currents along the Inside Passage. Some places it's so narrow there will be whirlpools that can reach up and suck a big boat right underwater."

"What do you do about that?" Her smile was thinning out.

"You just have to make sure you go through the narrow passages at slack tide, just when it's changing. I've got a good current book that tells you when to go through those places."

"That's good." Annabelle was smiling again.

"The Inside Passage is like a big river," Johnny said. "And it flows both ways. It's taking us north for another few hours. We'll be at San Juan Narrows when it's slack, then it will be flowing back toward the south."

"It's a big both ways river," the girl said happily.

"That's right," Johnny said. The waves pushed against the bow and Annabelle steered around a swirling bunch of kelp. A gull stood on a small piece of wood as if he were waiting for a bus.

"So what do you folks do when you're not bobbing around in a boat?"

The girl slid her glasses up her nose and squinted toward the horizon. "My aunt Ellie is a Red."

"A Red? You mean like a radical?" Johnny asked, looking down at the girl.

"Well, actually, Ellie is a Communist. She believes that the workers should control the means of production. I guess, really she's an anarcho-syndicalist, but that's way too complicated to explain. Most people just call her a Red."

"Oh," Johnny said.

The girl wrinkled her nose and looked up at the skipper. "But what she really wants to do is fly an airplane like Amelia Earhart."

"I suppose that makes good sense," Johnny Desmond said, and he gently eased next to the girl and took the wheel.

TEN

≈≈≈

The captain didn't want George Hanson back at work. An unhappy man was not good for morale. Death belonged out on the streets. When it happened to someone on the force, it began to stink up the station.

Morale was low enough. There had been three murders in a week. The Seattle papers were concentrating on the trade unionist David Kept. There had been some splashy articles hinting at corruption on the docks. One of these articles ran a grainy photo of Kept getting into a car in front of an official-looking building. The photo had succeeded in implying that Kept had been in some trouble with the law, although there was nothing in the article, or in reality, to support that.

Floodwater had been able to shut down any inquiries about the death of Ben Avery and the man killed in the vigilante action in the hobo jungle. But the captain knew that George Hanson would lead the papers to both of those stories. Which was another good reason to get him out of town.

"You've got to go to Alaska and look for these people in the boat. Don't thank me. Just get out of here. Take some time; go fishing while you're up there." The captain slapped down a single sheet of paper on George's desk and stood over him without smiling.

"I don't fish," George said.

"Well learn, or take up dog-mushing, but I want you on the boat to Alaska tomorrow."

"What if I . . . ?" George started to say.

The captain interrupted George, thumping the desk with the tip of his index finger. "Your sister lives up there somewhere, doesn't she?"

"I haven't seen her for some years now," George said, squinting up from his desk.

"Well, you're about to see her again. Real soon."

"But . . ." George said, but the captain had walked away.

George began packing up his files. He took everything with him: the picture of his wife and son, and all of the reports he had compiled on the Kept and Avery murders. He took his badge. But he left his gun locked up in the drawer. He wasn't planning to shoot anyone, and the gun was too small to kill a polar bear.

The next day George stood at the dock. In the last twenty-four hours he had looked at the maps and charts. He had even read the newspapers about the dust bowlers headed north to build their new farms in Alaska. He tried out his warmest wool pants that he had used to go deer hunting one time with his in-laws. He even thought of buying a life jacket but then he figured the steamship line would provide him with one. He had sat on his bed the night before and looked at his bag piled up with clothes, with the silence of the house pressing down on him, and he knew he had to go somewhere and it might as well be Alaska.

But now that he stood on the dock looking up at the steel bluff of the *Admiral Rodman's* hull, his suitcase and leather grip sitting at his feet, it was dawning on him that there was no way he could ever be ready for such a trip. Alaska was just too strange and too far.

But he was going to go. He would telegraph his sister later, maybe in one of the towns along the way.

The *Admiral Rodman* carried cargo and passengers from Seattle up the Inside Passage to Skagway and returned home with cargo from the north country. From the dock, George watched a crane loading a stripped-down commercial truck into the hold. Then there were netloads of cement bags, slings of kiln-dried lumber. There were crates and pallets of flour, men yelling while the winch engine strained at the loads. There were the sounds of passengers rattling up the gangway. There was a light rain falling from dark clouds. All the activity seemed to lift him up the gangplank and onto the ship.

George had never left Washington State in his life. He had only ventured east of the Cascade Mountains to satisfy Emily's filial loyalty. To him the sheltered world of the Sound, with its blackberries and rhododendrons, moist ground and dripping cedar trees, was his reality. The world and everything to the north was hard and distant. Alaska was virtually empty on his imaginative map. There were gold mines and fishermen, brown bears that could fill a room in his small house, and now there were two adults and one kid who could tell him about the murder of at least two men.

George settled into the closet-sized stateroom, which became very warm after the ship got under way. George took off his overcoat and jacket and hung them up on pegs behind the door. He lay down on top of his blankets and stared at the painted pipes and ducts that crisscrossed the ceiling. All during the packing for the trip, George had to suppress his urge to ask Emily, *Three pairs of pants or two? Would she like two adjoining rooms so Benny could have a room of his own?* The questions would push through his foggy brain and almost bubble up out of his throat before they dissolved when he opened his mouth to speak. He reached out to her now in ways that he never recognized before. He didn't feel so much lonely or sad, but sleepy, as if he were just dozing through this part of his life. Soon enough he would wake up in the house on the crest of the hill, and the air coming through the open window would be full of a boy's shenanigans and the smell of a pie Emily had made from their good friend's berries.

The hull shimmied as the engines gained speed, and the inside of the ship clattered with the activity of people stowing their gear. His stateroom must have been near the galley because he could hear the echoing of pots being moved about. Soon the air began to smell like turnips and coffee.

George closed his eyes but he did not dream. He thought of Ben Avery and how he died. He thought of three people leaving Seattle in a small boat. He had asked around, and apparently it was not uncommon for fishermen to row small dories to the fishing grounds in Alaska. They were mostly Norwegians or Finns and they would meet up in early spring when the worst of the winter storms were over but the prevailing winds were still from the south. They would group up in fleets of twenty or thirty boats and would row their small dories up the eight-hundred miles or so of Inside Passage. Sometimes they would set their sails and get a few days of sailing in, but mostly it was hand-pulling some twelve to fifteen hours a day. They would certainly be in shape to hand-line for salmon or cod in Alaskan waters after their six-week trip.

But these fishermen were tough. Their hands were as dark and as hard as polished oak. They could sleep under a tarp in the rain as well as most people could sleep in a featherbed. The logger, this Jack Wilson, might be tough, but probably not tough enough to haul all the three of them eight-hundred miles. He would come into port with bleeding hands and probably at least one less passenger than he started out with. The *Admiral Rodman* made stops at every little port of call on the Inside Passage. The stops were only long enough to unload and load passengers and cargo, but there would be enough time for George to ask around about a bedraggled-looking bunch coming in off the water, with an injured man, a fast-looking woman who flashed her legs, a bookish little girl, and a yellow bird in a round wire cage. Even five minutes on the docks would be enough time to find out about a group like that. They would stick out like the Second Coming in any of the villages up the coast.

Deep within the interior of the *Admiral Rodman* and well below the waterline, three men were being shown to a storage locker by a nervous oiler who knew he was risking his job.

"There's a barrel of water and a bucket for your toilet. I'm the one who keeps the key and I'm the only one should be coming in and out. Each night you can go out on the crew deck for some air. Only one other person onboard is in on this with me. The others won't know you. If anyone sees you walking around, don't talk to them. Just come back here. They'll think you're new. Just don't talk to nobody. You get me?"

The three men nodded. Each carried a duffle bag. Each of them looked warily at the opening to the small storage locker while the oiler sorted through his keys. "It's going to be tight but there's a vent. You'll be all right."

"We appreciate this," William Pierce said to the man.

"I'm only doing this because I liked Dave Kept. He shouldn't have got it like he did." The oiler unlocked the door and swung it back to show the small space beneath a tangle of pipes.

"He was a good man," McCauley Conner said as he slid his bag into the tight space. "We won't screw this up."

"Will it be a rough trip?" Raymond Cobb asked.

"Not for a while. Puke in the bucket if you have to, but don't make a big deal of it. Someone hears you in here, they'll make me open up for sure."

"How rough?" the little fireplug of a man asked. His face was pale and a prickly sweat dotted his forehead.

"Don't worry about it," the oiler said, helping Cobb through the door. "It won't get bad for a few days." Then he closed the door, leaving the three men in a crawl space with a barrel, a bucket, and just enough room to lie down.

"How bad?" Raymond Cobb asked the darkness.

George didn't remember going to sleep until he jerked awake at the sound of a man walking up and down the companionway ringing a chime and telling the passengers that the first seating for luncheon was available in the dining room.

George found the clattering dining hall and sat at a table with a pastor and his wife. After grace they sat in silence and slowly ate the watery soup the waiters brought around in shallow bowls. George waited to see if he was expected to make conversation with his tablemates. When the reverend took out a Bible and began reading silently to himself, George took out an old packet of letters and a telegram from his coat pocket. All of the correspondence was from his sister, and the telegram had just been delivered before he left his house.

George's sister was named Rebecca. She worked at a mission school in Sitka, Alaska. George had corresponded with her over the years. But in the last twelve months, except for one letter after Benny's death pleading with George to come and visit, there had been no letters from Alaska. As children, the siblings had played in the brambles together and had made forts within the hedgerow of scotch broom running alongside a neighbor's yard. When Rebecca was sent away to live with an aunt and attend a Presbyterian school,

George became the sole and silent audience for their father's rambling lectures on the injustices of the world.

He opened the envelope and read her telegram.

"George—Have started making plans for you.—Love, Rebecca."

His stomach tightened. He folded the telegram on top of the older packet of letters from her that he had saved over the years. He didn't know why he had saved them all, each letter having only been read once.

"Why didn't we just buy a ticket?" Ray Cobb asked the others. "I can already feel myself getting seasick."

"Will you shut up about being sick," Pierce said. He laid out a blanket on the greasy steel deck.

"We been through this, Ray. We don't want to show up on the ship's manifest or on any customs forms. We're just going to slip up there and bring her back, and no one's the wiser." McCauley Conner dipped out a cup of water from the barrel and handed it to Cobb in the dark.

"How the fuck are we going to find her?" Cobb said before taking a drink.

"We go to Ketchikan and wait. It's the first big city in Alaska they'll come to," Pierce said.

"What if they stay in Canada, or cut inland?" Cobb handed the cup back.

Pierce flopped down on his blanket and crossed his hands behind his head. "They might stay in Canada for a while, and if they do, we just work our way south. They won't go inland because the country's too rough and too desolate. Some Canadian cop's going to notice them and start asking questions for sure. They're in a boat. They'll stick to the coast. But dollars to doughnuts they'll go through Ketchikan on their way to Juneau."

"Why Juneau?" Cobb started laying out his blanket.

"Cause they've got a messy mine strike happening up in

Juneau. She'll have Party members there, and plenty of buyers if she wants to stand on a soapbox. It's made for Ellie Hobbes."

"Why don't we just fucking kill her and be done with it," Cobb said. He rubbed the knot growing out of his scalp and swallowed hard just to keep the contents of his stomach in place.

Annabelle was sleeping on a pad on the floor of the forward compartment. It was the space where the curved walls of the hull met at the bow. Her head was two feet from the tip of the hull, and beyond that the anchor chain ran from the winch down through six fathoms of 43-degree water to the anchor buried in the muddy bottom. She could smell the pine tar and hemp calking in the planks as she lay in her new bed. The boat was a menagerie of sounds: the ticking of the galley clock and the flame in the oil stove rumbling through the darkness on leathery wings. At times a gust of wind shrieked through the rigging while the anchor popped in the bow roller and the boat swung to face into the wind.

As sleep came on she felt herself melting into the floor of the boat. But something clawing against the outside of the hull drew her up. She felt warm and light with worry now, imagining something clawing against the hull of the boat, trying to lift itself out of the icy water. She stumbled up the stairs and found herself on the deck looking out over the dark anchorage.

A cold wind needled through her jacket and nightgown. Her bare feet ached on the sticky decking. She hunched her shoulders and found thin pockets of warmth under her clothes. It was a night for seeing ghosts. But Annabelle was a serious girl and did not believe in ghosts. Even when she wished them to come.

The anchor light on top of the mast cast a pale glow over the water. She could see that down close to the hull there was a mat of seaweed with sticks laced through the rubbery fronds. As the boat swung on the anchor chain the mat pushed against the hull, and the pieces of wood, which were as varied in size as human bones, rattled against the hull.

"What you doing out here, girl?" Johnny asked from behind her.

She jumped and spun around. The rigging cut tangled shadows across his body but he was smiling and he had his hands out to her as if he were coming to take her someplace safe.

"I thought I heard something," she said.

"I did, too," Johnny said. He took her hand to take her back inside. "I heard you out here. Do me a favor, okay?"

"Okay."

"I don't want you coming out here by yourself."

"No. I won't," she said. She padded down the stairs to her bed on the floor of the forward compartment. Slip and Ellie were breathing deep and steady breaths. Dead to the world.

E L E V E N

≈≈≈

No one else was awake when Johnny started the engine and the anchor chain began to rattle in the locker next to the crew quarters. Annabelle scrambled up the steep steps to see what was going on. Slip and Ellie were slow to roll over in their bunks. The sunlight was just slanting in over the anchorage. The *Pacific Pride* was cupped in the crescent of a cobbled beach that was flaring gray and green as the thin new daylight washed across it. Annabelle padded up silently behind Johnny on deck at the anchor winch.

"Whatcha doing?" she asked.

"Criminy!" The skipper flinched and turned to her. "You scared me there." Then he looked over the moving anchor chain to the beach and spoke over his shoulder. "You go back inside. When the hook comes off the bottom the boat might turn toward the beach with the current. Just nudge her into gear and turn us off the beach. You remember the gear lever?"

"The one on the left . . . port . . . with the black knob?"

"That's the one. No need to give her any fuel. I'll get the chain up and the hook secure, and then we'll work our way out of the cove."

The deck was damp from the evening's dew. The little girl walked back, placing her bare feet in her just-made prints on the deck. She made it into the wheelhouse just as Slip was coming up from below.

"Where we headed?" Slip asked the little girl in her nightshirt.

"I can't talk right now. When the hook comes up, the boat might swing into the beach." Annabelle hopped back on her box in front of the wheel, and slid her glasses up the bridge of her nose with her index finger.

The anchor came up and Ellie came from the forward berth to give Annabelle a kiss on the cheek. The little girl barely noticed her aunt as she turned the big boat away from the beach. Johnny secured the anchor in place and then took the wheel. Annabelle uncovered Buddy and the yellow bird began to chatter and preen his feathers.

"So, do you cook?" Johnny turned to Ellie.

The woman looked hard at the skipper, her fists resting on the points of her hips.

"It's not what I'm best at."

"Well, rummage around. There's plenty of food and I promise no one on this boat gives any guff to the cook."

Ellie and Slip walked down into the galley and went to work making a big pot of mush and frying up some eggs that could be eaten on slices of buttered bread. Coffee boiled and slopped out on top of the iron stove.

Johnny steered around the submerged rocks at the entrance to the cove where they had anchored. Once out of the cove he gradually gave the single engine more throttle and the boat churned west.

"I've been thinking," Johnny said, with some trepidation. "I mean . . . I've made a decision of what I think is best."

Everyone turned to face him. Slip was drinking coffee and Annabelle was crunching up a sugar cube with a spoon in her bowl of mush. Ellie handed Johnny a fresh mug of coffee.

"We're going into Canada. I'm going to need to clear customs. I'm assuming that you don't have all your papers and that you probably don't want to stand up to a bunch of questions by the Canadian authorities. Is that right?"

"You have to clear customs?" Slip asked, chewing his toast.

"Yeah . . . well . . . they patrol this coast. Not all that often. Not all that regular. But if I'm going to deliver this wood up to the cannery, eventually I'm going to run into some government agents. What do I tell them? I got no reason not to clear customs." He was stammering a bit and clearly uncomfortable.

"I understand," Slip said, rubbing his hands across his sore chest.

Johnny cleared his throat nervously. "What I was thinking was that I'll take you up to the beginning of the Gulf Islands. Then I'll duck back and clear customs. You can just keep moving north and I'll catch up with you in a couple of days."

Slip handed Johnny a slice of buttered bread with a fried egg folded into it. "You think we'll run into any customs agents?" he asked.

"Just don't go into any of the villages. Stay to the back bays and try to keep to yourself. If someone sees you, they'll think you're local. Just don't talk to too many people."

"That sounds all right to me. A couple of days, you say?" Ellie stood with her hands on Annabelle's shoulders.

"A couple of days for sure. I'll show you on a chart where to start looking for me."

"We've got food and water in our little boat?" Slip looked at Ellie.

"Enough for a couple of days, I think." She looked at Slip and then at Johnny, working over this new plan in her mind. "We could manage," she said.

Annabelle was looking out the side window to where the waves were scrolling past. Just the thought of getting back in the little boat made her hunch her shoulders and shudder.

"I've got another idea." Johnny cleared his throat nervously. "I was thinking that Annabelle and Buddy can stay with me on the *Pride*. If customs asks any questions, I'll tell them she's my niece and that she's coming along for the trip to help me steer. That last part is the truth and I think they'll be happy with that."

Annabelle turned her head to Johnny. "That sounds all right with me," she said, and her spoon flipped out of her bowl, sending mush catapulting onto the deck.

"Jeepers, I don't know . . ." Ellie said slowly, as she bent over to clean up the mush.

"It doesn't matter to me," the girl shrugged, when in fact the excitement at the prospect was building in her voice.

"It's really the best plan," Johnny said with his mouth full of bread and egg.

"I don't know . . ." Ellie repeated. Her hands were gripping more tightly onto the girl's shoulders than she realized.

"Just a couple of days." Annabelle winced and moved away from her grip. She looked at Ellie and slid her glasses up her nose.

"I suppose," Ellie said finally.

"All right then," Johnny said, and he turned the boat toward the north.

The *Pacific Pride* wound a course up through the San Juan Islands. Past Shaw and Yellow Islands, Jones Island, and then Johnny set a course to the south side of Flattop and to the north of Johns Island to the south of Waldron. A few clouds gathered but the wind was mild and carried a slight chop. The high mountains to the east seemed to have crept closer and the others to the south and west had stepped back behind the close hills. The sides of the smaller islands were steep and they showed smooth granite faces. A swell was running from the northwest, and the waves crawled slowly up the smooth rock faces to break back on themselves in garlands of white. Just as they fetched up abeam of Flattop Island, a seal popped his head up ten yards from the boat and Johnny pointed it out to the girl. She stood up on her tiptoes and barely got a glimpse of the animal before it ducked straight down without a trace.

"It looked like a doll's head," she said, "except it looked like it was thinking."

They spent most of the day moving toward the northeast. There was one section of water where big swells rolled under the *Pacific Pride*. At the top of the waves Annabelle could see the hazy line of the far horizon and moments later she was looking up the hill of the glittering green wave. Something in her chest rose up as she felt the big boat break across the top of the wave.

For most of the afternoon the *Pacific Pride* rolled gently as it quartered across the easy seas. The little dory skittered like a water bug behind the big boat, rising and falling at the end of its line almost like the tail of a kite. Annabelle stood by the wheel and talked with Johnny, and Ellie and Slip did the dishes, ate the last of the loaf of bread, and lay down in their bunks. The boat crossed over into Canadian waters.

Early in the afternoon Johnny eased back on the throttle, and Ellie and Slip came up from their bunks. Slip pulled the little dory alongside the big boat and stepped inside to bail her out. He undid the clasps on the trunk in the dory and took out the leather case with the roll of charts, which he handed up to Johnny on the back deck.

Ellie was putting on her warm coat and Slip stood looking down at the dory as if he'd rather take another beating than get back into the little boat. Johnny began to explain the points on the chart to Slip, who wasn't paying any attention.

"See that island there?" Johnny said. He pointed to a steep-sided wooded island about three miles to the northwest. "That's Saturna Island there. Look here on the chart."

Ellie swung the big man's shoulders around so she could see the charts clearly. "I'll navigate. Slip's still a little rocky," she said.

Johnny looked over at Slip with a frown. "Okay, then. Here on the chart is Saturna. The one after that is Mayne and then Galiano. Just stay on this side of those islands. See? It's like a channel. I'll catch up with you before you get up here . . . Dodd Narrows," and he pointed to a narrow passage on the chart. "Beyond that is Nanaimo. Don't go through the narrows. There'll be lots of boats waiting to go through Dodd at slack tide. If I don't catch up with you before, I'll wait on this side of the narrows."

"Okay," Ellie said, looking out at the expanse of sea to the distant island.

"There's plenty of coves and places to tuck in. Just make sure you don't pick a place that's too busy. You'll be fine."

"Okay," Ellie said again. "You take good care of her," she said, with just the tinge of a threat. Then she turned, wrapped the girl in her arms for five seconds, and clambered over the side of the wooden boat into the dory.

Slip was the last to get in and he looked around as if he were lost.

"Two days?" he asked no one in particular.

"Two . . . three days at most. Just don't go through Dodd Narrows. I'll catch up," Johnny said, and he threw the bow line into the dory.

Annabelle waved as if she were on the deck of an ocean liner leaving New York.

Ellie looked at the far shore of Saturna Island, and Slip gave the girl a quick nod and a smile and then fixed the oars in the oarlocks.

"Safe journey," Johnny said. He put a big hand on Annabelle's shoulder and led her into the wheelhouse.

Johnny swung the boat toward the southeast. Annabelle stood on the skipper's short bunk and looked over the stern. Buddy was preening and pecking at his bell. She had given the bird two teaspoons of seeds that she had brought with her from the small boat. She stored the seeds in a green tonic bottle that she sometimes left in the bottom of the cage. She would buy some more seeds in Canada with some of the money she had kept in her shoe.

Buddy preened and worried his food while the little dory with the two adults grew smaller to the stern. Annabelle saw the long oars dipping slowly in and out of the water. They looked liked skinny little bug's legs, she thought. Then she remembered Slip's sore hands and thought she might buy him a pair of gloves when she got into Canada.

She watched out the stern until she couldn't see the boat anymore, and for a few minutes she stared anyway to see if she could catch the invisible tremble of their oars. When she couldn't, she cleaned her glasses on her shirt sleeve and tried again.

"You don't need to worry about them. Their kind always makes out. We got to worry about you," Johnny Desmond said as he steered toward the south.

"About me? Why?" Annabelle turned back toward Johnny.

"You don't want to get back in that boat do you? You'll be happier here on the *Pride*. Don't you think?"

Buddy kept tapping the silver bell, and Annabelle felt a tightness in her stomach as if someone were dropping BBs down her throat.

"It will be a lot better here with me," Johnny said, staring at the sea ahead.

It took almost forty minutes for the *Pacific Pride* to disappear behind the southern islands, and with each second Ellie felt the sea growing larger and more lonely. The little dory, which had once felt substantial when they were pulling away from the docks in Seattle, now felt like one half of an empty walnut shell. It felt to her as if her anxiety alone was keeping them afloat. Slip had torn up his one spare undershirt and had made wrappings for his hands. He pulled slowly and steadily, not trying to increase his speed once he felt the boat moving along the water but just working to maintain their momentum. The oarlocks creaked with each stroke and Ellie could hear him breathe in time to his labor. Far ahead she could barely hear the swells washing around the rocks off Saturna Island,

and behind the dory she could hear the winnowing flutter of the *Pacific Pride* disappearing.

"Do you see that rock breaking over there?" Ellie said, stretching her arm toward the bow.

"What do you mean?" Slip said.

"I mean that a rock is breaking through the surface of the water, farmboy."

Just ahead, an elephant-colored rock garlanded in slick green banners of kelp appeared. The waves rose and covered it completely, and when they sank away the rock seemed to stand up in the water, dripping in the milky sunlight of the afternoon.

"I see it," Slip shot back. "And don't call me a farmboy."

"Aye, aye, captain." Ellie leaned back against the stern of the dory and fished around for a cigarette and a wooden match.

Slip rowed into the strait between Saturna and South Pender islands. Once in the middle of the strait their progress slowed. Slip pulled harder on the oars and the boat pulled quickly through the water yet they seemed to make little headway. Ellie pointed off their starboard to a point and suggested that they take a diagonal course to bring them closer to the shore of Saturna. Slip pulled for an hour with very little forward progress, but he did not stop.

Ellie dug out four pieces of flatbread crackers and put some orange marmalade on each of them. She fed one to Slip as he rowed, putting a piece into his mouth each time he leaned forward on the haul back. She alternated bites with a drink of fresh water from a ceramic jug that was wrapped in burlap and kept cool in the bottom of the boat. Slip pulled and drank, pulled and took a bite of the stale flatbread. When he had eaten the last piece, Ellie licked the marmalade off of her fingers and settled in to eating her own. Slip pulled and never looked where they were going, but occasionally Ellie would point out the best heading and Slip would line the boat up until her finger was pointing straight at his face. Then he settled into his steady rhythm on the oars. The crackers tasted fine but caused his stomach to growl with hunger.

They made better forward progress the closer they came to the shore, the boat moving up the island with less effort on his part. Slip slowed his pace, shipped the oars, and stretched his shoulders.

"I've got a pretty good knot coming in my back," Slip said, wincing.

"Let me row a while," Ellie said.

"Get the hell out of here," Slip said softly.

"Your ribs are banged up. You were spitting up blood last night. I'll row." Ellie stood up and put her hand on Slip's shoulder.

"Just till I get this knot worked out. Then I can row again."

"Don't worry. I won't hog it all," she said. Ellie settled herself and began pulling on the oars.

They worked their way around the point. Slip drifted in and out of sleep most of the afternoon. He would wake up with a start, shake himself, then lean back against the seat of the dory and close his eyes.

"You sure she's going to be all right on that boat?" Ellie said out of nowhere.

Slip opened his eyes and took a moment to orient himself. "She'll be fine."

Boot Cove had a narrow entrance that opened up into a tight anchorage. There was a shallow beach with some flat ground at the north end where they pulled the dory. The water came up almost to the grass where big drift logs lay bleached out and picked clean. The sky was clearing and as the afternoon wore on, the sun slanted in on their camp spot. Ellie gathered wood and got a fire going while Slip tried to figure out how to put up the tent, eventually giving up in favor of using it as a ground tarp.

The truth was, no matter how optimistic Ellie had been about the food supply, there wasn't much food left on the dory. There was some dried beef in a tin that was powerfully salty but they ate it and then washed it down with gulps of water. The beef made them thirsty and they drank more water than they could afford, so Slip offered to hunt around for a stream. Besides the beef, there was a can of peaches and one tin of crackers.

Slip and Ellie lay on their backs and watched as the sky darkened and the stars began to wink in the purple screen above them. The fire hissed and sparked every once in a while, sending a lightning bug of ember out toward the water. They had tied the dory off to a stubby tree but there was no need. As the tide lowered, the dory sat dry on the sand and cobbles of the beach. A wind from the north was beginning to build from behind their backs but it passed over their heads and only rippled the water out past the stern of the boat. Slip grumbled as he closed his eyes, and soon he was dreaming of food: hotcakes, beefsteaks, and banana cream pie.

Slip woke up and a teenage boy was standing next to the fire. He wore a broad-brimmed hat and a wool coat with a thick collar. The bulky coat made his raw-boned face appear all the more gaunt. The firelight on his face cast more shadows on his skin than light. Slip didn't start and he didn't say a thing, feeling sure the boy was a phantom.

The boy kicked the fire and sparks funneled up into the sky. The apparition then turned and looked at Slip lying on the tarp. Now Slip could see that the ghost held a shotgun cradled in its arms.

"Private property. You know that?"

"No sir," Slip said, and sat up straight. "We'll be gone in the morning."

"What you have for supper," the kid asked, and hugged his shotgun as if for warmth.

"Some dried beef. We got extra if you want."

"You sure you didn't have some roast lamb?" The kid was scanning around the campsite. His skinny legs scissored over to where the mess kit was laid out against a beach log, and he pushed the cookware around with his toe.

"No sir, we didn't have any lamb. All we packed was this dried beef. Like I said, you can have some if you want."

"No, thanks," he said. "You won't be here in the morning." He shifted the gun in his arms. This wasn't a question.

"No sir," Slip said and he stood up.

"If you're gone in the morning I won't tell Carl about it. He's madder than a hornet 'cause people been stealing his sheep. If he knew you were down here with a fire going he'd make you pack up tonight." It wasn't until he said the word "sheep" that Slip heard the tinkle of bells. Up the beach and in the darkness he heard bells and the faint mewing of a flock.

"Take a look around if you like. There's no blood. No meat. We didn't bother your animals. I swear." Slip walked slowly toward him with his hands out.

"I believe you. I just think it would be better if you packed up your kit and were out of this cove by sunup."

"You can count on it."

The skinny boy lowered the shotgun to one hand and walked out of the firelight and into the darkness of tinkling bells. Slip could hear leather boots crunching on the mussels encrusted on the beach rocks. As soon as the kid was gone Slip turned back toward the fire and bumped straight into Ellie.

"Jesus," Slip sputtered.

"He gone?" Ellie was looking over her shoulder in the direction where the kid had walked.

"I think so. They've had some poachers around. He wanted to make sure we didn't help ourselves to any of their lambs."

"Ah," Ellie said. Her eyes seemed even wilder in the light from the fire. Slip was going to step around her and head back to his bedroll when he looked down at Ellie's hands. She was holding the long knife from the mess kit in her right hand. The knife was covered with blood. Slip turned Ellie toward the fire and saw that she was spattered with blood along her sleeves and dungarees.

"Then I guess we better be getting a good start in the morning," she said, and turned to wash off the knife in the salt water.

The next morning they had to push the dory down the beach to be able to reach the water before the sun came up. The tide wouldn't be in for hours and Slip was eager to get out of Boot Cove. They were able to use some small drift logs as rollers and a couple of green limbs for levers to push the dory across the mud and rocks of the exposed beach. The sun was brightening in the eastern sky as the dory floated in the shallow water. They loaded the gear in the dory, and the last thing to be put in was a burlap bag Ellie fetched from the woods. Slip was standing in the water in his bare feet and pants rolled up, holding the dory and waiting for Ellie to get in. He considered pushing off and leaving her there with the bloody knife and the skinned-out lamb to explain herself, but he thought better of it.

"Got it. Let's get going." Ellie threw the burlap bag into the stern of the dory and lifted herself in. Slip was still sore from the beating he had taken at the hobo jungle but he was able to arrange himself tenderly into the stern of the boat. Ellie settled in the middle with the oars in her hands and began pulling off the beach.

"With all the trouble we've got, why'd you poach that lamb?" Slip asked.

"I'm hungry. I figure this meat belongs to me as much as anyone."

"You thought it was a wild lamb?"

"This meat is better used in our stomach than going to some grocery store in Vancouver. You'll be happy enough when we get to shore and cook some chops."

"We could have got thrown in jail," Slip said.

"Then you should be happy that we didn't get caught," she said with a smile.

≋≋

The weather was gentle from the north as the sun came up. The new daylight cut through the strips of fog that lay in the main channel and pushed over the islands to the north. For a few moments of sunrise, the air was a silver halo surrounding the gray-green islands in every direction. The inlet was quiet, only disturbed by the dipping of oars.

Slip lay down as best he could in the stern and listened to Ellie pull on the oars. Her breath was even and filled her throat as she warmed to a rhythm. He sat up and took the chart out of its round case and put his finger on their position.

"How we doing?" Ellie asked.

"We got lots of choices. I don't know what's in all of these little coves but I think we'll find something before nightfall. Let's just see how far we get. Yesterday it was easier going close to the rocks. You want to go that way?" Slip leaned in so his head was close to hers.

"Look out there," Ellie said. "See those ducks just sitting in the water out toward the middle of the channel? They seem to be moving almost as fast as we are and I've got to be working harder than them."

Slip looked, and sure enough there were three black-and-white ducks sitting equitably in the current moving at an easy pace.

"I think I'll go with the ducks," Ellie said. She pulled on her left oar and took the dory out into the bigger water of the channel.

The morning wore on at the pace of the oars. A slight breeze from the north started to stipple the water and Ellie leaned into her work. Slip finally got into the burlap bag and unwrapped a section of hide. Using his pocket knife and some pieces of tarred twine, he fashioned some fingerless gloves for his sore hands. The lanolin in the lamb's wool would soften his hands a little but that was all right because of the relief the gloves would offer him for the next few days.

He was just finishing up lacing on his crude gloves when they heard a puff of breath by the bow of the dory. Slip sat up with a start and looked around as if someone had fired a shot. Ellie kept rowing but craned her head around to see. There was another breath and another, and Slip looked at three black-and-white porpoises passing under the boat, curling through the water and coming up on each side.

"Are they sharks?" he asked, reaching around for the gaff hook wedged under the center seat.

"No, I don't think so. Their tails don't look like a shark's," Ellie said as she shipped oars and let the boat glide along.

"Well, they sure like this boat," he said, standing up in the bow.

Slip could see underwater that the darkness was almost alive with the black-and-white creatures swimming faster and faster under the surface.

"I wish Annabelle could see this," Ellie said. She watched as the flashes of black and white zigzagged under their boat, which was now drifting slowly to the north on the incoming tide.

"What do you think they're doing?" she asked.

"Looks like they're playing tag or something."

Just then a massive black-and-white form broke the surface of the water some fifteen feet from the dory. Something shuddered against the bottom of the boat. Another massive animal, larger than the dory itself, churned to the surface, sending a hissing spray of water off its back and into the boat.

"What the hell?" Slip yelled, grabbing the little axe as if that would protect him.

Under the dory, porpoises were cutting back and forth as if looking for a way out of the sea. Slip was watching the small animals slashing through the water when suddenly a huge black-and-white form slid underneath, close enough for him to reach out and touch. This animal moved with the steady grace of a tree being felled. It rolled underneath the boat and Slip could see its great eye looking toward the surface of the sea and the tender little boat.

"Whales!" was all Slip could yell.

A killer whale pushed its head out of the water as if it were a large log bobbing on end, and then it rolled around so its eye could scan the length of the dory. Another whale came to the surface with a dagger-shaped fin that jutted almost six feet into the air. This one carried the carcass of one of the small Dall's porpoises in its mouth.

"Look," Ellie whispered, lost now in a collapsed moment of surprise, like a person in a train wreck who only manages to say "oh" before walking out of the wreckage unharmed.

Another whale surfaced and tossed the broken corpse of a Dall's porpoise into the air. Smaller whales swam after the dead porpoise, and a dark red slick bloomed up on the surface of the water.

"I don't think these real little ones are whales," Slip said. "But these whales sure as hell used this boat as a backstop to trap the little ones."

Two of the adult killer whales stayed still in the water and tore at the one corpse. The large male with the huge dagger fin swam around the dory with a skein of red flesh streaming from his mouth, and the smaller whales struck at the bloody streamer.

"Pull," Slip said, still gripping the camp axe in his right hand. "Pull hard."

Ellie was stunned, looking at the blood that spread like a storm cloud all around the boat, and could not move. Slip stepped around her and sat in the middle seat, and took the oars out of her hands. He began pulling hard, leaving the kill site behind.

The surviving Dall's porpoises scattered like panicked colts in all directions. One of the juvenile killer whales gave half-hearted chase but soon came back to the kill site where the adults were sharing the meal and the little ones were learning how to hunt.

Any tiredness Slip had felt had been replaced by adrenaline pumping through his veins. He pulled on the oars so hard he felt he might snap them at the oarlocks. He watched the whales milling in the slick of blood as he pulled away. Gulls began wheeling over the kill site, diving down to pick up any bits of flesh that might float to the surface. Once Slip thought he saw a killer whale lunge up at one of the diving birds, but the gull pushed off into the air and circled back around to scan the scene for food.

"Let's go in someplace and start a fire," Ellie said after a few moments.

Slip pulled on his left oar and made a course for the islands to the west. The northwest wind was quartering off their bow, and after half an hour Slip suggested they put up their sail and he would keep rowing and using the oars as leeboards. This seemed to work quite well. He found that with the light wind and the oars, he could set a course for the south end of North Pender Island and the small bay that looked to be hospitable for them and perhaps no other deep-draft boats.

"I don't know why I'm so hungry all of a sudden," Ellie said. She looked over Slip's shoulder and did not let the tip of North Pender Island out of her sight.

It was mid afternoon by the time they completed the crossing and pulled into the shallow cove of Davidson Bay. They were fairly well protected from the light northern breeze but the low valley to the south of the island would leave them exposed if the wind should change. Sheep grazed the hills above the beach and they watched to make sure there were no shepherds before they pushed their boat ashore. They agreed they would press on north to some anchorage on Mayne Island if the wind died down. When they had rounded the northern point of South Pender they had seen docks with some boats tied up. There were houses onshore and a tiny community. They didn't want to linger long, but they were hungry now, so Slip got the fire started and Ellie cut some green willow limbs to make a crude spit for their chops. The wind carried the smoke south, and they hoped it would not attract any attention. They wanted to eat quickly.

The chops were on the end of long narrow ribs with not a lot of meat so they cooked up almost all of the rib cage. The fire hissed as grease sputtered down onto the flames. The bones blackened and the two of them were hungry enough to pull the meat off the fire before it was cooked. Ellie took a piece off first and tore into it, but the warm raw lamb was so rich that it turned in her stomach. She put it back over the fire, but closer to the flames this time so that the outside of the meat began to crystallize in char.

Soon enough the chops were all blackened so they plucked them out and started gnawing on the bones. Slip burned the roof of his mouth and dropped one chop into the fire, and without thinking he reached into the flame to pluck it out.

Grease rolled down between their fingers and they ate greedily. A small stream flowed out into the bight, and Slip filled their water jugs. They drank the cold water, and the fat congealed on their fingers. They drank more water and ate the chops, even crunching down greedily on the bones to suck out the gooey marrow.

Slip filled the water jugs again and as he was making his way back to the boat he looked up over his shoulder and saw a horse and rider coming down a steep slope through a clearing. He didn't run but walked quickly to the dory. Ellie kicked the fire apart. She dipped her greasy hands into the cold salt water and climbed into the dory. They pushed off, then pulled out into the main part of the channel.

Annabelle made a sour face when the Canadian customs agent spoke with Johnny about his young niece making the trip north with him. The agent wasn't put off by the fact that Johnny had no identification for the girl. There didn't seem to be any reason to be suspicious. Johnny had his papers in order along with the freight bill and some letters from the manager of the cannery up the coast. All this seemed to satisfy the agent. He handed the papers back to Johnny, then with a handshake they were on their way.

The docks of Victoria were busy with freighters and fishing vessels taking on supplies. A row of stone buildings stood in the background like bluffs above the waterfront. Annabelle agreed to walk up to the shops with Johnny as long as he promised that they would buy some food for Buddy. There were tobacconists and mercantile stores, ship's chandleries, and down some of the long side streets Annabelle thought there must be factories because of the smoke and noise coming out into the road. They walked slowly through the crowds of people on the sidewalk. Johnny extended his hand several times but Annabelle would not take it. She said very little, but in everything she said she tried to include the plan to meet back up with the little dory.

"I'm going to need some more food for Buddy if we're going to row all the way to Alaska," she said, without looking up at Johnny as she ducked through the crowd.

"Uh-huh," Johnny said, scanning the stores.

They found a Chinese grocery that sold sunflower seeds and strange-looking crackers that Annabelle thought Buddy would like for sure. Johnny bought more food for the boat: tins of meat and a sack of potatoes, a box of apples and a cured ham. He also bought a large paper bag of peppermint sticks and set them on the counter in front of the old man totaling up the bill with an abacus.

Johnny handed Annabelle a peppermint stick as the old man took down the name of the boat so he could have the groceries delivered.

"This will be fine," Annabelle said in a flat tone. "Ellie likes peppermint candy."

"Uh-huh," Johnny said again. Then, "You left most of your clothes and things on the dory. You want to go buy some new clothes? I could get you a nice dress or something here if you like."

Annabelle looked down at herself. Clothes had never been important to her. She had seen the film stars in the magazines with their fancy evening clothes. She wondered for a moment if Johnny was talking about a dress like that? One that sparkled when she moved. Johnny couldn't mean such a thing, could he? Annabelle was wearing her play pants made of tough canvas and a flannel shirt. She had her hair in braids and her glasses sat firmly on the bridge of her nose. For a moment she considered what it would be like to wear a dress like Claudette Colbert, where her legs showed to the world and helped her stop cars when she needed one. Annabelle smiled, thinking of Clark Gable.

"No, thank you. I'll be fine."

Johnny walked around the docks and went into a shop and brought out a bottle in a paper bag. A man on the sidewalk was selling windup tin toys, and he and Annabelle stopped to watch them whirr and jerk back and forth on top of the man's traveling case. There were soldiers, stiffly high-stepping toward the edge, and tiny trains chuffing around on the sidewalk beside his feet. The barker tried to talk Johnny into buying one for the girl but Annabelle had just shook her head that she didn't want one, even though she smiled at the little tin terrier who bobbled and sniffed at the ground.

"I'd like to buy a pair of gloves for Mr. Wilson. He tore up his hands pretty good on that first day of rowing."

"I wouldn't worry, hon, his hands will toughen up soon enough," Johnny said. They walked back toward the waterfront where the *Pacific Pride* was tied up to the transient dock.

"How'd you fall in with that character anyway?" Johnny asked.

"Oh, he's a friend of Ellie's." Annabelle walked along swinging her arms.

"Oh," Johnny said, and he too swung his arms to match hers. "Here's what I've been thinking, girly-girl, and tell me what you think."

Annabelle stared up at him and squinched up her nose so that her glasses slipped. No one had ever called her girly-girl before.

"Those people aren't your parents."

"No," Annabelle said. She started looking for the masts of the *Pacific Pride* sticking up in the harbor.

"Then why don't you and me go deliver this load of box wood to the cannery and I take you back to live with your real folks."

"My real folks are dead," Annabelle said, and she took a couple of steps into the busy street. A beer truck rumbled by on the cobblestones just inches from the tips of her leather shoes.

"You don't have to tell stories," Johnny said, and he pulled her back up on the sidewalk by her shoulders. Annabelle took a bite of the peppermint stick and crunched the candy between her teeth.

"I'm not telling stories. My parents are buried in Montana. Ellie's my aunt."

"Then who's the fella?" Johnny asked.

"He's some man my aunt found to help us out. I don't know."

"You shouldn't be around such people," Johnny said. "Even if we can't find some other folks for you, you could come stay with my wife and me. We got some boys who would love to have a sister to look after."

"No, thank you," Annabelle said, and she darted across the street to a mercantile store where they had leather gloves in the front window.

Johnny didn't know what to do. He had no intention of stealing the girl but he couldn't bear putting her off the *Pride* and back into that little boat. There had to be something else he could do. But as he watched the girl with the braids skipping across the street ahead of him, his mind was blank of possibilities.

They made it back to the boat just a few minutes before the boy from the Chinese grocery showed up with the bag of food. Annabelle jumped onboard and poured some more seeds into a little dish for Buddy, who happily remained in his cage behind the skipper's short bunk in the wheelhouse. Annabelle slid the dirty paper liner out of the cage, then took the newspaper wrapped around the smoked ham and spread it out on the bottom of Buddy's cage. While Johnny brought the new groceries inside, she wrapped the seeds and the Chinese crackers into her coat, then she tied the bundle closed with a piece of twine she had picked up from the dory. Then she squished her foot around in her leather shoe to make sure she could feel the money she had secreted there.

The Chinese delivery boy was walking up the dock and Johnny was in the galley stowing the groceries when Annabelle quietly picked up Buddy's cage, tucked the bundle under her arm, and picked up her tightly wrapped umbrella. Then she walked over to the side door of the wheelhouse. She sat on the thick bulwark for a moment, and jumped down to the dock the boat was tied to. She stumbled once and dropped Buddy's cage, which caused such a commotion that the delivery boy from the Chinese grocery came running back down.

They met in the middle of the float.

"What you want?" the boy asked.

"Nothing, thank you," Annabelle said, trying to push past him quickly.

"I take. I take you. Where you go?" the boy held out his hand flat as if asking for money.

"What you want?" the boy asked again. And just as Annabelle was about to answer she felt the grip of a large hand on her shoulders.

"We're fine," Johnny said, and he flipped a nickel through the air to the boy standing on the dock, then pushed the girl back toward the *Pacific Pride*.

Slip rowed through sunset and well into dark. The light wind backed around from the southwest and soon enough they put up the small sail and rigged an oar over the stern as a rudder. As they proceeded north they saw more boats crossing the main part of the channel and each cove where they considered putting in had a light in it. Some of the lights were small and clear, perched on top of an anchored boat, and some of the lights were the soft flutter of a lantern inside a cabin on shore.

As the sun set, the rippled water turned a dark purple and the cool of night floated in off the gulf currents. Occasionally they heard geese laboring their way north and once they heard the sudden breath of some mammal rising out in the dark. Seabirds on their short wings would flutter by, making odd little squeaking sounds as they passed, and everywhere they could hear the multilayered hiss of the water against the hull, against the islands, and against the light wind that lathered just the tips of the small waves.

The dory moved slowly, no more than a stroll, but it was easy to keep a course. A few lights blinked up ahead; some moved slowly across their bow and some remained stationary. Some were clear and some were green or red. Slip just steered the way the boat wanted to go and away from the rocks. There was a small hand compass in the trunk that had two drops of radium, one on the arrow and the other on the "N" along the edge. Slip selected a course before sunset and was able to hold it by keeping the relative position of the glowing dots constant. The dory rose and fell evenly when a wake from a passing boat would overtake them and no water came over the sides.

Once, Slip found himself jerking awake and the oar cocked at an odd angle. The dory was fighting against the wind and the soggy canvas sail began to pop and flutter. Slip straightened up and Ellie came back to take the makeshift tiller.

"This looks like something I can do," she said.

"You mean besides stealing sheep," he said, and eased himself toward the bow.

"We both know that stealing sheep is not the worst thing either of us has done," Ellie said as gently as she could.

Slip just grunted and tried to plump up a rolled blanket to lean against.

By morning they were tied to a kelp bed off the point of a small island. To the north they could see the land coming together and boats funneling toward a low section of hills. They couldn't see an opening but they assumed that about two and a half miles ahead was the entrance to Dodd Narrows. The kelp bed sat in the lee of a rock. The wind was building from the south, but this bit of flat water offered a clear view of the main channel and the point to the east where the northbound fleet came to join the gathering of boats waiting to go through the narrows. They ate the soggy crackers and chewed on the salted beef until Slip took out three cooked chops he had saved from the night before and offered one to Ellie without comment. The two of them ate slowly, chewing on the bones until they were as clean as scientific specimens.

After they ate the lamb and salted beef, they drank fresh water and then lay back with round bellies. Ellie surprised Slip by standing up and unbuttoning her pants and saying, "You're going to want to look somewhere else a second." Then she proceeded to take her pants down, sat on the edge of the boat in the bow, and peed over the side.

"You better hope those whales aren't around," he said after a pause, with a lamb rib cocked back in his teeth.

"You would have to say that," she said, and stood up quickly, tucking in her blouse and staring down into the water.

The sun rose in the sky and the fronds of kelp lengthened on the surface as the tide went out. The clouds were stacking up from the south but not a drop of rain had fallen for several days. None of the passing boats seemed to pay them any mind. Occasionally a skipper would wave from a pilothouse and Ellie would gaily wave back as if she were a princess in a ticker tape parade.

They agreed that one person would stay awake and keep watch for the *Pacific Pride* while the other dozed in the bottom of the boat. Slip lay on his back and looked up at the sky. He felt a long way from anything else in his life. His face was still bruised from the insanity in Seattle but each day he felt a bit better, and just then a fine spring sunshine streamed down on him in the bottom of the boat and he felt better than he had in some time.

Ellie's thin arm shot out and she said, "There . . . I think. There."

Slip sat up and he was fairly certain he saw the *Pacific Pride* coming around the point of the islands to the north. There was the black hull and the large white wheelhouse. The big boat rolled through the water and a small cascade of foam angled out from the bow.

Ellie untied the dory from the tangle of kelp and Slip took the oars. Instead of trying to row directly for the boat, he followed the current and aimed for a course he hoped would bring them together. Ellie waved her arms and Slip pulled hard on the oars. Slip stared toward the pilothouse, and after a few minutes he said, "Something's not right."

The big boat was closing the distance between them but was not correcting its course to come close to the dory. The *Pacific Pride* was heading on a course far to their port side. Slip pulled harder but there was no way he could catch up with the *Pride*. Johnny was not slowing down and Slip could not come close. The *Pride* . . . and Annabelle . . . were passing them by.

Slip bore into the oars with so much of his weight that he felt the muscles knotting up under his shoulder blade. He wanted to lift the boat out of the water but the little dory just slid along.

"Slip . . . Slip . . ." Ellie said, her voice rising in panic, "he's not slowing down. Slip?" She was standing up in the dory now, waving her arms and whistling. The big boat was some fifty yards away from them now and was pulling away.

"There. What's that?" Slip said and pointed.

On the back deck they saw the door to the pilothouse open. Then there was a flash of movement: Annabelle was standing on the rail with her umbrella in one hand and the birdcage in the other.

"Don't do it," Slip said.

"No . . . Honey . . ." Ellie said softly. She held her arms out helplessly as the girl jumped off the rail and into the foamy wake hissing on top of the green water.

Slip pulled until he thought all his joints were going to give way. Ellie stripped off her shoes and was about to go over the side of the dory.

"We're going faster than you can swim in this water. It will only slow us down," he yelled.

The girl pumped her legs and flailed in the wake. She let the umbrella go and used both hands to try to support the cage. The *Pride* did not slow down, for Johnny was at the wheel and he assumed Annabelle was sleeping in the forward bunk where he had left her. The big boat rolled over the wake of another ship and the water was a crisscross of currents spouting up around the girl as she struggled. The cage sank into the water and the yellow bird screamed as he crowded to the top. The girl lay on her side with her mouth near the surface, trying to lift the cage up into the air, but the move only made her sink. She threw her bundle out in front of her and then she disappeared.

"Jesus, Slip," Ellie sobbed, and the logger pulled toward the girl.

"Point to her. Point to her," he wheezed, for he could not see her clearly now.

Ellie's arms were shaking as she pointed straight over the bow. They could not see her but were watching the small garland of bubbles that appeared just under the top three inches of the birdcage that cleared the water.

They were a hundred feet from her when Annabelle came to the surface, struggling to open the cage. She rolled on her back and, lifting the cage on her chest, reached up and opened the door.

The bird flew out of the cage like a flutter of dry leaves, his high voice piercing the air with a shrill whistle. His yellow feathers were vivid and out of place in this gray-green world.

Annabelle clung to the cage, then kicked ahead, retrieved her bundle and jammed it through the cage's open door. Her breath was blasting hard from her nose and she kicked with her legs like a panicked dog. With his back to the dory's bow Slip could hear her clearly now, her lungs loudly pumping air, each rattling breath ending with a high-pitched grunt.

She swam toward the dory and Ellie kept both arms pointing straight at her.

"Tell me when I'm close," Slip said.

Ellie said, "Thirty feet, maybe forty. Don't stop now."

Slip pulled five more strokes, and when he turned to see for himself, the girl was sputtering and coughing. She had sucked cold water into her lungs and wasn't swimming forward anymore but was flailing at the water as if she were trying to pull herself out of a hole.

Slip turned in the boat and jumped over the side. The water was stunningly cold and all of his muscles seemed to cramp at once. He curled into a ball and could not swim.

The world slowed down and he felt nothing but numbness and needles of pain. He rolled so that his face was barely out of the water. He knew he had something to say, but his mind had gone slushy. "Can't do it," was all he managed.

There was a splash behind him and then he felt the blade of an oar tapping against his chest. He was able to uncurl his arms and clamp them around the oar.

Ellie was swimming back to the dory with Annabelle sputtering in her arms. Ellie held on to the dory's stern with one hand and was able to get the girl and the cage up into the boat with her other. Then both Ellie and Slip were able to steady the dory and clamber in.

The *Pacific Pride* motored down toward Dodd Narrows as all the rest of the boats began to funnel through the tight passage at the beginning of slack tide. Slip lay cramped up on the bottom of the dory. Ellie wrapped Annabelle in a wool blanket and tried to rub her dry.

Above them Buddy flew in wide arcs around the dory like a yellow meteorite enjoying his first full moments of freedom.

TWELVE

≈≈≈

Slip's teeth chattered uncontrollably as he rowed the dory out of the current. Ellie and Annabelle clung together under a wool blanket. The *Pacific Pride* continued through Dodd Narrows, the skipper apparently oblivious of his missing passenger. Once through the narrows, unless he found her missing within an hour he would have to wait for the next slack to double back.

The yellow bird circled the dory, chirping and calling out as he worked his wings through the damp air hard enough for everyone in the boat to hear the pushing of the air in his feathers.

"Buddy," Annabelle called, and she lifted an arm out from under the blanket. "Come here, Buddy."

Slip scanned the islands to the east for an opening. The current was fair for them close to shore in the swirl, so he pulled toward the islands to the east, bumping and hopping along the changeable currents. His ribs and arms ached with each stroke but the familiar effort at the oars began to warm him.

Annabelle was shivering uncontrollably, her teeth clattering together and wet tendrils of her hair swinging back and forth in front of her eyes. Ellie dug out two dry undershirts from the bag stowed in the stern as well as her black coat. Then she held the blanket in front of Annabelle so she could change out of her wet clothes without embarrassment. But even through her shivering, the little girl only watched the yellow bird circling the dory.

Buddy was a strange flicker of yellow flame in the light gray sky. Slip pulled on the oars and looked over his shoulder as the bird rattled and whistled around. He shipped the oars and changed out of his shirt, putting on his scratchy wool jacket over his bare skin. Ellie watched and rubbed an edge of the blanket against Annabelle's wet hair. But the girl's eyes bore out into the air and tried to ensnare the bird.

They didn't speak as the current changed direction and the water flowed against them. They didn't speak of Johnny or the *Pacific Pride* as the sun began to slip behind the western islands.

Once the parade of boats had gone through the narrows on the tide, they saw no one else. The darkness eased around the dory, and in the twilight, before any moon or stars, the passageway seemed unnaturally black: no stars, no moon, no lighted ships. Only the rumble of the wind coming from the north and the hissing of the waves as they slapped the side of the dory, lifting it up like a runner jogging in place. Slip pulled with his arms but he could not bear his full weight into the oars. Finally Ellie sat next to him and, taking one oar, they rowed together, awkwardly at first, but eventually they pulled alongside De Courcy Island. As a sliver of a moon rose above the island, they were able to see a narrow beach just past the end of De Courcy where the water lay flat in the lee of the sloping side of Rink Island. They pulled hard against the current and the wind. The progress of the dory was agonizingly slow, but eventually they slid onto the calm water and the commotion of wind and waves hushed.

Slip leaned back and lay in the bottom of the boat, winded and aching from rowing against the current. Annabelle was wrapped in a tarp near the bow. While Ellie stood in her dark wool coat and tried to find a fair beach to land, the wind pushed high clouds past the scythe of a moon. A light flickered on the far corner of the beach.

"Hallooooo." It was a woman's voice sliding over the water and Slip heard it first, not sure if he could trust his senses.

"Hallooooo." The voice warbled like a loon's. Slip sat up and looked over in the anchorage that was just coming into view, where a fire blazed on the beach and a lone figure stood in outline against the flames.

"You've just about made it. Over here."

The dark form appeared to be wearing a long coat. Fire illuminated the back and shoulders while the face remained in darkness. The firelight dazzled across the water and cast a strange shadow on the surface, where it looked like the mast and rigging of a sizeable yacht stuck up at an odd angle from the sea. A raven perched on the end of the mast that slanted out over the light-smeared ripples.

"You've just a few more feet to go. Come on." The figure raised its thin arm and gestured "come," so Ellie picked up the oars and pulled the boat toward the firelight.

Annabelle stood up in the boat and hopped out just as the dory pushed into the gravelly beach. An old woman in a long wool coat came hurriedly to the shore and took hold of the bow, being careful not to step into the water.

"Looks like you were having a time of it," she said. "You must be the people who took the lamb from Carl's flock down on South Pender."

Ellie put the oars back in the water and turned to look at Slip, who had his hands in his pockets and didn't say a word to the old woman on the beach.

"Come on, child, come ashore. Don't have to worry. I never cared for Carl or his sheep neither. Just some talk off the mail boat. No one's after you. Come on ashore. You look like you all could use a cup of warm soup."

She said her name was Mary B. and she had a pot of fish stew sitting on a flat rock next to the fire. Slip and Annabelle pulled the dory up the beach and tied it off to a tree growing out of one of the steep bluffs that bordered the little anchorage. By the time Slip reached the fire, Annabelle had cantered up to Ellie and they both were sitting on a log hunched over their bowls, steam rising around their faces.

"Here," Mary said, offering Slip a bowl of soup. Looking up in the woods, Slip saw the dark forms of buildings that looked partially fallen in, the windows broken out and supporting timbers sprung through the walls like ugly compound fractures.

"This is the right place," Mary said. She watched Slip's eyes take in the scene. "You've come to the right place. Don't you worry." Then she put a big spoon in the bowl. "He will be returning. You needn't worry."

She was an old woman though sometimes in the firelight you could see her as a child again. She was waiting there in the desolate anchorage, waiting for the return of her savior, a man she called the Brother Twelve.

She looked around at the refugees the sea had brought her. The girl was shivering as she ate her soup. Firelight painted their faces and each of them moved as close as they could to the flames. "Let me tell you about the first time I laid eyes on him," the old woman said, and Slip wanted to leave the second she said it but there was nowhere to go in the cold, unfamiliar night.

She had been a college student when she first saw the Brother speak in a hall in Seattle. Her parents were both dead and she had inherited the money they had made from wheat over near Walla Walla. The executor had told her to go to college and she had been obedient.

"But when the Brother Twelve walked onto the stage, I knew, I just knew I had been saved."

In the darkness the raven on the mast of the sunken yacht tipped forward and flew to a branch above the fire. He rattled and called down at the humans as if he were demanding some of the stew, and in fact the old woman dug the dipper into the pot and flipped a piece of salmon and two small potatoes into the darkness behind the fire. The black bird leaped from the high branch and curved into the darkness as the old woman continued her story.

The Brother was a tall man, well over six feet, dark complexioned, with wide intense brown eyes that others described as "burning embers" but Mary described as "pools of wisdom." He had been the son of an English philosopher and an Indian princess. He had studied with swamis and saints and with brothers of wisdom in Italy, where he was accepted into their midst as a true seer and the twelfth brother in the Order of Wisdom. The Brother Twelve had received direction from God to build his following on the remote islands of British Columbia. There, he and his followers were living according to God's plan and waiting for their induction into Nirvana.

His eyes found hers during the lecture. He could see she was sitting alone, and after the talk he walked straight to her and took her hands in his, knowing they were meant to be connected.

She didn't have access to all the money in her trust, but she was able to funnel a sizeable sum into the Brother Twelve's good works. She had lived with him there in the cove for several years. She shared him with the others in their flock, but there was no doubt that he knew she was the most devout of all the women who loved him "body, soul, and spirit."

"God is larger than the divisions we try to foist on him," Mary said evenly into the firelight. "Christian, Protestant, Hindu, Jew . . . words . . . all divisions of our own creation. It wasn't until I saw it in his eyes, until I felt it in his hand that I knew God was an undeniable fact of life, much larger than our poor ability to describe Him. The Brother Twelve was like a bare electrical wire you could hold on to and feel the force of creation."

The wind blew in the trees and the raven flew up on the high limb and started cackling. Mary once again dipped into the stew and threw more food out into the brush behind her. She did this without any apparent forethought or explanation. Once again the black bird carved an invisible line through the air to the food.

"He destroyed his earthly compound here and he sank his yacht." She pointed at the mast that was sticking higher in the air since the tide had gone out. "He took his other wife but I have remained true. I am waiting here."

Slip looked over his shoulder at the sunken yacht. Now more ravens perched on the mast, perhaps having sensed that there was someone throwing out food.

"When I saw you coming across the bay, I knew you were coming here. I knew you were going to wait for him."

Ellie sat with Annabelle curled in her lap. The drowsy girl scanned the trees for her bird, and the punch-drunk seditionist drew stars in the sand with a stick.

"I know what you're thinking. You heard the reports that the Brother Twelve died long ago in Switzerland. 'He is dead,' you say. 'What's the point of waiting for him here?'"

Mary B. gestured around the anchorage with her arms. Slip stood up and took a long piece of driftwood from a nearby pile and placed it on the embers. Then he picked up two smaller pieces and set one alongside and another on top to form a wooden pyramid for the tiny tongues of flame to lick.

"We will wait for him here because we are the faithful," Mary said, and as she did, a bright yellow bird with vivid red dots on his cheeks landed in the tree above the fire.

Slip saw him first, nudging Annabelle awake, and the girl's gaze drifted upward into the trees where she saw the match-head brightness of her pet bird. "Buddy!" She stood up and stretched out her arms. "Buddy!"

"Well, I thank you for the stew ma'am, but I think we better get going," Slip said, and he stood up as well. Ellie looked at him as if he were crazy.

Annabelle ran down to the dory to get the cage.

"Don't be silly," Mary said. "You stay here tonight. I told you, you needn't worry about the gossip about that lamb. Isn't anybody going to care about it now. Won't you wait here with me for the Brother?" As the old woman spoke she looked up at the yellow bird with a confused kind of intensity, as if it perhaps wasn't really there.

"No . . . thank you very much but we . . ." Slip said.

"Slip, do you really want to go?" Ellie asked. "You want to go through Dodd Narrows in the dark?"

He stared back at her, not speaking, not wanting to admit that the old woman had spooked him.

"People call me crazy," Ellie said, and smiled at the old crone by the fire.

Mary stooped down and poured coffee out of a tin coffeepot by holding the wire handle with a rag and tilting the pot with a charred stick.

"It will be lovely. You'll see."

Annabelle came running up the beach with the cage rattling next to her leg. She had a handkerchief with some seeds folded inside. The yellow bird sat some thirty feet up in the dark tree and far out on the end of an overhanging limb. The firelight flickered around him and the luminous bird hunched up and trilled a song.

"Here, Buddy," the girl called, and she held out the seeds in her hand. She jumped up and down on her toes. "Come on, boy. Here's food for you," and some of the seeds spilled out onto the rocks.

"Here, child," Mary said softly, and put her hand on the girl's shoulders. "Let's just set the food back inside his cage and we'll rig a little thread to trip the door when he goes in."

And the old woman and Annabelle set about to do just that. Ellie got some blankets and tarps out of the dory while Slip scavenged some timbers from the old buildings for the fire. The stars were needling down through the night sky and only an occasional wisp of a fast-moving cloud ran past the moon.

The old woman saw them making their beds by the fire and turned away from the girl who was laying out a trail of seeds leading up to the door of the cage. She walked up into the woods and came back with a long-handled shovel and gave it to Slip. Then she explained how they should move the fire about twenty feet over and dig out the rocks where the old fire had been. They could lay their blankets on the warm sand and even have a few of the warm rocks under the blankets with them.

"Makes it a bit more comfortable," Mary said.

"Where do you sleep?" Ellie asked.

"I'll be in the chapel. I've got a fine bed and a little stove up there."

"Come on, Buddy. Come on, boy," Annabelle called up into tree. She slowly backed away from the cage. She had gotten some tarred twine from the dory and had attached it to a stick that held the door of the cage open. She had several small piles of seeds laid on flat stones. The grownups were moving the fire down the beach and as they did she eased into darkness until there was only a film of light cast over the rocks. They scoured the sand for embers and Annabelle waited. They laid out their blankets and she crouched in the darkness, holding on to the end of the tarred twine.

Buddy flew down from the tree and ate the pile of seeds farthest from the cage. Annabelle could barely breathe. The yellow bird ate and preened and hopped back and forth at every possible sound coming from either the fire or the beach.

"Come on, boy," the girl whispered.

Buddy cocked his head back and forth and flew up into the forest and disappeared.

They slept comfortably that night. The warm sand was a luxurious comfort. Only once did Slip wake up to the smell of burning wool. He flicked an ember off of his blanket, rolled over, and went back to sleep.

They slept close together to share the warm sand and rocks. Slip slept on the edge with his back to Ellie and Annabelle lay on the other side. The girl lay listening and watching the sky where the black treetops spiked up into the horizon. She lay listening for perhaps ten minutes, then slowly warmth eased into her icy bones and her eyes closed.

Ellie rolled over and put her hand on Slip's shoulder.

"You awake still?" she asked in a whisper, and the tired man grunted.

Ellie touched Slip's hand with the tips of her fingers, "Do you want to go home?" she asked.

"Home?" he asked. "You mean the state of Washington?"

"I guess."

"I don't know," he said, not opening his eyes as he spoke. "I can't even imagine where my home might be now."

"What do you mean 'now'?" she asked.

"Now that I met you," was all he said.

The next morning Mary was up before the sun. She built a new fire on the beach. The wind was sizzling over the island and the clouds were shredding through the tops of the trees. The sand had cooled from the outside of the fire ring toward the center, so they were now all curled next to each other like sea lions on a rocky ledge. Slip was the first to open his eyes. His left arm was over Ellie's shoulder. Annabelle was tucked around Ellie's waist. Slip gently lifted his arm away and eased out from the tangle of legs.

The fire flared and danced up from the logs Mary had dragged down from the trees. The flames seemed sick in the damp air. Where once the sky was a dome of stars, it was now a closed lid of clouds. Small waves were breaking on the beach. Far back in the trees he could hear the voice of the yellow bird squawking for his seeds.

"Good morning, sunshine. You bring to mind a litter of puppies down there on the sand." Mary smiled up at him as she leaned toward the fire to take the coffeepot off its hanger.

"Good morning, ma'am," Slip said softly. He put on his wool coat, which was still damp but it kept him serviceably warm.

He hunched his shoulders against the wet wind pushing into the anchorage.

"Change in the weather," he said.

"Oh Lord, yes," the old woman said. "Changes its mind more often than a girl in a hat shop." She smiled and handed him a tin mug of coffee.

This had always been his favorite time: these few moments before the day began. These early mornings, when the damp grass began to unbend and the birds began to stir.

Slip sipped the bitter coffee and shuffled back and forth in front of the fire, letting the heat from the tin cup warm the palms of his hands. He had always thought of his life as happy. His memories were sunlit and apple red but now . . . Now he wasn't sure.

He thought of his parents waking up to a cold room every morning. He thought of his father's thin face and how he bore the pain of the farm's failure. He thought of the chalky dust that spread over his mother's skin as the gardens withered and blew away. His belief in his childhood had been his faith up until now. Now he had killed a man. He was in a strange and cold country, with a woman who vexed him at every turn and a crone who was waiting for a salvation that would never come.

All he had ever wanted was a place on this earth. A home where he understood himself. And it was beginning to seep into his bones that this would never happen.

"You know we can't stay," Slip said softly to the old woman.

She looked down the beach where Slip was staring. "I suppose that's true," she said, and her voice was sad. "But I wish you would. We could keep each other company."

"We could take you into Nanaimo."

"Oh, thank you, child. But the Brother was none too popular in Nanaimo before he left. When he returns he won't be sharing himself with those people."

"Is there something else we can do for you? Cut wood? Haul water?"

"I'm fine, child. Just wait with me here a bit for the weather to clear. It's not right for you to take that girl out into the narrows when the wind is up and the tide is wrong. The current will run fair for you about mid morning."

The rest of them woke and came around. Despite Mary's protests, they split and carried wood up to the broken-down chapel back in the woods. The floor she slept on was at an angle. A fir tree leaned in through a hole in the roof. Ellie carried water from the rainwater cistern and filled up all Mary's available pots. Annabelle was exempt from chores so she wandered through the woods and called for Buddy with a handful of seeds.

With each load of wood and dipper of water, Mary told them stories about the power of the Brother Twelve. She told of his command of both the Christian scriptures and the holy books of Asia. "He had seen Nirvana, you know," she whispered. "That's not a place, child, like Vancouver or Tacoma. It's a condition. It's the keystone at the top of the arch. Nirvana is the heaven we can find for ourselves, right here on earth."

"I'm sure you're right," Ellie said. She was making up the blankets on the cracked floor where the old woman slept.

Slip took Ellie by the elbow as they both broke from the woods onto the beach.

"I don't know . . . Ellie . . ." Slip stammered, "but I have to get out of here."

The wind was building and the trees were flailing against each other. They creaked and snapped as the wind blustered around them now. Out past the opening of the anchorage the water was a mass of whitecaps.

"We might have to wait out the weather," she offered.

"This place is giving me the heebie-jeebies, I swear."

"No sense getting killed."

"I'm not saying that. Just . . . I'm saying we go at the first chance."

She looked at him for several moments. She wanted to choose her words carefully. "We're going to be all right, Slippery Wilson. You know that, don't you?"

"Do *you*?" A shudder of desperation crept into his voice.

"Yes I do." She held on to his hand and turned him back to their work.

In the woods Annabelle wandered with her head cocked back as she whistled up into the trees. The violence of the wind brought her to a kind of panic. She hated to think of Buddy out in this pounding wind. In the interior of the island she could hear the boom of waves from every direction. The forest floor undulated as the roots of the trees shook with the wind. Annabelle called Buddy's name.

She walked far enough into the woods that she didn't know the direction of the beach where the dory was tied. She looked around her and saw nothing but a circle of trees. The top of the island was flattened out with small second-growth fir thickly packed together. In places she had to crawl through a thicket, and when she stood up she had to pry the limbs apart. She fought her way into a small clearing in the bracken and sat down on the moss.

After her parents had died Annabelle understood that she was an orphan. She knew she needed to be smart and do well with her studies. She had memorized her times tables at least a month before any of her classmates. She knew the names of the flowers that grew around her house and she could make change from any denomination of money handed to her. She knew she had to be ready to live anyplace in the world and be able to make her own way there and back. But right now she didn't want to be anywhere. She didn't want to get back into the dory, and neither did she want to stay on the island. She didn't want to be back in Seattle in the room that overlooked the street, and she didn't want to be back in Montana where the tire swing hung from the willow tree in the yard. She just wanted to be in the presence of her pet bird. She wasn't sure why. He could be cross and objectionable. He didn't speak and would only whistle a catcall occasionally. But there was something about Buddy that made her hopeful. His company was all she wanted.

The wind continued to shriek through the trees as she sat cross-legged in her damp dungarees. She wanted him to come down to her now. She wanted him to fly down from the limbs and curl up in her hands, and the more she suffered for it the more she believed it would happen.

But it didn't, and she sat for an hour listening to the trees sizzle and the waves pound against the rocks. She thought she heard the voices of the adults calling somewhere in the wind, but there was no direction to the sounds entering her bower. She sat and waited. She didn't think and she didn't remember anything from her past. The surge of the wind pushed against her clothes and she felt it move around her as if she too had become a tree. She waited without any faith and without promise.

But still she was not rewarded. Even when she emptied her mind of her cravings, they were neither fulfilled nor diminished when she returned to her desiring mind. She got up and walked away.

Soon the voices of the adults percolated through the trees from the direction of the beach. She walked past the ruined buildings of Brother Twelve's compound, past the outhouse and the electrical plant. She walked past the chapel and the stone fence around the massive house in the center. She walked through the beach fringe where the driftwood piled in windrows, where the wreckage of the holy man's compound had drifted out into the inlet and then back again. She walked right up to where Slip was lashing the sail rig to the outside deck.

"Hey, girl, where you been?" Slip asked, turning from his work.

"I was looking for Buddy."

"You have any luck?" Slip brushed the twigs off the back of Annabelle's dungarees.

"No." The girl shook her head and looked down at the sand.

"Let me show you something. Come on," Slip said. He took her by the hand.

Even before they got close to the dory Annabelle could see him. There, in the bow of the dory, standing on top of the cage, eating from a cup that Slip had wired in place, was Buddy.

"I don't think he'll go back in the cage," Slip said.

She ran to him, and as she thrust her hands out toward him the bird lifted up and flew away. Then she slumped onto the sand.

"Just sit quiet," Slip whispered in her ear.

They sat by the dory for some minutes. Soon the yellow bird curled down out of the trees and landed on top of the cage once again, and calmly pecked seeds from the cup.

"Guess he's not much for the grub the other birds eat," Slip said, stowing a bundle of blankets.

"Are we going to go out in this storm?" Annabelle asked.

"It's calming down some. And if we don't, we're going to have to wait another day to go through the narrows in daylight."

"The wind's with us. I'll row if you want," Annabelle said.

Slip turned back to the dory. "That's all right. Thanks."

"Do you think he'll ever go back in his cage?" Annabelle asked.

"Don't know," Slip said. "But my guess is he likes the taste of freedom."

"Then why'd he come back?"

"Where the heck else is he going to go, other than with you?"

Slip finished securing the dory and then went back to hauling wood for Mary. He made a tremendous pile near the door to the chapel. He wrapped up a hindquarter of the lamb and put it in the cooling box she kept near the cistern. Just to be sure he secured his tools in the dory. He retied the lanyards on the U-shaped oarlocks to make sure they could not fall overboard and sink. He made sure the mast and the extra oar were well tied to the narrow deck. He secured the trunk of cooking gear and filled the jugs with fresh water. He tried to even out the load so the boat would ride level through the chop.

Annabelle slipped quietly into the bow. The yellow bird allowed her to come close, but as soon as she moved her hands toward him he would ruffle and back away. She sat as still as a photograph, looking at Buddy as if her eyes could bind him.

Ellie put on her warmest coat and several dry shirts underneath. She double-checked Slip's work on the oarlocks and pulled the leather bindings tight on the oars.

Finally, Mary and Slip walked down to the beach together. Mary was speaking steadily, calmly, not as if she were arguing or trying to convince but as if she were holding on to Slip with her words. She nodded and smiled. He nodded and kept walking.

Ellie walked over to Slip with a sheaf of yellow papers in her hand. "Hand me that little tin of yours," she said.

"Why?"

"Just get it. Quick now. I'm not crazy for Annabelle to see."

Slip dug under the middle seat and got the tobacco tin from his tool kit. He handed it to Ellie. She folded the yellow papers into a tight square and jammed them in on top of the money.

"This is how I'm going to take care of you," she said. "You keep these papers."

Slip was about to argue. He was at least going to take them out and read them. But Mary stepped closer and interrupted him.

"You should stay until tomorrow at least," Mary said.

Slip turned to secure the axe in the dory. "We'll be fine. If we have any trouble we'll come back and eat some mutton with you," he said, knowing they both were aware this was not true.

Slip finished with the axe and put the tin back in his kit. He stood next to the small boat, ready to slide it into the water.

"God bless you, children," Mary said. "Take good care of that bird."

Slip and Ellie pulled the dory down the beach with Annabelle and Buddy in their places. Ellie got into the stern with the chart and the steering oar and Slip took the middle seat.

Annabelle waved to the old woman on the beach and she waved back. "Is she going to be all right?" the girl asked.

Ellie said, "Just worry about yourself there, missy. You get settled and get that tarp over you."

Slip worked the oars and Ellie began to steer. As the dory poked out into the main channel, the waves hit hard on their port side and they turned to put them to their stern. There were other boats lining up once again to travel through the narrows. The dory cantered easily up and down the waves with the wind pushing it along. The drowsy mood of the island where Mary waited for her holy man gave way to turbulent motion once again, the foaming of the sea and the slap of water.

The wind was too strong for Buddy to stand on top of his cage so he hopped down under the tarp where Annabelle covered her head. Soon Slip could hear the girl singing under the muffling canvas, and he smiled at Ellie as he pulled on the oars.

Dodd Narrows was indeed a thin passage. A small child could throw a rock across it at its narrowest point. Even at slack tide the water boiled up on the surface. The wind set up a nice chop that was crosshatched by the wakes of the boats going in both directions. Slip pulled and Ellie steered the dory close to the rocks to give the fishing boats and the larger cargo tugs room to pass them. In the narrowest part, the water was a mass of colliding waves and crosscurrents, and in places the surface spouted straight up into the air. The bruised logger pulled the dory through thousands of pointy water spouts and roiling wakes. Great rocks kept smooth by the powerful currents passed underneath the dory, and they slid through the final narrows and out into the sound just south of Nanaimo. The waves were now a lather of white.

Ellie ground her teeth together as she looked at the waves building beyond the narrows. The current was changing and the boat seemed to be sliding down a slope like a sled. The current was carrying them out into the bay and straight into the collision of current and wind. She pushed the steering oar to port, hoping to take them back into shore, but the boat only moved sideways in the current.

They pulled all day without making much progress. The northerly weather humped up the seas. Clouds built up behind them and suddenly the winds shifted with a chaotic swirl of crosscurrents. The afternoon wore on in a rumble of wind and water splashing in the boat. Ellie dug into the food box looking for something to feed the girl. There was a jug of what was marked as lantern fuel but when she opened it to see if she could use it in the little stove, she found that it was rum.

Annabelle ate pilot bread and moldy cheese while Ellie and Slip drank from the jug. They even let the girl have several sips of rum to warm her up. But Annabelle winced when she swallowed it and even preferred the cheese gone bad to the sourness of rum.

Soon the wind was spraying water up their stern and lifting the little boat higher on the crest of the waves. Slip and Ellie were singing and their cheeks were red. Annabelle hunkered down in the bow and pulled the tarp over herself and the bird.

Voices arguing and singing, flirting and laughing mingled in the shrieking wind. Annabelle peeked out from the tarp while the wind battered down on them through the cresting waves. One moment the horizon was above them churning the water white as if they were lumbering uphill, and the next the dory fell away into a valley and all she could see were the green sides of the waves that were scratched by the fingernails of the wind. In the distance she could see the black hull of another boat following a course parallel with theirs.

Buddy stayed in the most forward point of the dory. He sat there calmly as the boat heaved and fell and the wind rumbled over the top of them like a train. Annabelle held out a handful of seeds and Buddy ate from her hand as calmly as if he were sitting in a restaurant. Annabelle liked looking at him. She was happy now that he wasn't in his cage. She imagined that if the dory sank, Buddy would fly up and away from them, and that was all the reassurance she needed in the middle of the storm.

Slip rowed only to keep the dory in a stable position in relation to the waves. Ellie helped him steer. But they were both too drunk to do much of anything. Ellie was trying to steer a course for the lee of two islands to the west, but the wind and the seas were not kindly to her course. All they could do was keep the dory upright and let the storm determine their course, and hope that it didn't take them into the shallows where the waves would grind them against the rocks.

Slip pulled, and as he did he butchered the words to a popular song, "When You Wore a Tulip and I Wore a Red, Red Nose," as he smiled at Ellie. He was pulling on the oars out of a kind of fatalism now. He might as well die right here, right now. He was growing tired of the suspense.

As he looked over the stern, the sea looked like a moving stretch of prairie, the hills pushing and moving all around him. He was too drunk to see the black hull coming from his stern quarter. He pulled against the oars, and with each stroke he felt an iciness easing around the false warmth of the rum. This must be the way the world looked to Noah, he thought, the mounting waves having washed the sinful world away. This must be what it looks like when the world ends. The tops of the waves were shredding off into white foam that carried down the water like broken teeth.

To the south he could see a steamship pulling out into the straits. It was late afternoon and the ship was lit up like a birthday cake. As the dory rose and fell, the steamship churned steadily along to the north, its stacks laying a black streamer down on the bottom side of the fast-moving clouds.

Slip nodded with his chin to the steamship. "I think we should have taken a bigger boat."

Ellie looked back and smiled. "I'm not sure," she said. "I doubt that they would have let me steer."

THIRTEEN

〜〜〜

In the dining room of the *Admiral Rodman*, a steward was pouring hot water on the tablecloths. They were expecting only a few passengers in the dining room for an early supper, but even so they didn't want the china to slide off the tables into their laps. George Hanson sat by himself at one of the tables and glanced at his reports. He read quickly and scanned his notes when he could, for he didn't like the sensation in his head and stomach when he read for too long on the rough seas.

George had been ashore in Nanaimo and had asked questions along the docks. There was no report of a small boatload of Americans traveling with a child. The RCMP had been polite but not particularly enthusiastic about his investigation. The customs officers were even less than forthcoming. All they said was that they had no records for any of the names George offered.

He spoke to several fishermen and was met with friendly interest but not much in the way of information. A man had told him there was a group of people traveling in the Gulf Islands who were said to have poached a lamb, and that the owner of the lamb had discovered the gut pile and was quite upset, but this was all by way of mail boat gossip.

The ship was lurching side to side. George gathered up his files, walked to the outer deck, and stood at the rail. The sea was a mass of gray and white, he could see no birds flying, but low on the water the tops of the waves were ripping off and the lather rolled downwind.

Just three hundred yards to the port of the ship he could see a small boat sliding up the face of a swell, the stern rising and the bow pushing down into the trough. George leaned forward. He squinted, and held his hand in front of his face to block the wind from his eyes. The wave overtook the dory and lifted it into the air. He saw a man at the oars and a woman steering. As the dory rose up on the face of the next wave, George thought he saw a small pair of legs in the bow of the boat. The stern sank into the next trough and the rower put his weight into the oars as foam flecked over the dory.

A man, a woman, and a child.

George burst onto the *Admiral Rodman*'s bridge. "Captain, you must pick up the people in that dory."

"Have they signaled an emergency?" the man standing beside the helmsman said calmly without turning his attention from the bow of the ship.

"They are suspects in a murder investigation." George's voice was not quite as calm.

"In this seaway and in these conditions, it would be reckless to try to maneuver the ship to take them aboard."

"Captain, I must insist. I am a police detective." He reached into his pocket for his badge and identification.

"Save yourself the trouble, detective," the captain said, turning to him. "You are nothing more than a passenger on my ship—in Canadian waters I might add—and outside of an emergency rescue I will not even consider slowing our progress toward Campbell River and the narrows up ahead."

"Captain . . ." George could feel the absolute certainty of the Captain's position. He stopped in mid sentence, saw a pair of binoculars on the chart table, picked them up, and walked back on deck.

"You can wait for them in Campbell River if you like," the captain's voice reached out to him through the swinging door. "And bring back those binoculars." George heard the captain's words in the screaming wind.

George walked quickly toward the stern, buffeting between the rails and the bulkhead walls. He zigzagged as fast as he could to the stern deck and scanned the sea.

The little boat was a toy in the ocean. The churning wake of the steamship crossed the direction of the waves and sent a violent spout up some ten feet into the wind. The dory's bow jumped straight up into the air and then was gone into the trough of the next wave. George stood on his toes, desperate to get another look. Then the dory slid up the front side of the next wave and he glassed it with the binoculars. He saw a blonde woman in the stern gesturing to someone in the bow. There was a man pulling on the oars, and just as the dory was about to pitch up and under the next swell, George saw the figure of a little girl with braids in her hair poke from under a canvas tarp in the bow.

"Goddamnit," George said under his breath, just as the first officer came to retrieve the captain's binoculars.

In the dory, Slip was still too drunk to recognize the seriousness of the situation they were in, but he was beginning to sober up.

The dory plunged and bucked like a carnival ride. At the top of a wave the wind rumbled down the seas and wrapped its arms around them, and then they'd plunge into a sizzling trough and the wind would lose its grip. When Slip opened his eyes, the world was spinning both inside and outside of his head.

"Wait just a goddamn minute," Slip said and turned as if he were going to climb out of the dory.

"You damn fool." Ellie lurched over the seats and grabbed onto his leg. "Just sit down and stay low," she yelled, though the wind sucked up her words.

"Where in the hell are we?" Slip yelled back to Ellie.

"Just head with the wind. Get us to land," Ellie screamed.

The dory had been a remarkably dry boat up till then. Now every third wave was breaking over the bow and there was enough water in the bottom to start floating the boxes off the floor. The wind drove through their clothes and the fifty-degree water ran down their necks spreading a gnawing cold like the pain of toothache. At first the cold water felt like sobriety but after a few strokes with the oars Slip thought he might be dying.

"Shit," he said, and he started bailing.

"Let me ask you, Ellie," Slip yelled. "Have you ever converted anybody to the cause?" He stared at her as he splashed water out of the boat.

"Don't start in on me now."

"Come on, admit it, you've never converted anyone."

"Don't start with me, I'm telling you."

Ellie hefted a bucketful and this time got about half of the water outside of the dory as another wave sloshed over the side.

"I've brought lots of workers into the Party. Don't start in on that stuff with me."

"Ellie broke the miners association over in Butte. They had to call in federal troops," Annabelle chirped, her head peaking out from under the tarp.

"Thank you," Ellie said. "You see?" She nodded to the girl.

"She must have used a better line of bullshit in Butte than I've ever heard from her. That's all I've got to say."

Annabelle jumped out from the tarp and started sluicing water out with her hands. The large steamship was passing them on their right. Annabelle wished they could row over to the ship and be taken aboard. She wished it with such an urgency and passion that she almost imagined it was happening; the ship was coming to a stop and the crew were lowering rope ladders for her to climb onboard. She could almost feel the dry bedding in a narrow ship's bunk. Then she opened her eyes to the gray-green prairie of water undulating around her and knew nothing good was going to happen.

"Ellie, stop bailing and help row," Slip said. "I'm just thinking that this ship is going to throw one heck of a wake."

A gust of wind sucked up the last of his words but she understood. She threw down the bucket and struggled to get into position.

Both of them pulled and with the increased speed the boat lifted its bow. Annabelle took up the bucket. She was able to get three half buckets of water out of the boat in the time it would have taken Ellie to throw one. Buddy peeped and screeched from under the tarp.

"Hush, Buddy," the girl said. "We'll be okay." Hers was the only reassuring voice in the ocean.

The bow wake of the *Admiral Rodman* grew like a mountain range rolling into view. The other waves now looked like foothills. The ridge of the wake peaked up in front of them, gray-green and icy, with what looked to be snowcapped peaks.

"Pull now," Ellie said easily. She kept looking to her right as the wake bore down on them. "Just keep pulling."

Slip felt a shadow fall across the boat as the wake thrust up behind them. Ellie turned the dory and the waves crashed on their backs. Then they sank down for a moment before being pushed up the face of the wake.

"Pull now, Ellie."

The crest cascaded down around them. White water churned its way into the boat. Annabelle ducked back under the tarp, the wake passed under them, and the two drunks gave out a cheer.

The bow wake was the smaller of the two that the *Admiral Rodman* was churning. The ship had smoothed some of the seas. Ellie grabbed the stern oar and steered the dory back toward the stern of the big boat, thinking the way would be easier. Then she looked over and saw the first of the stern wakes, which was nearly twice as high as the last.

The wake was shredding through the seas like an underwater explosion. Slip and Ellie had stopped rowing and were twisted around, staring at the stern of the ship. The soaked blonde looked once again to her right and was the first to see what was coming.

"One more."

And they pulled, but the boat was wallowing in the seas and they barely had time to regain their momentum when the wake hit them, filling the little boat with water.

Half-filled jugs floated up off the bottom of the boat. There were six precious inches of freeboard keeping the sea out and the dory afloat. All three of them splashed at the water, spooning it out with their hands at first, and then Slip went to work with the bucket, but the next waves hit and the dory lost momentum. The sea poured in over the sides.

Ellie waved her oar up in the air and screamed at the stern of the passing ship. "Hey! Hey! Here!"

The dory began to sink below the surface now. The bow was tugging into the sea as if a long thread of gravity were pulling the dory down. A cask bumped over the side and floated away.

Ellie turned around and began waving in the other direction. "Hey! Hey! Here! Here!"

Slip, now no more sober in his life, threw buckets of seawater until his shoulders ached. Annabelle scooped water with a corner of the tarp but with little effect for now they were wallowing just below the surface of the waves.

"Can we swim to the islands?" Slip asked.

"Maybe if we all clung together and used the wind to help. You are a good swimmer, right?"

"Not really," Slip yelled back.

"Once we push off, you hold onto my neck. Annabelle, you stay close," Ellie said, her voice cracking as a wave washed over her head. The little dory still had some buoyancy and they held on to their seats with their feet. Annabelle was holding the cage above her head and the yellow bird sat on top of it yawping and whistling as if to scold the weather. Slip turned and looked at his toolbox sitting like a stone under the water beneath the middle seat. He reached for the strap and pulled it up out of the water.

"Hell, you can't swim with that," Ellie yelled over the rumble of the waves.

"I'm not going to try." Slip opened the top and took out the tobacco tin. He was about to put it in his shirt pocket, but he gave it to the girl.

"You hold on to this. It's important and you're a better swimmer than me." The shivering girl took the tin and stuffed it down the front of her shirt. Then Slip lifted her up and he leaned forward as if he were about to pour himself into the sea.

"There! There!" Ellie was waving the oar above her head. To the south she could see a hull pushing through the seas a quarter mile off. "Hold on to our stuff!" she yelled.

The three of them gathered as much of the floating gear in their arms as they could manage. Ellie took turns waving the oar in the air and paddling the stern around to face the seas. The hull of the approaching boat rose and fell on the water but kept coming in a straight line toward them. Another water keg floated away and the food kit and tent floated up under the seats. Slip grabbed them before they could float away.

The black boat pulled close to the dory and then swung abeam to the seas. Johnny Desmond walked out onto the deck of the *Pacific Pride* with a tight grip on the rigging.

"I've been looking all over for you. Do you have Annabelle?" Johnny called out.

"Yes! Yes! She's here!" Ellie shouted, and pointed to the girl in the bow. Annabelle stood up on the bow seat and waved, perhaps a bit defiantly, to Johnny.

He clutched his chest and sank down into himself in thanks. "Let's get you all onboard," he yelled.

FOURTEEN

~~~

"I don't care what you say. I'm getting off this goddamn ship." Raymond Cobb was standing on the back deck of the *Admiral Rodman*, which sat at the dock in Campbell River. His skin was pale and his face was noticeably thinner after several days of vomiting and dehydration.

"Let's at least get off and take a look around," pleaded McCauley Conner, who looked to be in much the same condition.

"All right, let's grab our gear," Pierce said. "I could use a solid meal at least."

"All I want is solid ground," Cobb said, and he pushed past his mates and headed to the gangway.

&

The dock was crowded with men. There were white men in their stiff canvas work clothes calling out to one another, while Haida and Kwakiutl men, their skin as dark as kelp, sat quietly around the edges of the pier. The Natives sat on top of their bundles, and said nothing to the white men who pushed past them carrying their bedrolls under their arms. Men signaled the cranes to come toward the ship while teamsters jostled their paired workhorses in front of their wagons. George pushed past the rest of the passengers to get down the dock.

George had found the office of the Provincial Police Department, but there was no one there. He had only a few hours to ask for help finding the dory. He asked a kid on the dock where the cheapest place to buy a drink might be.

George walked at a good clip down to the commercial harbor, then turned uphill toward a street off the waterfront where a small red building had a sign advertising beer and sandwiches. There were no windows on the front and the door sat cocked out of its frame on broken hinges. The policeman had to jerk the door to get it open. The warm smell of mildewed sawdust, sweat, and spilt beer rolled out of the place like a cloudburst. George walked into the bar and squinted around in the gloom. The low ceiling sagged in the middle of the room and only a few bare lightbulbs hung on cords near the back. A strangely elegant chandelier hung above the ornate bar, where a stout man with a handlebar mustache stood wiping out the inside of a beer mug.

"What's your pleasure?" the barman asked.

George's eyes worked to adjust to the light. Three men sat in the corner hunched over their glasses. "If you have a cold beer I'll buy one from you."

As the barman pulled on the spigot and filled the mug, George told him that he was a policeman from Seattle and he was looking for some people in a small boat. A man, a woman, and a child. They were probably pretty bedraggled, and the girl had a yellow bird.

The barman smiled and stepped back as if George were pulling his leg. He started cleaning another mug. Then George offered to pay for the information, and the barman stopped cleaning and stuck his hand out to introduce himself.

"Tom . . . Tom Stanton. I'm your man, officer."

The three men hunched in the corner picked up their bags, left money on the table, and walked quietly to the door.

The storm had blown up the Inside Passage and the sky was a blue dome over Campbell River. A light wind carried the smell of cold salt water and wood sap up from the sawmill's holding pond. The three men turned the corner of the muddy street and the steamship dock came into full view. The *Admiral Rodman* sat against the backdrop of the wooded islands like a stately hotel.

"I ain't getting back on that fucking ship," Ray said.

"That was a Seattle cop back there," Pierce hissed.

"So? That don't settle my stomach none."

"Would it settle it if he recognized you and started asking about what the hell you're doing up here?" Conner was breathing hard as he pushed toward the crewmen's gangway.

"How the hell's he going to recognize me?" Cobb stopped in his tracks.

"You're the one told us that a Seattle cop was snooping around. He came out and talked to your wife. Isn't that right?"

"So?"

"Listen, Ray, don't you think your wife might have given him a picture of you or something?"

"She ain't got no pictures of me."

"Great, Ray," Pierce said. "You stay here and explain it to him."

"We ain't done nothing wrong," Ray blurted out, a steady whine building into his voice.

"Not yet. But we're planning to kidnap someone and obstruct an official investigation."

"He don't know that."

Pierce stopped and turned to Conner. "I agree. Just let him stay. I'm sick of his bellyaching anyway. I didn't want him coming along. He forced his way on this trip. Let him stay here and make friends with the Seattle police." Then he turned to Ray. "I'll see you around, buster. Write when you get out. We're taking the whiskey with us." Pierce took the bottle that Ray had bought at the package goods store and walked toward the ship.

McCauley Conner shrugged his shoulders, picked up his bags, and hurried to follow his friend.

The two of them grew smaller against the backdrop of the ship. Hundreds of gulls were paddling in the calm water around the ship, and when the steamship's whistle blew they rose into the air, filling the space between the men with their lonely cries.

"Oh, for Pete's sake," Ray Cobb finally said. He grabbed his bag and started running toward the gangplank.

The *Pacific Pride* was traveling past Campbell River on its way to catch slack tide at Seymour Narrows. The narrows moved a great area of tidal current through its gap. Johnny was anxious to be past it before the flood could bring some sixteen knots of current along with the spring tides. There were also the notorious rocks that lay barely submerged under the low tide mark: they caused whirling pools along the surface. The *Pride* was just able to make the low slack. The *Admiral Rodman*, because of a loading delay in Campbell River, had to wait eight hours at the dock for the next chance to go through the narrows. When the steamship passed the boat again, it would be in the middle of the night.

Johnny stood at the wheel and continued wiping the glass port in front of him. There were wet gear, clothing, tarps, and a tent strewn all over the interior of the boat. Moisture was rising off the gear and becoming trapped on the inside of the boat's ports.

"Darn it," Johnny said. "I should rig up a fan." He opened the side port next to his elbow to let the moisture out.

They had said very little once they all got safely onboard. Johnny hugged Annabelle and touched her hair, and tears streamed down his face. He said he couldn't have lived with himself if she had drowned.

He would have been hard-pressed to explain what he had done. He didn't want to steal the girl. He had seen the dory back by Dodd Narrows, but he didn't want to give her back. The current was fair, the boat was running well, and he assumed she was sleeping soundly. He would wait for the dory on the other side of the narrows, or maybe not. He didn't know what was best but it just didn't feel right to bring the rough-looking blonde back on the boat. By the time he realized Annabelle was gone, the current had turned against him and there was no way to go back until the tide changed. He had spent the next day fitfully searching the waters on both sides of Dodd Narrows, but he had missed the dory when it had pulled into Mary's cove and the ruined compound of the Brother Twelve.

The blubbering skipper crouched in front of her, and Annabelle patted the top of his cap. "It just wasn't right, Captain. I'm supposed to be with Ellie."

"I know," he said.

Even with her hard feelings about Johnnie trying to steal her, Annabelle was happy to be back onboard the *Pacific Pride,* and she showed it. She put Buddy's cage on the shelf above the skipper's half bunk. The defiant bird sat atop the cage, still refusing to enter. Ellie, on the other hand, remained frosty toward the skipper, and this, in a strange way, gave her the run of the boat. She pointed and ordered where to hang all the wet gear, and the hangdog skipper did nothing to resist.

As the storm blew itself out, Slip and Ellie agreed to travel with Johnny up through the outer island passages to the cannery just south of the Alaska border. There they would see if there was any work and make their choices. They would travel long days to make up his lost time, and they would have to hit every narrows at the optimum time even if that meant pushing past daylight. It would take three days to get to the cannery.

As they passed Campbell River, Johnny opened his side port all the way and looked over the waterfront. The black hulk of the *Admiral Rodman* hunched in front of the town. Smoke from a dozen chimneys rose a few hundred feet, then smeared to the north over the ridge. There was a slight ripple on the water and the lights of the houses built against the hill were beginning to blink on. Johnny was tired and wished he were going to sleep in a bed on land. He wanted to be able to walk away from his troubles, but of course he couldn't. He set his course for the mouth of Seymour Narrows. As the sun moved low against the hill, he closed the port to save some of the heat in the old boat. He reached out to wipe the moisture off the glass so he could see the water sliding under the bow.

Johnny had heard many stories of the tidal currents along the Inside Passage. Old men who had fished the northern grounds told stories of whirlpools big enough to tip a seine boat on its side and suck a skiff straight down only to shoot it up again in pieces. There were Indian legends about spirits that lived under the water and reached their bony fingers to embrace unwary mariners. Johnny hadn't given much weight to these stories but it was easy to be dismissive when sitting around an iron stove in the chandlery back home. As he traveled north and the familiar country gave way to densely forested hills wearing different shades of green, he began to feel the iron grit of fear build up in his stomach. The cedar trees dripped over the steep-sided passages and the current blossomed up in cauliflower forms. Sometimes rips came when he didn't expect them and the water moved quickly in two directions at once. The ravens that sat on the branches were as big as cats and some of them seemed to grow horns as they heckled the boat from their perches.

Despite its fearsome reputation, when they got to Seymour Narrows the waters were mild. The rock that had claimed so many ships was a benign ripple in the channel, leaving plenty of room to maneuver. Once they were past the narrows a steamship overtook them. Johnny put his hand outside the port and waved it up and down. There looked to be half a dozen people standing on the back deck of the ship and one of them waved in return.

They spent two days drying out their gear in every warm part of the *Pacific Pride*. The smell of boiled coffee and mildew saturated the wheelhouse. Slip and Ellie slept long hours in their bunks and dozed off at almost any time of day. Annabelle played with Buddy and looked at pictures in catalogues piled in one of the drawers. Johnny gave them all lessons on steering and assigned them all, including Annabelle, regular shifts to stand watch. But Johnny never was long off the bridge and if he slept during the day, it was only lightly in his half bunk near the helm.

The big both ways river pushed and pulled at the boat so that when the current was against them they slowed considerably and the trees along the steep-sided fjords seemed to creep past. But as they learned to ride the current to their advantage they were able to slide along as if they were sitting in a streetcar. Ellie loved steering the big boat and often stood watch for Slip. Annabelle would not relinquish her turn at the wheel. She kept a close eye on the brass clock above Johnny's bunk, and when the first second ticked of her watch she would haul her wooden box out, stand up on it, and begin to review their course.

Turnips and corned beef simmered in the pot all day long as they drove up the narrow passages. They passed tugs with barges and fishing boats with men sleeping on the webbing piled on the back decks. Annabelle would wave and most often the men would raise their heads and wave lazily back. Slip drank coffee and mended his clothes. He put salve on his blistered hands and cleaned the cuts on his face. His bruises were turning from dark purple to jaundiced yellow. Each morning he made coffee and flipped pancakes on the big diesel stove. They all ate, stayed dry, and became drowsy in the hum of the engine.

⌒⌒⌒

It was a little past three o'clock when they pulled into the Inland Packing cannery. Johnny was happy to see it, partly because he was eager to get off the crowded boat. The fjord was so deep that there had been no place to anchor for more than twenty miles. Along this stretch of the coast there were a few trees clinging to the sheer rock at waterline. Streams fell down bluffs for more than a thousand feet. A deep-draft boat could motor directly under these falls and take on fresh water. But the walls of rock were so steep both above and below the surface, no boat carried enough anchor chain to put in for the night anywhere along this fjord.

The cannery was built back in the only shallow bay. The mountains came down in three walls around the bay with one opening directly behind the massive wooden cannery buildings. A river pushed down the narrow valley and rumbled down a rock falls into a shallow estuary.

The little anchorage was a bluster of sounds, the white noise of the falls echoing around the mountain slopes and the churning of the cannery machinery rolled on underneath everything. A pile driver on skids worked on the dock replacing a piling, the iron hammer rising and falling in a heavy rhythm, and somewhere in the midst of it all Annabelle could hear children playing.

There was a floating raft with a narrow ramp to shore, and small vessels were moored in the back bay. Johnny decided to tie up first and talk to someone at the plant to see where they wanted him to unload his cargo of box wood. It took only a few minutes to secure the *Pacific Pride* to the float and tie the dory alongside. Then Johnny was up the slick ramp to find a supervisor. Ellie slowly packed her dry gear into a suitcase.

"Now what?" she said aloud what each of them had been thinking.

"Do you think Johnny is going to kick us off the boat?" Annabelle said. She sat cross-legged on the short bunk, not giving any indication that she would leave willingly.

"We can look for a job, get a spot in the bunkhouse," Ellie said. "Didn't you hear the kids here?" She touched the girl's knee with the tip of her finger.

The girl pushed her glasses up and scuttled out of the boat without a word to anyone.

As they walked up the ramp Slip combed his hair with a pocket comb, wiped it on his pants, and handed it to Ellie, then placed his cap on top of his head at a jaunty angle. "Got to try and look good," he said, winking at her.

Ellie rolled her eyes but she took the comb and made a couple of passes through her hair.

They walked through the barn-style doors off the loading dock into the cavernous production line. There was a clatter of chains and sprockets. Belts whirred off of the main shaft that ran high up the center of the room. The shaft spun and turned the belts that ran to each of the machines. At each machine a person stood with a stub of a pencil and a notebook counting cans as they slipped past. There were clutch handles by each machine to stop the mechanical apparatus and a man in an apron standing near each one. There were white people and Filipinos, some Chinese and some Indians. At one end of the room Indians stood at steel tables cutting up salmon. Down the line, the Chinese were stuffing cans, and the Filipinos worked the steam cookers, labelers, and boxers. And most of the people holding the pencils and notebooks appeared to be white.

"It's a split shop," Ellie shouted over the clatter.

"What?" Slip cupped his hand to his ear.

Ellie pulled him closer so she didn't have to yell. "All these people belong to different unions: the Indians, the whites, the Chinese, and the Filipinos, they're all represented by different unions. Management can play one against the other."

"Please, Ellie," Slip beseeched. "We need some money and we need a place to live for a bit."

"Relax. Your good looks are going to get us work, right?"

They walked through smaller rooms where caldrons of steam vented out across the floor. There was a carpentry shop where a crew of men hammered boxes together. Slip looked around and everything was in place; the hammers had numbers branded into the handles and the bins of nails were neatly marked. Ellie walked out the door and down a hall. She walked with such purpose none of the tired men or women in the hall asked their business.

At the end of the hall there was a door to the machine shop. "Let me just take a look and don't do anything," Ellie said, grabbing Slip's arm. He made a sour face and turned away from the door Ellie was ducking into.

The shop was cramped with machines, most of which Slip didn't recognize. There were lathes, presses, band saws; there was a forge and a man standing at an anvil with a rounding hammer. He was wearing goggles and he looked up at them as they stood in the doorway.

"Excuse me," Ellie called out with a singsongy tone that Slip had never heard before. "Have you seen the super?"

The man with the rounding hammer wiped his nose and then wiped his hand on his leather apron. "You try his office?"

"Oh, of course, but I was wondering if he was around here now." She smiled and took a half step in, leading with her hip and curling one arm behind her back almost as if she were going to ask the man to dance.

"Christ, I hope not," the big man said. "You seen the super around here, Clyde?" he turned and yelled over his shoulder. Back behind some gray humming piece of machinery, a greasy-looking man squinted up from a shower of sparks.

"What, are you crazy? He don't come around here. Go back to the office."

"You two do all this work around here?" she said round-eyed and gesturing into the room. She stumbled over a pile of sprockets and a rusted pair of pliers, then stopped to pick them up.

"You're looking at it. Both shifts, if needs be. The bastards."

"Well, you must be good at it," she said, and looked at them both in a kind of sex-infused wonder as if she were deciding which one of them she wanted to eat. "Thank you," she whispered, then backed out and closed the door.

"You know what you are?" Ellie said, looking straight at Slip.

"No," he said.

"You're a goddamn machinist's assistant."

He rolled his eyes and walked on. They found a door to the outside and turned toward the loading dock at the front of the cannery. Johnny was moving the *Pacific Pride* from the float over to the main pier to unload his box wood from the hold. Annabelle stood on the bow holding a line. Annabelle saw the two of them standing at the bull rail of the wharf, and she jumped up and down waving.

A surly man with a black watch cap and a leather windbreaker stood by the davit winch. From there he could lower a hook and some chokers into the hold of the boat and lift the flats of lumber up onto several steel carts. As Johnny eased up to the wharf the man rolled a cigarette and lit it.

"So, you bring your family on vacation then?" he said with a thick French Canadian accent. "Bunch of yachtsmen, I suppose."

"We just hitched a ride. Who do we talk to about a job around here anyway?" Slip asked.

"That'd be Charlie, up at the office. But don't get too excited 'cause he ain't been hiring in weeks. Unless you're a crooked bookkeeper, I doubt he could use you." Then he spit into the water, just barely missing the bow of the *Pacific Pride* as it eased up against the pilings some twelve feet below where they were standing.

Slip and Ellie turned and walked up the outside stairs to the office that had big windows overlooking the operation. The French Canadian yelled down at Johnny and Annabelle, telling them how to tie the boat while he unloaded her. Ellie went in after Slip and closed the door on the commotion. Slip asked to see the boss. He didn't say that he wanted a job but when the woman at the counter asked his business he started stammering. Ellie eased around his shoulder and said they had a proposition she was sure Charlie would want to hear.

Inside the office the walls were painted green four feet up from the floor and white all the way up to the ten-foot ceiling. The front-facing wall had three large windows and a windowsill with several pairs of binoculars resting on it. The other walls were dotted with ephemera from the fishing fleet: calendar photos of boats in foreign ports and snapshots of fine-looking boats unloading their catch at the cannery. There were pictures of schooners and dories. There were a couple of shots of massive halibut hanging from hooks with men in their oilskins smiling next to them.

Finally Charlie Hayes walked out of his office. He wore a vest and his tie was unknotted. Both of his sleeves were rolled up.

"I'm sorry," he said loudly, and he gestured toward the big front windows. "We're just not taking anybody on." He started to put on a wool coat and walk out the door but Ellie stopped him.

"My man's a machinist's assistant. A good one. I can help him. You got a mess down there in the machine shop and we'll fix it up for you in a couple of days. You give us food and a cabin for a week and we'll work for free. If you don't like what we do then you can send us down the road." And when she came to the end of her sentence she smiled sweetly and crossed her ankles so she teetered there in front of him.

Charlie Hayes stared at her for a moment as if he were judging a show horse. Then he said, "Hell with it. Check with housing. The machine shop's a fright. No pay for now but food and a bed." Then he turned and walked back out the door.

The French Canadian winch man was unloading the wood from the hold. Johnny was down in the boat rigging the pallets and Annabelle was the go-between signal for the winch man.

"Up just a teensy bit," she called up to him.

"Is that a teensy bit or a teensy-weensy bit?" he called down in his gruff tone.

The girl squinted down into the hold and looked back up, shifted her glasses back up her nose, and held her fingers about an inch apart. "Just a teensy bit will do, thank you."

"Don't mention it at all, miss," the winch man said, popping the handle back on the winch for half a second.

Ellie and Slip helped with unloading the wood. Then they loaded their personal gear into the dory and talked the winch operator into hauling it up onto the dock and onto a dolly. The dock boss let them wheel the dory over to a far corner of the dock where they let boats that delivered fish store their gear. Ellie, Slip, and Annabelle took their gear out of the dory, including the cage with the defiant yellow bird sitting on top, and went in search of the housing manager.

Within half an hour they were walking down a row of cabins along a boardwalk back where the mountain shouldered against the cannery. It didn't feel like the sun ever shone down where the cabins lay. Six kids ran across the soggy ground and up onto the boardwalk.

"Is that your bird?" a towheaded boy asked.

"Yes," Annabelle replied, unable to conceal her pride.

"You gonna eat him?" another blurted out.

"No!" she said, and walked away from the group of children with her head held high.

The cabin was about twelve by sixteen. Two walls had wooden bunk beds. The bottom bunk by the back wall had been modified to be a double bed. There was an electric heater, a table, and four straight-back chairs. Nails were driven into the walls where it appeared people hung their clothes. The room smelled of boiled vegetables, tobacco, and mildew. Buddy flew up from his cage and came to rest on a two-by-four rafter.

The housing manager told Ellie to keep the wet clothes well away from the coils of the electric heater and that they could eat their meals in the dining hall. There was no smoking in bed, and he pointed his index finger at each of them, even Annabelle, as he said, "And don't let me catch anyone drinking spirits in camp."

Before he left, the housing manager stopped by the open door and said, "I'd keep your girl here pretty much to this part of camp. Not really safe around the Indians or the Chinks. Filipinos won't hurt her but it would still be best if she stayed in this part of camp." Then he was gone and Annabelle looked up at Ellie and Slip with round eyes.

"Ellie, is he a management stooge?"

Slip shook his head and set his bedroll down on the double bunk. Ellie fiddled with the electric heater, then motioned the girl to come close.

"You know, honey, we've got a pretty good setup here for a bit. It wouldn't do for you to talk that way around here for a while."

"You're not going to try and unite the workers?"

Slip looked back over his shoulder at Ellie, and she brushed him off. "Well, not straight off. I got to get them listening to me, and you know . . . liking me first. Otherwise we'll just get run out of here and nothing happens. So we take it slow. Try and make friends. Okay?"

"My Lord!" Slip jumped back as the prongs of the cord sparked in the socket and the exposed coils of the heater began to glow.

"Okay, then," Ellie clapped her hands together and stood up. She didn't look at Slip, who was spreading blankets out on the bottom bunk. Annabelle climbed up onto the top bunk. She was able to hang Buddy's cage on a nail in the rafter just above her feet. The yellow bird walked over and hopped onto the cage and pecked in through the bars for a few seeds. The little cabin began to warm to the heater's glow.

Out on the boardwalk they could hear people walking back from the cannery buildings. The housing manager had told them that because there were no boats with big loads due in, they were running just one ten-hour shift. Later when the big runs started coming in, they would stretch that out to a sixteen-hour shift. If the boats backed up at the dock they might work straight through.

The sound of footsteps thudded to a slow rhythm, tired men and women coming home to clean up for supper. Ellie opened the door to their cabin and greeted some of the folks walking back. They still had their aprons on, and they nodded but didn't stop to talk. White folks and Filipinos, Indian and Chinese walking together. The whites' quarters were closest to the plant. Then the Filipino and the Chinese. The Indians had built their own village back up by a small tributary of the main stream. The Filipinos and Chinese each had their own kitchens and communal dining halls. The Indians fended for themselves, with each family cooking for itself. Sometimes a grandmother stayed home to cook the wild food they put up themselves or to open a can of stew they bought at the company store. Ellie nodded to them all and said hello to the ones who had the energy to look up at her and smile.

She turned back inside the cabin and looked over at Annabelle. "Nice setup," she said.

Slip nodded, walked over to a bunk, and wound his watch. He bent over and tied his shoes. There were four bunks, two upper and two lower. Annabelle had already claimed the bunk above Ellie's. Slip had thrown his bindle on the opposite top bunk. He watched as Ellie rigged a curtain around her bottom bunk, and when she saw him looking at her she smiled in a way that made him stop breathing.

Ellie tucked in the corner of the curtain, smoothed out the shirt she was wearing, ran a comb three times through her hair, and walked to the door. Slip watched her as if by studying the way she moved he could discern some distant part of his own emotions.

For weeks now, when he lay down to sleep he thought of the bower on the beach south of Edmonds. That world of Puget Sound seemed distant and vague to him now. But the memory of her body had invaded his mind and everything that came after seemed more sharply in focus, even if it were more dangerous. She was reckless and bad luck, but still, when she walked out the door ahead of him, he followed. And he felt better about things when she turned to make sure he was coming along into this new and glittering world that seemed to widen out in her wake.

FIFTEEN

≈≈≈

No one asked for their last names. That first night they ate rice and boiled fish with buttered turnips and slices of white bread. The men and women sitting at the plank table didn't ask questions, and if they responded at all to Ellie's or Annabelle's questions they did so with single words. The smell of the boiled fish wound its way around the whites' dining hall. They chewed their food in big mouthfuls, washing it down with mugs of cold water.

Johnny came in and sat with a big Norwegian in the corner. After trying to engage him in some cheerful conversation he gave up and ate his food in silence. As they carried their tin plates to the counter by the kitchen, Johnny waved at Annabelle and the little girl waved back and ran out the door ahead of her aunt.

Annabelle roamed the boardwalk in front of her cabin, looking for the wild boys who had been running loose when they had arrived. She passed her cabin, and when the grownups went through the door, Ellie said something to her about not going too far, but the girl didn't hear her instructions.

Annabelle skipped down the boardwalk, her leather shoes slippery on the damp wood. She skated around corners and fell off into the soft damp moss on either side. Beyond the whites' bunkhouse and through an arbor of young alder trees stood the Filipino bunkhouse, which smelled like cooking oil and celery. Music came from the open door where a dark-skinned woman wearing a broad apron was drying her hands. Annabelle waved as she skipped and the woman waved in return. She ran past the Chinese camp, where a long line of men stood out on the porch with towels draped over their shoulders. Some of them had long braids and she wanted to stare but she didn't. She ran past a dilapidated building she would learn later was an opium den.

Eventually Annabelle came to the rocky beach. The calm water from the bay slid up and down on the gravel. Three boys were skipping rocks. Half a dozen cabins with chimneys pumping white smoke sat just under the canopy of trees. This was the Indian village where the company provided nothing but a muddy path up to the cannery. The boys smiled and laughed and spoke English quite well. They invited her up to the dump with them. There they climbed a tree to watch a black bear sow gnaw on the discarded skull of one of the dairy cows that had fallen sick and had to be put down.

Annabelle was happy to be up in the tree. She was happy to be on dry land and in the company of someone her own age. She clung to the trunk of the spruce tree and smiled, feeling the permanent heft of its mass.

The sow held the skull with her front paws. She worked the hide with her teeth, and her flame-red tongue scoured the bone. Annabelle sat fascinated as the three boys watched and spoke their own language to each other, sometimes miming that they were bears themselves gnawing on a fine big meal.

Footsteps approached from the cannery side and they all heard the voices of two adults. The boys jumped down from the tree and ran toward the dump. The sow lifted her head and in three long bounds was gone. The boys were scouring through the crates and barrels left in the dump. Annabelle climbed down and ran up to the dump just as the littlest boy pulled out a glass bottle of Karo syrup. The top of the bottle had broken off and there was a thick plug of mold on top of the amber liquid. The middle boy got a stick and scraped away the mold then dug deep down into the bottle, pulled the stick out, and began licking it as the other two tried to wrestle the bottle away from him.

The big boy found a clean stick and made sure there was not a trace of bark or mud on it. He dipped it into the syrup bottle and he gave the stick to Annabelle. She thanked him and licked the sweet syrup. The boys were clearly proud of themselves.

"Thank you," Annabelle said to the three of them.

"That's nothing," the big boy said. "We do this kind of stuff all the time."

He grabbed at the syrup bottle again just as they noticed the watchman standing at the end of the dump road with Ellie.

"Hey, you goddamn rodents, get out of the dump. This ain't your stuff to be scrounging through." The watchman shouldered his shotgun and fired in the direction of the boys but well over their heads. The boys ran like the sow back into the woods, leaving Annabelle standing with her sugary stick.

Ellie walked toward Annabelle. She wasn't listening to the watchman rant about the unruly Indian boys or about the three black bear cubs he had shot just a week ago.

Ellie walked slowly, stumbling over the refuse. Annabelle could tell Ellie wasn't mad. Ellie hardly ever got mad, at her at least.

"It's getting late. I started to worry," Ellie said, her voice more tired than angry.

"It's still light out," Annabelle said, and she finished the last of the syrup on the stick.

"I know but it's still late. Funny that way up here. Sun stays up a long time."

"Lots of things are funny up here," Annabelle said. She took Ellie's hand and walked back to the cabin.

Ellie and Slip started in at the machine shop the next day. He had no idea what they would be doing or what they should be doing for no pay.

"I think we should organize first," Ellie said in a whispery voice, and Slip's stomach tightened up. Slip's distress must have shown on his face for Ellie looked him in the eye and stopped walking just short of the machine shop door. "Listen," she said softly, "I'm sorry about all this," and she gestured with her hands, taking everything in the world into the scope of her words. "But we're still above ground, aren't we?"

Slip looked away from her beautiful battered face. "That's a plus, I agree," he said.

"Yes it is," she continued over his attempt at humor, "and right now we've got to work this job. Trust me. I can do this. I can do this better than anything else." Slip nodded, and Ellie opened the door to the machine shop.

The shop was a dark hole in the back of the cannery building that whirred with rattling lathes and hissing compressors. It was run by a big Swede named Nels and his assistant, Clyde. Nels had been a blacksmith in Saskatchewan, but in his early twenties he killed a man in a bar fight and rode a freight train west to Vancouver. Nels liked working in a small shop. Clyde was dumber than a bag of hammers but at least he didn't talk much and when he did it was almost always to say something in agreement with Nels. He didn't ask for a couple of scarecrows to help out in the shop but the super had told him they were coming down. Nels had no idea what they could do.

When Ellie walked into the shop she saw nothing but things to do. There were piles of drill bits on greasy benches, broken sprockets on the floor, calipers and metal rules, punches and hacksaws, cold chisels and deadweight hammers, bent shafts and broken motor mounts scattered on every flat surface and the floor. There were punchboards where the tools had once hung but the brackets were all empty now. There were buckets with solvent, and some with water for cooling heated parts. There were buckets just for spitting in. There was a calendar with a different inspirational Bible verse for each week of the year hanging on the wall. There were three hanging lights that pulsed with the uneven revving of the camp's electrical system. There were drifts of sprocket chains snaking between the machines and a broken chain hoist swinging like a gallows from the ceiling.

"What you think you gonna do in my shop?" Nels asked.

The light pulsed on the big man wearing the leather apron. Clyde had his head down and was running a hand file up the notch of a short motor shaft.

"We're going to do whatever we can to help you out," Ellie said with a smile sweeter than berry cobbler.

"Just stay out of my way. I didn't ask for no help." He turned away and went back to the lathe where he was turning a shaft.

"Let's get out of here," Slip said. "They're never going to let you and me work in here," and he turned to walk out the door.

Ellie touched his elbow. "Hang on. Let's watch a bit."

They sat in the back corner and watched the two men work. Slip had no idea what they were going to do and his eyes wandered all over the clutter. The room was so heaped with tools and broken metal that he could not differentiate the individual tools or what was useful and what was being discarded. It was a junk drawer that had spilled and taken over an entire room of the cannery.

Ellie nudged him on the shoulder and said, "Grab that broom. See there, the greasy one over by the barrel. Go in the back and start sweeping the floor. I'll find a dustpan and an empty barrel. We'll start slow."

Nels scowled at them as they went about sweeping the floor. Occasionally he'd bark out, "Don't be moving nothing. I got things where I want 'em."

And Ellie would ask, "So you want these shavings on the floor right where they are?" Nels would turn away and go back to straightening a shaft or welding a new section of a chipped sprocket.

Soon Ellie and Slip were working together, sweeping and moving around piles of tools and broken metal. They swept around the lathes, then wiped the big machines with clean rags. They threw the rustiest pieces of metal in the barrel. Slip kept his head down and swept because he felt that Nels was going to throw a hammer at him at any moment. But after about twenty minutes of sweeping and scooping metal shavings into the barrel, Slip looked over at Clyde who was staring straight at Ellie. Clyde was standing at a vice holding a ball-peen hammer and looking at Ellie as if she were going to burst into flame.

"Whacha doing this for? He don't want no woman's help," Clyde said softly, and as he spoke he turned away from the blonde.

"I don't figure it hurts to help you guys get organized," Ellie said, and she slid the barrel closer to the vice and started sweeping under the workbench. "I won't say a thing or bother you at your work. I'm just going to make life easier. That's what I do, boys. I make life easier." Then she winked.

Slip stopped sweeping. Clyde was turning pale. It seemed to Slip that no one had ever winked at Clyde or spoken to him in a civil tone and the poor man simply didn't know how to respond.

The little greasy man couldn't bring himself to look at Ellie again, but he said, "I suppose not."

Clyde was suspicious of Ellie and Slip for a lot of reasons. One was that a skinny blonde woman had no business in his shop, but she and her beat-up boyfriend could have been stooges. The owners were always hiring private dicks to snoop around the workers to make sure there weren't any agitators in the bunch. They would be friendly as hell and they'd start asking around about who was having meetings and they'd even start complaining about the food and the bedding to see who piped up. Then in a couple of days, whoever it was who had piped up was gone on a boat down the coast or sometimes flown out on an airplane to a hospital.

Clyde was watching Ellie. Clyde recognized the way Ellie had said the word "organize" as if it were a ringing bell, and he knew Ellie was up to something. Clyde wouldn't say anything to Nels. He would just keep his eyes open.

Late that evening Ellie and Slip walked down the boardwalk to the cabin. They had greasy hands and their boots scratched along the slick walkway because of sharp curls of steel stuck into their soles. They found themselves in the parade of tired workers at the end of the day, and Ellie nodded to people she had seen at dinner the night before. If they nodded back she would follow it up with a soft "hello." Slip tromped back, saying nothing.

As they turned the corner of the main cannery building something caught Ellie's eye and she ran ahead. Slip kept walking slowly and found Ellie standing at the rail, looking down at the float. She was shading her eyes and gazing at something intently, her hands gripping the top of the rail and her knuckles showed white.

Slip stopped beside her, but she didn't acknowledge him. He followed her gaze and saw a man and a boy unloading cartons off of a floatplane tied to the float.

"Hey," Slip said. "We had a good day in the shop. I have to admit you knew what you were doing," and he patted her on the back. She stared out to the dock without responding to his touch. He ran his hand down to the small of her back where her work coat hung over her dungarees. He stopped his hand when he felt the hardness of the revolver tucked into her belt.

"What the hell you carrying this for?" he whispered into her ear.

She didn't acknowledge his question. "That's a Lockheed Vega," she said. The tone in her voice was softer and more loving than Slip had yet heard. "It's got a Pratt and Whitney Wasp engine."

"Really?" Slip said, flummoxed.

"It's fast," she said, as if she were describing a mythological animal. "Some of them will cruise at a hundred fifty miles an hour and still carry a big payload. It's got three gas tanks."

"No kidding." Slip had taken out his pocketknife and was cleaning grease from under his fingernails.

"Amelia Earhart flew one," Ellie said. She pushed back from the rail and began walking away. She bumped into people walking the other way because she couldn't take her eyes off the plane.

Slip kept scraping his fingernails for a moment, then he shook his head and walked off in the opposite direction.

"I'm going to get cleaned up for supper," he said, without looking back.

Ellie waved absently in the general direction of the cabin. "Sounds good. I'll be along." She walked down the ramp toward the Vega, pushing past the chain of kitchen workers who were carrying cardboard cartons from the dock to the dining room. As she walked toward the pilot she swept off her kerchief, tossing her hair back and running her fingers through it. Slip hated himself for doing it but he watched her from the dock and he recognized a swaying in her walk, a fluid motion from her hips and arms that danced into her stride as she approached the pilot. The pilot came down off the ladder from the passenger door to hop on the float as she came closer. Soon they were engaged in a conversation, the pilot pointing to the wings and then the tail section, Ellie taking in every word. Her hands reached out to touch the skin of the plane even though it was too far away.

When the pilot held Ellie by the waist to help her inside, Slip turned away and walked back to the cabin.

The yellow bird was sitting on the two-by-four rafter when Slip walked in. The bird gave a great shriek and buzzed the top of his head. He flapped and waved the bird off. Annabelle sat up on her bunk reading a book.

"Can't you get him back in his cage?" he said, too tired to really sound fierce.

"I guess he doesn't want to get back in his cage."

"I could get him back in there. Just throw a towel over him, and jam him through the door." Slip sat on his bunk and started unlacing his boots.

"He'd just find a way to get out." Annabelle didn't look up from her book.

"Well if he's so fired up to be free, why doesn't he fly away and live in the woods with the rest of the birds?" Slip stripped off one boot and threw it on the floor.

"I dunno. I guess he doesn't want to. I bet those wild birds scare him."

"Well if he craps on my stuff one more time I'm going to cook him in a stew." Slip threw his second boot under the bunk.

Annabelle put her book aside and dug down beside the mattress where she kept a notebook and a pencil. She took the pencil and stood on the bunk, holding out her hand to Buddy. She made kissing sounds and Buddy walked the rafter over to the pencil and hopped onto it. Then the girl lay back down and held the bird up in front of her face. Buddy loved to look at himself in the reflection of Annabelle's glasses and he stood cooing and chortling a lovely song to himself.

"Where's Ellie?" the girl asked.

"She's down looking at an airplane." Slip clambered up onto the bunk opposite her.

"I went down and looked at it when it came in. It's a Lockheed Vega. It's like Amelia Earhart's plane."

"I know," Slip grumbled.

"It's made of wood."

"Really?"

"Yep, and when it gets cold in the winter the wood pops and creaks as the plane flies over the mountains. It can go a hundred and fifty miles per hour."

"I heard."

"That's a lot faster than we go in that little boat."

"No kidding."

"We'd be where we're going a heck of a lot faster if we went by plane."

"That's true." Slip was staring up at the unfinished ceiling.

"Slip?" Annabelle asked.

"Yes."

"I gave you your tin box back, right?"

"Yes, you did. Thank you."

"There's a lot of money in there."

"Yes, there is."

"You could probably pay that man in the airplane to fly you anywhere you want."

"I suppose."

"Slip?" she asked.

"Uh-huh," he mumbled, growing sleepy now.

"Just where are we headed?"

"I don't know," he said, and his voice dropped away.

They both lay there without speaking. The yellow bird was cooing and pecking at himself in the girl's glasses. People walked slowly past the cabin, and they could hear the clatter of the clean-up crew working in the plant.

"Then I guess we don't really need an airplane," she said sleepily.

"No, I suppose not."

The pilot's name was Willie Lee, and he had been taking a nip out of his pocket flask when Ellie started down the ramp. He had helped unload the groceries and next he had to fly south and pick up a party of geologists and take them on to Campbell River. When Ellie came down the dock he quickly wiped his mouth and put on a big smile. When he saw the pretty blonde approaching he was glad he had worn his leather windbreaker and military-style cap this morning. There were lots of dames who loved aircraft. It wasn't all about Lindbergh anymore. The planes were bigger and more powerful, and there were more of them too. He could imagine a pretty girl stuck in some dump like this cannery. He could imagine what she must feel when she heard the plane landing. She could climb up beside him in the plane and she'd instantly be somewhere else. This plane could take to the sky. The same sky that covered Seattle and Los Angeles. Hell, it was the same sky that covered Paris, France, and there weren't no tollbooths or stop signs anywhere.

This girl had a wild look in her eye. She also knew about the Vega. She knew the horsepower and the carburetion. She knew who had flown them and who had set distance records. This girl was different. She stood close and he knew she could smell the brandy on his breath. He almost reached into his pocket and offered her a slug, but he didn't because she might be the kind to tell somebody about it and he didn't need that kind of trouble. But there were several other kinds of trouble this girl brought to mind. She was friendly enough, and he let her crawl up inside. As she stepped in front of him, he put his hands around her waist and she didn't flinch or look back. She sat in the pilot's seat and named the instruments. She pulled gently back on the yoke and sat up straight so she could see the prop. He asked her if she had flown before and she said "not in a Vega." She said she wanted to fly in a Vega almost more than anything.

He asked her, "anything?" and tilted his cap back and gave her a look that left no doubt about what he was saying.

"Well," she looked at him and her eyes seemed to be burning pure oxygen, "almost anything."

He explained that he had to go and pick up a load of scientists and their gear. He said if he had room sometime when he came back, maybe she could ride along and keep him company. He could tell she was trying not to act too excited, but her eyes widened and she twisted around with her knees together like she had to go pee.

Then she said, "Well, maybe. That might be fun." She kept her eyes on the plane, as if she were trying to burn the image of it into her mind. "When do you think you'll be back?" she asked, as if it were not a matter of life and death.

"Can't say for sure. But as spring picks up I'm sure I'll be back out here soon enough."

"In the next week?"

"Could well be," he said. He undid the lines from the dock. "You'll hear me when I do. I'll buzz your cabin." Then he pushed away from the dock, climbed in through the rear passenger door and up to the cockpit, pumped the throttle, then levered the switch to turn the prop over. Even though he didn't need to, he stuck his head out of the side panel and shouted "Clear!" just before the big radial engine whined, rattled, then settled into a steady roar.

Ellie stood on the dock. Once the engine fired, the big plane shook itself like a wet dog. In the last weeks she had been scared and tired, she had been scheming and exhilarated, but for the first time she was angry. Her body shook as she squinted into the prop wash as the Vega began to move away from the dock. *Why is it men get to do these things?* she thought to herself. She had seen the gas drip from the air scoop on the bottom of the engine, so she was almost prepared for the ball of flame blasting between the floats when the exhaust manifold ignited the fumes of the spilled fuel. Willie gunned the engine so that the prop wash put the fire out. She knew that pilots called this "torching." In fact she was sure that she knew more about that plane than the smarmy oaf with the big hands who got to fly it. She stood in the prop wash and watched it blare across the water, bounce a few times, then pull up into the air. She shaded her eyes with both hands as Willie banked the Vega high and tight, then circled back around to buzz the water just off the float. He waved to her through the window as he passed.

"Stupid bastard," she said through smiling teeth, as she waved gaily, working her hips and her chest as she did. "Know nothing, stupid bastard."

In the next few days Slip and Ellie had the machine shop cleaner than it had ever been. Nels was spending less time rooting around in the mess and swearing at Clyde, and Clyde had more time to sit and "put the think on" a project. Ellie had watched the men work and she started putting the tools on the tables and by the machines where they were most often used. She cleaned the lathes so the wheels would turn more easily, then rounded up all the metal rules and calipers so that no one would have to hunt through the drifts of screwdrivers and wrenches each time they needed to make a measurement. Slip built a row of shelves on the back wall and he piled up end pieces and things that looked as if they could some-day be useful again. He sorted them solely by appearance and size, without knowing exactly what their function was. Ellie even dedicated a shelf for the problem projects: the jammed clutch assembly or the stubborn motor winding. She called it "The Healing Shelf" and labeled it such. Here were the parts that, when taken by them-selves, often didn't work. But when the larger piece of the mecha-nism was put back in order, the "broken" part would slip in and function as if it had been miraculously healed. Clyde smiled and whispered to Slip that he was thinking about "putting his pecker up on that shelf to see if it could do any good," then he elbowed the logger in his sore ribs.

By the end of the second day Clyde was showing Ellie how to do simple jobs on the metal lathe and how to do the setup for some of the more delicate jobs, such as cutting the shiv plates from the haulers. Clyde would reach around her shoulders with both arms, talking softly about calibration and how slow and steady to adjust the cut. Ellie would lean back into his chest just enough to let him know she was paying attention.

Slip made countless trips to the dump, using a wheelbarrow to take the oily filings and the butt ends of shafts out the boardwalk to where the black bear sow still rummaged around the clearing. Slip sometimes took his break at the dump, sitting on a stump and watching the trees, hoping the bear would wander out. It usually had to be late in the afternoon or early in the morning, but often she would come.

He was sitting on a stump one day and picking metal slivers out of his fingers when a twig snapped to his right, and when he turned, the black bear sow was some fifteen feet from him. Her fiery tongue flicked inside a shiny tin that had once been full of lard. She had carried the tin up from the dump and was now lying under the fringe of trees working the can around with her front paws. Slip watched the bear and he thought again about making his own home. Maybe if they stayed here the bosses would let him build a house on a little piece of ground up the beach from the cannery. He would build it on a little flat up the hill. He could make adzes and drawknives to work the green timber. It would have massive posts and beams with finely chiseled joinery. They would all live there, with a big woodstove and places to hang clothes and water piped right to the house. It wasn't the Grand Coulee country but it was someplace far from their troubles.

A gun boomed just over his shoulder and the bear seemed

to pop and settle to the moss as if she had been a balloon. Bright red blood eased into the moss. Slip dove down onto the ground and looked up to see the watchman shucking an empty shell from his shotgun.

"You better get back to work, young fella. This company don't pay you to sit on your can and watch the wildlife."

Slip stood up and walked past the watchman without saying a word.

By the beginning of their third day the cannery superintendent gave Slip and Johnny a job working on the pile-driving crew. Johnny got the job because he could run a boat and Slip got one because there wasn't a need for a second cleanup boy in the machine shop now that Ellie had become some kind of princess of the metal workers. Slip and Johnny would make fifteen cents an hour. Ellie would stay in the shop as an apprentice and make twenty. Ellie was dry and warm all day long, and as the new guys on the pile-driving crew, Slip and Johnny got the worst of the jobs, which often had to do with working under the wharf, standing in a leaky skiff and trying to wedge a new piling into place.

After the second day, Johnny quit and stole some fuel from the cannery and took off in the *Pacific Pride*. He had heard from his wife that she wanted him back soon or he would have no home to come back to. Johnny still wanted to head north to see how the new town of Cold Storage, Alaska, was doing, so he pumped the stolen fuel and headed north. He ended up only saying good-bye to Annabelle when he brought by her bag of peppermints and two bags of bird food she had left on the boat.

Annabelle took care of the cabin and tried to make friends in the cannery. Ellie didn't like the idea of Annabelle wandering around by herself. There was nothing else to do but let her read and explore the camp, as long as she was back before the evening meal. On Sundays she and Ellie borrowed fishing poles from a

Filipino man and learned to jig for halibut. There was one fallen tree that had wedged between two others and cantilevered out over the bay. There, with enough weight and the fish heads on circle hooks, aunt and niece could get their line some hundred feet down and they would jig for fish.

The first day they caught nothing but a small flat fish that seemed to have become impaled on the hook by mistake. The second day Ellie got a fish so large that there was no way to land it on the steep shore. It came to the surface slowly and looked about as big as a car door. The fish swam languidly and they both shrieked. Then the fish flipped violently and was gone. Annabelle immediately put her baited hook down in the water. Ellie went into the woods and fashioned a club then found a flat spot to stand near the water's edge.

An hour later Annabelle hauled up another fish, this one about the length of the girl herself. She teetered down the log and when the fish was resting between runs, she handed the pole off to Ellie, who slowly brought the sixty-pound halibut up to the shallows, tied off the thick line to a stump, and then clubbed the thrashing fish to death.

That night they cooked the fish in the Filipino kitchen. Two brothers played guitars on the porch of the Filipino bunkhouse while the crew of the little dory ate their fill sitting outside listening to the music. Ellie talked with Mr. Caroca, who was one of the three patriarchs of the Filipino workers. They talked about union business and working conditions. Ellie mostly asked questions, never pushing for conclusions or offering opinions. If Mr. Caroca offered a complaint against management Ellie took it in silence as if she were considering the truth of the man's words.

Slip ate the halibut and rice and looked around at his new family. Ellie sometimes sat with the women, gossiping about the single men of the camp and who they were seeing, but tonight she was deep into a conversation with Mr. Caroca. Annabelle played jacks in a circle of girls. She would eat a bite of fish, then bounce the red ball and grab a jack, eat another bite, then bounce again. Ellie leaned on the rail of the porch, laughing and asking questions. Slip took another mouthful. The fresh fish was moist and sweet with spices. He leaned his head back against the house where the spring sun gathered and warmed the damp wood. *Lucky,* he thought to himself. *Lucky.*

"Why not go talk to the boss?" Ellie asked Mr. Caroca.

"No good will come of it," the dark man offered. "We got jobs, better than most. No reason to risk that."

"True, but they can't run this plant without you." Ellie set her plate down on the porch rail.

"They always get another Flip, that's what they think."

"Maybe, but we're a long way from Manila." Ellie watched Mr. Caroca's face. He was suddenly disengaged from the conversation as if his face had turned to stone. Ellie followed his eyes out to the boardwalk in front of the house. Clyde stood there with a young Finn who worked on the slime line. Clyde was looking at Ellie sitting with the Filipino boss. He stood flat-footed and stared at her as if he couldn't quite believe what he was seeing.

Ellie raised up her arm and called out to them, "Hey boys, we're eating the halibut we caught. Wanna try some?"

Clyde turned and walked toward the white workers' cabins without saying a word. The young Finn smiled and half-heartedly waved as if embarrassed, then he too walked away.

"Maybe not such a good idea, you being here," Mr. Caroca said. He stood up with his plate.

"Any man who turns down a free meal of fresh-caught fish doesn't have the sense that God gave a duck," Ellie said, and she picked up her own plate to take it into the kitchen.

≈≈≈

Two more days passed. A high-pressure system pushed in from the north and settled over the Canadian coast. Wind from the north whipped the waters of the channel into a washboard of short white waves, and the newly budding trees waved their limbs about as if they were waking up from a long sleep. Slip's pile-driving crew spent the time shoring up the wharf and driving pilings for a new section of dock. Ellie worked in the machine shop and Clyde silently allowed her to sweep, organize, and take on the easiest and most tedious projects. Ellie whistled while she swept the metal filings and never once provoked a confrontation with the machinists.

The bookkeeper in the business office found a trunk of *National Geographic* magazines in a storage locker and gave them to Annabelle in place of some regular schooling. Annabelle was quite pleased and would bring treasures to the bookkeeper whenever she came across them. After the second day the bookkeeper had a fragile sea urchin nest and a raven's skull on her desk.

Annabelle kept one ear cocked for the sound of the returning Lockheed Vega. Buddy spent most of his time either trying to look at himself in Annabelle's glasses or preening and chuckling to himself on the center rafter of their cabin.

On a Thursday, Ellie was setting up a shiv plate in the lathe for Nels. The big Swede had showed her how to center the chucks and get the plate level. It was a slow process, with hundreds of slight adjustments. Ellie had a feeler gauge mounted to read whether the plate was running perfectly parallel with the chucks of the machine. Once she got it tight and even, Nels would run the lathe and take some twenty-thousandths of an inch off of the plate so that the lines running between them would be pinched down tight and not slip off the puller.

Clyde was working on forge-welding a broken sprocket. He stood under the forge hood and gripped the tongs with leather gloves. Then he brought the glowing pieces out of the coals and set them in a jig he had set up on the anvil. He was pounding the parts together as Ellie finished up the preparation on the shiv plate. The shop was clean and most of the tools hung in their proper places on the walls and benches. Nels had been in a good mood that morning and had offered to teach Ellie this new skill.

Nels stood next to Ellie and eyed the feeler gauge as he spun the mounted plate by hand. Ellie watched with satisfaction as the indicator needle barely flickered, showing that the plate was parallel to the chuck. The chuck of the big lathe weighed close to three hundred pounds and was driven by a ten-horsepower electric motor. The motor had more than enough torque to start the plate spinning with a tug on the lever and a quick whir of the chucks.

"Now get the carriage back out of the way and we'll cut this thing." Nels made adjustments to the cutting tool and Ellie turned the wheel to move the carriage. Nels had his back to her as he said, "Now push the lever down and get her spinning." Ellie reached back and pushed the lever, and as she did, she leaned against the machine and put her left hand on the inside edge of the carriage.

At first she felt nothing except a tug on the edge of her hand. Then there was the whining of the ten-horse motor as it bound up. She felt a numbness and a sense of urgency as Nels flew over the top of her to hit the cutoff switch. Then pain was shooting up her arm and Ellie felt a kind of stupid regret as she looked over to see her hand pinched between the chuck and the carriage table. Blood pooled out on the table like cutting oil, and Ellie leaned over and saw the little finger and ring finger of her left hand on the floor, nestled in a pile of metal shavings.

Of the rest she retained little memory. Nels had said, "Oh, good Christ." Then he forced the big machine out of gear and the big chuck swung lazily in the opposite direction, and Ellie slumped to the floor. Clyde walked slowly around the edge of the big lathe with a broom in his hand. He stopped for a moment, walked slowly over to the workbench, and flipped over the main electrical breaker for the shop, thinking that they would be done for the day. Then he walked out the door to get the superintendent and the big greasy bohunk who was supposed to be the camp nurse, though no one trusted him with any of their ailments.

The superintendent fired Ellie on the spot. He told her he'd put whatever wages she had coming toward the cost of the airplane to come take her out of camp. The plane could take her up to Ketchikan or down to Campbell River. If there was anything left over, the super said he'd send the wages on, but of course they both knew he never would.

Ellie sat in the office with her hand wrapped in gauze. The bohunk had given her morphine, which made her feel warm, sleepy, and sick to her stomach. Once she started to throw up in the trashcan and the bookkeeper told her to wait outside on the dock. Clyde helped Ellie up and they walked slowly to the airplane dock.

"This is a tough break for Nels and me," Clyde said. "We were just beginning to be able to stand having you around."

Clyde supported her by her good arm as they walked to the dock. Ellie hobbled down the ramp and smiled weakly up at Clyde. "Am I going to fly in the Vega?" she asked.

"I believe you are," Clyde said softly. "Listen, tell them to take you up to Ketchikan. Give 'em my name at the border. It's clean. 'Course it's not my real name but it's clean all the same. Tell them you're my daughter. Use my last name. You know what I'm saying."

"Thanks, Clyde." Ellie eased herself down onto a dock bench and leaned against the rail. "I'm not on the run," she said.

"Like fun, you ain't," Clyde said. "Just give 'em my name. Then get yourself down to Creek Street and ask for Yvette. She'll take care of you."

"I thank you for that, Clyde," Ellie said as she wobbled back and forth on the bench.

"Then you get yourself up to Juneau. The Party's looking for you, I bet."

Ellie looked down at the bundle of gauze around her hand. The blood was beginning to seep through the outer layers.

"You Red son of a bitch," she said, and her voice sounded thick with shock. Then she leaned over the rail and wretched.

Slip came running down the dock.

"You won't believe it," Ellie said as he came near her. "I get to fly on the airplane."

"Lucky break," Slip said. Then he looked over at the blood seeping through the gauze. "I better come with you," he said without thinking.

"You stay with Annabelle and the dory. I can't take care of her. I'll get a setup in Ketchikan, and I'll send word."

"I suppose so," was all Slip said by way of an argument.

Soon the buzz of the Lockheed Vega wheedled its way above the sound of the wind in the trees. Then the big red plane passed overhead, tipping its wings in the direction of the dock. As it did, Annabelle came running down the ramp. She was holding something in her hands.

"I got your fingers for you, Ellie" she said. Her glasses were fixed well up on her nose and her expression was stern. "Maybe you should take them along to the hospital?"

"That's nice of you, honey," Ellie said, and her voice was sadder than the girl had ever remembered. "I'll take 'em with me. Can use them for something, I guess."

"Yes. I didn't want to leave them on the floor," Annabelle said, her voice quavering with both exhilaration and fear. The plane came in low over the waterfall and put down on the bay. Green water hissed and turned white around the big aluminum floats.

"That's right, young lady. Those fingers would have just sat there waiting for the next cleanup man." Clyde patted Ellie on the shoulder and walked up the ramp toward his own life in the machine shop.

"You go on up to Juneau. They got some work for you up there," Clyde yelled over his shoulder.

The plane came in close to the dock and cut the engine. Willie jumped out the door behind the cockpit and stepped down onto a float. He unhooked a long paddle from a sleeve on the float and took a few strokes with it to help the plane reach the dock.

"So, we going north or south?" he called out.

"North," Ellie said to him.

"That's fine with me. I won't even charge you for the ride, Blondie."

"Every cloud has its silver fucking lining," Ellie said just under her breath, and she threw her severed fingers into the water so the girl couldn't see.

Ellie turned to Annabelle. "It'll be a week or so, I bet. You stay here with Slip and Buddy and I'll either send for you or come get you myself. Okay?"

"Okay," Annabelle said, then added quickly, "a week."

"A week, sweetie. No more."

Slip helped Ellie up into the plane.

"Don't be puking in the plane. Okay, beautiful? Use the paper bag I got here," Willie said, and he started to strap her into one of the passenger seats. But Ellie pushed her way up from the seat and climbed up into the copilot's seat, leaving a faint spatter of blood on the floor.

"All right then," Willie said, and he tilted his cap back and followed her to the cockpit.

The prop spun and the engine clattered. The wind from the plane pushed Annabelle's braids back over her shoulders. She held the side of her head to hold on to her glasses. The plane moved out into the bay, the wings tipping slightly back and forth as it floated over the small waves rolling in from the inlet. Then the engine blared so that it rang off the side of the mountains, and the floatplane skidded over the water and lifted into the air. It banked toward the inlet, then rose above the level of the ridgeline and disappeared to the north.

Slip and Annabelle stood there looking after the Vega. The storm of the plane leaving was replaced by the everyday shoosh of the waterfall and clatter of the plant.

"Well, I got to get back to work. You going to be okay until dinner?" Slip asked without looking directly at the little girl.

"I'll be fine," she said, and she walked slowly up the ramp, passing the superintendent coming down.

He looked in the direction of where the plane had disappeared and asked, "She get out of here okay?"

"Yes," Slip said. He took his work gloves out of his back pocket, slapped them against the side of his leg, and made a motion to walk up the ramp and to work.

The superintendent kept looking in the direction where the plane had disappeared. "We lost half a day's work in the shop because of this."

"She got hurt pretty bad." Slip slapped his gloves against his legs again.

"Then there's all the whispering and gossip that goes on when an accident like this happens. It slows everything down."

"I suppose so," Slip said. Now he was staring down at his feet. He was half-expecting what the superintendent was going to say next.

"You can draw your wages. I'll be expecting you and the girl to be out of here by tomorrow night." The superintendent started to walk away without waiting for a reply.

"Now, hold on," Slip called out to the man's back. "Why in blazes are you firing me? I didn't have a thing to do with that accident."

"I knew you were a couple of Reds when I laid eyes on you.

No woman like that works in a machine shop unless she's up to something. Well, you can leave together. Draw your wages and I'll have somebody help you put your boat back in the water. You can get some grub for the little girl, but I want you out of camp."

"I ain't no Red, mister," Slip called to the man's back as he walked away. "I'm just trying to get by."

"Get by somewhere else," the superintendent called out over his shoulder, then disappeared into his office.

∽∽∽

SIXTEEN

When the *Admiral Rodman* came toward the dock in Craig, George Hanson was standing on the deck drinking a cup of coffee. Craig was a small fishing village on the outside coast of Prince of Wales Island. The ship had made a stop the night before at a large cannery and would put in at Craig to deliver cargo and pick up a few passengers. This was an unusual route for the steamship line, but there was a delivery of livestock for Sitka in the hold, and the captain had decided to come up the outside coast and then go to Ketchikan on the return trip down the inside.

George had spent the morning watching birds. He had never watched birds before in his life but this particular morning he had watched birds and finished reading a novel. He even talked with a young couple on their way to Alaska for the first time about the healthful benefits of rain for the skin. None of these things really held any interest for him but somehow on the ship they were pleasurable diversions.

George watched the small boats paralleling the *Rodman*'s course toward Craig and he waved from the deck. They had crossed Dixon Entrance the day before and he had been up to walk the deck in the easy swells that rolled in from the Pacific Ocean. He wore light cotton pants and a pair of old tennis shoes he had last used when he and Benny had gone surf casting on the coast at La Push. When he put the shoes on he remembered the day with happiness and he even rolled the cuffs of his pants up to walk on deck.

As the village came into sight, George heard the engines on the steamship slow and felt a new vibration in the deck. A moment later there was a shrill grinding clatter coming from belowdecks and a bell sounded in a compartment somewhere under his feet. Then the ship slowed even more and an alarm bell sounded on the deck where he stood.

A ship's steward came walking briskly along and asked all of the passengers to please report to their lifeboat stations. He said repeatedly not to go back to their rooms for any of their luggage but to report immediately.

George stood in a crowd and put on his canvas life preserver. He smelled no smoke and the *Admiral Rodman* didn't show any sign of listing. It was a fine morning and the winds were calm. The older passengers fanned themselves and did not laugh when a young man called for a band to play "Nearer My God to Thee." Men smoked cigars and women stood on tiptoe, trying to see over the shoulders of the people around them and hoping for a sliver of information. A sailor came to the station to explain that the ship had lost power but there was a tug coming to tow them to the dock in Craig. Once the tug was alongside, the passengers would be allowed to go back to their business on ship. A steward started handing out cups of bouillon to the crowd and the atmosphere took on the nervous gaiety of a temporary crisis.

The old reverend who shared George's table at dinner came walking down the covered deck with his life jacket wrapped tightly around his narrow chest.

"I overheard the engineer tell the steward that the bolts in the main coupling have failed. He'll be able to make repairs in Craig but it will take several days at least." The reverend seemed pleased with himself—comfortable, George supposed, in having privileged information.

"Several days?" George asked.

The reverend said "yes," then continued walking down the covered deck with a peculiar pigeon-toed gait, looking for some other lucky soul to share his information with.

The steamship line served wine with a special dinner of salmon and halibut the night after the ship was taken to the wharf for repairs. Some of the passengers spoke of disembarking and finding other means to travel north. Although he knew he should be eager to get to Juneau and establish his headquarters for the search, George was secretly grateful for the time to spend in the village.

They had not been allowed to disembark that night while the ship was getting settled in for repairs. The next morning George got up early to clear customs and be one of the first ashore. He had planned to walk directly to the small boat harbor to see if any dories with a woman and girl had been seen down the coast. But as he turned the corner of the wharf onto the commercial street fronting the pier, he heard someone's voice rising above the clatter of cranes and carts rolling along the planks.

"Detective," a young man called out, and George turned. The red-faced boy was carrying a dispatch case slung over his shoulder and as he came to a stop he fumbled with it. "Detective Hanson, from Seattle?" the boy asked, straightening the front of his shirt.

George heard the young man's voice, but he did not respond right away. He knew the young man would have news from Seattle, and he didn't want news from Seattle. George was just realizing that news from Seattle was the thing he was trying to outrun onboard the steamship headed north.

"I have come from the territorial marshal's office in Ketchikan," the young man blurted out, and he stepped forward and tugged on the bottom of his suit coat in hopes of straightening out his appearance. "There are several telegrams here for you, and a package addressed to you came up on the plane. My chief wanted you to get them as soon as possible since the ship won't be in Ketchikan for some time."

"All right," George said, looking at the young man who continued to fidget with his uniform. "What's your name, son?" George asked in a calm voice.

"I'm Walter Tillman, sir."

"Good. I'm George," he said, and extended his hand. The young officer pumped George's hand up and down enthusiastically. Then they both stood silently for a moment. People getting off the ship pushed around them on the muddy street.

"Do you have something for me, Walter?"

"Oh . . . yes." He dug in the dispatch case to get out the papers. "Here you are, sir."

"Good," George said, taking the packet of papers. "Now, is there a place where we can sit and maybe get a cup of coffee? Policemen in Alaska do drink coffee, don't they, Walter?"

"Oh yes, sir. We can mug up across the street." The young man pointed timidly down the street, and gestured for George to walk ahead of him.

"Lead on," George said, and waved as if the young police officer were a sheepdog and he wanted him to work.

He opened the envelope Walter Tillman had given him, and the murder that had brought him north settled like a fog down the street. A folder was topped by a telegram from the captain and it was short: "See Ketchikan P.D. package, to follow."

They walked into the café that was in a log cabin slumped along the mud street of the village. The front windows were hazy with steam and the air inside smelled of grease and cigarettes.

There were two stools at the counter next to a narrow door back to the kitchen. Two men were eating breakfast and looked to be nursing hangovers. The waitress wore a white jumper with a red ribbon in her hair. The jumper was snug around her waist and the top two buttons of her blouse were undone. She smiled at the policemen as they entered, but her eyes lingered on young Walter as they sat down.

The young man was tongue-tied, leaving George to ask the waitress for two cups of coffee and two pieces of pie. George wanted to just sit and enjoy the day, but the envelope in his hand felt as heavy as lead. He undid the brown ribbon on the file folder, reached in, and took out the photographs and telegrams.

The police photographs spilled out on the red countertop. The waitress, who was rounding the corner from the kitchen, got a glimpse of the pictures as they spilled out. She sucked in her breath and turned away quickly. They were black-and-white photos of crime scenes: men with skulls caved in and distorted faces like stretched rubber masks, overturned rooms, phone cords wrapped around soft flesh, and blood that looked black in the overexposing flash. On the backs of the photographs were names, dates, and Party affiliation. Someone had been busting up the radicals in Seattle.

There was a handwritten note clipped to the last photograph from George's captain. "Sorry to mess up your vacation. Hell of a mess. You were right. Can't rely on the Fs. Find Ellie Hobbes and the man she is with. Bring them in alive and we might be able to straighten some of this out. All the best," and he signed his first name.

As George looked over the photographs, a dense sadness settled down through his head and into his chest. The waitress set his coffee down and he looked into the dark round reflection in the mouth of the cup.

"Was there anything else?" he asked Walter Tillman.

Walter reached into his pocket and took out a telegram. George read it while the young policeman awkwardly tried to chat up the waitress.

"Departed for Alaska May 29: William Pierce 32, dock boss / McCauley Conner, 29, stevedore. / Raymond Cobb, 31, club fighter. You have friends in common, but not for long.—Fatty."

"I can arrange a flight for you to Juneau if you like," Walter Tillman said.

"No," George said, "I'll stay on the ship a bit longer."

Ellie was almost blind with nausea. The throbbing pain in her hand spread up her arm and sluiced all over her body. She listened to the harmonic thrum of the radial engine. The wooden Vega had a single overhead wing held on to the main fuselage by means of a steel strut that coupled inside the main cabin. While flying the plane, Willie made a show of reaching around and tightening the nut half a twist.

Ellie was caught in the push-pull of agony and exhilaration and she seemed to be slipping into some giddy fever dream of the first time she had been up in a plane. She had been sixteen and the pilot had a gold tooth tucked back in his smile. The first lift of the plane away from the dusty field had almost made her pass out. She could see the shrinking barn and cars, the dumbstruck kids staring up into the air with their mouths open and their hands shading their eyes. She had never seen the river from the sky, how it wound like a snake across the flat land, how the sections of corn and wheat were cut into straight lines like a checkerboard. A part of her would always be airborne from that day forward.

Now she was in the Vega and the sensation was exquisite. Taking off from the sea was smoother than the rutted field in Spokane. The inlets flowed out beneath her and the plane stayed in the corridor between the mountains. Mountain bluffs fell away under the plane, giving her a heightened sense of vertigo. Willie turned in his seat and gave her a bag to throw up in and she used it.

The Lockheed Vega was traveling at more than a hundred miles per hour past the stone faces where ice still clung to high rock ledges. She felt as if she were standing on the lip of a cliff about to be pushed over. The plane lunged up over an ice cornice. Ellie dug her fingers into her legs. Then she threw up again. Willie turned around and yelled something to Ellie, but she only nodded her head that she understood when in fact she hadn't. The mountains passed by the wingtips of the Vega and Ellie's eyes tried to grab hold of them. All of the tethers between the earth and the sky seemed to be frayed, and she had the giddy, panicked exhilaration of being out of control. Blood dripped from her bandage and she scuffed at the droplets on the floor with her shoe.

The Vega buffeted up over another ridge and a huge expanse of water lay before them. Cumulus clouds sat fat-bellied and satisfied above the sea. Beneath them the ocean waves curled around the breaking rocks on the coastline. Three fishing boats rolled toward the north. They quickly slid under the wings of the plane and disappeared behind them.

They flew for an hour, and when Ketchikan came into sight Ellie leaned forward to see what to expect. A steamship sat at the pier and small boats cut across the channel. There was a church on the hill and cars were lumbering along the narrow waterfront road. White wooden buildings lay out in a small grid and tiny houses clung to the sides of a creek. It was a little wooden town set down on the spongy earth between the mountains and the sea. Ellie wondered how long the plane would be in town.

Willie swung around and yelled over the roar of the engine, "We'll land in the channel. You can get a cab up to the hospital. I'm going to get some fuel and groceries, then I'm going to take off. You check in with the customs people when you get to the hospital."

"When will you be coming back?" Ellie yelled.

Willie was looking straight ahead and picking his landing spot between the boats in the channel. "Don't know that I'll ever be back. Don't get up here all that much." He pulled the throttle back and nosed the plane down toward the water. As the water came closer, the weight in her stomach increased. There would be the hospital and questions, what names to use, and how to get back to Annabelle.

Ellie pushed back in her seat and felt the easy bump of the Vega's floats settling down on the water. Once the weight of the plane settled, Willie advanced the throttle and the big plane scooted on step across the water's surface toward a floatplane dock. He climbed out onto the float, took a line dangling from a strut, and tied it off to a dock cleat. He opened the passenger door and half carried Ellie down the ladder to the float, being careful not to get her blood on his jacket.

"Thanks," was all she could manage.

"No problem, Blondie. I'll ask around about you if I come back this way," he said, still flirting with the injured woman, as if that was the only context he had for conversation with a female.

"Yeah, great," Ellie said, and she let go of his arm.

"Oh, Christ," Willie said, as Ellie began to pitch headfirst onto the dock. The pilot lurched forward and caught her by the shoulders. "Jeeze . . . you're a mess," Willie said. Blood dripped from the bandages and Ellie's looked pale. "You want me to call an ambulance?"

"Don't go to the fucking trouble," Ellie said, and she lurched toward the ramp.

She walked south along the waterfront. No cabs came. When Ellie finally slumped down against a broken fence beside the harbor, a kid driving a beer truck stopped.

"Creek Street . . . Yvette," was all Ellie could say. And the kid gave her a lift.

Halfway to town Ellie let out a low moan when the kid shifted gears and lurched along the narrow street near the wharf. He was in a hurry because he didn't want to be caught with a dead whore in the boss's truck.

The next morning Slip sat in the dory with Annabelle and her empty birdcage. Slip was wedging his tool kit underneath the middle seat with his money tin safely in place. The damned yellow bird stood on the gunwales of the dory, peeping angrily as if every decision Slip made was the wrong one.

"Can you shut him up?" Slip asked the girl, who was squinting through her glasses at the chart.

"He won't go in his cage. I tried."

"He doesn't have to get in his cage. I just meant could he quiet down a little. It's hard to think."

Annabelle started whistling. It wasn't a tune so much as a meandering kind of warble that eventually settled into a sort of tune, and the bird began to sing along in his own way.

The two of them trilled away as Slip pulled on the oars and they glided past the waterfall. No one waved to them from the cannery. The kid who ran the hoist to lower the dory back into the water didn't wait around to watch them go but had to get back to the line. Fishing boats were starting to come in more regularly now and the foremen were pushing their crews hard.

They passed their cabin and then the Filipino bunkhouse and the Chinese. A few women were hanging out laundry on the lines along the side of the house but no one bothered to wave. They swung wide past the Native encampment where some of the boys were rolling a barrel hoop along the ground. It toppled and spun on the hard-packed ground and the boys laughed, then stopped to look out at the dory. One of them recognized Annabelle and he waved frantically. Annabelle waved back.

Out toward the point of the Native encampment an old woman stood with a couple of sealed buckets on each side of her. She waved to the dory and motioned them to come in to the beach. Slip thought that perhaps she had some news from the camp, and he brought the dory in close to the beach. The closer he got, the more she urged him on with her gestures. When he got close enough, she threw the buckets into the dory and jumped into the boat with surprising agility.

"Okay," she said, and she pointed to the north.

"I'm sorry, ma'am, but we're headed out. We've been thrown out of camp. We can't take you anywhere," Slip said, in a voice that was too loud.

"Okay," the woman said, gesturing north and smiling at Annabelle. The bird whistled and cheeped. The old woman clapped her hands together and laughed when she saw the yellow bird standing on the gunwale.

"It's okay. Just go." Annabelle waved forward and Slip started to pull. The old woman gathered her pails together and put them in front of her feet. Then she lifted the canvas tent and put it behind her and settled comfortably into the stern of the dory. She was as dark as oiled walnut and her cheeks hung like coin purses on each side of her face. She was speaking in a language that Slip had never heard, but the tone was friendly and conversational. She pointed, laughed, and pointed some more. It became clear that she was explaining where they were going and Slip kept pulling.

At the mouth of the bay a strong current was pulling down the inlet. The rocks at the point jutted up into the current as if they were sitting in the middle of a slow-moving river, and a small wake spread out in a V from the rocks. The old woman gestured around the corner of the bay in the direction of the current. She kept talking and as she did Slip began to fear that perhaps she was feeble and didn't know where she was. Annabelle sat in front of her and watched the old woman intently as if she could understand every word of what was being said.

"She's talking to you," Slip said to the girl.

"I think she's talking to Buddy," the girl said, and sure enough the old woman turned her head and it was possible that she was addressing the yellow bird.

It was a calm morning with high overcast that sank down over the tops of the mountains on each side of the narrow inlet. It almost seemed that the Inside Passage had been tented over so that once they came around the point, the waterway ahead seemed like a long hallway.

The old woman wore a man's wool jacket and a long cotton skirt. Her head was wrapped in a blue scarf that set off her dark skin. She was speaking louder now and she gestured toward the middle of the inlet. As he pulled, Slip could feel the tug of the current carrying the dory along faster than the pull of the oars. Once out in the center of the channel, she nodded and gestured straight down the middle, then she sat back and surveyed the dory and the water around her calmly, almost imperiously, as if she were being borne along by her minions. Slip pulled on the oars and she nodded and muttered a few syllables but said nothing more.

It was almost eerily calm, the surface of the water was oily, and whatever wind there was came from the stern so that the sensation of movement was muted. The boat could have been flying, carried aloft by the rhythm of the oars. A puff of breath came from the port side as a seal bobbed to the surface. The animal raised its head to watch the dory. Slip turned and watched as he rowed. The animal's dark eyes sparkled with intelligence so that its face took on a weird kind of humanness.

"How long will it take to get to Ketchikan?" Annabelle asked. She watched the rings of water where the seal had disappeared.

"I don't know," Slip said. "I guess it depends on the weather and whether anybody gives us a ride."

"There's a section on the chart where it looks like we have to go out into the big ocean." Annabelle was squinting down at the chart.

"We'll skirt along the shore," Slip said.

"That would take a heck of a lot longer, I think."

"Well, if the weather's good we'll row all night if we have to. If not we'll just go ashore and wait for the right weather to come along. We've got enough food, don't you think?"

"Boy, I guess," Annabelle said. She reached into the basket under the tarp in the middle of the boat and pulled out a cinnamon roll. "You want a piece?" She held out the roll to Slip, who shook his head no. Then Annabelle split the roll in half and held it out to the woman in the stern of the boat. The woman took the roll, nodded, and bit into it. She smiled and chewed, holding up the piece of roll in a gesture of thanks to Annabelle.

The morning passed and the sunlight stabbed off the water so that Slip had to squint to keep his eyes open. The old woman gestured toward the western shore of the inlet. Slip ignored her and kept pulling on the oars. The girl and the yellow bird sat chatting at the side of the boat, and the old woman chuckled from time to time. Slip pulled and his body warmed with sweat as his muscles seemed to oil up, and he began to feel good about the day.

Then he looked to the sides of the inlet and he saw that his progress had slowed. Where once they were making a fair passage along the inlet, they were now slowing down. He had been pulling toward a rockslide to the north for some time, and when he looked over his shoulder the rockslide seemed no closer. They could have drifted backward for all he could tell. The old woman gestured to the western shore again, and she made a rowing motion with her arms. George pulled to the west, and as he came closer to shore he felt the pull of the current taking them north. The woman smiled

and leaned back. She reached forward and held out her finger to
the yellow bird and the feisty thing pecked at the finger. She leaned
back and frowned. Then Buddy hopped onto Annabelle's finger
and the two of them laughed at the bird.

The dory rounded the northern point where the current was
running nicely. They came to the mouth of another bay and the old
woman stood up and picked up her buckets. Slip thought she was
going to step right out of the boat. She was looking over the bow,
and Slip turned around. There in the middle of the bay was a canoe
with two men in it. She pointed, called out to the men in the canoe,
and they waved in return. Slip rowed toward them. They had been
out on the water some three hours now.

As they got closer Slip could see there was an old man with
someone much younger. They were pulling line hand over hand
from the sea into their canoe. Slip could see the tails of several
large fish sticking into the air. The woman called out and held up
the buckets. The two men looked almost embarrassed, yet happy
nonetheless.

As they pulled alongside, the young man said, "Grandma, we
made a lunch. We're fine." The old woman crawled across the gunwales and stepped into the canoe, which was surprisingly stable for
so narrow a boat.

"My grandmother worries about us. But we're fine really,"
the young man said to Slip. "She thinks we're getting too thin."

The old woman sat in the stern of the canoe and handed food
out. Slices of dried fish wrapped in cloth and some berry cobbler
in a pan. She was speaking in an animated way to the man Slip
assumed was her husband. She pointed at the dory and the old man
shot back his comments quickly as if he were not even considering
her arguments.

"What are they saying?" Annabelle asked.

The young man was holding on to the gunwale of the dory
now. He had tied off the line he had been pulling from the bottom.

He turned and looked at his grandparents. "Oh, he's saying that she shouldn't have come. That she didn't know anything about you. She's saying that you got fired from the cannery for eating with the Filipinos. She said she knew that you were headed north to meet up with your friend who hurt her hand and flew out yesterday. She knew just where you were going and thought she could catch a ride."

"We were glad to do it. I just had no idea how long she'd be with us."

The grandson laughed. "You thought you had just inherited an old lady?"

"I didn't know for sure." Slip grinned, and leaned back on the seat and stretched his arms.

"What are they talking about now?" Annabelle asked.

"My grandpa is asking about your bird."

"What is she telling him?" Annabelle looked over at Buddy.

The grandson paused, not sure how to translate, or whether to translate at all. "She's saying that it's some kind of white man's bird. She's saying that it's a pretty thing but probably wouldn't taste like much to eat. That it doesn't really live anywhere but white people keep them just the same."

"What's he saying now?" Annabelle asked.

The grandson bowed his head. "Oh, he's just an old man."

"But what's he saying?" Annabelle was looking at Buddy, strutting back and forth across the top of his cage.

"My grandpa says your bird isn't smart enough to fly away."

"Oh, don't listen," Annabelle cooed to Buddy.

"They don't mean harm. She's grateful for the ride."

"That's all right. He's right about the bird too," Slip said, and started to fix the oars in the locks.

"Here," the young man said, and he spoke with his grandfather for a moment and then dug around in the bottom of the canoe.

"Take this with you." And he slung a small halibut into the dory.

"Appreciate it," Slip said. "Can you tell me the best way to cross Dixon Entrance?"

The young man stared at Slip, then at Annabelle. "In a steamship," he said.

"Thanks for the tip." Slip smiled, and then he began pulling away.

"Wait for the weather," the young man called out. "If it's sunny like this, wait behind an island until the north wind stops blowing. Just when it starts to change, get an early start and go like hell."

Both Slip and Annabelle thanked him, and Slip rowed north. Buddy flew up and away from the dory. Annabelle reached out to grab him but missed. He flew up in a wide arc and around the canoe three times and then settled back on top of his cage, where he could get a peek at himself in the shiny bell.

The long inlet offered few beaches or anchorages. Slip rowed for hours until his back and arms began to ache and then seize into a spasm. They were in a section of the inlet where the current was running steadily to the north along the shore. Slip lay down in the front of the dory and Annabelle swept the oars through the water keeping the dory heading north. She sang to her yellow bird and watched the dappled sunlight along the rocky shore. As soon as the last of the fair current had turned against them, they tried to anchor but the anchor line hung straight down in the water never finding bottom. Even when they were close enough to the rock walls that Annabelle could reach out and pick a white wildflower from a patch of moss, the sixty feet of anchor line still never touched bottom. After an hour, the current began to push them backward and Slip rowed over to a tree that had fallen down a rock chute and was cantilevered over the water. Slip was able to tie to the tree with a long line for the night.

The moon rose late and even though the twilight was long, the fjord cooled off quickly. Annabelle and Slip wrapped themselves in blankets and then in the tarp. The dory rocked gently in the current as they made themselves comfortable in the boat.

"You think Ellie is going to be okay?" she asked.

"Yeah, I think she's going to be fine." Slip rolled over and the dory rocked a bit.

"You think she got to fly the airplane, even for a little bit?" the girl asked.

"She was pretty sick honey, but . . . I don't know. It wouldn't surprise me if she talked that guy into letting her fly a little." Slip laughed, as he curled as deep as he could into the warmth of the blanket.

Yvette's establishment was a sad excuse for a whorehouse. It was a sagging wood-frame house that smelled predominantly of sweat on wet wool. The flooring was soft and the walls were thin. Even before she woke up on that stinking parlor divan, she knew exactly where she was when she smelled talcum powder and mildew.

At first Yvette wasn't about to give up a room, but when she saw Ellie's bleeding hand drooped over the truck driver's shoulder she softened. When the injured girl mentioned Clyde's name, Yvette knew she didn't have a choice. Clyde had helped her out of a jam in Tacoma years ago. She had seen worse trouble since, but Clyde had saved her from a stint in jail and she had never paid him back.

"If she dies, we throw her out with the trash. You understand?" Yvette said to the kid, as he plopped Ellie down on the parlor divan.

"Don't matter a goddamn to me," the kid said. He wiped his hands down the front of his pants and took off without looking around the room.

She called herself Yvette but her real name was Carol. She wasn't showing sympathy by letting Ellie sleep in a small back room. It was purely a business decision. If she died, there wouldn't be much expense to that, and if she got better quickly, this girl would owe her something. Having a pretty girl in her debt was always a good thing.

The parlor was cramped and the floral pattern on the wall-paper was water-stained and splotched with mold. Wet wood hissed in the woodstove while two anemic girls with dark circles under their eyes smoked cigarettes and played cribbage next to an open window. A fisherman was passed out in an overstuffed chair. He was wearing wool pants and suspenders over his bare chest. His whiskers lay against his chest and looked to be spotted with vomit.

"Have John get him dressed and out the door. He's bad for business, stinking up the place," Yvette called to one of the girls, who took a drag on her cigarette and then counted out her points before even acknowledging her boss's voice.

Then Yvette turned to Ellie. "Okay. I can make more money on this room if I let a girl work it, but I can let you have it for ten dollars a night."

Ellie reached into her pants pocket and gave the madam a quarter. "That's what I got right now," she said.

"It's a start," Yvette said. "I've got a doctor who will come and take a look at your hand. I'm assuming you don't want to go to the hospital."

Ellie nodded in agreement.

"I don't blame you. I got a doctor who is pretty much sober. He looks after all my girls. I'll add whatever his bill will be to your bill here. What you can't pay, you work off, you understand?" She stared hard at Ellie.

Ellie nodded.

"Good," said Yvette.

"I'll clean up shit," Ellie said, fighting back the urge to throw up again. "But I'm not fucking anybody for thin wages." She was slurring her words and going in and out of consciousness, and this was the only reason Yvette even listened to her foolishness.

"I suppose we'll just see about that," Yvette said, with one hand on her hip. "Let's get you upstairs and out of sight. You're worse for business than that pig John just lugged out of here."

Blood dripped from her bandages as they pulled her down the hall. The blood looked black under the bare lightbulbs spaced down the hall. The lights throbbed with intensity as if they were keeping time with the motion of rusty springs behind the doors.

Yvette opened a door where there was just enough room for a bed and a nightstand. After Ellie flopped on top of the coverlet, the madam turned to a skinny girl who stood in the hall with her arms folded over her housecoat. "She's going to die. So don't get used to having her around, honey." The skinny girl shrugged and walked back down the hall.

Doctor Williams had a drunkard's nose, which looked like a tender testicle. He wore a rumpled black suit and his breath smelled of cigars. When he first walked in, he stumbled over the end of the bed and pain flared through Ellie's hand. He stood at the side of her bed jingling the change in his right pocket. Ellie thought he was going to say something dismissive or make a pronouncement, but without preamble he started to work on her hand.

First he washed his hands and used an alcohol rub on them. Then he cleaned Ellie's hand tenderly. She was in and out now, feverish and sweating. Her face was as pale as the threadbare sheet she lay on. The doctor asked for another light, and one of the little whores fetched a lamp from the parlor and set it on the nightstand. When the doctor used what appeared to be gardening shears to trim the ragged bone and flesh around the wound, Ellie cried out, with pitiful sobs she had been holding back ever since the machine had clamped down on her hand. The doctor folded a piece of cloth and placed it over her nose and dripped two drops of ether on it. Then he handed the bottle to the girl, who stood by Ellie's head and continued dripping ether onto the cloth.

Doc Williams did not engage in conversation while he worked. He murmured to himself, "Poor hand. Goddamn shame. Poor broken hand." Once he asked for a glass of water and Yvette brought him some cool water from the tap. He thanked her and took a long drink. Then he smiled at her and said, "Thirsty work," and turned his attention back to Ellie.

The left hand was swollen and blue-black, turning a sickly yellow up the arm. The doctor pulled and sutured the skin around the trimmed stubs. He cleaned after every step and cleaned again. He asked for a bucket of ice to be brought up, and John, a big black man, came in a few minutes with a champagne bucket filled with shaved ice from the fish house. The doctor then wrapped Ellie's hand with gauze, and then he cut a piece of a rubber sheet, which he laid on top of the ice. He made sure to get the ether back from the little whore, who slunk out of the room like a house cat, leaving only John standing by the bed like the shadow of a church tower.

"She won't need this," he said to the big black man holding up the ether. "Let her lay the hand on top of the ice for tonight. It might help with the swelling. And give her one of these." He poured a tablet out onto his palm. "I will come tomorrow with more tablets. She may cry out or have strange dreams. She's feverish. But don't get too excited. If she doesn't come around by morning or if she starts getting more pale and taking real shallow breaths, send around for me. I'll come."

"Yes," John said.

"She's pretty beat up. But it looks like she's been beat up before." He rolled down his shirtsleeves and put his jacket back on. The black man went to attend to some girl crying down the hall, and the doctor kicked a flimsy chair into place and sat by the bed.

In a few minutes Ellie opened her eyes.

"Good evening," the doctor said, with evident pleasure in her company.

"If you say so," Ellie managed.

"Yvette says you are not a working girl." He was standing now.

"No," Ellie said, as she watched him open his black bag.

"That's a sound decision. These girls don't prosper for long." He took the tools and wiped them with a clean rag and put them on top of his black bag. Then he wiped his hands on one of Yvette's clean hand towels.

"Would you consider having a drink with an old man?"

"If we can have it up here," Ellie said.

"You're in no shape to go anywhere anyway," he said, watching Ellie lifting up her tender hand from the ice.

"Where are my fingers?" she asked, confused and forgetting that she had thrown them into the sea.

"I suppose wherever you left them," the doctor smiled.

"How about that drink?" she coughed out.

"Of course. I believe I have a bottle of port stored here. I will bring us some glasses."

Ellie closed her eyes as he left the room and didn't remember him coming back. She only remembered waking up with a glass in her right hand.

She sipped slowly. Her right hand shook violently but she was able to crane her neck forward to take in a bit of the sweet liquor. She closed her eyes and listened as the doctor talked about the rain in Ketchikan and the things he missed by living there. He had once lived in San Francisco and he missed the musical theater and the lecture halls. He missed the smell of eucalyptus in the early mornings and the taste of ripe yellow pears. They drank their port and Ellie told him about the qualities of the Lockheed Vega. She told him everything she knew about Amelia Earhart and of her own desire to fly around the world.

"What would you do on such a trip?" the doctor asked, as he poured her another glass of port.

"I would just look down on everything." Ellie beamed drunk-enly though she had only sipped her second drink, and the doctor smiled.

He downed the last of his drink, then slapped his thighs and stood up. "I'm going to totter home. It was a pleasure speaking with you. I'm sure I'll see you tomorrow." Just as he was about to walk through the door he turned back and said, "I'm sorry but I never asked your name. Would you mind telling me? I'd rather keep you in my books by name, seeing as you're not one of Yvette's girls, which is how I usually note them down."

"Ellie Hobbes," she said, flush with port and good feeling toward the doctor.

"Really? Ellie Hobbes?" he said, and he scratched the top of his head before putting on his hat. "I know that name for some reason. No. Wait. There was somebody asking after you," he said.

"Really?" Ellie's voice cracked slightly. All of the good will she had felt for the doctor was chilling in her bones. "Who?"

"I'm not sure, but it was someone who was downstairs this morning . . . uh . . . taking advantage of the services here."

SEVENTEEN

~~~

Slip woke up before the sun appeared over the ridge. The dory was dawdling at the end of its tether. The sky was the color of lead, with a few clouds smeared across the tops of the ridges. His arms ached and his hands felt numb. It was the rowing, he thought, and the repetitive motion of swinging the maul on the piling crew. Each morning now his arms ached and he would have to throw his hands over his head and shake them to get the feeling back.

Annabelle was sleeping under the tarp and the yellow bird sat hunched in his damp feathers under the forward thwart. The dory had swung under the overhanging tree during the night as the tide turned, and now the current was running north. There was a slight breeze from the south and the dory pulled against its painter line. The tide was lower now than it had been when they had first tied up for the night, so the line hung at a right angle to the water and was tied high over Slip's head.

He was in no hurry to be going except for the fact that the current and the wind were fair and the combination of the two would make for some good headway to the north. He dug down into the food trunk and found one of the sweet rolls Annabelle had stored away, and he ate one as the dory tugged on the painter line and the sun eased up above the ridge.

The immediate problem was that the end of the painter line was almost a foot beyond his reach. He could pull the dory so that it was directly under it, but he could not reach the knot that he had tied so easily when the tide was higher. The wind was building and everything in the inlet seemed to be wanting to push them on their way. Slip pulled on the rope and lifted his feet just a few inches clear of the rowing seat. He reached the knot but the boat drifted back so quickly that he was hanging above the water.

"Annabelle," he said, "honey, can you give me a hand here?" Only the yellow bird responded by poking his head out and scowling at Slip, giving a short noncommittal peep.

Slip bent himself in half and wrapped his legs around the trunk of the overhanging tree. The tree bobbed a bit with his weight but seemed solidly wedged between its torn root wad and a sturdy outcropping of granite that kept it from falling into the inlet. Now Slip hung like a dead monkey being carried back to camp by porters.

"Annabelle. Wake up. I need a hand."

Again, only Buddy responded with an indifferent peep.

The sides of the inlet at this spot were near vertical and so smooth that it was impossible to go to shore. He was able to hook one of his legs around a limb of the snag and leverage himself onto the upper side of the log. Now he sat astride the log as if it were a pony.

"Slip? What are you doing up there?" The sleepy girl was sitting upright, rubbing her eyes, with the tarp still wrapped around her shoulders.

"I'm in a fix. Can you row the boat so that it's underneath me? I'll untie the line and then drop into the boat. Just pull as hard as you can and row up underneath me."

She looked up at him as if he were some improbable figure from a dream she might still be in the middle of. She rubbed her eyes once more, then lay down in the boat and pulled the tarp up over her shoulders.

"Hey now, listen, I'm serious. Wake up," Slip called down from his perch, and the girl sat up again with the same expression of sleepy surprise to be back in the same dream.

Eventually she rustled around and got the long oars in the oarlocks. The wind continued to pick up and the waves coming down the inlet were building. She pulled on the oars but could make no steady headway. What she gained into the wind with one stroke was taken away during her glide back for the next one. The boat barely jogged against the painter line. Slip finally untied the painter line from the snag and was able to jerk the line so that the bow of the dory swung directly under him for a moment. He told her to row as hard as she could to keep the boat moving toward him. He would jerk on the line and then lower himself back into the dory before it drifted downwind.

"Are you ready? One . . . two . . . three!"

Annabelle pulled on the long oars and Slip jerked the rope. The dory slid more than halfway under the snag and Slip scrambled to lower himself down into the boat. Annabelle took short fast strokes with the oars, splashing the water and straining as hard as she could. Slip rolled under the tree and dangled just inches above the boat for a moment. But a gust rumbled down the inlet and the dory moved off. The sleeve of Slip's coat was tangled in both the tree limbs and the dory's painter line. The dory eased downwind.

"Pull on the line," he called out, and the girl set the oars down with a clatter and pulled on the line to bring the boat back under the dangling man. With one hard tug the painter line snapped the twigs in the snag and zipped past the fabric of Slip's sleeve. The end of the line fell in the water, and the dory went drifting away from his kicking feet.

"We can try it again!" he called out to her through the bluster-ing wind. "Just row up underneath me."

She scrambled back to her seat and picked up the ungainly oars once again. The dory wallowed in the waves and the wind pushed the bow toward the middle of the inlet.

"Pull, honey. You can do it."

But of course she couldn't, and by the time Slip saw that it was impossible for her to row back to him, she had drifted so far he knew he would not be able to swim to her. He knew enough from his recent experience to know that the cold water had a way of gripping his muscles in a kind of seizure. He might be able to survive in the water for half an hour or so but he would never be able to make up the difference between himself and the wind and current-borne dory.

"Slip!" the girl called out. "What should I do?" Her voice was becoming faint in the rumble of wind but he could hear the shrill edge of panic in her voice.

"Don't do anything crazy," he shouted.

"Yeah . . . like crawl up into a tree," the girl yelled back, obvi-ously angry to be left alone in the moving boat.

Slip waved to her as she shrank into the distance, and he could barely make her out as she waved back.

A shipping agent came into the little café and informed George Hanson that the *Admiral Rodman* would be delayed at least seven days and perhaps ten. Parts were not available locally and would have to be found, then flown up from Seattle or Vancouver. It was regrettable, the agent said, but there was nothing to be done.

Walter Tillman offered to fly George anywhere he wanted and George knew that would be the responsible thing to do. But he thanked Walter Tillman and sent him on his way. George said that he would do his best looking for the dory there in Craig. He would ask around, he said, and would be in contact with Walter as soon as he made landfall in Juneau.

Young Walter Tillman looked at George and said, "You won't get much out of these folks here, sir. They're a hard bunch." George smiled at the young man and thought that surely his experience would count for something.

But in the next few days George discovered that the young man was right. He walked the docks and drank coffee and tried to talk with the fishermen and beach loggers, but all he got was a series of courteous dismissals. When he asked about the small dory and the girl with the yellow bird, the conversations went dead.

The Indian people he spoke with gave him nothing at all, denying any understanding of his questions but giving him the impression of full cooperation. The white people simply turned him off. After the first such interactions George began to see something familiar about these folks tucked back along the wild coast. There was something of the Big Finn in all of them: the wariness of authority and a stiff-necked defensiveness around anyone who dressed in expensive clothes and asked questions without a long and proper introduction.

Then George remembered the history his father had taught him. After the Centralia debacle back in 1919, the state of Washington had started enforcing the Sedition Laws. Anyone could go to jail for ten years for just having once been a member of the IWW. Anyone found with a Red card or a pennant with the words ONE BIG UNION emblazoned across the fabric could be arrested. The Big Finn kept no radical materials either on his person or in his home. He stayed in Washington and kept the fire alive. But many of the most public of the radicals began to scatter. There was more than one island off the wild north coast that held old seditionists. They fished, and strung radio antennas above their cabins to pull in the scores of the distant ball games, and they kept to themselves. The islands around Craig had a fairly high density of hermits and folks with new names and histories, and their neighbors knew to give them both their privacy and their loyalty.

During George's days in Craig, the weather was fair with only a few showers blowing through. He stayed on the ship, where he ate meals of fresh fish and crab that the galley prepared to keep everyone's spirits high. George even rented a small skiff and a fishing pole to spend days out on the water, telling himself he was looking for the dory with the little girl and the yellow bird. But in fact he was not looking for anything that reminded him of Seattle and the corpses there.

William Pierce and McCauley Conner had indeed been drinking downstairs in Yvette's sporting house, while Ray Cobb was eating at a soda fountain down the creek. They had gotten a ride on a fish-packing boat that left Craig the same afternoon the *Admiral Rodman* had arrived.

The three men were an ill-suited bunch, dirty and mismatched. Pierce had a certain stiff-spined dignity. He was tall and he stood up straight and appeared to always be scouting the space around him. Conner was a rheumy-eyed dreamer who always had at least half his attention turned inward. He stood with a slouch as if he were looking for something to lean up against. Cobb was a short cairn of hard-packed flesh and muscle. Wherever he stopped he seemed to be affixed to that one spot until some stimulus, food usually, would tip his bulk forward and he would shamble back into motion.

David Kept had been a good friend to the members of his local. He had gotten them more money and had kept them focused on attainable goals that seemed to grow closer with each month. Kept had stood on the bull rails and made the members only promises that they all could keep, and they had believed him because their lives continued to improve under his leadership. There were better money and predictable hours, fairness in the hiring hall, and no special treatment for "friends of friends" from the outside. David Kept ran a good shop and he was well liked by a group of working men who had no other friends like him.

So when his body was found in the trunk of the Lincoln, the membership commissioned its own investigation. The national office wanted to work through the police, but the boys on the docks were in a hurry. Besides, no one trusted the police. Even if David Kept had made inroads with the local cops, the boys boosting the bales and slings had no more use for the cops than they did for a dose of the clap. They would handle it themselves without the police and without the Floodwater boys who oiled through every public meeting and informal gathering. Even though David Kept had no wife or children, he had family . . . and they would take care of his interests now.

So as Ellie had been flying over the mountains in the Vega and Slip had been packing his and Annabelle's belongings for their dory ride north, William Pierce and McCauley Conner were lying naked on either side of a sleeping whore named Beatrice. Ray Cobb was down the street drinking one glass of soda water after another and belching so loudly that some of the patrons were moved to complain.

"Christ, I miss my home," Conner said, his skinny hairless shin draped over the sleeping woman's backside.

"Listen to you. You got a bed and money in your pocket. Hell, there're men all over the world who would envy us."

"I still wish I was someplace else. Doing something else." And he rolled over onto his side, away from the girl, who stirred slightly and murmured something from her dreams.

"This is different from the usual. I grant you that. But it's got to be done. You said so yourself when it first came up." Bill Pierce was stroking Beatrice's neck, hoping she'd stay asleep. Even though the men had bathed the night before, the sheets were still sooty with coal dust and smelled of fish oil. Bill wiped his nose. "You said so yourself," he repeated.

Out the open window they heard an airplane passing overhead.

"I know what I said, but goddamn, Bill."

"We're just going to take her and the kid back south." Pierce spoke softly, rubbing the white skin of the woman's thigh.

"Why'd we have to bring Cobb, anyway?" Conner asked. "I thought he was going to die down there in the bottom of the ship."

"Cobb insisted he come along. He says he's got more reason to stick up for Dave than anybody."

"I don't like him," Conner said, and the girl began to stir. "He's got too big an appetite or something. I don't know." Conner brushed dark hair away from the girl's face.

Pierce sat up on the edge of the bed. "We'll keep an eye on him. We'll get this done and be home."

"No killing. You sure of that?" Conner put his hand against the girl's cheek.

"Not if it can be avoided." Pierce pulled up his pants.

"God, I miss my home," Conner said. Then he kissed the girl and she opened her eyes and smiled.

Ellie stayed feverish for several days. She drank water and nibbled on stale bread that John brought to her from the restaurant down the street. On the third day he brought a proper dinner —rice, fish, and onions—and it was hot and had a fine hint of salt and ginger.

The whorehouse was quieter than Ellie had expected. There were footsteps padding down the hall, creaking floors, and the continued opening and closing of doors. If she listened she could hear the creaking of the box springs and the murmur of women's voices uttering encouragements. Outside, the noisy creek became silent twice a day as the tide came up high enough to fill the narrow rock basin with seawater. She started using the tides as a clock to keep track of the day. On the fourth day she used a radio telephone downtown to call the flight service in Campbell River, trying to get news from the cannery, but all she could find out was that Slip and the girl were no longer there. The phone line hissed and popped, and when the flight service secretary slammed down the receiver, the silence on the line scared her.

Yvette changed Ellie's bandages once a day, and each time she gave the invalid one more day before she would have to start turning tricks. Ellie shook her head and said she wouldn't, and Yvette would threaten to throw her out and Ellie dared her to. Yvette would storm out of the room leaving an angry wake of silence. Then Ellie would walk down the backstairs to help John and the crippled Chinese girl with the laundry.

On some afternoons while she waited for sheets to dry, she read magazines on the porch. Sometimes Doc Williams would come to check on her and they might drink a glass of red wine and visit about the news of the day. Williams liked to converse, which was fortunate because he was good at it. He favored art and politics. He liked Roosevelt and the New Deal. Ellie avoided politics but was happy to listen to him talk about French painting and German composers. Sometimes during their conversations she dozed off with her head propped against the porch railing, dreaming of music she had never heard.

Some men came into the whorehouse early in the day. They usually walked quickly and ducked into doorways hoping no one would notice them. Late at night men would sometimes come in groups, arm in arm and singing. Judging by what she could hear through the thin walls, the quiet men during the middle of the day were more voluble in the rooms with the girls. They would sometimes call out names or begin to plead and order specific attentions. Once she heard a man, visiting at what must have been his lunch hour, recite the Lord's Prayer as he made the bed frame rattle against the wall.

The louder party boys were generally quieter once they came upstairs. Many of them, she suspected, were essentially scared of women and hence the need for the big show out on the sidewalks. But occasionally these party boys became violent, and John would bound up the stairs and, with a thudding of their bare heels on the uneven floor, the big black man hauled them outside as if they were sacks of coal. Doc Williams would come then and soothe the girls with paregoric, or morphine if the injuries were serious enough. Most often he calmed them by simply sitting at their bedsides, listening to them talk about their fears and about their plans for their future.

"There'll be far too many millinery shops in the world if all of these girls were to achieve their dreams," he told Ellie.

Mindful of her need to repay Yvette, Ellie found ways to be useful. She carried coal for John or she helped the girls with the laundry. When they were blue she would sit and play cards with them or simply listen to their rambling stories. They were decent girls, mostly immigrants from Europe, sturdy girls who seemed to bruise easily but didn't enjoy complaining. Their given names were often long and difficult to pronounce so they adopted American names with their customers. They were Betty or Sally and sometimes Claudine upstairs, but playing cards back in the kitchen or running their clothes through the ringer washer, they would call each other the pet names of their youth. They smoked hand-rolled cigarettes and drank whiskey from their own clean glasses and talked of the lives they had left behind in Budapest, Prague, or Dublin—the dirty stone streets and the roofs that leaked. All the while the rain pattered down on the shake roofs of Ketchikan and the lonely men queued up under the clogged, overflowing gutters until Yvette let them in.

It was there that Ellie brought up the idea of forming a trade union. "It would be the most powerful union on earth," she said. "Imagine a strike. My God, what a beautiful idea. Jesus, girls, imagine it."

"The wives would be the first to beg us to come back," a sad-eyed girl spoke up.

"Explain to me why you need Yvette," Ellie asked the girl named Petroska.

"Shut up, Ellie. You'll get us bounced out of here," another whore called out from the porch, where she was helping Alice wring out her second load of sheets for the day.

"I'm just asking. I like Yvette as much as any man."

"Any man?" Petroska asked with a smile.

"Perhaps not any man. But I like her, and I can understand why you like her too. But she gets paid for being generous to you. When you are generous to her, it comes out of your pocket, and when she is generous to you it *also* comes out of your pocket. That's all I'm saying."

"You'll get these girls in trouble," John said, smiling. He was turning the crank on the old wringer and feeding a wet sheet through.

"These girls are already in trouble. That's all I'm saying." Ellie made an emphatic gesture with her left hand and it bumped the edge of the table. Wincing in pain, she pulled her arm back and cradled it against her chest. "Damn!" Her eyes were clamped shut and tears squirted out the corners.

"Poor baby." Petroska patted her cheek with a pale hand. "Poor Ellie. There will be no revolution in America," she said, as if she were comforting a baby.

"Why's that?" Ellie shot back, still cradling her throbbing hand.

"Because Americans are children. They could not endure a revolution. Trust me, Ellie, this I know for sure. Americans are babies, big and fat and happy. There is no revolution for such people."

"You haven't seen much of the Depression over here."

"Pagh! This is nothing. This is as bad as it's been and it's still wonderful. No, sweetheart. No revolution. You should try selling something else."

"What, silk stockings and tractor parts?" Ellie did not like being condescended to by a whore. A whore who was being exploited whether she knew it or not.

"I like silk socks. Very good," the Russian girl said.

"All right, you two, enough. Help me with these sheets," John called out. He had a basket of laundry and was backing up against the door to hang it out to dry along the side porch of the building that had a wide eave and got springtime sun. Most of the laundry for the house was picked up by a Finn to be done over at the steam laundry in town, but Yvette charged the girls for that service so many of them paid John a lower rate to save a few dollars. Ellie pushed against the back door with her back and stepped out onto the porch. John set the wet laundry down and walked back inside.

"Hang it, then you can come back. I'll make us some coffee and I'll take a look at that hand again."

"You know what I'm talking about, don't you, John?"

"I do," he said, "and I agree. But the laundry needs doing." He turned to her with a smile. "Then I'll change that bandage for you, comrade." The door swung shut.

It was afternoon and a soft rain was falling. The clogged gutters continued to drip thirty feet onto the low-tide rocks of the creek bed. Ellie walked toward the front of the house, listening to the patter of rain on the boardwalk.

She was reaching for the first clothespin when a large, dirty hand reached around and covered her mouth. At first she screamed but the hand clamped down harder and pinched off her nostrils. Then she bit down hard onto the fleshy hand, which tasted like coal dust. The owner of the hand let out a hissing sound and someone slugged her in the stomach hard enough for her to black out for a moment.

"Let her breathe, Ray," someone said, and when she opened her eyes she recognized William Pierce and McCauley Conner standing just in under the dripping eaves.

Ellie tried to kick Pierce in the crotch but whoever was behind her choked off her air again, and all she could sense were her heels hitting the top of the steps as someone dragged her off the porch.

≈≈≈

Annabelle pulled against the big oars but they were awkward in her hands. When she did manage to get a good bite into the water with both of them, the combination of the wind and the current continued to push her down the inlet, away from Slip hanging on the tree.

Buddy sat on top of his cage, ruffling his feathers and calling out in his high irritating voice. The girl pulled on the oars and looked at the yellow bird with the bright red spots on his cheeks. She watched him and dreamed of being able to fly. The ends of the oars skittered over the top of the water and she splashed the stern of the boat. Buddy shook himself and started to fly.

She watched him fly in wide circles around the boat, dipping toward the water and it looked as if he were mesmerized by his own reflection. He was like a bolt of tropical sunlight in this muted gray-green world. The circles got bigger and bigger around the boat.

"Buddy," the girl called out softly, short of breath. "Hey, over here."

But the vain yellow bird, for whatever reason, flew away. He rose up into the canopy of tall trees and disappeared like a spark.

Slip sat very still. He knew that if he fell in the water there was a good chance that he would be able to claw his way up onto the face of the rock. There were ledges, after all; some ferns grew out of the rock and somehow this tree had taken root before it had fallen over. Or he could cling to the rock so that he might not die in the cold water. But still, he would not be able to go anywhere. His only real hope was that there would be a passing boat that would see him and somehow offer help.

A kingfisher flickered up to him and settled on the snag. He looked at the bird and tried to imagine changing places. He thought of flying out over the water and into the wheelhouse of a warm boat, where there was coffee boiling over on the metal grates and the cook had bread in the oven. Slip thought of Johnny on the *Pacific Pride* and wanted nothing so much as to see its black hull push around the point and come over to him so that he could simply step off the snag and onto the front deck.

By late afternoon the wind was calm. His legs were cramping. He had decided to try to snap the log all the way off by breaking it with his weight and twisting on the branches so that it would float free. He stared straight down where the calm water was flowing now in the opposite direction from when he first climbed up there. He began to bounce. The tree crackled and back near the fulcrum he heard a sharp popping. Just as he was about to stand up and plan his last push, he heard the girl's voice.

"Slip? Hey, Slip, you know what?" She was rowing the dory easily now in the calm water and fair current. She was a hundred yards away.

Slip waved. "Come on," he yelled, and she pulled against the oars.

He watched her approach, and he felt an aching love for her. Soon she floated just a few feet underneath him, and he was able to easily lower himself into the dory.

"You know what?" she asked.

"No, honey, I don't."

"Buddy flew off." Her eyes were red and she looked older to him now, her frown having grown stiff.

"I'm sorry to hear that," Slip said, and his voice was broken from not having much use for most of the day.

"He just flew off," she said.

"Well, let's take a look around for him," Slip said. "He's going to be around here someplace," Slip said. And he put his arm around the little girl, who broke into tears, sobbing into the dirty wool of his old red jacket.

~~~

John lost track of the afternoon. He worked on laundry, and then did a short carpentry job of shimming a new door for one of the girls' rooms, which took him much longer than he expected because nothing in the sagging old whorehouse was square. He finished that job and lay down on the cot he had set up by the kitchen, took a drink of wine, and closed his eyes in gratitude for getting some rest before the night's work.

When he woke, the sun was slanting down the back of the building. The tide was out, so the creek was snaking between the algae-covered rocks. As he woke he remembered that he had never changed the girl's bandage. It would be getting ripe by now and he should take care of that before Miss Yvette caught wind of it.

He went down to the kitchen, where the Chinese girl with the bad leg was stirring a large pot of stew and listening to the old Victrola she had sitting on a stool.

"Where is Ellie at?" the black man asked.

"No, sir, don't know," the girl said, without raising her eyes from the pot. "Whores mad, though."

"Why's that?" John asked as he sat in a straight-backed chair by the big table.

"Did not hang clothes."

John looked at the girl. "What do you mean? What'd she do with them?" John shot back.

"Just leave basket of wet clothes on porch. Now some are saying they'll be wearing dirty unders tonight. That make Miss Yvette angry and it ain't their fault."

"Where'd she leave the basket?"

"Just out there by the door. Left the basket and walked off. But I take care. I take care."

"How?"

"I find the basket out there and I hang clothes. Girls will have clean unders."

"Well, that's good. Thanks for that," he said, but his voice was drifting off with some indescribable concern for the girl with the mangled hand.

"I'm wondering where she went. You have any idea?"

"No, I don't."

John stood up and went out on the porch. The clothes hung in the shade under the eaves. They had missed the direct sun on this side of the building and the evening sun was slanting around the corner. He touched the sleeve of a cotton nightshirt. The fabric was still damp. He stood on the porch fingering the material and looking out toward the alley. There was music seeping out from under the doors of the parlors along the creek and he could hear the footfall of two men wandering up the boardwalk with tentative steps. The blue sky was darkening to a purple bruise and the fat crows stood sentinel on the wires overhead.

His eyes followed the clothes down the line and then to the edge of the steps. Then he turned and walked back upstairs to her room, and lifted Ellie's suitcase out from under the bed to see that it was still there. He looked in the drawer of the bedside table and found the revolver he knew would be there. That she had a gun didn't bother him. He felt it in her waistband that first night he carried her up the stairs with Yvette. He had put it in the drawer. It was a good thing for a crippled-up whore to have a gun but it was not wise to tell Yvette about its existence.

He went back to the porch and sat down on the steps. He looked in the dirt near the path. There were footprints scrambled in the mud and gravel. Two men, and between them the dragging heels of a woman.

Thirty feet down the path he found her shoe, and twenty feet past that he found the button from a man's coat, the thread still holding in its holes. The tracks were scattered and then confused. There was a bit of blood on the handrail of the boardwalk, and John was hoping that Ellie had bitten someone and made a getaway. Then he saw a hank of bleached blonde hair caught in a splinter of the decking and a larger stain of blood. He stopped and looked around. He put her shoe in his pocket. The crows were hopping down the boardwalk as if they were following him to food. This was probably a good sign, for if there were a fresh body dumped somewhere, the crows would not be waiting around for him.

The creek made a musical tumble over the rocks and up on the hill behind the creek the tops of the trees swayed gently in a light breeze. John turned his head around and slacked his jaw. His ears were ringing from the exertion, but still, under the music from the whorehouses and the wind through the trees, he could hear it: the soft percussive chopping of shovels striking rocky ground.

"I told you we should have just dumped her in the river," Ray said, as he leaned into his short-handled shovel. "This ground is too damn rocky. We'll never get her deep enough."

"Goddamnit, we are not supposed to kill her," Bill Pierce said. He was sick to his stomach. "I mean, what the hell are you thinking, Ray?"

The short man with the barrel chest leaned on the shovel. "Don't worry, boys. I'll kill her then stick her in the ground, then we go catch the *The Swan* up to Juneau. It leaves in an hour and a half. Hell, boys, we'll have time enough to get a beer and maybe a bath before she sails."

"Is it solid, Ray?" Conner asked, his voice trembling with fear. "I mean, they know we're coming?"

"Hell, yes, he'll be there, but he damn sure won't wait all night. So, let's get back to diggin', boys." Ray threw the shovel over to McCauley Conner, who was sitting on a rock with his head in his hands.

"Fuck it, Bill. I ain't doing it," Pierce said.

Just off to his left John could see the trussed-up body of the little injured whore. She was breathing hard and snot ran down her face and dripped down onto the gag stuffed in her mouth.

"Crap, Bill, seems like I'm doing all the work in this outfit," Ray brayed at the others.

"Quit your bellyaching, Ray. Either way, killing her is not the right move. If we shoot her and then dig a hole, no telling who will hear the shot and come running. You dump her in the creek, especially now at low tide, she'll be found in ten minutes and the cops'll be all over this place."

"They'll just think she's a whore. They won't do nothing," Ray said. He rolled a rock out of the hole they were making on the steep-sided hill.

"Now see, that's where you're wrong again, Ray." Bill Pierce stared down at him from above. "I happen to know that these local cops are softhearted when it comes to their whores. They don't so much mind when one of their customers gets killed, unless it's a judge or something. But it's plumb bad for business when a whore gets killed. It's just another good reason not to kill her."

"Well, she ain't a whore anyway," Ray muttered from the bottom of the hole.

"You're as dumb as a stump, Ray," Bill said.

"Well, I'm not dumb enough to let you be the boss of me." Ray threw down the shovel and stepped out of the hole. "I'm going to get a beer. You deal with it." And he stepped over the white heap lying next to the narrow hole he was digging.

"Now hold on, don't sulk up like an old cow," Conner called after him.

The footing was steep and uncertain. The slope above the creek in Ketchikan may have been the poorest place on earth to bury a corpse. Besides being uneven and hard, the thin layer of moss and dirt supported a thick bramble of berry bushes and stems of broad-leafed devil's club with thorns like slivers of glass. Ray's hands had dozens of these tiny thorns in them and they were making him grumpy while he dug the grave; the thorns and the fact that he was being treated like Bill Pierce's own personal slave. He was not going to put up with it much longer, he thought to himself. He might as well just kill the lot of them and head out on his own.

"Them bastards can do some of the heavy lifting," he muttered to himself, and he pushed back another thorny stalk. He stumbled a bit, twisting his ankle. "Goddamnit," he swore. "These pantywaists will wet themselves before they take care of this Red." Then he looked up and saw the flash of the muzzle from the shot he never heard.

Bill Pierce tried to run but the steep rocky ground threw him down and he tumbled. The second shot caught him in the neck.

McCauley Conner jumped in the hole and tried to hide. The third shot burrowed across the scattering of fresh dirt and tore out the side of his head.

The breeze blew, and the music still drifted up from the street. The sun slanted through the trees from the west and the understory of brambles glowed golden with the smoke from the revolver. John stood over Ellie. Her blue dress was ripped and her head was bleeding but she did not struggle or call out. He bent over her and gently straightened her dress. He set her shoe beside her. When he saw that her underwear was missing, he pumped another shot into McCauley Conner's head. Someone might hear him. Hell, he was sure that someone had heard the shots. But he didn't care. He put one more shot into each of them and took the gag out of Ellie's mouth.

"Thank you," was all she could manage to say.

"Peckerwoods were right about one thing for sure."

"What's that?"

"It's bad for business trying to kill a whore around these parts."

"That seems true enough," Ellie said.

She stood and took the gun from the big man standing next to him. "I'll take this. Anyone asks, this is my gun and I did the killing."

"I can't do that."

"Hell you can't. I'm not saying you have to offer it up. But if it comes to it, I'll take the blame. You saved me and I'm grateful." Then she stood on her tiptoes and kissed him on the lips.

"I'm gonna catch a boat. If a beat-up guy and a little girl come looking for me, tell them to try Juneau. Only them. You understand?"

"I do."

She kissed him again and stumbled down the hill with the gun dangling from her hand like the head of a dead snake.

EIGHTEEN

〜〜〜

Ellie walked across town to the wharf and climbed the ladder down to the deck of the little troller called *The Swan*. A sorry-looking man named Larry was standing in the door of the wheelhouse.

"You're not Pierce are you?" Larry said, backing up a bit into the shadow of the tiny wheelhouse.

"Those boys ran into some bad luck. I'm here to take their place." Ellie's thin voice echoed under the drippy high ceiling of the wharf.

"What kind of bad luck?" Larry almost whispered.

"They got gunned down," she said.

Larry didn't look up as he untied the line. "I heard they were supposed to meet up with a woman and bring her back."

"Yeah, well, I'm bringing myself back." Ellie sat down heavily on the deck hatch. She put the gun in the cradle of her housedress and then she rubbed her good hand against her cheek. "Do you got some warm clothes I can wear?"

"I ain't got no girl clothes. Maybe I should wait for the others," Larry said without looking at Ellie as he walked up to the bow. The little one-lung engine on *The Swan* was thumping away at idle. Water from a broken pipe dripped down under the wharf. Ellie leaned back and lay on the hatch cover. "No use waiting," she said. "They're dead. I'm supposed to go up to Juneau and meet the rest of the them, give 'em my report."

"Well . . . I don't know. I was supposed to meet up with a guy named Pierce and them other two."

Ellie could see that the sorry man didn't have much conviction about hanging around, so she didn't have to sell the idea of leaving very hard. "Well, if you like you could wait and see if anybody comes looking for us, then you could explain to them what your orders were."

"Naw, that's fine. I'm running late as it is." Larry put the little boat in gear and eased away from the wharf.

Larry had been enlisted by a union man in Juneau to bring these boys and the woman back to Juneau, and he took the job only after he was paid half the money in advance. Larry didn't think of himself as a radical. He just didn't like the cops and the rich swells who treated him like a mule. Larry didn't care a whit about the plight of the brotherhood of workers. Larry was motivated only by his hatred of people who were better off than he was, and they were many. All of them, it seemed, had come into their good fortune by some advantage of birth. Even when he was enjoying it, Larry railed against privilege.

"You all right back there?" Larry called out, but Ellie did not answer. When he looked back he saw that the woman with the wrecked left hand was lying on the hatch cover rocking back and forth with her mouth open. At first he didn't recognize the sound and thought that something might be wrong with *The Swan,* but when he listened more carefully he could hear the keening sound of the girl's wild crying coming from the hatch cover. He looked back once more and noticed that she had a handgun gripped firmly in her right hand. Larry closed the door to the wheelhouse, then looked below to make sure his .30-30, as rusted as it was from years on the boat, was still in its place above the galley table.

They would travel north for a few hours and anchor for the night, but before he would lie down in the fo'c'sle he would make sure his gun was loaded and well within reach.

The sea swell was large but gentle on the outside. The ship had rolled easily in the long-period swells, so the passengers were able to get their sea legs beneath them when they walked down the narrow corridors. In the dining hall George and the reverend sat on opposite sides of a round table. George was looking through his files and making notes. The reverend stared down into his teacup.

"What are you working on?" the man of the cloth asked.

George put his pencil down on the table and watched it roll back and forth with the motion of the boat.

"Murder," he said.

"Ah," the reverend said as if he had been expecting the answer all along. "I best leave you to it." He stood up and walked away at a brisk pace.

Outside the ship an albatross was gliding the surface of the waves with the tips of its wings dipping close to the foam of the ship's wake. The wake rolled out from the stern of the ship in two waves that cut across all others, then those waves curled out on opposite sides of the ship and once set in motion they would never cross again. Belowdecks, passengers rolled in their bunks with the motion of the ship. Couples clung to each other so as not to fall out of their narrow beds. The oiler from the engine room stood out on the stern of the crew deck and smoked a cigarette. When he was done he flicked the butt into the sea and it winked out in the rush of the waves. George Hanson sat at the table in the dining hall looking at the photograph of the union man with the crushed skull. He sat there for another thirty seconds before he rose and walked away from the table and out onto the open deck.

The next morning the ship was moored at the small pier at the end of Sitka's main street. A misty rain fell on all sides as if the ship had moored in the middle of a cloud. From the uppermost deck George could just barely see the Russian Cathedral and the steep mountains that rise behind the town. Tlingit women sat with their backs against the buildings selling craftwork laid out on their blankets. The hems of their dresses were muddy from walking in the bog of the street.

A boy from town came onboard and brought George an envelope that had been flown over from Ketchikan. The envelope had two separate letters in it. One was from young Walter Tillman and another was from Campbell River, British Columbia. Tillman's letter said that he would be meeting him in Juneau. The miners at the Alaska-Juneau mine were going on strike and there was going to be trouble. Management was bringing in replacement workers, and every day more radicals were showing up on the docks of Juneau. "I know you've had more experience in these areas but it looks to me like your people would end up in Juneau," the young policeman had written.

The letter from Campbell River was from the bartender. George smiled as he opened the grimy envelope as if he were reading something from an old friend.

"Dear Det. Hanson," the letter read. "I been keeping an eye out for you and I thought I'd let you know what I found. The little dory you was looking for never came into Campbell River but I heard that they got a lift on a fishing boat out of Washington. I learned this from talking to the skipper of one of the mail boats. He came into my place and tied one on when he was heading home. He said that he heard from a pilot that the blonde woman ended up in a cannery up the coast a ways. Then I heard from a friend who worked on airplanes that a woman was flown out of that cannery up to Ketchikan. My friend said that this lady had boogered up her hand pretty good and the cannery fired her. I haven't heard anything about the man, the girl, or the bird. I'm writing you this because I told you I would. So that's what I'm doing. I don't expect no more money, but if you have other things you need looked into I'd be happy to work something out. Sincerely, Tom Stanton.' "

George went to the ship's purser and bought an envelope and paper and wrote a short note back to Campbell River. He put ten dollars in the envelope, folded the note around it, and gave the letter to the purser, asking that it be hand-delivered to Tom in Campbell River on the *Admiral Rodman*'s return trip. The purser said he knew the establishment and would make sure Tom received it.

There was construction going on close to the dock, so along with the ship lowering its cargo onto the wharf, there were workers carrying buckets of concrete and the slap of hammers filled the air.

George knew his sister lived somewhere in town. Perhaps it was his work, perhaps it was his new-found connection to the ship, but he decided not to go ashore to find her. He had known for a few days now that he didn't want to see her. All familial connections felt like the outriders of grief. He did not want to retell his sad story. He did not want to hear the undertone of unsought forgiveness that would almost certainly be in his sister's voice. He did not want to know the details of her plans for him.

He was in Alaska now. On a ship floating the current. This little town, which was building for the future, could go on and do just that, without him and his sad story. It was not time to go ashore.

The stevedores whistled up at the winch operator as a black-and-white dairy cow hung in midair on the end of a sling. The animal's wide eyes seemed to be pleading. Her sides fluttered with panic as her lowing wound down the street like a traffic jam. A kink in the line finally slid through the block and the animal was lowered to the dock, where a man unhooked the sling and led her away. Her small feet made a chunking sound on the timbers.

George turned and walked back to his cabin to reread his telegrams and enter the information into his own reports.

From that day on, Slip and Annabelle did not fight the tide. When the wind or the tide was too strong against them they would find a calm bight in the lee and rest. They both learned to fine-tune the technique of milking the tide by following the fair currents as they ebbed and flowed through the passage. At high flood they could ride the current in a broad band down the middle of the channel, and at slack water when the tide was changing they would pull in closer to the shore where the vestiges of the fair current still swirled. They could get almost seven hours of fair current this way when the wind didn't collude with the moon to stop them dead in the water. They slept on the boat, sometimes drifting through the night with Slip keeping a sleepy eye out for boats and sometimes pulling against the anchor when they could find a place shallow enough for their short anchor line. When they needed water they would row under a waterfall coming down the side of the mountain and funnel the water with the tarp into their keg. When they had the need for privacy they used the tarp and one of the oars as a screen.

They rowed early in the morning when the wind was calm, and on a few days when the wind was from the south they put up the sail. Annabelle would steer when they sailed and sometimes she rowed at the peak of the current. Slip would rest, often lying in the bottom of the dory as the girl pulled on the long oars.

They never found Buddy. Eventually Annabelle stopped looking for him. The fate of the yellow bird became a story to which she did not know the ending. All she could do was study the charts and keep the remote possibility of his return alive in her heart.

The inlets were widening out as they moved toward the open ocean. Islands started to appear in the distance. Boats rolled past them: fishing boats churning toward the open sea and towboats headed up the Inside Passage. When they saw a new boat, Slip would wave the end of the painter line tied to the bow, hoping they would recognize his need for a tow, but each boat they saw kept right on going.

They were going to head for the farthest island and wait there for perfect weather to cross Dixon Entrance. The current here was harder to milk. As the inlet widened, the changing current swirled in less predictable ways, and sometimes the distances were too great to change course for the chance of a favorable current. So they pulled on the oars, sometimes together, and made their way toward the island.

One early morning the water was exceptionally calm as if they were rowing through a blue-green oil, and as they pulled, little silver fish boiled to the surface. When it first happened Slip thought it was some kind of freak wind disturbing the waters around the boat. The water hissed with the roiling of millions of small silvery fish. Slip pulled the dory toward the boiling surface and both he and the girl looked down into the water to watch the kaleidoscopic swirl of fish.

From the surface it appeared to be a single organism, shifting and darting beneath the boat. The school of small fish flashed silver as they swam in one direction then flattened to green as they all changed direction at once. They moved as with one mind, a single entity made up of thousands of individuals.

"How many are there?" Annabelle asked.

"I dunno. Lots of 'em. Maybe a million. I don't know."

"Do they always stay together like that? In a big ball?"

"I suppose so," Slip said.

Then a larger flash of silver torpedoed through the silvery fish and the one organism shattered. A salmon darted into the group and came close enough to the surface that Slip could see the small flash of silver in the salmon's mouth. The single school became several smaller schools, each turning frantically. More salmon circled

in from the deep. It was hard to see the little fish as individual creatures until one of the salmon blasted in and Slip could make out a
few individuals that had been stunned by the salmon charging into
the mass. The stunned fish became fixed points in the fluid motion
of the sea. Then the salmon came in hard and snapped them up in
their jaws, setting the whole school churning and roiling again.

The commotion of the feed near the surface brought in the
birds. Soon gulls wheeled and screamed over the dory. They collapsed their wings and fell onto the sea. The white birds were like
darts, their feathered bodies pushing the points of their bills into
the biomass.

Annabelle tried to count the birds as they gathered, first one
and then another, until there were too many to count, bickering and
crying, diving down and coming back up with fish draped in their
bills. They shook themselves and gulped the wriggling fish down,
only to dive again. Slip kept watching the school weave and split
beneath them. The salmon slashed through and finally Slip saw a
massive form rocketing through to take a salmon in its jaws.

A sea lion rose to the surface, whipping the big fish violently
back and forth on the surface. The male sea lion might have weighed
twelve hundred pounds. He took no notice of the two people in
the dory some twenty feet away and shook the salmon again, then
paused and lashed the fish back and forth once again until a chunk
of red flesh became visible along the silver body. Blood from the gills
bloomed out on the surface and the small silver fish beneath the dory
swirled and disappeared, leaving a few stunned and dying individuals on the surface for the birds. The sea lion came to the surface twice
more with smaller and smaller pieces of the salmon, until eventually
it was gone. The birds wheeled up as a group and scattered. The air
became quiet and the water regained its oily calm.

Slip began to pull on the oars once again. Some three hundred yards to the east Annabelle spotted another mass of silvery
fish boiling on the surface. Again the birds gathered and again the

sea lion worked the edge of the feed. This time they did not slow down, but as he pulled Slip imagined the individual fish underneath his feet endlessly combining and splitting apart, the frantic individuals finding protection in the group, each one trying to hide behind the other until the frantic mass became one living thing. There was protection in the group, but it still could not forestall the threat of death from the big fish or the sea lion. It was going on all the time, in infinite combinations, he thought. He tapped his feet nervously against the bottom of the boat and pulled harder toward the island on the edge of the wildest crossing along the coast.

Late that evening they pulled into an anchorage behind an island, where there was enough shallow water for them to moor the dory. Just the two of them would have a hard time pulling the loaded boat up the beach to clear high tide. They waded in to the beach and built a fire, keeping a close eye on the boat. They were too tired to put up the tent so they just threw the canvas tent over their blankets and slept on the warm sand near the fire. They ate the last of the halibut they had tried to dry in the sunlight, but Slip knew that they would have to either bum some food off someone along the coast or they would have to catch a fish of their own soon. A little stream cut through the rocks along the upper beach, and they were able to top off the water cask once again. Water was plentiful in this green world along the edge of the rain forest.

That night Slip woke up and saw a black form waddling down the beach snuffling and grunting toward the smell of their cook pots. He stood up, shouted, and waved his arms and the little black bear ran up into the woods. It took a few minutes but he gathered the pans and rinsed them in the sea then waded out to the dory to store them in the cook trunk. His legs were prickly with cold when he got back under the canvas and lay once again on the warm sand. Annabelle stirred only when he lifted his edge of the blanket.

"What?" she asked, still asleep. "Is something the matter?" and she brushed her raggedy braids away from her face.

"No, honey, everything's fine. Go back to sleep," Slip said. He rolled over with his back to her and watched the embers pulsing until he went to sleep.

Early the next morning they tried to cross Dixon Entrance, but the north wind came up and beat them back. The current cut against the wind and the sea was a violent jumble of waves. It only took a couple of hours for them to decide to come back to their anchorage. After pulling against the wind and watching themselves lose ground with every stroke of the oars, they put up the sail and eased downwind and back into the snug little bight behind the island.

The next morning the wind blew so hard they didn't even attempt leaving the beach. They got some logs for rollers and with each of them using a lever they were able to move the dory up the beach. It made for more comfortable nights knowing that their boat was on solid ground rather than bobbing against the single frayed anchor line.

There was plenty of anxiety to be had, however. Though he never gave voice to his concerns, Slip was not certain that they could make it across Dixon Entrance unless they had near perfect conditions. There were islands off the coast but the coves looked shallow on the chart and nothing there indicated much shelter. They could curl in along the coast but they would have to make some significant crossings or risk going down into the long fjords that cut inland to the Coast Range. The sail was basically only good for a light downwind run and the weather didn't look promising for that. The weather coming from the north was dry, but it was going to be hard to push against it. A shift from the south would have been all right but it would have brought rain, bigger seas, and the possibility of a full-fledged gale. Or at least that was how the weather had seemed to behave so far. Slip wasn't sure about the weather patterns here on the border between British Columbia and Alaska, but nothing he had heard or seen caused him to believe that the sea would become more benign the farther north they traveled.

That night the winds shifted around from the southwest. Early in the morning it seemed as if they should make a break for it, but by the time they got the dory loaded and down the beach the gusts were bending the treetops around them and they could look out and see the waves humping up and rolling into the anchorage. By mid afternoon it was blowing a gale and the anchorage was a froth of white except for one calm spot behind a small point where the water lay down in the lee. They rolled and levered the dory back up the beach and gathered more wood for the fire. When the rain came they put up the tent and moved their blankets inside. The tent leaked, especially if a person rubbed against the inside of the soaked canvas, but it was still better than being outside. They lit candles and Annabelle read the charts and looked at some of the old magazine pages she found stuffed down in the cooking trunk, which had been used to wrap the dishes. The little black bear came back that evening and scuttled around in their pots and pans, and Slip ran outside to chase him off. He bundled the small bit of food together in another small case and hung it up in a tree. Then he washed the dishes once again and put everything back in the dory.

The next morning the fire pit was a lake of ashes and floating charred sticks. One corner of the tent had a three-inch puddle on the floor. Slip lay under his damp blanket and didn't want to get up. They had to get across Dixon Entrance, but now they had so little food that he began to wonder whether he should take the dory out and try to jig up some kind of fish before even thinking about heading north.

When he stepped out of the tent he saw a small wooden boat in the little anchorage behind the point. It floated in the lee of the point as if made for it. The boat wasn't rigged for fishing but had a large back deck with high sides and a high bow. It looked like a little tug that had been converted for some kind of specialty work. On the stern of the boat was the lettering, THE SHEPHERD, and under that was written BOOT COVE. Slip dug a trench in the fire pit to drain out the rainwater and he used the little axe from the dory to split dry wood. When he got the fire going he held his hands out into the smoke and rubbed them together. Although the temperature was not all that cold, the dampness was seeping into his bones.

The smoke curled around the anchorage, and soon enough a man lowered a dingy into the water from the workboat and rowed toward the beach. He was a big man with hunched shoulders. He wore a broad-brimmed hat and a substantial sweater with a thick collar pulled up around his neck. When he got out of the dingy, Slip could see that he wore leather work boots that looked to be well oiled. Even so, he didn't seem to mind walking through the shallow water while pulling the dingy up onto the sand.

"I'm just putting some water on. Got a little coffee left if you want to have some," Slip called out, surprising himself with his friendliness.

"Don't mind if I do," the man said. He was an older man who looked as if he had lived a lifetime working out in the weather. They shook hands and Slip thought the man's hand might have been made out of oak.

"Carl Tisher," the man said.

"Good to meet you, Carl," Slip replied, as he turned to pour a little more water into the blackened coffeepot.

"You folks headed across the Entrance?" Carl asked, then squatted down near the fire with his hands spread to the flames.

"Yes, we are, if the weather breaks for us." Slip poured the last of the coffee from the can into the pot.

"Could be a long wait. All you got is that dory?" The man gestured over to the boat sitting on the sand.

"Yes sir, that's it. Just me and a little girl. We're headed up to Ketchikan to find her aunt."

"Split up, did you?"

"Yes sir, this little girl's aunt got her hand hurt bad on a job in Canada. She's in Ketchikan. We're just trying to catch up."

"Well, I think I can help you. Weather should die down this morning. I can pull that dory up on the back deck. I can get you across."

"Wouldn't be out of your way?"

"Naw. I'm headed to Juneau to get a son of mine. He got mixed up in some foolishness and I'm going to take him back to my place."

"Where you from, then?" Slip asked, as he poked sticks under the bottom of the coffeepot.

"South. Just a little place down in the Gulf Islands. Boot Cove."

A chill crept up Slip's spine. He propped the coffeepot up on a couple of rocks and reached for the axe to split some more wood.

"Boot Cove, you say," he said.

The old man squinted into the fire and took off his hat to fan the smoke away from his face. He didn't look up at Slip as he said, "Yes sir. That's back down where you folks poached one of my lambs."

NINETEEN

~~~

"The hell you say?" Slip muttered as the girl crawled sleepily out of the wet tent.

"Yes sir, and don't bother trying to deny it neither." Carl Tisher moved around on the other side of the smoke and sat down on a piece of driftwood. "I saw you and your dory down in that cove. I heard from Mary up the way there that you was headed north. I know it was you."

"Well, sir, I'm sorry. We was hungry back there," Slip said as he poured the man some boiled coffee.

"Lots of hungry people don't steal my lambs."

"That's true, but I don't have enough to pay you for it now," Slip said.

"You're going to get me up to Juneau and help me load up my boy."

"But . . . we've got to go to Ketchikan and find her aunt," Slip motioned to Annabelle, who was wrapped in the wool blanket and staring into the fire, her braids a tangle on the top of her head.

"I'm going to fuel up in Ketchikan but you're coming with me. I'm too old to drive this damn boat all day and half the night without some help. I 'bout piled it up three times just getting this far. Sleepy, don't you know."

"I got to get her back with her family," Slip insisted.

"I'll give you half a day in Ketchikan. That's it."

"Or what? You'll give us over to the cops? They're not going to care about some old lamb in Canada."

"No," Carl Tisher said as he sipped his bitter coffee, "I won't go to no cops. I'll just knock a hole in your dory 'bout the size of both your heads and leave you here."

Slip looked at the old man. His eyes were steady and his voice betrayed not a note of humor. He was a man who meant exactly what he said, and Slip was certain that he would do exactly what he promised.

"Did you follow us all the way up here because of the lamb?" Slip asked.

"No, I told you the truth. I'm headed up to get my kid. He's working in a mine in Juneau and is about to get hisself shot because of some miners strike. He ended up scabbing for management and he's going to get himself killed if I don't get there first."

They didn't say anything for a few moments. The smoke swirled around the little circle of space between them. Annabelle leaned against Slip and closed her eyes again. Carl cleared his throat and softened his voice out of respect for her.

"I just kept an eye out for you on the way up. It's a big country all right but it skinnies up in places so I thought I might see you, though I have to say, it wasn't on my mind much."

"How mad are you about the lamb?" Slip said back.

"You ain't the first to poach a lamb from me. I'd be hung long ago if I killed every hobo who comes along and eats my lamb. I just need a hand to get to Juneau and get my boy back on my boat."

"Well, I'll do it. I'll leave the girl with her aunt in Ketchikan and I'll get you to Juneau, if it'll help you out." Slip took out a crust of moldy bread and started to cut the green spots off.

"Let's get you loaded up and you can cook breakfast on my boat. Looks like you're down on your tucker again. Nobody raising lambs around here, I guess," Carl said, through a smile.

Slip took a swig of coffee and stood up.

Annabelle stirred and spoke in a sleep-muddled voice. "Did Brother Twelve ever come back for Mary?" the girl asked. "You know, that lady on the island with the sunken boat out front. Did he ever come to save her?"

The old man looked away from the girl and spit in the fire. He did not answer the child.

"Is she still waiting?" Annabelle asked again.

"Yes, I suppose she is."

"Is he ever going to come back?"

"That fellow was a stick and not a boomerang. She's seen the last of Brother Twelve." Carl Tisher stood up and slapped his old felt hat against his thigh.

"But you came to save us, didn't you?" Annabelle said and stretched.

"That I did, young lady." He chuckled and motioned toward the dory, and said to Slip, "Let's get you loaded up. Sooner we get going, sooner we can have something to eat."

The Swan was a slow and smelly boat. When Larry felt like it, he would stand at the wheel and pee down a crack into the bilge. If there were any seas at all, his aim would suffer and the piss would cascade down the steps and all over the diesel stove. Larry liked to drink whiskey and beer while he traveled, so it was a blessing the boat was so slow. *The Swan* would simply bounce off most everything it ran into.

Ellie slept out on the deck. There was a small cover over the trolling cockpit and she wrapped herself in a fetid blanket that Larry threw out to her. She kept the revolver close and never let herself drift into deep sleep. She was out of live rounds but Larry was too dumb to know that. The seas were calm on that first day so when they ran out of daylight Larry just found some shallow water, threw out his anchor, and went to sleep without taking his clothes off.

When the sun rose, Ellie got up and ventured down into the galley where Larry was lying tangled in a pile of dirty coats. There was a wet paper bag on the deck of the wheelhouse. A can of beans was breaking through the sack and was ready to fall down onto the bilge. She took the beans and a nasty-looking spoon from the table. Then, unable to tolerate the smell, she took the can back up on deck. Ellie's hand hurt too badly to hold the can and open it with a knife, so she poked a circle of holes around the top with a gaff hook and, after cleaning the spoon with salt water and the hem of her dress, Ellie ate the beans for breakfast.

The commotion of opening the beans woke Larry, who rolled over, drank the last of his beer from the night before, peed in the bilge, then hooked his arms through his suspenders and greeted the day.

They traveled like this for four nights and three days. They didn't speak much. Larry drank until he couldn't steer and then Ellie would take the wheel. There were minimal charts, and by the time Larry was ready to finish his watch he couldn't speak clearly enough to give Ellie a proper heading, so *The Swan* went down a few dead ends. Eventually they wound their way up through Behm Canal and Clarence Strait, through Stikine Strait, Wrangell Narrows, and Frederick Sound, all the way up past Glass Peninsula and into Stephens Passage. The days passed in a tableau of silver to gray to light blue, gray clouds scraping the green trees and the currents whirling through the narrow passages. Tugs with barges of lumber and stone headed south. Fishing boats with their poles up motored toward the coast. Men in dories rowed with their gear balled up in tarps, and small gas boats hauled freight with a few passengers bound for the villages. There were whales diving through the surface of Frederick Sound, and a schooner with a dozen dead eagles strung up on the boom waiting to be turned in for bounty. Each muddy little town was made lively with the shriek of a steam whistle and the thump of a pile-driving hammer, and every harbor had a scattering of hungry men wandering the docks looking for work.

Ellie was at the wheel when a humpback whale came up near the bow of the boat. She cut the engine because she wasn't sure that the poor *Swan*, despite its resiliency regarding sandbars and pilings, might not come off the worse in a collision with a forty-ton beast. The whale's great gaping mouth came to the surface and Ellie could see the haze of silvery fish inside. The rubbery creature closed its jaws and the birds dove down on the leftovers. As the whale rolled back to right itself, the eye broke the surface and Ellie felt the queasiness of being watched by a warm-blooded creature bigger than a fishing boat. The gearshift lever was a box-end wrench elaborately lashed to the linkage. Ellie kept her good hand on it as she watched the whale blow, rest, blow again, and then raise its tail to dive under the boat.

She turned for a moment to say something to Annabelle. She wanted her to see the whale. Then she grimaced, realizing that she was alone on *The Swan*, with the drunken skipper curled up in the bunk below cradling a rusty saddle gun.

The Alaska-Juneau mine dominated the mountain on the east side of Gastineau Channel just south of the town of Juneau. The old Treadwell mine on the other side of the channel had flooded with seawater and collapsed in 1917 and was now abandoned, leaving the Alaska-Juneau as the richest place for gold in the territory. The Klondike gold rush had made a few prospectors rich, but had made the fortunes of many more who were quick enough to sell supplies to the frantic gold hunters. Many of the biggest buildings in Seattle and Portland had been built with money made from selling gear to Alaskan fortune hunters, many of whom limped home broke if they made it home at all. Mining had always been more profitable for the storekeeper than it had been for most of the miners themselves. So when Alaska's biggest gold mine was standing idle because of a strike, the merchants of the territorial capital were incensed. This was their livelihood the miners were fooling with.

The A-J mine, as it was called, was made up of a honeycomb of tunnels back in the hard rock of the mountain. These mines were riddled with seeps of fresh water and rotten shale. There was some quartz and microscopic amounts of gold. To make any profit at all, hundreds of tons of rock had to be jackhammered and blasted away, carted through the tunnels, rolled down into the stamp mill that was built in stair-step fashion on the side of the mountain, and crushed into dust. When the crushed rock floated away, flecks of gold were left to settle. It took hundreds of men stooping and straining in damp rock crevices to get a pouch full of gold. On May 22, 1935, the miners voted for a raise, a forty-eight hour work-week, some kind of hospitalization plan for the injuries they knew were part of the work, and finally they wanted more than two days off a year. A squall rose up from management. They insisted that this would make the Juneau miners the most coddled miners in the world. Alaska had jobs. More miners would come. They didn't care if the president of the United States was driving the country toward socialism; they were not going to pay.

The miners had stayed out and blocked any scabs from entering the shafts. By June, a "miners association" had formed with the help of the Juneau city attorney. The men belonging to the

Arctic Brotherhood, a fraternal order of middle-class merchants and professionals, stood four-square behind the new miners association, as the scabs were called. The city fathers assured the scabs that they would be allowed to cross the picket line and go to work. Carl Tisher's son, Amos, was one of these replacement miners. He just wanted to work and he didn't like the threatening taunts of the strikers who stood defiantly out in front of the Union Hall.

Once Amos had walked by the hall and a miner stepped in front of him, blocking his way. "Where you headed, bub?" the man asked, and he took a tobacco pouch out of his shirt pocket.

"I'm just going for a walk," Amos had said in a tone that was more defiant than he had intended.

The man sprinkled tobacco in his paper, licked the edge, and rolled his smoke. "You got a match?" he asked Amos.

Amos said, "No."

Then the man took a section of pipe out of the back of his pants and slashed it across the boy's head, splitting his ear and laying him out on the boardwalk. Amos lay on the planks of the sidewalk, dimly aware of his blood dripping between the cracks in the planks.

"You better stay the fuck away from the mine, or it will be worse the next time," the man said. He lit a wooden match with his thumbnail, fired up his smoke, and threw the match on the boy's head. The dull eyes of the men beside the Union Hall stared at Amos as if he were a rabid dog. They didn't really care who put him down, just as long as it was taken care of quickly.

Amos limped away. He had made the mistake of writing his mother that night. He sat in his boardinghouse room that he shared with two other men, and scribbled out a few lines in pencil, while the two men sat on the single bed watching him work.

They had taken the single room thinking they would be working shifts and able to avoid each other, but now that none of them was working their quarters were tight. The landlady didn't mind because she was charging them each the same rent as she would have for the single bed. She could live with tripling her money as long as they didn't break the bed. If they did, of course, she would charge them for it.

Amos was hoping to get a job and find a girlfriend in Juneau. He hated the life in the Gulf Islands back home. He hated the smell of sheep and cedar chips. He hated the feeling of being bound up on the tiny island. Juneau was landlocked, but there was plenty of activity, cars churning up the hills in summer and the rumble of oar trucks on the plank roads. There were people walking into restaurants wearing tailored clothes and women with strange accents calling down to you from second-story windows. These women had beautiful dark eyes, and when he looked up at them his heart would tighten with the thought of walking up those narrow stairs. Amos didn't care how many times he got his head cracked, he was going to work in the Alaska-Juneau mine.

It was late evening by the time *The Swan* made it into Gastineau Channel. The A-J mine was as quiet as the pyramids as the little troller sputtered past. Trucks rumbled up and down the wharf along the front of town. They had passed shacks along the edge of the channel where Tlingit boys were throwing sticks into the water and their mothers stood watching with a pail in one hand and a baby on their hip. The smell of coal dust eased down the channel toward them and the lights from the little wooden buildings seemed as yellow as rotten teeth.

As they pulled in toward the wharf, Ellie could hear men arguing and women laughing back up the side streets. Dogs barked on the hill and someone was breaking bottles on the rocks in the scrubby trees above town. Ellie again cupped her bad hand in her good one. Then she put it gingerly into the pocket of the wool coat she had borrowed from Larry. She checked the revolver in her pocket and pulled a filthy cap down on her head. As the boat got near enough to the dock, Ellie jumped and took the mid-ships line to wrap around a cleat.

"I'm going to go find the boys. They'll be looking for my report. I'll tell them you did good, Larry."

"Not so fast there, little missy." Larry was holding his .30-30 at his hip and he was pointing it straight at Ellie's belly. "You're not going anywhere."

"What is this? You don't know who I am, do you? When they find out you've been threatening me you're going to be in a whole new world of hurt." Ellie stood with her right hand on the cracked wooden grip of the revolver plainly showing above her pocket.

"Yeah, that may be so. But I'm getting paid to deliver you ... or at least somebody from Ketchikan, and I ain't gonna risk not gettin' paid the rest of my money by having you run off somewhere leaving me with only my word on it." Larry tried to pull back the hammer on the rusted rifle and Ellie could see he was having trouble.

"Well what you gonna do, parade me up the street at gunpoint?" Ellie leaned forward as if talking to a child.

"Yeah, well . . . I don't know. I just know I ain't letting you go uptown."

"All right, then. I've got an idea. I'll stay here and you go get the boys."

Larry mulled this idea over. He wanted to go uptown in the worst way. He had run out of beer a day before and he was about as dry as dirt. He liked the idea, but there was something in the back of his mind that was bothering him. "What do I get as security so you won't run off?" Larry asked.

"I'll tell you what. I'll give you my gun. I don't go anywhere without it. I'll wait to get it back. Look . . ." And she pulled out the revolver, showing Larry how the cylinder spun and the hammer actually pulled back. "You can even use it to shoot me if you want. Hell, it's a damn sight better than that rusted-up fowling piece of yours."

Larry smiled. He knew he could trade the rifle for whiskey uptown and keep the new pistol for himself. He'd get himself a drink and Ellie would have to watch the boat.

"It's a deal," Larry said, walking slowly off the boat still holding the rifle in front of him. Ellie took out the revolver and turned its handle out to Larry. He smirked, and tucked the pistol in his pants. Then with some effort, he cranked the three cartridges out of the saddle gun and dropped the empty rifle onto the deck of the boat.

"You stay with the boat now. I got your gun, and I'm gonna kill you if you wander off."

"I understand, Larry. I'll be right here," Ellie said. She looked over her shoulder at a steamship slowly churning up the channel toward the wharf just ahead of *The Swan*. A few crows darted out of the shadows and sliced the air under the wharf. One of them was holding a mussel in its beak.

"Yeah, you better be here. I'm gonna get the boys up at the Union Hall right now."

"All right," Ellie said. And she stepped back onto the boat, waving as Larry labored up the ramp of the rickety floating dock.

Once the drunkard was out of sight, Ellie hopped off the boat, walked up the ramp, and headed away from the clatter of the barrooms. She smiled to herself as she walked down the boardwalk, thinking of how much the cops would believe the sorry man's story when they found the gun that had killed three men in Ketchikan and two in Seattle tucked away in Larry's pants.

George Hanson had been gloomy during the trip from Sitka to Juneau, and the sight of Juneau on that early evening did nothing to raise his spirits. The big empty mine on the hillside seemed to suck the sound out of the air. A motionless layer of smoke hung just above the rigging of the ship, and this gray cloud had thin appendages reaching down into the blackened chimney pipes of town, so that there appeared to be a giant spider walking along the rooftops. Sunlight did not seem to brighten a town like this; it only highlighted the shadows.

There was the usual commotion when the *Admiral Rodman* tied up at the wharf. After some jockeying around with the tugboats getting her turned around and into her place, the crew threw the lanyards to the dock boys and they pulled the heavy hawsers to secure the ship to the dock. There were men yelling back and forth, teasing and laughing. There were several families waiting for the ship to dock and a group of men in dark suits holding on to manifests waiting to check off some important cargo. A white bull terrier walked through the small crowd gathered on the dock. The local people seemed to defer to the fat dog as if it were an important personage. It wasn't until much later George learned that the old dog was, in fact, a revered member of the community who was rumored to have the uncanny ability to predict, and be at the dock to greet, unexpected ships.

George scanned all the faces at the dock wondering if the dog was to be the only one to great him. But soon enough he found the grim young face of Walter Tillman cutting through the crowd.

"I flew up here yesterday. My captain said I was to bring you this report myself," Walter called out, as George walked down the gangway.

"It's good to see you, Walter," George said, reaching out his hand to the young police officer.

"Yes sir, I wanted to tell you about the murders we had down in Ketchikan. I think they relate to your case and to the people you are looking for. On June third we got a report . . ."

"Let's take care of my bags first," George interrupted. "Then let's go someplace private where I can give you my full attention." George handed Walter his briefcase and they walked over to where the crewmen were starting to unload the first sling of passenger baggage. "It's best that people don't know our business here, don't you think?"

"Oh, yes." Walter stood with the detective's satchel clutched to his chest. George could tell that the young man had been ready to give his full report and to not do so had created a kind of vacuum in his brain.

George gathered up his one leather case, gave the crewman a dime, slapped Walter on the back, and started to walk uptown.

Later, after he had shown the Seattle detective to his boardinghouse, Walter cleared his throat and started in on his report. "On June third the department got a call concerning some loud noises down on the creek. No one from the department responded, but the next morning one of our officers was speaking to a woman who runs a sporting house on the creek. She reported that one of her employees, named Ellie, had disappeared without telling a soul."

"Did this woman have an injured hand?" George Hanson asked.

"Yes sir, she did."

They were sitting in the empty parlor of the boardinghouse built against the hill. It was a clean house with rooms sharing a bath. It seemed to George that every flat surface in the room was covered with decorative lacework. The room smelled of coal dust, and all of the doilies seemed to have a light film of soot over them, so that if he traced the tip of his finger along the lace it would leave a faint line.

"The woman apparently had lost some fingers in a cannery accident and this . . . uh . . . proprietress of the establishment . . . was helping her back to health. A local doctor had treated the badly wounded hand."

"This girl, Ellie, was she a longtime whore there in Ketchikan?" George asked, as he fingered one of several white satin roses set in a china vase.

"No sir, she had come there quite recently, just a matter of days I think. I don't know if she had been actually working as a whore. I didn't check on that."

"That's all right," George smiled.

"Well, sir, I went down to the creek to look around and I saw that there were eagles feeding back up in the woods and that's real strange unless someone dumps a carcass or something. So I went up and found them."

"Them?" George put the rose down and stared at him.

"I found three men shot to death. Two slugs in each of them. Two men shot in the body and one shot in the head. The man shot in the head was in a small trench that someone had dug out on the hillside."

"What else?"

"There were some women who worked along the creek who said they knew the three men. They had arrived together and they said they were from Seattle on their way to Juneau. One of the girls got a name that she believed was a real name, because you know, many of the men don't give correct names. She said his name was Ray and that this Ray was not very . . . how did she put it . . . he was not very genteel."

"What's that mean to a Ketchikan whore?"

"She said he used rough language with her and was violent during the performance of her duties."

"He beat her?"

"In a way that made her think he was enjoying himself."

"Ah." George leaned back and looked out the window of the boardinghouse. Trucks rumbled down the wooden streets downtown while up in the woods there were songbirds trilling.

"This woman, Ellie, was she blonde?"

"Her hair had been dyed blonde some time ago, according to the women she worked with."

"Anything else?"

"One of the girls at the house where Ellie stayed said that she was polite and sober. They said that she had encouraged them to start their own sporting house."

"Start their own?"

"Yes, one of them told me that the injured girl had told her that she owned her body and that the madam of the house was exploiting her."

"Well, bless her heart. How about the other three men, the ones you found dead. Had they tried to bring any of the whores of Ketchikan to the revolution?"

"No, sir, it appeared that they were pretty much all business." Walter Tillman was blushing as he reached into his own satchel and took out some grimy-looking photographs. George glanced down at the top one where McCauley Conner stared up into the lens with half of his skull blown out into the dirt. The flashbulb's glare put a glaze on his face. His mouth was open in a misshapen oval that appeared to be frozen in place.

"All business," George muttered.

He flipped through the pictures. George knew that photos somehow captured the essence of a murder more than any story could: the little man splayed out on the stones, head cocked awkwardly and his soap-white limbs pinwheeling from his body, his mouth stuffed with darkness. Policemen caught in the glare, walking around the body as if they were burglars. Then the photos of two other men with their faces pulled apart and their bodies so askew that it looked as if they had been dressed in someone else's clothes: their bellies peeking out from their shirts, their ties flopped up into their eyes. Most people died in one bright flash of chaos. Murder wasn't a story, George thought, it was that moment when a story ended. This moment of ending was where a homicide detective lived.

George pushed the photographs aside. The landlady had put out a plate of sandwiches. There was a pitcher of buttermilk in the icebox, she said. George offered Walter a sandwich and they sat without speaking for a few moments. Somewhere up the hill George could hear water running in a creek. A boat horn blasted in the harbor. The photographs of the bodies sat between the two men.

"Anything else?" George asked the young policeman.

"Your office in Seattle wants you to contact them. It sounds like there are revenge killings going on."

"Who is dead?" George looked around for a glass to put some buttermilk in.

"A man named Francis Miller was killed in the steam baths. He was a Floodwater operative."

George let his hand dangle in the air above a dust-coated glass. "Yes . . ." he said, "I knew him. He was called Fatty."

"I'm sorry, sir, I didn't know he was a friend of yours. He's dead, sir. Shot in the head three times."

"Not a friend exactly." George took up the glass and walked to the icebox. "But a shame nonetheless."

George poured the buttermilk, then looked over at the young man. "Tell me your impressions of the case so far."

"Well, sir, I think the woman with the bad hand is Ellie Hobbes. She is one of the people you were looking for in the Seattle matter. I think the three men were sent to find her and she killed them and then left town somehow. Maybe stowed away on a ship or just headed up into the woods. We've got officers in Ketchikan working on that now."

"Have you identified the dead men?"

"I haven't got a good I.D. from Seattle. They had some gear stored in a bar along the creek but there was nothing printed. No identification or letters, no radical leaflets, nothing."

George dug into his case and brought out his thin files on the union men. "Here," he said. "These are photos of Pierce, Conner, and Cobb. It's a good chance these three are your victims."

"Thank you, sir," the young officer looked down at the photographs, a little stunned.

"What about the logger and the little girl?" George asked.

"I'm not sure, sir. I was going to check the cannery in B.C. They might still be there. The girl's just a niece. Ellie must have left her with the logger, when she was hurt."

"Why'd your captain send you up to Juneau?"

"One of the whores said this is where the three dead men were headed. My captain supposed that Juneau is where the case would be made. He sent me here to help."

George set aside his gristly pot roast sandwich and leaned back in his chair. "Now all we need is a yellow bird."

"Yellow bird, sir?"

"Once the yellow bird gets here we'll have the whole congregation."

The Shepherd rolled across the opening of Dixon Entrance without rattling a single cup. Annabelle took her turn at the wheel and Carl watched to make sure she could steer to a compass bearing. The sea swells were smooth and well spaced, so the boat rolled like an old mule with a light load on her back. Carl carved out a direct route into Revillagigedo Channel and north into Ketchikan. It was late in the afternoon when Carl pulled the boat up to the fuel dock and turned to Slip.

"Annabelle can stay here on the boat with the dory and your gear. You go see if you can find her aunt and you bring her down here to get her. If I can't tie up right here, I won't be far," Carl called over to Slip, who was making fast the stern line.

Slip understood and waved to the girl before he turned and climbed up the iron ladder to the wharf. Then he took off running to the hospital.

Annabelle stayed in the wheelhouse on *The Shepherd*. She was looking forward to being with Ellie again. Annabelle had been frightened by Ellie's injury. She found it hard to think that Ellie would never have all her fingers again. Maybe the doctors could do something, but Slip said it was pretty bad. She shook her head and tried to shake the ugly thoughts out of her mind.

She missed Ellie's company. She missed the way she did impractical things. The dory trip had been full of practicality: pulling on the oars to a steady course. Annabelle wanted to talk with Ellie about the virtues of hot fudge and flying airplanes. She wanted to talk to her about what it was like to be in a Lockheed Vega. Annabelle had heard some men talking in the cannery that the Vega was like a flying log. What did they mean? Ellie had told her that Amelia Earhart had flown in a Lockheed Vega early in her career. Now Amelia flew a Lockheed Electra. Were they going to live in Ketchikan and buy a plane? She slid her glasses up her nose and took a deep breath. Asking questions raised her spirits.

Annabelle had hung a set of clothes to dry in the engine compartment of the boat as it crossed Dixon Entrance. The heat from the engine had dried her shirt, pants, socks, and unders completely for the first time in what felt like weeks. As she sat waiting for Slip to bring Ellie down to the boat, she decided to put on dry clothes in case Ellie wanted to go out to get ice cream or something. That would be like Ellie to do something like that, ice cream rather than dinner or unpacking their things in this new place that might be home.

Annabelle put on the clothes and the faint smell of diesel didn't reduce the pure pleasure of wearing warm clothes. She came back out on deck and wrapped her arms around herself. She felt good for the first time in days. Ellie would come and she could braid her hair nice and tight again. They would talk over things while she did it. She would tell her about meeting the man with the stolen sheep, and about Slip's adventure on the snag. She would tell about Buddy flying off, and Ellie would understand and she would know just the right way to think about it so that it wouldn't hurt so much.

Annabelle fell asleep on the skipper's berth in the wheelhouse. The oil stove in the galley kept her warm without a blanket. She dreamed of flying in a Lockheed Electra around the world. Slip and Ellie were eating ice cream in the back of the plane and all they did was laugh. Yellow birds roosted in the treetops wherever she flew, and if she came down close enough they all flew up in a shuddering yellow haze, yellow birds chirping and calling out louder than the roar of the big radial engines.

The door of the wheelhouse slammed shut and Carl was starting the engine of the boat. Cockatiels fluttered around in her head and her eyes were half open. The door opened and slammed shut again. Slip was pacing back and forth in the wheelhouse.

"Is Ellie here?" Annabelle rolled up on one elbow. She could still feel the pull of gravity as she flew the Lockheed Electra. She could hear Ellie laughing.

"Go back to sleep, now," Slip said. His eyes were red and he looked pale. For a second Annabelle thought that maybe he had hurt himself, like Ellie.

"Are you okay?" she asked. "Did you find Ellie?"

"Go back to sleep, I tell you," Slip barked at her, and then he went out on the back deck, slamming the door once again.

"Just lay down, honey," Carl Tisher said. "I'll wake you up for some supper in a bit."

She could raise herself up just enough in the bunk to look out on the back deck where Slip was hanging on to the dory. He was leaning out over the water. He looked as if he were vomiting, which seemed strange to her because it was hardly rough here in the channel.

"Everything okay?" Annabelle asked, as she put her head back down on the pillow.

"You just go back to your dreams, honey. We're just going to head on up to Juneau," Carl Tisher said in a voice that seemed soft and wet.

He is a nice man, Annabelle thought. Ellie is going to like him.

Her clothes still felt warm to her and the steady vibration of the engine thrummed through her body. Once again she pulled back on the yoke of the Electra's controls, while a down of yellow feathers fell like snow from the sky.

≈≈≈

TWENTY

To Annabelle, Juneau looked like a little town you might find in a snow globe: wooden buildings clinging to the side of a mountain. The big crooked building clung to the steep hill like a giant staircase someone thought to enclose. She sat on the skipper's berth, bouncing in her seat, thinking that this looked as good as any place to wait for Ellie.

Slip hadn't said anything since Ketchikan. He didn't eat supper when Carl cooked up a rockfish he jigged up at anchor. Slip sat on the back deck as *The Shepherd* motored up past Petersburg and out into Frederick Sound. He slept on the back deck even when Carl told him there was a bunk for him up forward. Only once did Annabelle poke her head out onto the deck and she saw him sitting in the pen that Carl had used to transport his sheep.

"Hey," the girl said above the motor, "come inside."

He waved her back into the wheelhouse.

By the time they arrived in Juneau, Annabelle told herself that Slip was crazy and it was definitely time for her to find Ellie. As they eased up to the wharf, Annabelle could see black dust hanging in the air. When she turned to look at Slip she saw a meanness in his face that brought a chill to her heart.

"I'm going to head uptown," Slip said, helping Carl tie the boat. The girl stood on the back deck next to the dory and he looked at her for a second, filled his lungs with what he knew he should tell her, then stopped.

"I'm going to head uptown," he repeated.

Carl Tisher grabbed onto Slip's elbow. "I'll anchor out tonight. You find Amos. I know you got things on your mind but I want you to find him, understand?"

"I'll get someone to ferry me out to the boat if I find him," Slip said. He turned away without a word to the girl.

The pressure building in her chest kept her planted to the deck and unable to speak. Up the hill by the stamp mill, a man walked across a steep sidehill. Rocks clattered down like damp fireworks. Annabelle raised her hand and waved at Slip, who was climbing up the ladder to the top of the wharf.

"I wouldn't worry, detective, we'll clean out the damned Reds. We know how to run our own affairs." The federal magistrate sat across his oak desk from George and Walter. The magistrate was cleaning his fingernails with the point of his Barlow pocket-knife. He was a portly man whose chin was sunk back under several folds of fat. As he ripped the tip of his knife under each nail, he would flinch just enough so that his entire face jiggled. Beside the magistrate sat Tom Delaney, the head of Floodwater's office in Seattle.

"The strike's been going on for a month?" George asked.

"Something like that. I don't suppose it matters how long they stay out; they'll never get those kind of wages to work in a mine." The magistrate didn't look up from his nails.

"They got replacement workers coming in?"

"They even got some stump speakers down there building a fire underneath them. It's like they got a new union to replace the old one." He jerked back his hand and looked at a thread of blood winding down the little finger of his left hand. He put the finger in his mouth and sucked at the blood.

"I don't know. If they did happen to get those wages I might be tempted to be a miner myself." He looked at the soft white tip of his finger and wheezed out a flatulent laugh.

"Do you have people inside the union?" George said, looking at Delaney who was keeping conspicuously silent.

The magistrate looked a bit confused, and spoke for Delaney. "People?" he looked at the shamus with basset hound eyes. "You mean, like spies?"

George nodded and Delaney was about to open his mouth when the magistrate interrupted.

"Don't really need spies. Guys come up here to my office and tell me anything I want to know."

"Just come up here during the day to tell you what the union is planning?" George smiled at the thought.

"They know enough to have their bread buttered on both sides."

Tom Delaney flicked at a piece of lint on the knee of his wool trousers, cleared his throat, and spoke up before the magistrate had anything more to offer. "We've got everything under control, George. You don't have much to do up here."

"You looking for Ellie Hobbes?" George asked.

"I'm here to help with the strike situation and head off any civil disturbance. It's a pretty simple job."

"Then you aren't after Ellie Hobbes or Slippery Wilson?"

Delaney shook his head slowly as if he were gently stirring his next thought. "I'm not worried about Hobbes, and I don't care about Wilson," he said. He opened his mouth and it looked as if he were going to say something more but then he leaned back in the chair. "I'm not worried about either of them, actually."

George stood up and dusted off the brim of his hat. He looked from the magistrate to Delaney and back. "All right then," George said, putting his hat on.

As he turned and walked to the door Tom Delaney said, "Did you hear we lost another operative?"

George turned. "I heard about Fatty. It's too bad. I suppose it will be hard on his family." George looked closely at the brim of his hat.

"He didn't have much of a family left," Tom Delaney said, though his attention was already turning elsewhere. "You be careful out there, George." The Floodwater man reached over and closed the door and the edge of the door brushed George's shoulder on his way out.

George walked down the hill from the courthouse. He knew that if Ellie Hobbes were still alive she wouldn't be hard to find. The magistrate was a fool—that was plain to see. There were two miners unions in Juneau that summer: the original local that had gone out on strike and the new workers association that was backed by management and the Arctic Brotherhood boys. It wasn't uncommon for management to try to organize strikebreakers but it was a new twist to masquerade scabs as radical union men. If they had tried that down in the states, the town would have been overrun with agitators from all over the country. But Juneau was a long way from anywhere. It was a landlocked town with its back against the Canadian Coast Range. Any Red who wanted to come here to organize had to run the gauntlet of boatmen and night watchmen. They had to bring everything they needed with them on their back and survive in the town once they arrived.

George guessed that Ellie Hobbes would be drinking. She had a mangled hand and she was separated from the little girl and her running partner. She had a death sentence hanging over her head, and she was running out of places to run. Hobbes was not going to become a radical hermit out on one of the islands. She was a natural born speech giver.

Slip didn't want to tell Annabelle about Ellie. He didn't want to say that she had murdered three men and was on the run. After he had come up with nothing at the Ketchikan hospital, a cabby had directed him to the whorehouse on Creek Street. There, John told him Ellie was on the run and under suspicion of murder. The tall black man watched his words carefully so Slip knew he wasn't telling everything he knew. But one look at the newspaper the black man held out told him that the essentials had been true. There were the three names that the enterprising reporter had tracked down— Pierce, Conner, and Cobb—and then there were some photographs of the men that had been taken on the Everett docks. Slip recognized all three even though he had only a glimpse of Conner and Pierce at Ellie's meeting hall. But he remembered Cobb as the fireplug on the porch that first morning driving the black car with Ellie. Slip slapped the paper against his leg. Somewhere over his shoulder a withered laugh fell out into the street and a radio played dance music from some distant station. He thanked the man and walked away.

Even though it had only been two days, Ketchikan seemed a long time ago now. Slip had to put the past out of his mind or he would be sunk down with the gravity of all his mistakes. Now he was walking down Franklin Street in Juneau looking for Ellie. Slip had been standing right there when Clyde, the machinist at the cannery, had told Ellie about heading to Juneau, and Slip figured that Juneau was a big enough town with trouble enough for Ellie to hide in. Ketchikan was too hot for her now and Seattle was too far away. Ellie had to be in Juneau.

The late evening sun filled the street like canyon light. People wove their way around the legs of the men sprawled on the sidewalk and heavy trucks rumbled up the street toward the mine. He was walking down the sidewalk when he came abreast of an open doorway. A short man with steel-rimmed glasses stood squarely in the opening and he flipped a cigarette in front of Slip's legs.

"You looking for work?" the short man said as he adjusted his visor above his eyes.

"Naw," Slip said and he turned away. "I'm looking for somebody."

"They're hiring up at the mine. There're going to be good jobs up there and plenty of them."

"Naw," Slip said. He looked behind the man's shoulders where he saw the dark forms of men sitting around a card table. Slip could hear the chatter of poker chips and the creaking of wooden chairs against the floor.

"This the hiring hall?" Slip asked.

"Just go over to the new miners association building, down the block and to the left. You'll see it. They'll fix you up. Unless you're in the mood for a card game." A cob of yellow teeth appeared in the man's face. He stepped aside and Slip could see women bringing drinks to the players.

Slip shook his head and started to walk on again when the little man took him by the elbow.

"What's your name, friend?"

Slip looked down at him and pulled his arm back. "I'm just looking for Ellie Hobbes."

"You a friend of Ellie's?" The man looked at him and then spit on the plank sidewalk.

"In a manner of speaking."

"What you say your name was?"

"That's all right. I'll just keep looking," Slippery Wilson said, and he hurried down the street, right past the next open doorway where Walter Tillman had been standing listening to their conversation.

George had walked into the bar and saw a blonde wearing three dirty shirts sitting hunched over a bottle in the corner. Her right hand gripped the bottle's neck and her bandaged left hand was cradled in her lap. This was the unhappiest soul in a town of unhappy souls and George knew it had to be Ellie Hobbes. George walked past the barman, tapped his finger on the mahogany counter, and asked for a clean glass.

"Hello, Ellie," George said, and sat down. "Having a rough time of it?"

Ellie didn't look up from the glass. "Get away from me."

"I bet you're tired of rowing, Ellie. I'm here to help you."

The barman walked over with a glass and set it on the table. George took the bottle from Ellie's hand, poured himself a drink, and left the stopper off the bottle.

Ellie swung her head up and tried to keep it level with the horizon but without much success. "How can you help me?"

"I'm here to take you into custody as a material witness in the killing of Ben Avery." George took a drink and winced as the whiskey scoured its way down.

"You have to be a Seattle cop."

"Why's that, Ellie?"

"Because the Floodwater boys don't want to be seen talking to me." Ellie took another long drink.

"And the local cops?"

"This town doesn't have local cops as far as I can tell. They got miners association thugs and Floodwater. That's all they need."

"Ellie . . ." George moved his chair in closer and lowered his voice. "Ellie, this is awful whiskey. Why don't you let me buy you something better."

Ellie waved her good hand across the table as if to clear everything away. "Sure. Why not?"

George craned his head around and called over to the barman. "Get us two cups of coffee, some kind of sandwich with meat in it, and a two shots of your best brandy."

"You buying?" the barman asked.

George nodded, then turned back to the broken woman at the table. "You killed Ben Avery, didn't you, Ellie?"

Ellie covered her eyes with her uninjured hand. Her body was shaking now.

"What about those boys in Ketchikan?" George asked.

"I don't want to talk about Ketchikan." Ellie looked around for a new drink.

"You should understand. I'm not saying you did it alone. You had some help there."

"I'm not going to talk about Ketchikan."

"Let's talk about Seattle then. You were working for Floodwater, weren't you, Ellie? Your name was on that informants list."

"I don't have the list . . ." Ellie looked around the room half-expecting to see Avery coming from the afterworld with a club. "And besides it wasn't all about the list," she said, her shoulders slumping forward, her voice starting to crack.

"Then what was it about?" His voice was low, confidential, as if no one else would ever need to know.

"It was about staying alive, I suppose," she said, and slumped deeper into the chair. "Or I suppose you could say I whored myself out to Floodwater."

An empty ore truck rolled past the bar and the building shook on its pilings.

"Did Avery kill David Kept?" George leaned in.

"David Kept . . ." she said, letting the words escape like a long held breath.

"Tell me about it," was all the detective had to say.

The drunken Red stared down at the bloody wrappings on her hand.

"Everybody was selling information to the Floodwater ops. Hell, it was like there was no real organizing being done anymore. The Party, even the unions, were making up their shortfalls selling secrets to the private detectives."

"But the good union man, the crusader David Kept, didn't like the arrangement," George offered.

Ellie looked up at the police officer, whom she hadn't seen before but had always known was on his way. She spoke softly and slowly, not a speech and not a confession but a statement of fact. "There was someone in his own union on Ben's payroll. David Kept was going to confront Ben Avery. David Kept had an informants list. I don't know how the hell he got it but he had it. Ben Avery killed Kept. Used his own gun and put the body in the trunk of the car and then told me to get rid of the evidence. I was on the hook with Ben already. Just as you said, I was on the list. He figured if things went bad with his alibi he'd pin the killing on me."

The barman brought the coffee. Ellie pushed it away with her left hand, then winced with pain, keeping her eyes shut for several seconds.

"Why did you stop at the little farm near Everett?"

"I don't want to talk about anybody else."

"Come on, you met Ben Avery there?" George raised his voice and the bartender's eyes flickered over to their table for a moment.

"Christ, no," Ellie said. "Ben screwed up. Kept had the papers in a case. Ben had the case in the trunk. Ben forgot to get the papers out of the trunk when he turned over the car to me. He needed those papers back. But I had them."

"But Floodwater would need those back," George offered.

"Sure, but why should I give him back what he was using to blackmail me?"

"So who was the stooge in David Kept's union? Come on Ellie, you had the list."

"I lost the list."

"Come on, Ellie."

"All I wanted was to get out from under. Money for flying lessons. Money to just fly away."

"Were the men in Ketchikan on Avery's informants list?"

"I'm not talking about Ketchikan," Ellie said articulating each syllable in a drunkard's diction.

"Why talk at all? Why not keep on moving? Head to Canada. Ship out on a freighter."

"You know as well as I do, I'm not making it out of this town. Not after Ketch-i-kan," she said in a loopy stage whisper. "I'm just hoping they keep my niece out of this. But hell. I don't know now . . . . Floodwater owns this town."

George walked over to the bar and asked for a pitcher of milk. He stirred some into both of the coffees and pushed a cup close to Ellie. He wrapped his hands around the warm coffee mug. Ellie pushed her coffee away.

"What about the revolution, Ellie? Will it come?"

"Bits at a time maybe. I don't know."

"What about these poor saps out on strike. What will they get?"

"They'll get a beating. Then they'll get a token raise."

"So they get what they want."

"They get a few more cents. But they'll die down there, slaving for someone else's prosperity."

"But for better pay."

"It doesn't matter what the pay is. They'll never jump ahead in line. They'll never be the ones deciding who lives and who dies. Paid slaves."

The barman brought the sandwiches and the glasses of brandy. He set the tray on the table and laid out the sandwiches and shots before them as if it were a banquet.

"Three dollars for everything," he said, and George paid him.

"Ellie," he said, after the barman walked away, "I don't want you to tell me about Ben Avery and how he died. I don't want you to tell me until after you hear my proposition."

Ellie took too big a bite out of the sandwich. She could only hold it in one hand and a slice of greenish-looking meat fell out onto the table. The dirt on her hand rubbed off onto the soft white bread.

"All right," she blurted through her stuffed mouth.

"Because you are right. You're in a dead end here, Ellie. Either these union boys are going to kill you or Floodwater will."

Ellie chased the bite of sandwich down with the shot of brandy. "So?"

"I want to take you into custody here. I book you as a material witness to Ben Avery's murder."

"So I can be hung down in Washington?"

"Listen to me, Ellie. You are a material witness. I get you out of here. You give me everything you have on Floodwater's operations and you testify truthfully in the Ben Avery murder investigation and we set you up with something nice back down in the States."

"I testify truthfully in the murder investigation?"

"That's right, Ellie. The way I see it, Slippery Wilson probably killed Ben in self-defense. Ben was going to kill him for protecting you."

"Slippery Wilson. He's my hero, all right." Ellie rattled the empty brandy glass around on the table. George turned, whistled to the barman, and waved his finger over the glasses.

"All right then. You testify truthfully that you saw this Slippery Wilson character kill Ben Avery."

"I suppose I could do that," Ellie said. The barman brought her another drink and she stared down into it as if it were a wishing well.

≈≈≈

Slip never found Ellie that night. He wasn't even sure he wanted to find her. He should slip up into Canada. Leave the girl with Carl on *The Shepherd*, she'd be better off anyhow. As the darkness came on, the bars got louder with the clatter of glasses. Some of the bars had phonograph records that hissed out their thin music through small paper speakers. As the evening went on, fights started. Two men were grunting and rolling out into the street, pulling each other's shirts over their heads and throwing roundhouse punches that flailed into the dirt like parts of a broken combine.

From the gutter a half-naked man with blood running down his chin put his bottle down for a moment and looked up at Slip. "Whachyou looking hat?" the drunk blurted.

Slippery eased around the corner and out of sight. He had to go back to the boat for his tool kit and he was not going back without something to show, something to talk about so he wouldn't have to face the silence of avoiding Annabelle's questions. So he started asking about Amos Tisher, the boy from Boot Cove who never wanted to go home.

Amos wasn't hard to find. There was only one bar where the workers of the new miners association felt safe to drink. They all were given temporary memberships in the Arctic Brotherhood Hall. The hall itself was easy to find because of the hired thugs standing around the front.

Slip asked the barmaid and she pointed Amos out. The young man was by himself in the corner watching the billiard game. He was chewing tobacco and spitting in the coffee cans that were set around the back wall. He spit like a kid eating watermelon and he rolled his shoulders when he thought someone was watching.

Slip walked up to the young man. "Your father's down in the harbor," he said. "He wants to talk with you."

"Excuse me?" the kid said with a silly tone that he probably thought sounded tough.

"You heard me. Let's walk down to the harbor. Your father wants to talk with you."

"Yeah, well maybe I don't want to talk with him," Amos said, rolling his shoulders and smirking like a guilty child.

Slip was not in the mood. He reached up, grabbed Amos by the throat, and whispered in his ear. "Listen, son, if you don't walk out with me right now, I'm going to tell all your scab playmates that you are a Red and that you work for Ellie Hobbes."

"I don't know no Ellie Hobbes, mister." The kid leaned back and pulled Slip's hand away. "Go peddle your papers, bub. I ain't going anywhere."

"You filthy Red bastard," Slip yelled at the top of his lungs, and the two billiard players put up their cues and stared. "I ain't selling out my friends for no radical claptrap," Slip then swung down hard on Amos's chin and stepped back to watch the kid fall.

There was a scuffle in the Arctic Brotherhood Hall, but most of the drunks sided with Slip, who loudly asserted that the kid was an informant for the striking miners union. He insisted that the kid had been pumping him for information about when the scabs would make their move. Drunkards swore and spit on the boy in righteous indignation. But soon enough the scuffle was getting bad for business and the Floodwater boys threw them both out on the street.

Amos sulked as they walked down to the harbor. "I ain't going back. I hate sheep," he muttered.

"You like dying in the mines?" Slip pushed him along.

"I ain't gonna die. I'm careful."

"I don't think you know how many ways there are for a scab to die on the job." Slip pushed him down the wharf, where they found a kid in a skiff just coming back from fishing who was willing to take them out to *The Shepherd*.

～～～

Ellie Hobbes woke up on a cot set up in the back of the bar. George Hanson had paid the barman two dollars to let her sleep there and a couple of bucks more for a good breakfast when she woke up. Ellie woke up feverish. She had had vivid dreams about dead people walking up from the water carrying signs. They walked slowly and didn't speak. Their signs were blank. Ellie was sick. Her hand throbbed down in the bones and the skin burned against the wrappings.

When she sat down at the bar a new barman stepped back, held his nose, and waved his hand as if Ellie's dressings were crawling with flies. "I tell you, doll, you better get that thing cleaned up or you'll lose the whole mitt." Ellie thanked him for his concern and ordered some corned beef hash and a beer.

Ellie had been drunk when the policeman from Seattle had been buying drinks. Her memory of the night was slurred with the images of her dream and the pain pounding through her body. She remembered his offer. Go into his custody and provide information. Tell a tale about the night Ben Avery died and live in peace.

The beer was warm and the hash was mostly salty potatoes, but she forced them both down. The cop had been selling a fairy tale. Ellie Hobbes knew there would be no peace. She ate the hash, tapped the top of the bar and fished into her pocket, but the barman waved her off.

"It's covered, doll. Go get that hand looked at."

Ellie nodded and stumbled out of the bar. The morning was overcast, the clouds still shredding up through the spruce trees just in back of town. The air felt like a cold steam bath, so she put up her collar and asked a boy where the scabs were holed up.

Outside the new miners association hall, men in clean work clothes stood two deep. Some had their arms folded. Others shifted from foot to foot watching everyone around them. Two had homemade bats in their hands, the fat ends resting lightly on their shoulders. Ellie tried to push past them but men crowded around. She told them her name and they moved aside so Ellie could step inside. Three guards stopped her on the way to the back room. They didn't search her because two of them didn't want to get near the smell of her bandages. When they asked after her business she told them her name was Ellie Hobbes and that's all they needed to know. One of them went to the next room, came back quickly, and jerked his thumb over his shoulder.

"In there," he snapped. When the door opened a man with wire-rimmed glasses sat behind a card table. He was rolling a cigarette. There was a revolver on the table and a chipped ball bat leaning against the back of his chair.

"It's about time you came in, Ellie," he said.

Ellie sat down in the chair across from him. "I need to see your doctor," she demanded.

"I can see that," the man said. He licked the seam of his cigarette and rolled it between his fingers. "We can arrange medical services for members in good standing, Ellie."

"I must be in good standing." Ellie slid her hand across the table. The dressings were crusted with black and smelled like rotten meat. A bloody smear pointed across the table at the man with the wire-rimmed glasses, who lit his cigarette and pushed back in his chair.

"I guess we'd have to ask Pierce, Conner, and Cobb about your standing."

"Yeah, we could also ask Dave Kept."

"True enough," he said, and blew smoke down onto Ellie's hand.

"There are Floodwater ops all over this town. Why haven't they wrapped me up?"

"Ask them, Ellie."

Ellie thought of her dream: dead people walking across the water, hundreds and thousands of them shoaling like fish. She rubbed her eyes, realizing that she hadn't been really awake for a long, long time.

"Go ahead, ask them, Ellie." The man with the glasses leaned across the table and blew a plume of smoke into her face.

"What do you want from me?" Ellie asked.

"We've got a favor to ask," the man said. "You've got to make a speech."

"Get me a doctor, will you?"

"Sure, Ellie. Just so you give a barn burner, something that gets them out of their chairs."

"I can do that," Ellie said, and she fell forward onto the card table, her eyes closed and the dressing on her left hand dripping blood onto the tips of her shoes.

Legions of the dead were walking up the river valleys, no one saying a word, each in lockstep with the other, each indistinguishable from the other. And their signs were blank.

Amos Tisher sat sulking in the wheelhouse of his father's boat.

"I can make you come back with me, by God I can," his father said.

"I got my own life," the young man muttered.

Carl Tisher walked to the helm and started the engine. "You got everything you need?" He looked at Slip and Annabelle sitting at the chart table. "I wrapped up some jars of peaches for you. I put them in the dory."

"That's fine," Slip said, and he stood up to take the last bit of Annabelle's gear to the dory, which was tied off *The Shepherd*'s stern. The little girl carried the empty birdcage, which she had insisted on bringing into the wheelhouse. She still liked to fiddle with the silver bell hanging inside the cage.

Amos stood up and walked down to the forward berth.

"He'll be all right. His time will come soon enough. Just not now. Not here," Carl said to Slip, standing by the stern doorway. "Thank you for finding him."

"That's okay," Slip said, nodding to the old man. "Thanks for the lift, and again I'm sorry about the lamb."

"It all worked out." Carl walked with him back to the stern and helped him and Annabelle into the dory.

As they pulled toward the wharf in Juneau, Annabelle watched *The Shepherd* pull anchor and motor away. She watched intently, one arm resting on top of the empty cage, not taking her eyes off the boat.

"What you looking at?" Slip asked.

"I'm waiting to see if Amos jumps off the boat."

Slip shook his head as he stroked the oars. "No, I don't think he has it in him."

Slip looked at the girl in the stern. She was sitting in the spot where Ellie had sat. She was pointing toward where she wanted Slip to steer. She seemed older now. It was something in how she narrowed her eyes when looking forward. For the first time he could see just how much she looked like Ellie.

"I have something to tell you," Slip said. The girl turned away from his voice and looked down into the water. A gull flew down beside the boat and plucked a silvery fish out of the sea.

"I don't think we're going to see Ellie no more," Slip said. He took a long breath and started to say something more, but he couldn't.

Annabelle picked up Buddy's cage and dropped it into the water. She didn't appear angry or impulsive. She just put it overboard. Slip stopped rowing and they both watched the cage drift down into the gloom until it disappeared completely.

"You don't want that?" Slip asked.

"Don't need it," the girl said. "Where's Ellie, then?"

"I don't know. I guess some rough men in Ketchikan took her up into the woods and she killed them."

"We better go find her," Annabelle said, with the heft of certainty in her voice.

The Shepherd was disappearing down the channel and two gulls wheeled above its stern. Whatever was in Slip's heart to be hard against Ellie for his troubles, or against God for that matter, had dissolved into steam.

"We'll find her then," he said.

"Where are we going to sleep tonight?" she said, her eyes glittering with tears.

Sip stopped rowing and looked at the girl, her braids hanging down on her shoulders and her glasses tilted on the bridge of her nose. "I'll think of something," he said.

They found a rocky beach on the north side of the wharf and they pulled the dory above the high-tide mark. Slip lifted the girl out of the boat and sat her on a rock. He stowed their gear in the bottom of the boat and covered it as best he could with a tarp to keep it dry. Then he took her hand and they walked up the steep bank and into the woods.

They walked toward the sound of a truck and ended up going down a steep ravine. Clouds moved past the sun and pools of light appeared on the forest floor, illuminating sometimes a single tree or the broad leaf of a devil's club plant. Among old hemlock stumps fallen trees lay in a chaotic pattern. Soon they couldn't hear a truck or the rumble of town. All they heard was the running water of a creek.

Soon they were disoriented and their bearing swirled around them so they couldn't be sure where the boat or the beach was. They walked downhill until they met the creek and then followed the direction the water was flowing. They clambered down some steep pitches but soon enough they came to a footbridge. Just under the bridge a black bear was digging around the roots of some skunk cabbage plants, its red tongue curling around its teeth. It grunted and snuffled down the creek bed when it heard their footsteps on the rocks. They could look uphill and see houses with flagpoles and kids playing in the street.

"Let's go back in the woods," Annabelle said.

"Come on, don't you want to get something to eat downtown?"

"No," she said. "Let's just go back into the woods." Her jaw was quivering again and she began to cry.

They walked back into the woods and sat down on a dry log near the stream. They sat there until the sun moved down toward the mountains across the channel and the sky opened up with rain.

The rain was soaking through their clothes when he talked her into walking out of the woods. At first he tried holding her hand but she tugged away so he let her go. He walked a few paces ahead of her and she lagged behind, trudging down the wooden steps of the steep trails into town.

Slip went into the new union hiring hall. It was crowded with men nervously standing around. They shifted from foot to foot as they waited, without looking anyone in the eye. A man with a broken arm sitting behind a desk gave Slip an application form and asked him if he could read. Slip nodded and walked out the door. He turned the corner where he had left the girl, and there was Annabelle talking to two men in dark suits. One was a young man showing the girl a badge.

"Mr. Wilson," George Hanson said, and reached out to shake the logger's hand. "I was just telling the girl how sorry I was to hear that her bird flew off." Then he knelt down so that his eyes were at Annabelle's level and he spoke to her as he would to an adult. "I'm going to ask Officer Tillman here to take you over to the drugstore fountain for some ice cream. Would that be all right with you?"

"I don't want ice cream," she said solemnly.

"What would you like?" George knelt close to her.

"Hot chocolate," she said, and then added, "if you don't mind."

"Of course." George stood up and gestured to Tillman to take the girl.

"Will Slip come too?" the girl asked.

"Yes. After we have a talk, we'll both come in for a cup."

"I don't have money," the girl said.

"Officer Tillman will pay for it," George said firmly, then nodded once again to the young policeman.

The girl walked around the corner with Walter Tillman. He put his hand out for her to take but she jammed her hands into her pants pockets. Slip watched her until she was around the corner and out of sight.

"Ellie Hobbes says you killed Ben Avery. What about it, Slip?"

Slip felt something collapse inside himself. He was tired and wanted to lie down.

"You have Ellie?" he asked the man in the blue suit.

"Ellie's here in Juneau. She's working for Floodwater. Did you know that?"

"Like fun she is."

"No. It's true, Slip."

"They almost killed us at the hobo jungle," Slip's voice had gone up an octave.

"I didn't say they were good people to work for," George said without a smile.

Slip fell back against the wall of the union hall and rubbed his eyes as if he were trying to shake off a particularly disturbing hallucination. "Are you going to arrest me now?"

"I don't think so. You've got no place to go. You're not going to get back in that skiff and take off with the girl. Where would you go?"

"All I wanted was to buy a little place and raise a cow or two," Slip said, still rubbing his eyes and starting to slide down the wall. George stepped over and held him up by the elbow.

"That's not a bad thing to want." George helped him to his feet.

"You think there's any chance it could still happen?" His voice sounded thin to his own ears.

"Not if you're hanged for killing a Floodwater op in Seattle." George's voice was growing harder.

"Why don't you just arrest me?" Slip blustered.

"Because I don't see why you would kill Ben Avery."

"You ever meet him?" Slip's eyes glazed with the effects of a bad memory.

"Yeah, and I'm not saying he wasn't worth killing. I'm just saying that between the two of you, Ellie had the motive."

"You say Ellie was working for Floodwater?"

"She was trying to beat them at their own game. She lost, but I guess that's pretty obvious now. She'll sell you out, Slip. You can come with me now and it'll be her in jail and you can start finding that piece of land."

A breeze blew some damp grit down the street, flopping the pages of a discarded newspaper over and over like a dying fish.

"I want you to think about it overnight." George stood close to him and nudged Slip's chest with his index finger. "Think about how Ben died . . . exactly how he died. Then tomorrow I'm going to ask you what happened. You understand me?"

Slip nodded. He was too tired to run. His legs felt rubbery and his hands were shaking. George dug into his pocket and took some cash out of his billfold.

"There's a place up the hill. The lady rents out rooms. It's a nice spot and she'll look after the girl. Get her off the street, Slip. You may be the only family she's got."

"What do you mean?"

"Tomorrow Ellie is going to break the strike deadlock. She's going to lead the scabs up the hill."

"What's that to me?" Slip asked.

"I thought maybe you'd want to talk to her one more time before I came to lock you up." Then George slapped Slip on the shoulder and turned him toward the corner. "Let's get some hot cocoa."

As they turned, two men shouldered past them on the sidewalk. One of the men was a thin man with steel-rimmed glasses and the other was Tom Delaney. The tall Floodwater chief didn't acknowledge George as the front of his coat brushed up against the policeman's chest. Delaney put his hand out to fend off the policeman, and as he did his tight Masonic ring glinted in the sunlight. Slip turned around and watched the men's backs as they walked away.

"You know him?" George asked.

"The tall man. I saw him down in Washington before I got in the dory."

"Where'd you see him, Mr. Wilson?" George asked.

"We made a stop."

"You and Ellie?"

"That's right." Slippery was stopped now, staring at the shoulders of the tall man lumbering up the hill.

"At a farmhouse near Everett and that man was there?" George stood close, his voice excited now.

"The tall one with the big ring. He was there. He took some papers from her." Slip said softly, digging into his memory.

"That's good, Mr. Wilson. Let me buy you something hot to drink," George said, and he slapped him once more on the back.

Slip didn't accept the policeman's generosity. He waited for the girl to come outside, and then he left the cops standing on the corner without saying good-bye. Annabelle started to thank the policemen but Slip took her hand and walked away before she could get the words out. They walked through town and over to the dory, which was still tied to the stump where they had left it. The little boat seemed as patient as an old horse standing in her stall. Slip thought of getting in and pushing away from the beach. He thought of rowing down the channel and putting the sail up for whatever wind would push them the farthest. He looked down the channel where the wind riffled on the surface. The tide was fair for them and there was enough daylight to get well away before all hell broke loose tomorrow.

"What about Ellie?" Annabelle asked. The sweet taste of chocolate was still in her mouth. She pushed her glasses up her nose. "What about Ellie? Shouldn't we go get her?"

Slip looked at her. Her pants were ripped and the tail of her shirt hung halfway out her pants. Her braids were loose and fraying. She seemed smaller than she actually was.

"Yes," Slip said, knowing that if he disappeared from Juneau now he would be convicted for the murder of Ben Avery. "We better find Ellie." And he started back toward town with the girl.

That evening Slip went back to the dory and got his bindle and a suitcase of clothes for the girl. He had no idea how long they would be in Juneau. A light rain fell on him as he walked back to the boardinghouse. Rain ran down the windows as he got Annabelle settled on the folding cot in the room. The girl didn't want to read the Oz book Slip had found in the house for her. She didn't want to play with any of the kids who were swinging from a rope swing behind the house. She lay on the cot with her glasses on and her eyes open as if she were afraid to go to sleep.

Slip took a shower down the hall. He put on a different wrinkled shirt and combed his hair. When he came back, the girl was asleep. He reached down and took off her glasses.

Slip was bone tired. He tried to think of a way he could leave this town and his troubles behind him. He didn't want to go to jail. All he wanted was to wake up in his own bed on a cool morning of a warm day. But that wasn't going to happen. He sat down on the edge of his bed and watched the girl sleep until the sky flared silver and settled into its long summer twilight.

Downstairs George Hanson withstood the silence of the young police officer from Ketchikan. The landlady had poured them each a glass of iced tea and had excused herself to go back to her room to read. All that passed between the two men was the clicking of ice.

Finally George said, "After we finish this, one of us should take a chair and sit out by the back door. You can see the window to his room from there. One of us can stay here at the front."

Walter nodded his head as if he understood. The young policeman reached into the bag at his feet and lifted out a revolver in a burnished leather holster.

"Brought you a weapon. My captain told me you would need one," the young man said.

George took the weapon and pulled the gun from its case. "Thank you," he said, "though I doubt it will be of much use. Once the shooting starts, I don't think a pistol will do much good."

Walter Tillman leaned closer to the older officer. "Why is Ellie Hobbes going to lead the scabs up the hill to the mine?"

"She's got no choice. The strike's at a deadlock. People are losing money. Management can't just force them to cross the line at gunpoint. They need it to seem like it's the workers' idea."

"There will be hell to pay."

"That's true, but management won't be paying. Violence gives them an excuse to break up the strike."

"What about Ellie Hobbes?" Walter rattled the ice in his glass.

"They're throwing Ellie out with the trash. Besides a battle right now works to everybody's advantage, even the strikers. Some of them are starting to have second thoughts. Head cracking will radicalize a few of them."

"Why don't we take Wilson and Hobbes into custody right now, tonight?"

George Hanson stretched and settled into his chair. He sighted down the barrel of the pistol. "I don't have enough to hold either of them, even if we could get someone here to authorize an arrest. We need one of the two to come running into our arms."

"One of them is going to be killed," the young man said, staring at the floor.

"I think it's probably worse than that," George said as he spun the cylinder of the gun. "If we don't do things just right tomorrow, lots of us may be killed."

TWENTY-ONE

〜〜〜

The two policemen traded shifts during the night so that by the time Slip and the girl clambered out the bedroom window, Walter Tillman was sleeping lightly on a straight-back chair just off the porch. He woke up when Slip threw a bundle of clothes down into the bushes below his window.

It was early morning and the sunlight had a syrupy warmth to it as Slip and the girl wound their way through lanes, empty lots, and interconnecting trails. Twice Annabelle fell behind and he turned to take her hand, and twice he saw the policeman duck out of sight.

All through town men were waking up and leaving their houses early. The city attorney, who was also the lawyer for the mine, had drafted a police protection act. People could not gather in groups larger than five without being subject to arrest. That morning men tapped on windows and whispered to their friends. Miners were spreading the word about the scabs marching on the mine. Businessmen were reporting to the Arctic Brotherhood Hall to work as deputies. Kids climbed trees to get a good view of the street. Police were unlocking the trunks where they kept the tear gas, and firemen checked the hydrants for water pressure and made sure their hoses were ready.

Slip and the girl passed two men in an alley smoking cigarettes and speaking intently to each other. The men caught sight of them and ducked into a doorway. Through another open window Annabelle heard a man arguing with his wife. The sound of breaking crockery rained down on their shoulders as they walked past.

Slip took Annabelle to the dory. He pulled back the tarp and moist air billowed out of the hull. He made a nest in the bow and tucked the girl down where she could pull the canvas over her head if she needed to hide.

"I'm going to go uptown," Slip said. "I'll try and find Ellie."

"I want to come," Annabelle said with ambivalence.

"You wait here. No matter what. You say it back to me now."

"I'll just stay here," the girl said and she sat still in the boat.

Slip looked down at her and she seemed so still that the world could have stopped moving. The clouds could have been hung from hooks and turned to ice. He reached down and touched her cheek. "That's fine. You stay here," he said. He stuck the handle of the axe down his pants leg so the axe head hooked into his belt. He walked a little stiff-legged but that was okay, because he didn't feel like sprinting anyway.

Men were beginning to gather in front of the new miners association hall. Everyone wore their hats. Some even had ties on under their work coats. They were going for jobs but few expected to dig rock that afternoon. Floodwater operatives in their long wool coats and newly deputized store owners walked the perimeter of the block, waving anybody through who said they wanted to go to work. They checked their names against lists of the striking miners. They had no need to enforce the police protection act here. This gathering was sanctioned, and the deputies were walking the sidewalks like barkers trying to get more workers to join the crusade.

"You going to let them radical bastards tell you to go hungry?" one called out to a skinny old man with tobacco stains down the front of his shirt. The old man shifted from foot to foot and mumbled some excuses for why he needed to leave. But dozens of men pushed past the men with the lists and once inside the block the deputies would not let them leave. There were a few men who looked like they were ready for work, but there were far more who weren't. They had on slick-soled shoes and hunting jackets.

"I'm just here to take a look. I've got to run back to the house in a second," one man in a grey fedora said.

Over by the hall someone was passing a flask, and someone brayed to his friends, "What right they got to say that I can't work?" Some men nodded and some walked away. Up a side street they heard a slurry of swearing and baton blows thudding down on someone's ribs. Three more men drifted away. Two more men showed up.

Ellie Hobbes sat in the front window of the miners association office. The doctor had changed her dressings and given her some sulfa tablets. Ellie had on a new skirt and a clean white blouse. She had dark rings under her eyes and when she smiled her mouth couldn't quite stretch over her teeth. Even in the fresh clothes she had the sad countenance of a beaten mule.

A kid ran out from the back room and brought her a glass of brandy. Ellie gave him a nickel tip and watched him jam it into his pants pocket with a grin. As the kid started back Ellie called him over and gave him another dime.

"Thanks, lady!" the kid said. He flipped the dime end over end and caught it as if he were James Cagney or a big city swell.

"That's okay," Ellie said. "You got a hole to hide in back there?"

"Are you crazy?" The kid stood flat-footed with his face screwed up.

"I used to work in a bar when I was a kid, and I always had a hiding place for when fights broke out. I had a little spot beside the cooler where nobody could get to me. You got a place like that?"

"I can handle myself," the kid said, and he put the dime in his pocket and swaggered off.

Ellie watched him go and she felt sick to her stomach. The doctor had said she should be in the hospital, but there wasn't much need for that now. She looked out the window at all the working men milling around. The atmosphere was charged and tentative at the same time.

"They should have some music or something, maybe a vaudeville comic, something to keep their minds off of what is going to happen next," Ellie said aloud, though no one was listening.

Tom Delaney walked from the back room and stood over her. "We're losing them," he said.

"Yes, you are," Ellie said, taking a drink and watching the nervous men looking for a way out.

"We need these spineless sons of bitches to go over to the hiring hall."

"They just don't look too anxious to take a beating," Ellie said without looking at the shamus.

"What the hell's the matter with them? If enough of them go there, no one would have to take a beating."

Ellie smiled broadly and set the empty glass down on the table. "Why don't you go out and tell them that?"

"Why would the strikers put up a fight? They know they'll get stomped."

Ellie laughed. "They are thinking the exact same thing about you," and she waved her hands at the scene on the street. "They think you're bringing the revolution to them."

Outside two more men joined the group passing the flask. A man in work clothes glanced at his watch and looked nervously at the deputies. Delaney tugged on Ellie's shoulder.

"Well, nothing's going to happen if somebody doesn't build a fire underneath these boys."

"We've got a deal?" Ellie said again without looking up.

"We'll talk about that later."

"What if I don't go out there?"

"You feeling suicidal, Ellie?"

"Not particularly."

"Then it looks like we have a deal."

Walter had lost Slip in the crowd that was flowing through the streets toward the miners association hall. Deputies pushed away gawkers with their batons and waved through any scabs who said they wanted to go to work. Walter pushed against the crowd and held his badge in front of him but the crowd was too tight. Slip had somehow hit a clearing in the crowd that closed in behind him.

Slip kept walking toward the front of the miners association hall. Someone had turned over a crate on top of a couple of pallets and deputies were clearing a space for a speaker. Slip kept one hand on the axe head and leaned into whatever body was blocking his way.

"Christ, buddy, ease up, will you?" someone yelled, but Slip pushed toward the front of the crowd, the blade of the axe hard against his hip. He thought about being arrested, about tight handcuffs and the long months of waiting until someone led him up the thirteen steps where a long-faced executioner stood ready. He thought of Ellie and whether she had made a deal with the cops.

There was some logic in killing her, once all hell broke loose, just as it surely was. Nobody would stop him. Then he thought of that first moment he saw her beside the Skagit River and he thought of all the wild country he had seen since then. Like it or not, he was living in that wild country now.

No one introduced her. Ellie got up on the overturned crates, looked out into the crowd, and waited for them to settle. There were men and a few boys. Some were waiting for her to speak. Some nervously looked at their watches. Some looked up the hill where the silent mine sat like a monument. One by one their attention turned to Ellie, maybe out of curiosity, maybe just because there was nowhere else to look.

"Brothers," she said loudly, but no one looked up. "I been asked to talk to you today because I've been here before."

"You ain't *my* brother!" someone called from the crowd.

"That's true," she said smiling, her bruised face apologetic. "You don't know me. But I've been here." She cleared her throat and held up her bandaged hand where fresh blood was already weeping through. "I used to have a good hand but a machine took off most of it," she yelled. The man who had been catcalling stepped back and pulled his hat down on his head.

Ellie scanned the faces. "A plain, stupid machine. Just a machine in a cannery, like a million others up and down this coast. It was my own fault and I'll live with it. I might even get me a job posing for exit signs." Ellie held up the deformed profile of her hand with the index finger pointing up the hill. A few men chuckled.

"You know, they fired me for cutting my fingers off." She paused and looked around. "But they didn't do a thing to that machine. It's still working there if I'm not mistaken." A few of the boys laughed out loud.

Slip was close enough now that he could see Ellie clearly without having to stand on his tiptoes or lean around the hulking kid who had blocked his way. Slip pulled the axe out slowly and kept it under his coat. He bumped a fat man standing next to him, but the man never turned his head.

His fingers turned white against the head of the axe. He looked at the battered woman he had come so far with. *Who am I kidding?* Slip thought to himself, letting the axe swing loosely at his side. *This is not my time to change.*

"I guess I'm going to jail," Slip muttered, and the big man in front of him turned to give him a sour look.

"Then stay the hell away from me, buddy," the big man said.

"I ain't going to lie to you, boys," Ellie continued. "I don't really care if you go hungry tonight. I got my own troubles."

Men started grumbling, looking around to see if this was the real speaker or some crank.

"You know what else? Nobody cares. Nobody cares if you get lung disease working up in that mine. Nobody cares if your kids die young from something that a rich kid just gets a couple of shots to fix. That gold is just a bunch of rocks without your labor, but you think they're going to pay you enough to fix your teeth or feed your family if you get hurt? If you don't know it yet boys . . . ain't nobody cares about you, as long as they get their gold."

"Who the hell are *you*, lady?" someone yelled.

Ellie snapped right back. "I'm just a lady who wants a good life. I want a man who doesn't come home too tired to make babies at the end of the day."

And a wild cry went round the crowd, some laughter, some booing.

"I want a good life for me and my man. I want something more than the promise that if we work hard we'll get rich. That if we cough up our lungs down in a hole or change the diapers for rich women's children, then we'll get rich. 'Cause that's a lie and you know it."

"We know that the only way anybody gets rich is by exploiting the hard work of people just like you." Ellie pointed to an old man standing in the front of the crowd. "Hey, pop, you know anybody ever got rich working in a mine?" The old man shook his head and spit on the ground.

Ellie raised her voice so that the men in the back standing on their toes could hear. "Just look around, boys. You see anybody here who's gonna get rich? You see any Rockefellers in the crowd today? Hell, you see anybody who's going to make babies tonight?"

A couple of men elbowed each other and laughed. One guy pointed his own thumb at his chest. Ellie picked up on the gesture and looked straight at him.

"You aren't going to make babies. Hell, you'll be lucky to live through the week."

Some boys were grumbling. The deputies were scowling and tapping their batons against their legs.

"I'll tell you something else. You ain't going to start a revolution neither. The union says you'll get justice if you stick with them. Well, they're sticking together, but nobody's working, nobody's getting any justice."

Ellie pointed down to a dark-haired kid with a patched felt hat. "Did they ask you if they should go on strike?" Ellie yelled out to the crowd, "Are you going to share in the profits if they end up getting a raise? Hell, no. You just want a job so you won't have an empty belly tonight. You just want to start work and maybe get a say in things. But the trade unions won't feed your kids tonight."

"You're goddamn right!" the man next to Slip yelled.

"You think those union boys care a whit about you? They don't. Truth is, all you boys are going to die broke. The union don't care as long as they get their dues. Management don't care as long as they get their gold, and the government don't care as long as you stay quiet. So where's that leave you sorry sons of bitches?" Ellie looked out at the crowd and they didn't speak. They didn't step forward and not one of them would look another in the eye.

Ellie stepped forward and took a breath, and then stopped. "The hell with it," she said, and stepped down off the box.

Men started yelling insults. They had their fists pumping the air.

"Goddamn Red bastard," screamed the man next to Slip. He started pushing the smaller men out of the way. Another called her a "management spy" and surged in behind the other, yelling, "I'll show you where that leaves us." Men were fighting their way over to Ellie, and they knocked her to the ground.

Slip walked forward and swung the axe toward the men surrounding Ellie. A man with a pick handle knocked the knees out from under Slip and the axe clattered out of his hand. The big man crouched over Ellie and swung away at her with roundhouse punches. A couple of older men tried to pull her attackers off. Men were yelling and swearing, their mouths flecked with spit. People in the back of the crowd pushed forward to see what was going on. Someone in the back threw a rock into the crowd. A bottle arched over the street and exploded against a man's skull, and a roar went up from the crowd.

And then, just as if a dam had given way, the mob became dislodged and surged up the street: a current of shabby men flowed up the avenue toward the union hall and the mine.

Tom Delaney ran out into the street and sapped down a big man beating Ellie. Others ran away and followed the charge to the hiring hall. Deputies jumped over men lying in the street, trying to stay ahead of the crowd. The men in the front of the crowd had their fists in the air. They jostled each other as they stormed up the street.

The scabs rounded the corner near the union hall and a wave of union boys with pick handles waded into the crowd. Sticks smacked against skulls and men fell limp to the ground; some tried to pick them up, and others stomped them with their boots. Firemen turned on hoses and tear gas canisters spun in the streets.

Three scabs had Slip on the ground and were kicking him while he curled and tried to roll away. Walter Tillman pushed his way out of the current of men heading up the street and pulled the men off. Slip stood up and ran, and he became indistinguishable from the other men running through the streets.

George Hanson pushed and punched his way through the crowd until he got to where Delaney was lifting Ellie Hobbes to her feet.

"I'm taking this woman into custody," George yelled above the din.

Two Floodwater ops pushed toward George. Both of them were wearing heavy leather gloves. One punched him in the gut to double him over and the other caught him on the chin with a right upper cut. George rolled on the street, then looked up for a moment and saw a dazzling field of blue diamonds. Then he went limp.

Tom Delaney grabbed Ellie by the infected stumps of her lost fingers. "What the hell was that?" Delaney hissed at her.

Ellie was doubled over in pain. She could not walk. Delaney shifted his grip and Ellie straightened up.

"I built a fire under them," Ellie said, finally.

"All I know is I wouldn't want to be you," the Floodwater man said, jerking Ellie's bad arm through the door of the bar.

"That's a comfort to me, Tom," Ellie said, as the red-faced detective led her into the back room where the supplies were kept.

Inside the dark room they could hear the shouts and splashes of men being hosed down, the sound of boots thumping the wooden sidewalks in both directions, men running toward the fight and men running away. Shouts and curses. Glass breaking. Tom pulled on the chain of the overhead light. Then he took out his revolver, pulled the hammer back, and put it to Ellie's ear.

"You got to answer for what you did to Ben Avery," Tom said.

"Go to hell," Ellie spat out.

Delaney said, "I'm not saying that Ben didn't screw things up. I never told him to go ahead and kill the union man, and now it's fallen to me to clean all this up." The barrel of the gun was quivering against the thin skin of Ellie's scalp. "You were a good little bum, Ellie, but you're dog meat now."

"Least I've been some use in this sorry world."

"You're a cocky little cunt, aren't you?"

"You can't kill me." Ellie was breathing hard, her wide eyes were darting around the room.

"Let's just see about that," he said, and picked up a bar towel. "Here," he barked. "Wrap this around your head. It will be easier to clean up that way."

George Hanson opened his eyes slowly. The din of the riot was a thin sizzle in his head. A crowd of men ran past him down the hill with bandannas held to their faces, their eyes red and streaming tears. George rolled over and pushed himself up. There were no policemen on the street. The clattering in his head grew louder. Men were running down the street from the union hall, and one bumped into George and nearly sent him to the ground.

"Sorry, bub," the man slurred. "I wouldn't go up there," he added, then took off back down the hill.

George limped his way to the new miners association hall and stumbled in the front door. Handbills for the speech were scattered on the floor along with the glass from one broken window. George took out his revolver and walked the edges of the room toward the back. He heard only his own weight squeaking against the floorboards. There was a door to a back room on the first floor, and he heard a thump, then the scuffle of feet. He took out his gun and pulled the hammer back and put his ear to the door. A glass clattered to the floor. More footsteps. Then nothing.

"Ellie," he called out. "Ellie Hobbes, you in there?" George stood to the side of the door, reached slowly for the knob, and eased the door open with his back against the wall.

A buffalo of a man came from behind him. He had one hand resting on the gun by his belt. From his angle he couldn't see

George's revolver, and as he walked straight toward the policeman he reached out as if he were going to throw him in the street. "Push off, pal" he said, and his left hand grabbed at George's shoulder.

The policemen turned and hit him with the butt of his gun, once across the nose and once again on the back of his head as he fell. George rolled him over and took the pistol from under the man's coat, and then turned to the door leading to the back room.

The door creaked on its hinges and cool air carried out of the open door. He could smell spilled beer and old cigars mixed in with the unmistakable tang of gunpowder.

George pushed his revolver into the room as if it were a flashlight. He shined it in every corner. "Hobbes?"

First he saw the legs splayed out on the floor. Then a blood-spattered towel against the side of a wool coat. George stepped into the room.

"Goddamnit," he said just under his breath.

A thick smear of dark blood and brain matter spread like a halo beneath the tall man. Nothing moved except a few flies buzzing around the widening puddle of blood. Tom Delaney lay dead on the floor.

A glass fell behind the counter and George swung his gun. "Police officer. Let's see your hands. Hands up, damnit, or I start shooting."

Two small hands trembled into view. They were holding a sawed-off shotgun with smoke still curling from both barrels.

"Stand up." George barked, and the boy Ellie had tipped so generously stood up with the gun over his head.

"He was going to shoot her, mister. I swear. He had his gun out and he was going to shoot her." Tears streamed down the boy's cheeks as he blubbered. "She just got up and ran out of here."

"Where'd she go?" George uncocked his gun.

"I don't know. She said 'thank you' though. And she gave me two dollars. Can I keep it? Can I keep the money?"

The tired police officer holstered his gun and slumped down on a beer keg.

"I suppose so," he said. "Just show me the door she used."

Outside, the fire brigade was rolling out the last of the hoses, and men were shouting orders over the rumble of people running in every direction.

Annabelle curled up in the dory and pulled the canvas over her head. The sounds of thudding boots and sirens tumbled through the streets and out across the beach. Peeking out, she saw the wisps of gas drifting down the side of the hill, like the clouds sliding through the trees. She hated the sound of sirens. She crawled to the bow of the dory and opened the kitchen box to find a sharp knife. She groped in the dark until she clutched it in her hand. She heard someone step right up to the dory and stop. Annabelle held her breath as a white arm reached into the gloom and touched her face with cold, sticky fingers.

Slip ran north and away from the roar of men's voices. He made his way under the wharf and along the beach. Once he reached a quiet street he pulled himself up onto the sidewalk and started walking back toward the dory. He walked fast, but not fast enough to call attention to himself. By the time he came within sight of the dory the riot sounded like a high school football game and a small one at that. Men were beginning to drift away in twos and threes. The police were lining up bleeding union men and placing them under arrest, and a few scabs were freely milling around the mine employment office where there were no employees to process the men who wanted to work. All the same the strike was over.

Slip walked down to the dory and called out Annabelle's name but no one answered. He threw back the tarp and dug around in the bottom of the boat. He ran around to the other side. Then he slumped down with his back against the dory. He had lost the axe in the riot and had a fresh set of bruises on his face and ribs. Ellie was going to the cops and she would testify against him. The girl was gone, and he was a thousand miles from Grand Coulee country. Slip lay down on the gravel beach. Small waves, panting like a pack of wolves, moved closer and closer as the tide came in.

The world refused to stop for Slippery Wilson, and that's all he had ever asked of it. There was a cabin near a river and a beautiful woman who loved him. These things had been anchored, unchanging in his heart, for as long as he could remember. As an adult he thought he had been moving toward them, but of course he hadn't.

"Maybe I just need a nap," he said aloud as the chill crept through his clothes, and he closed his eyes.

"Whatcha sleeping for?" Annabelle asked. She was leaning over him, with her frazzled braids hanging toward his face and her glasses on the tip of her nose.

"I got some ice cream," she said. "Want some?"

He kept his eyes shut, not knowing how much more curious his life could become. Then he looked over at the leather shoes and long skirt standing next to the girl, and his eyes moved up to the battered but still beautiful face of the woman, who was holding a folded cone of butcher paper with what looked like vanilla ice cream melting down the sides.

"No time for napping, pal. We got to make the tide," Ellie said.

Slip said nothing. He didn't move. As the tide rose it came closer and closer to his shoes. In another hour the Pacific Ocean would cover him completely.

"Where in the hell did you get ice cream?" he finally asked.

"I guess fishermen like to make their own ice cream when they come into port," Ellie said. "I got some ice for my bruises and this old boy gave me some. Good-hearted guy."

The little girl blinked at him, licking the sweet white cream off her fingers. Ellie reached down and put her own sweet finger to his lips.

"You know what I just figured out," she said.

"No," Slip murmured.

"The nice thing about being alive is that it can always get better. Let's get the hell out of here."

Slowly Slip stood up, and the three of them together pulled the dory down the beach as the shadow of the ridgeline crept up from the sea and dipped down into darkness.

T W E N T Y - T W O

~~~

A demagogue, like a broken watch, can always hope to be right at least twice a day. But a revolutionary wants to smash the watch altogether, which, no matter how often it's done, never succeeds in stopping time.

Ellie Hobbes had been both right and wrong about the trade unions. They sapped the strength out of the class struggle but they went on to improve the lives of most of their members. It took more than a year, but the newly established National Labor Relations Board finally turned the scabs out of the mine and reinstated the union boys at a better wage. Of course to this day, men keep dying in the mines; but at least management keeps raising their wages.

But this was the summer of 1935. That summer like all the summers before was atomizing into the past. It was the middle of August and already the emerald days were giving way to fall. The fireweed blossoms were turning to seed and pink salmon were churning up the rivers to spawn. George Hanson sat on the stone corner post set back in the woods. It had taken him five and a half weeks to trace them to this spot, about a mile and a half from where the new settlement of Cold Storage, Alaska, was being built. George had scrambled over fallen trees across a steep hill to get to their building site. There were skinned logs sitting under a shed roof and three stone slabs on a scoured-out patch of forest floor. Two drawknives were wrapped in cloth on top of a makeshift table. Three sharp axes leaned against a stump near the fire pit, a few feet from a snugly pitched canvas tent. It was a tidy enterprise.

George had stayed in Juneau, just long enough to make sure the kid at the bar didn't take any heat for killing the Floodwater boss. That had been easy enough to do. The town fathers were ready to have everybody get back to work and forget the ugliness of all that had been done to break the strike. That summer, ore trucks rumbled, the stamp mill howled, Juneau's air filled up with dust, and money jingled in pockets all over town.

George had sent his resignation by telegraph to Seattle and there was not much fuss in accepting it. Floodwater had made enough of a mess that their political muscle was not eager to flex. But neither was George's captain looking forward to seeing a report from Alaska that included dead operatives and young boys with shotguns. Better let it all stay in the far north.

The seas were calm back in the inlet where Cold Storage was being built. Five miles to the northwest the inlet opened into the North Pacific. Fat swells broke on black rocks and gulls busied the air. Just off the cabin site the water was smooth and a few cormorants paddled the current down the beach. Just beyond, a dory pulled into view around the rocky point from town.

George sat and watched as the girl hopped out to pull the painter line up the beach. Slippery Wilson steadied the boat with the oars and Ellie Hobbes stepped off the bow with an armload of groceries. Her hair was cut short now and almost all of it was her natural color of black.

Slip was the first to see George and he nodded to Ellie, who blanched and took two quick steps back toward the boat. Slip sat with the oars still in the water.

"I didn't mean to startle you," George said, and the two adults stared at him, eyes wide like two deer having come across a hunter.

Annabelle cantered up to him, her braids flying. "Want to see where I'm going to sleep?" she called out.

"Of course," the policeman said, and he took her hand for the grand tour of the imagined house emerging from the forest floor.

"What are we going to do?" Slip asked Ellie softly.

"We got enough food. We ask him for supper," Ellie said. She went to the toolshed to set down the groceries.

George looked over everything around the building site. Slip and he walked back in the woods to the stand of straight old trees. They walked along the stream near the house and talked about their water supply and the materials they were going to need. George asked questions about costs, and tools, and how to hang trusses with only a few people to help, and Slip answered slowly and carefully, always afraid about what the next question might be.

Ellie was threading venison on sticks and poking up the fire. Onions were frying in the pan and a coffeepot was burping its contents into the coals, as George and Slip walked back down to the beach fringe where the cabin would sit. Annabelle, having showed him where her area would be in the loft with a window to the north, had gone back to the log pile where she sat reading a book about canaries.

"So," Ellie said, handing him a cup of coffee, "you come to arrest us?"

"I don't know," George said, blowing over the top of the mug. "I'm not really a cop anymore. But there are a couple of things I'm curious about."

"All right," Ellie said, "shoot." She squatted on a log round and hung the meat over the fire.

"Ben Avery killed the union man, David Kept. You told me that back in the bar. Kept was not going along with Floodwater and he was going to blow the whistle on all the informants in the union."

"Yes," Ellie said.

"Why did you agree to get rid of the body?" George sat across the fire from her.

"I needed the informant list. Avery owned me as long as he had the list. I agreed to dump the body and give everything to Delaney while Ben took off and established an alibi."

"Do you still have the list?" George asked.

Slip bent down into his tool kit and took out his tobacco tin. The paper was damp and creased from being folded up so small but George could still make out the names.

"Then who killed Ben Avery? You, Mr. Wilson?" George sipped his coffee.

"I swear to God I didn't mean to," Slip said, with more sadness than defiance. "He had a knife. I had his gun. We wrestled a bit and it went off."

Slip stood up, his hands shaking at his sides. "I swear to God that's what happened."

"It's true," Ellie said.

George looked at them both, one to the other. "I know it's true," he said finally. "The way the path of the bullet lined up in his body matches your story. The muzzle blast on the clothes and the point of entry—all of it . . ." His voice faded away, and he stared into the fire for a moment.

"And the three men in Ketchikan?"

"I'm sorry but I'm still not talking about Ketchikan," Ellie said. "If you want to hang somebody for it you can hang me."

"I just thought I'd ask, you know, because I'm curious, is all."

"Well . . ." she said, "you asked."

"You see . . . there's a Negro at a cathouse in Ketchikan who seems a little nervous about it, is all. I just thought I'd ask you if he has any reason to be."

Meat sizzled above the fire and scented smoke swirled around their legs. A river otter scrambled over a stump on the edge of camp then stopped a moment to look at them.

"Nobody I know has any reason to be nervous," Ellie said. "If you have to make an arrest you can do it now." And she held out her wrists as if to be cuffed up.

"Naw," George said, and waved her off. "I guess I can send along that message to John down in Ketchikan." And the otter slipped into the inlet.

"If you aren't a policeman anymore, what are you?" Annabelle poked her head up over the log pile, and pushed her glasses up her nose to squint at him.

"Well . . ." George let out a sigh, "I was going to live in Sitka. But, you know, I've got a sister there." The four of them looked at each other as a soft wind teased the trees around them. "You know . . . you don't choose family, really."

"What about Seattle, don't you have a house there and everything?" Annabelle called out without taking her eyes off her book.

"I guess I don't want to go back there, miss," George offered.

"So?" Slippery asked. "What are you going to do?"

"I was thinking about staying here for a bit. Brand-new town. Plenty of fish. No bosses stealing their cut from your catch."

The girl slid up her glasses one more time, nodded, and turned the page of her picture book with the colorful birds sitting on their pure white pages.

"When do we eat?" she called out.

≈≈≈

It was the summer of 1935. In Germany, Hitler had abrogated the Treaty of Versailles and the Third Reich had instituted the Nuremberg Race Laws forbidding Jews their humanity. Soon enough Will Rogers and Wiley Post would die in a plane crash near Point Barrow and Amelia Earhart would disappear into the Pacific. Soon enough German tanks would roll into Poland, the Japanese would bomb Pearl Harbor, Mr. Roosevelt's social programs would be subsumed into the vast engine of the war machine, and the rhetoric of the American class struggle would likewise be subsumed into the nation's comfortable memory of what we still call "life before the war."

But none of that would matter to the four of them as they sat eating fresh venison from charred sticks. Time and history would roll across them in waves, pushing them forward then dragging them back. Soon enough, George Hanson would partner up with Johnny Desmond to run their own tug carrying supplies from Cold Storage to Sitka, where George would spend one pleasant evening at a time with his sister before catching the morning tide home. Soon enough Johnny Desmond's wife would leave her relations down in Tacoma and move into a place in town where their kids would play with Annabelle after school.

Soon enough Slippery Wilson would be landing on the beach in Normandy, scared once again and shivering, but with the cabin by the creek securely anchored in his heart.

Soon enough Ellie Hobbes would learn to fly. She would build the first and most profitable bar in Cold Storage. She would save her earnings until she had enough to buy a reconditioned de Havilland Beaver and she would fly her family up to the high lakes above the inlet to go fishing, including her two girls and a boy she raised with Slip.

Soon enough Annabelle would grow up to become one of

Alaska's first female owners of a flying service, and she would fall in love with a kind man who fished a cedar-plank troller that he anchored off the beach near their cabin down the inlet from Slip and Ellie's.

And soon enough Annabelle's children would gather up in the woods beyond the old house to tell the stories and tend the graves of the people their mother had loved and traveled with that turbulent spring when she first came to Alaska and lost her yellow bird.

ABOUT THE AUTHOR

John Straley is the author of six novels featuring the Alaskan private investigator Cecil Younger. The first book in that series, *The Woman Who Married a Bear*, won the 1992 Shamus award for best first novel. Straley is a criminal investigator, a poet, and is currently the twelfth Writer Laureate of Alaska. His work has been featured on *Fresh Air with Terry Gross* and *CBS Sunday Morning*. He lives on the beach in Sitka, Alaska, with his wife, Jan, and their son, Finn.